The Famine

A Saga of Survival and Rebellion

By Ryan Donaghy

Release Date: March 2025

Language: English

*To the memory of those who endured the Great Famine,
and to the indomitable spirit of the Irish people.*

*More personally, I dedicate this book to my
grandmother, Ailish O'Hagan, who passed away while
I was writing it. My wee nanny would sit with me for
hours, patiently listening as I rambled excitedly down
countless historical rabbit holes. She was always there,
nodding along, sharing in my enthusiasm, never once
growing weary of my endless discoveries.*

*One of the most cherished moments of my life
was reading her the first completed chapter.
A tear welled in her eye as she listened, and
now, as I write these words, I feel my own. That
moment will forever live in my heart—a quiet,
beautiful memory of my grandmother's love,
and the stories that bound us together.*

CONTENTS

AUTHOR'S NOTE

The Famine: A Saga of Survival and Rebellion is a work of historical fiction. While the characters are fictional, the events they encounter are rooted in the realities of the Great Irish Potato Famine and the broader context of British colonialism. Extensive research was undertaken to ensure historical accuracy, particularly in portraying the social, economic, and political landscape of Ireland during this period.

However, this novel is not a historical treatise but a story, a narrative exploring the lives of ordinary individuals caught in extraordinary circumstances. The characters' experiences and choices are meant to be believable, even as they grapple with the tumultuous events that shaped their lives.

It is my hope that this tale will resonate with readers, not only as a fictional journey but as a reminder of the enduring strength of the human spirit in the face of adversity.

PREFACE

In the midst of Ireland's darkest days, when famine and despair gripped the land, the O'Donaghue family emerged as both victims and heroes of a tumultuous era. The Famine weaves together the harrowing struggle for survival with tales of love, betrayal, and the unyielding spirit of those who dared to dream of a free and united Ireland. Spanning continents and generations, this novel follows the O'Donaghue's from the fields of Cork to the salons of Paris, and from the bustling streets of New York to the unforgiving outback of Australia. Through their eyes, we witness the indomitable resilience of the human spirit and the enduring power of hope. This is a story not only of famine, but of rebirth, revolution, and the quest for justice. As you turn these pages, may you be transported to a time when history was forged by the courage of ordinary people.

This novel is a product of many hours, days and months of research and reflection on one of the most harrowing chapters in Irish history: the Great Famine. It is a story inspired by the resilience of the Irish people, their ability to survive unimaginable hardship and to fight for a better future.

My goal has been to capture the complexity of this

period, not just as a historical event but also as a human experience. The characters in this novel are fictional, but their journeys are based on the real-life experiences of countless individuals who endured the Famine and its devastating consequences.

THE GREAT IRISH POTATO FAMINE OF 1845 – 1851 - CORK

The Great Irish Potato Famine, which ravaged Ireland between 1845 and 1851, was one of the most devastating periods in the country's history. In the Cork countryside, as in much of rural Ireland, life was already fraught with challenges long before the blight struck. The vast majority of the population depended almost entirely on the potato as their primary food source. This crop, which was both easy to grow and nutritiously dense, sustained millions of Irish families who lived on small plots of land, often rented from absentee landlords.

When the potato blight (Phytophthora infestans) appeared in 1845, it spread with alarming speed, turning healthy potato fields into stinking, blackened wastelands. For the rural poor, the loss of the potato crop was catastrophic. The blight destroyed the only reliable source of food for many families, plunging them into a state of desperation and starvation. Unlike other parts of Europe, where agriculture was more diverse, Ireland's dependence on a single crop left the population uniquely vulnerable to such a disaster.

As the blight returned year after year, the situation in the countryside became increasingly dire. The small tenant farmers and laborers, who were already living on the brink of poverty, found themselves unable to pay rent or feed their families. The British government's response to the famine was widely viewed as inadequate and indifferent. Relief efforts were slow, and when they did come, they were often woefully insufficient. Policies that favored economic principles over humanitarian aid, such as the continued export of food from Ireland even as the population starved, only exacerbated the crisis.

Absentee landlords, many of whom lived in England and were insulated from the horrors unfolding on their lands, often chose to evict tenants who could no longer pay rent. These evictions were ruthless, leaving countless families homeless and destitute. The roads of rural Cork became filled with the displaced, their few possessions piled onto carts as they wandered in search of shelter or admittance to overcrowded workhouses, which themselves became sites of death due to disease and malnutrition.

Emigration, perilous as it was, offered one of the few possible escapes from the famine. The so-called "coffin ships" that carried Irish emigrants to America, Canada, and beyond were notoriously unsafe, with many dying from disease and starvation during the journey. Yet, for many, the risks of emigration were preferable to the grim certainty of death by starvation at home.

The Great Famine left an indelible mark on Ireland. In Cork, as in other parts of the country, the social and economic fabric was torn apart. The population was drastically reduced, and the landscape was dotted with the ruins of abandoned cottages and fields. The trauma of the famine, compounded by the perceived indifference of the British government, fueled a growing sense of resentment and nationalism that would have lasting effects on Ireland's future.

The Famine was not just a period of hunger and death; it was a profound human tragedy that altered the course of Irish history. The Cork countryside, once a land of small farms and close-knit communities, emerged from the famine a place of loss and desolation, its people forever changed by the hardships they had endured.

CHAPTER 1:
THE END OF INNOCENCE

The summer of 1845 was the kind that would linger in memory, not for its warmth, but for the way it held the world in a deceptive stillness, as if the earth itself was holding its breath. The O'Donaghue family, nestled in their small cottage outside Reenascreena, near Rosscarbery in County Cork, felt the uneasy quiet like a shadow stretching across their lives. They had always known hardship—each stone in their field seemed to carry the weight of generations of toil, their 1.5-acre plot a bitter reminder of what had been taken from them centuries ago. The land was their life, their struggle, and their hope, but now, it seemed to tremble under a threat that could not yet be named.

Patrick O'Donaghue (Irish: Pádraig Ó Donnchadha) was a man shaped by the land he worked. In his late forties, his body was sturdy, marked by the rough labor that defined his existence. His hands, thick and calloused, were the hands of a man who had spent his life fighting against the earth's reluctance to yield. Yet, as he made his way home from England that late August, working extra to make up the rent, his steps were heavy, not with physical exhaustion, but with a burden of a different kind—a creeping dread that gnawed at the edges of his thoughts. He carried with him the news that might as well have been a death sentence for his family: the blight had come.

In his satchel, crumpled and worn, were two newspapers—The Freeman's Journal and The Gardeners' Chronicle and Horticultural Gazette. The words on the pages were burned into his mind: "A blight of unusual character" ... "a fearful malady." The blight had ravaged crops in England and Belgium, and now it threatened Ireland. Patrick's hands clenched involuntarily around the reins as he urged Puddles, their loyal horse, forward. The familiar landscape of home drew closer, but with it came the fear that this might be the last time he saw it as it was—green, alive, full of promise.

The cottage came into view, a modest structure that had weathered countless storms, both literal and metaphorical. Ann (Irish: Áine Ó Donnchadha), his wife, stood at the doorway, their youngest, Rebecca (Irish: Ríobhca Ó Donnchadha), cradled in her arms. At just over a year old, Rebecca was a beacon of light in a world that seemed to grow darker by the day. Her laughter, soft and innocent, floated through the air, momentarily dispelling the weight on Patrick's heart.

Ann's eyes met his, and in that brief exchange, Patrick saw reflected back at him the same fear he carried. Ann was a woman who had aged beyond her years, the lines on her face etched by worry and sacrifice. Yet, there was a strength in her—a resilience that had kept the family together through countless hardships. She had been the anchor while Patrick was away, but even anchors could be worn down by the relentless tides of life.

"Christopher has done a good job with the fields," Ann said, her voice carrying a forced lightness as if speaking the words aloud might make them true.

Patrick nodded, his eyes scanning the horizon. "He's a good lad. But there's talk of trouble, Ann. The blight's in the north, maybe even closer. We'll need to be careful, watch the crops like hawks."

Christopher (Irish: Críostóir Ó Donnchadha), their

eldest at fifteen, emerged from the barn, his face streaked with dirt and sweat. He had taken on the mantle of responsibility with a gravity that was both admirable and heartbreaking. Childhood had been a brief chapter in Christopher's life, one that seemed to close the moment he realized the burden he had to carry. His hands, much like his father's, were rough from the work that needed doing—tending to the crops, repairing the tools, keeping the small farm running in Patrick's absence.

"Da," Christopher greeted, his voice steady but his eyes betraying a flicker of uncertainty. "The fields are holding up, but I've seen some of the plants ... there's something off about them. I didn't want to say anything until you got back."

Patrick's heart sank. He had hoped, against all reason, that the blight might spare them. But the land, like an old friend who had turned hostile, was already showing signs of betrayal. "We'll take a look tomorrow," Patrick replied, forcing strength into his voice. "Tonight, we'll have supper together. We've got to hold on to what we can."

As they gathered inside the cottage, the familiar scents of peat smoke and boiled potatoes filled the air. It was a meager meal, the kind they had grown used to —potatoes, the ever-present staple, were accompanied by a small piece of salted fish that Ann had managed to procure. The children—Christopher, Ryan, Seamus, and little Rebecca—sat around the table, their faces reflecting a mixture of weariness and fleeting joy at their father's return.

Ryan (Irish: Rian Ó Donnchadha), thirteen, had spent

the summer in Cork with his mother and younger siblings. He was a boy on the cusp of manhood, filled with restless energy and a longing for adventure. The bustling port town had been a revelation to him—a place where he could lose himself in the excitement of the docks, where ships from far-off lands came and went with the tides. But now, as he sat at the table, his gaze shifted between his father and the uneaten portion of his meal. "Da, did you see any ships from America?" Ryan asked, his voice betraying a mixture of curiosity and a desire to escape the harsh realities of life on the farm.

Patrick shook his head, a small smile playing at the corners of his mouth despite the dread in his heart. "No ships for you, lad. But we've got work here that needs doing. There's no adventure like keeping a farm running."

Ryan sighed, clearly disappointed, but he knew better than to argue. His father's tone, while gentle, brooked no room for debate. The farm was their world, and it demanded every ounce of their strength.

Seamus (Irish: Séamas Ó Donnchadha), just four years old, sat quietly beside his mother, his wide eyes taking in the scene around him. He had been a lively child, full of questions and laughter, but since the blight had first been mentioned, something had changed. The brightness in his eyes had dimmed, replaced by a silence that was unnerving in one so young. He clung to his mother's skirts, finding comfort in her presence, though the world around him seemed to grow more uncertain by the day.

Ann reached out and gently brushed a lock of hair from

Seamus's forehead. "Eat up, love," she urged, her voice soft but firm. "You'll need your strength."

Seamus obediently picked up his spoon, but his movements were slow, almost reluctant, as if he could sense that something was terribly wrong.

After supper, as the children prepared for bed, Patrick and Ann sat together by the hearth. The fire crackled softly, casting flickering shadows on the walls. The silence between them was heavy, filled with the words they didn't dare speak. Finally, Patrick broke the silence. "I'm scared, Ann. I'm scared of what's coming."

Ann reached for his hand, her fingers intertwining with his. "So am I, Patrick. But we've faced hard times before. We'll face this too, together."

Patrick squeezed her hand, drawing strength from her unwavering resolve. "We'll get through this. We have to."

But even as he spoke the words, a part of him wondered if they were enough. The world outside was changing, darkening, and no amount of determination could hold back the storm that was coming.

The days that followed were tense, each morning bringing with it a fresh wave of anxiety. Patrick and Christopher inspected the fields, their worst fears confirmed as they found the telltale signs of blight spreading through the plants. The leaves, once vibrant and green, were now mottled with brown and black, the tubers beneath the soil turning to rot. The stench of decay filled the air, an oppressive reminder of the disaster that was unfolding.

"We'll salvage what we can," Patrick said, his voice grim.

"But it's not enough. It'll never be enough."

Christopher nodded, his face pale as he watched his father dig through the ruined crop. He had always believed that his father could fix anything, that there was no problem too great for Patrick O'Donaghue to solve. But now, as he saw the defeat in his father's eyes, Christopher felt a cold fear settle in his chest. The world was slipping out of their control, and there was nothing they could do to stop it.

Winter came early that year, the cold settling in with a ferocity that matched the despair in the O'Donaghue household. The blight had taken almost everything, leaving the family to scrape together what little they could to survive. Each day was a struggle, each night a test of their endurance.

Patrick grew weaker with each passing day, his body ravaged by hunger and disease. He had always been the rock of the family, the one who held them together through the worst of times. But now, as cholera took hold, he was fading, slipping away like the last embers of a dying fire.

Ann did what she could to care for him, but the resources at her disposal were pitifully inadequate. She watched, helpless, as the man she had built her life with succumbed to the illness. The children were no better off—Christopher and Ryan worked tirelessly to gather firewood, to find any scrap of food that might keep them going, but their efforts were increasingly futile.

The day Patrick died was a day that would forever be etched into the minds of the O'Donaghue family. The cottage, once a place of warmth and love, was now a tomb, filled with the echoes of their grief. Ann sat beside Patrick's body, her heart shattered but her resolve hardening into something steely and unbreakable. She had lost her husband, but she would not lose her children—not if she could help it.

"We'll get through this," she whispered to herself, her voice barely audible. "We have to."

But even as she spoke the words, she knew that their chances were dwindling with each passing day. The winter was relentless, the cold seeping into their bones, the hunger gnawing at them from the inside out.

It was in the depths of that brutal winter that Ann made the decision to slaughter Puddles. The horse had been with the family for years, a faithful companion who had seen them through many trials. But now, Puddles was weak, his once-strong body reduced to little more than skin and bones. He could no longer work the fields, could no longer pull the cart that had carried them to market and back. He was, in the cruel calculus of survival, expendable.

When Ann told the children of her decision, the reaction was immediate and intense. Seamus, who had been so quiet for so long, erupted in a fit of rage that took them all by surprise. "No!" he screamed, his small fists pounding against his mother's legs. "Not Puddles! You can't do this!"

Ann knelt down, her heart breaking as she tried to comfort her son. "Seamus, love, we have no choice," she whispered, her voice thick with tears. "We have to survive."

But Seamus was inconsolable. The loss of Puddles was

too much for him to bear, the final straw in a year that had taken so much from him. He cried until he could cry no more, and when the tears were gone, a deep, unsettling silence settled over him—a silence that would last for many months to come.

That night, as the wind howled outside, they slaughtered Puddles. The meat sustained them through the worst of the winter, but it came at a great cost. The light that had once filled their home was gone, replaced by a darkness that seemed impossible to lift.

As the snow melted and spring approached, the O'Donaghues were left with little more than their memories and their grief. The land that had once been their lifeline was now a source of bitter reminders, each furrow in the earth a scar left by the blight.

June brought with it a new terror. Major Denis Mahon, the landlord's enforcer, arrived at their door, his presence a cold reminder of the debt they could no longer pay. The sight of him, tall and imposing in his military uniform, sent a chill through Ann. She had heard the stories—tenants across the countryside were being evicted, their homes burned, their possessions destroyed. Now it was their turn.

"You've got one day to clear out," Mahon said, his voice devoid of emotion. "This house will be burned tomorrow. Take what you can and leave the rest."

The words struck Ann like a blow, but she did not let it show. She had lost too much already to be cowed by this man. "We'll go," she said, her voice steady, though her heart raced in her chest.

But Ryan, now fourteen, could not hold back his anger.

"You can't do this!" he shouted, stepping forward with fists clenched. "This is our home!"

Mahon sneered, his expression one of disdain. "Not anymore."

In a flash of movement, Ryan lunged at Mahon, his anger boiling over. But Mahon was prepared. With a swift motion, he knocked Ryan to the ground, his boot pressing down on the boy's chest. "You need to learn your place," Mahon growled, drawing a knife from his belt.

The world seemed to slow as Ann watched in horror. She could see the knife, the glint of steel as Mahon prepared to strike. Without thinking, she grabbed the kitchen knife from the table and moved with a speed born of desperation. The blade found its mark, sinking deep into Mahon's back. For a moment, the room was silent, as if the world had stopped turning. Then Mahon crumpled to the floor, his life ebbing away in a pool of blood.

Ann stood over him, the knife still clutched in her hand, her breath coming in ragged gasps. She had done what she had to do, but the reality of it hit her like a wave, threatening to pull her under. "We have to go," she whispered, her voice trembling. "Now."

Christopher was the first to move. He grabbed Ryan and pulled him to his feet, then began gathering what little they had left. Ann scooped up Rebecca, who had begun to cry, and wrapped her in a blanket. Seamus stood frozen, his eyes wide with fear, but there was no time to comfort him now.

"Seamus, come on," Christopher urged, his voice steady

despite the fear that gripped him. "We have to go."

With that, they fled the only home they had ever known, the place that had been their sanctuary now a scene of violence and death. They didn't look back as they hurried down the darkened road, the cold night air biting at their skin. Their only thought was to reach Cork, to find Uncle Michael, and to pray that they could somehow start again.

As they made their way through the night, Ann's mind raced. She had killed a man, and now they were fugitives. The weight of what she had done threatened to crush her, but she forced herself to keep moving, to put one foot in front of the other. For her children's sake, she had to be strong. But in the back of her mind, a single, terrifying thought loomed: what would become of them now?

Michael O'Hagan (Irish: Mícheál Ó hAodhagáin) stood in the doorway of his small shop in Cork town, gazing out at the familiar streets that had once bustled with life. Now, they seemed quieter, as if the very soul of the city had been hollowed out. The year was 1847, and Ireland was a land of whispers and shadows, where hunger stalked every corner and fear gripped the hearts of its people. Michael let out a slow breath, his thoughts drifting back to a time that felt like a lifetime ago—the summer of 1845, when his sister Ann and her children had visited.

The memories of that summer were bright and clear, standing out against the bleakness of the present. Michael could still see the joy in Ryan's eyes as they set out to sea, the boy's spirit unburdened by the worries that now weighed him down. Ryan had always been the adventurer, eager to explore the world beyond the confines of his family's small farm. Michael had taken him under his wing, teaching him the ways of the ocean, how to read the wind and the waves. Those days on the boat had been a respite, a time when the future had seemed full of promise.

Seamus, too young to fully grasp the complexities of life, had been content to sit quietly, watching the seagulls wheel overhead and the water sparkle under the sun. Rebecca, still a baby then, had been the heart of the family, her laughter a constant reminder of the innocence they all fought to protect. Ann had been strong, as she always was, but Michael could see the weariness in her eyes even then, a subtle sign of the burdens she carried.

But that was before the blight, before the land had turned against them and the famine had tightened its grip on their lives. The boat—his pride and joy—was sold in 1846, the money lent to Ann to help pay the rent and keep the family from starving. It had been a difficult decision, but Michael had known it was the only choice. The sea had been his escape, but family was everything. He had hoped, foolishly perhaps, that things would improve, that they would find a way to survive the coming storm. Instead, the storm had consumed them.

Now, the boat was gone, and with it, the sense of freedom that had once defined his life. In its place was this small shop, a meager source of income that barely kept him afloat. He sold basic goods—wheat, salt, whatever he could scrounge from the docks. Every day was a battle, a struggle to haggle with the traders from England who saw the Irish as little more than beggars. Some days, there was nothing to sell, and Michael would go to bed hungry, his stomach knotted with hunger and worry.

It was on one such morning, weak from lack of food and weary from the endless grind, that Michael was handed a copy of The Freeman's Journal. The paper was tattered, its edges frayed from passing through too many hands, but the headline was clear and bold, searing itself into his mind:

"WANTED FOR MURDER: ANN, CHRISTOPHER & RYAN O'DONAGHUE."

Michael's breath caught in his throat as he read the article, his hands trembling. The story was one that had already begun to ripple across Ireland, gaining attention even in England, where the gentry watched with growing concern. The murder of a landlord's enforcer was not just a crime; it was a spark that could ignite a firestorm of rebellion across the land. And now, Ann—his sister, strong and unyiclding Ann—was at the center of it.

The article detailed the events in cold, detached prose: how Major Denis Mahon, the enforcer for the local landlord, had been killed in a confrontation with Ann and her two eldest sons, Christopher and Ryan. The authorities had been swift in their response, issuing a warrant for their arrest, and the hunt was on. The police were everywhere, their presence a constant reminder that the O'Donaghue family was now fugitives, with no place left to hide.

Michael's shop had become a regular stop for the police, who questioned him relentlessly about the whereabouts of his sister and her children. Each day, they would come, their questions sharp and their eyes searching for any sign of deception. Michael had learned to school his features into a mask of indifference, denying any knowledge of his family's movements even as his heart pounded with fear for their safety.

But the constant pressure was wearing him down. Every time the door to his shop opened, he tensed, expecting to see the uniformed figures of the constables. The fear that they might discover the truth —that Ann and the children had sought refuge with him—was a constant, gnawing presence.

Then, one day, Ann appeared.

It was early morning, the sky still tinged with the soft hues of dawn, when she slipped into the shop. Her face was gaunt, her eyes hollowed by exhaustion and fear. She looked nothing like the sister Michael had known, the woman who had faced every hardship with a strength that seemed unbreakable. Now, she was a shadow of herself, worn down by the relentless pursuit of the law and the ravages of starvation.

"Michael," she whispered, her voice hoarse. "I had no other place to go."

Michael's heart broke at the sight of her, but he knew the danger they were in. The police came every day, and it was only a matter of time before they found her. He had to be strong, for her and for the children. "You can't stay here, Ann," he said quietly, his voice betraying the pain he felt. "They're watching me. Every day, they come asking for you."

Tears welled in Ann's eyes, but she nodded, understanding the truth in his words. "I know," she replied, her voice trembling. "But I can't take Rebecca and Seamus. They're too young. They need you, Michael."

Michael's resolve faltered. The thought of turning away his niece and nephew was unbearable, but the risk was too great. Yet, he couldn't bring himself to refuse her. He reached out, pulling Ann into a tight embrace, feeling the thinness of her frame, the weakness in her limbs. "I'll take them," he whispered fiercely. "I'll keep them safe. But you, Christopher, and Ryan— you have to stay away from here."

Ann pulled back, her eyes filled with gratitude and sorrow. "Thank you, Michael. You don't know what this means to me."

Michael shook his head, his throat tight with emotion. "I wish I could do more. I wish I could protect you all."

"You've done enough," Ann said softly, her voice breaking. "You've done more than enough."

With that, they made their preparations quickly. Ann handed over Rebecca and Seamus, her hands lingering on her children as if she couldn't bear to let them go. Rebecca, too young to understand, clung to her mother, her tiny fingers grasping at the worn fabric of Ann's dress. Seamus, on the other hand, understood all too well. His silence, once a comfort, now seemed to echo with the weight of unspoken words.

"I'll come back for you," Ann promised, her voice choked

with emotion. "I'll come back."

But even as she spoke the words, Michael knew that they were empty, a comfort spoken to soothe the pain of parting. He watched as Ann, Christopher, and Ryan slipped out the back door, their figures disappearing into the early morning mist. The fear that he might never see them again gripped his heart, but he pushed it down, focusing on the task at hand.

Days turned into weeks, and the tension in Cork grew palpable. The story of Major Mahon's murder had spread like wildfire, inflaming the fears of the English landlords and the ire of the Irish peasantry. It was more than just a crime; it was a symbol of resistance, of the desperate lengths to which the starving and oppressed would go to fight for their survival. The papers in England decried the act, calling for swift justice, while in Ireland, the story took on a life of its own, whispered in secret meetings and spoken of with both fear and reverence.

Ann, Christopher, and Ryan had to stay hidden, their faces dirty and soot-streaked to disguise their identities. The police had stationed officers at the entrances to the workhouses, knowing that the desperate often sought refuge there. Posters with their faces plastered across them were hung in every public space, a constant reminder that they were hunted. The three of them, already weakened by hunger and exhaustion, found it increasingly difficult to evade capture. They could not stay in one place for long, always moving, always hiding in the shadows of the city.

Michael did what he could to help, slipping food and

supplies to them whenever possible. But he knew it was not enough. Each day, Ann grew weaker, the same illness that had claimed Patrick now taking hold of her. The signs were unmistakable—her gaunt face, her hollow eyes, the fever that burned through her body. She was fading, and there was nothing Michael could do to stop it.

It was late one evening, under the cover of darkness, that Michael found Ann huddled in an alleyway, her body wracked with shivers. Christopher and Ryan sat beside her, their faces pale and drawn with fear and fatigue. Michael knelt beside his sister, his heart breaking at the sight of her. "Ann," he whispered, reaching out to touch her forehead. It was burning hot, and the touch seemed to jolt her back to awareness.

"Michael," she murmured, her voice barely audible. "I can't … I can't go on."

"Don't say that" Michael urged; his voice thick with emotion. "You'll get better. We'll find a way."

But even as he spoke, he knew the truth. There was no getting better. Ann was dying, just as Patrick had, and the end was near. "Christopher, Ryan," Ann said weakly, turning to her sons. "You must … you must go on without me. Stay together. Protect each other."

The boys nodded, their faces etched with grief. They had watched their father die, and now they were losing their mother too. The weight of that loss was almost too much to bear, but they had no choice. They had to keep going, just as she had taught them.

"I love you," Ann whispered, her voice breaking. "Never forget that."

And with that, she was gone.

Michael held her as she took her last breath, his tears falling freely as he mourned the sister he had lost. The boys clung to each other, their grief too deep for words. The world felt emptier, colder, without her, and the thought of facing it without her guidance was terrifying.

The night pressed in around them, cold and unforgiving, as Michael cradled Ann's lifeless body. The grief that had been building within him broke free, and he allowed himself a moment of vulnerability, tears streaming down his face. Christopher and Ryan, huddled together beside him, were silent, their faces etched with a pain that words could not convey.

After what felt like an eternity, Michael gently laid Ann down, closing her eyes with trembling hands. The city seemed to grow quieter, as if even the distant sounds of the night had stilled in respect for their loss.

"We can't stay here," Michael finally whispered, his voice hoarse. "Not tonight."

Christopher, who had been holding his brother tightly, looked up at his uncle, his eyes filled with a resolve that belied his years. "What do we do, Uncle Michael?"

Michael took a deep breath, forcing himself to think clearly. He knew that time was against them, and they needed to be careful. "I'll help you leave the city," he said, his voice steadier now. "But we can't do it tonight. It's too dangerous, and I need time to make arrangements."

Ryan glanced at his mother's still form, his voice small and trembling. "Where will we go?"

Michael placed a hand on Ryan's shoulder, his touch firm yet gentle. "Tomorrow night after dark, come to the shop. We'll get you out of Cork, to somewhere safer. But until then, you have to stay hidden. You have to stay safe."

Christopher nodded, the weight of responsibility settling on his young shoulders. "We'll be ready."

Michael's gaze lingered on his nephews, his heart heavy with the knowledge of what they had already endured and what lay ahead. "Stay alive," he urged, his voice thick with emotion. "No matter what, you stay alive until I come back."

Their faces became solemn as they absorbed the gravity of his words.

Michael stood, looking around the darkened alley one last time before turning back to the boys. "I'll be here tomorrow night," he repeated, as much for his own reassurance as for theirs. "Be ready."

And with that, he disappeared into the shadows, leaving Christopher and Ryan alone with their grief and the cold night. The two brothers sat in silence, the weight of the world pressing down on them, knowing that they would have to survive just one more day—and then, somehow, beyond that.

But for now, they had to wait. They had to endure.

They had to stay alive.

As the first light of dawn crept into the sky, Christopher sat alone in the shadowed corner of an alleyway, the cold seeping into his bones. Cork, which had once been a place of familiarity, now felt like an endless maze of threats and uncertainties. With his mother gone and Ryan the only family member by his side, the burden of survival had fallen squarely on Christopher's young shoulders.

Christopher had barely slept. The weight of responsibility, coupled with the grief that gnawed at his heart, made rest impossible. He kept replaying the events of the previous night in his mind—his mother's last breath, the promise to his uncle, and the sheer terror of what lay ahead. They had to make it through just one more day. Tonight, they would meet Uncle Michael at his shop, where Seamus and Rebecca were already safe. Then, maybe, they could find a way out of this nightmare.

But first, he and Ryan needed food. Christopher's stomach churned with hunger, a dull ache that had become all too familiar over the past weeks. Ryan, who had spent the night beside him, was equally famished, but his eyes held a mix of fear and determination. Christopher knew that his younger brother looked up to him, and the thought both comforted and terrified him. He couldn't let Ryan down. He had to be strong, even if he felt like the world was crumbling around him.

"We need to find something to eat," Christopher murmured, breaking the heavy silence. His voice was steady, though inside, he felt anything but calm. "We can't meet Uncle Michael tonight on empty stomachs."

Ryan nodded, though the worry in his eyes was evident. "But how? We've got no money, Christopher."

Christopher took a deep breath, his mind racing. The market wasn't far—he knew that from wandering the streets the day before. It would be crowded, noisy, the perfect place to grab something without being noticed. But the risk was enormous. If they were caught, the consequences could be devastating. He looked at Ryan, seeing the same fear mirrored in his brother's eyes. "We'll have to steal something," Christopher said, his voice dropping to a whisper. "It's the only way."

Ryan hesitated, the moral weight of the decision hanging between them. "What if we get caught?" he asked, his voice small, the vulnerability of his youth seeping through.

"We won't," Christopher replied, trying to sound more confident than he felt. "We'll be quick. I'll keep watch, and you'll grab a loaf of bread. Just one. We don't need to be greedy."

Ryan swallowed hard, then nodded. "Okay. Just one loaf."

Christopher stood, pulling Ryan to his feet. The city was beginning to wake up around them, the streets slowly filling with people going about their day. The brothers moved through the alleys, sticking to the shadows, their hearts pounding in unison with each step they took toward the market.

When they arrived, the market was already bustling with activity. Stalls lined the streets, filled with goods that seemed like a distant dream to the boys— fresh fruit, vegetables, meat, and, most importantly, bread. The smell of freshly baked loaves filled the air, making their stomachs twist with longing. Christopher scanned the area, noting the position of the stall owners and the guards who occasionally patrolled the market.

He found a stall that was particularly busy, the owner's attention split between customers.

"Now," Christopher whispered to Ryan, nodding toward the stall. "I'll be right here, keeping watch. You just grab it and run. Don't stop, no matter what."

Ryan took a deep breath, steeling himself. Then, with a quick glance at Christopher, he moved toward the stall. Christopher watched as his brother edged closer, his heart thudding in his chest. Ryan's small hands reached out, trembling slightly, and then he grabbed the loaf of bread, tucking it under his arm.

But as Ryan turned to flee, the stall owner's gaze snapped to him, eyes narrowing in suspicion. "Thief!" the man shouted, his voice cutting through the noise of the market like a knife. "Stop, thief!"

Panic surged through Christopher as he saw the owner take off after Ryan. "Run!" he shouted; his voice hoarse with fear. The two brothers bolted, weaving through the crowd as the market erupted into chaos around them. Christopher's heart pounded in his ears, each beat a frantic rhythm urging him to move faster, to escape.

But as they rounded a corner, disaster struck. Ryan stumbled, his foot catching on a loose cobblestone, and he went down hard, the loaf of bread tumbling from his grasp. Christopher skidded to a halt, torn between helping his brother and saving himself. But in that split second of hesitation, the stall owner was upon them.

"You filthy little thief!" the man snarled, grabbing Ryan by the collar and hauling him to his feet. The man's grip was ironclad, and Ryan's struggles were futile against his strength. Christopher, frozen in panic, didn't notice the constable approaching until the officer had already grabbed Ryan, yanking him away from the stall owner.

"You're under arrest for theft," the constable declared, his grip on Ryan firm and unyielding.

Ryan struggled, but he was no match for the constable's strength. "Christopher!" he cried out, his voice laced with terror.

Christopher started forward, ready to fight for his brother, but another constable stepped in his path, his hand gripping Christopher's arm with surprising force. "And where do you think you're going?" the constable growled.

Christopher's heart pounded in his chest as he stared up at the constable. "Let him go! Please, let him go!" Christopher pleaded, desperation clawing at him.

The constable studied Christopher for a moment, his eyes narrowing. "You're lucky, boy," he finally said, his voice cold. "You weren't the one who took the bread. Get out of here before I change my mind."

With a rough shove, the constable pushed Christopher away. Christopher stumbled back, his mind racing with panic and guilt as he watched Ryan being dragged away. "Ryan!" Christopher shouted, but his voice was drowned out by the bustling crowd. Ryan looked back, his eyes wide with fear and desperation, but there was nothing Christopher could do. He was powerless to stop it.

Tears burned in Christopher's eyes as he watched Ryan disappear from view, the realization that he had lost his brother crashing over him like a tidal wave. Guilt gnawed at him, a bitter, corrosive feeling that settled deep in his chest. He had failed to protect Ryan, failed to keep their family together.

With a heart heavy with guilt and despair, Christopher made his way to his uncle's shop, his steps slow and filled with dread. Uncle Michael had entrusted him with the responsibility of getting the family to safety, and now Ryan was lost to them, taken by the very authorities they were trying to escape.

When Christopher finally reached the shop, the usual hustle and bustle of the marketplace seemed a world away. He pushed open the door, the bell above it jingling softly as he entered. The shop was quiet, and the familiar scent of flour and grain hung in the air. Seamus and Rebecca were inside, their faces lighting up with relief when they saw Christopher.

"Christopher! You're back!" Rebecca cried out, rushing to his side. "Where's Ryan? Is he with you?"

Christopher's heart clenched at the question, and he could only shake his head. "They took him," he whispered, his voice trembling. "The constable... he took Ryan."

Rebecca's eyes filled with tears, and she clung to Christopher, her small body shaking with sobs. Seamus stood beside them, his face pale and stricken with fear. "But... Uncle Michael said we were all going to leave together," Seamus whispered, his voice cracking.

Christopher knelt down, pulling his siblings into a tight embrace. "I'm sorry," he choked out. "I'm so sorry. I tried to stop them... I tried."

At that moment, Michael emerged from the back room, his expression growing grave as he took in the scene before him. "Christopher," he said quietly, stepping forward. "Where's Ryan?"

Christopher couldn't bear to look his uncle in the eye. "They arrested him," he admitted, his voice thick with guilt. "We tried to steal some bread... I thought... I thought we could get away. But we didn't. They took him."

Michael's face drained of colour, and he ran a hand over his face, visibly shaken. "God, no..." he muttered, sinking into a chair. "I had it all arranged, Christopher. I bribed a dock worker with the last of my grain to get us two passages on a ship to America. We were supposed to leave tonight."

Christopher's heart sank even further. "I'm sorry, Uncle Michael... I didn't know..."

Michael looked up at Christopher, his eyes filled with a mixture of sorrow and determination. "It's not your fault, Christopher. None of this is your fault. But we can't change what's happened. We don't have time to waste. We have to get you on that ship tonight, or everything we've done will be for nothing."

"But what about Ryan?" Christopher asked, his voice desperate. "We can't leave him behind!"

Michael's expression hardened, his jaw set with resolve. "I'll take care of it, Christopher. I'll do everything I can to make sure Ryan is safe. But right now, you need to get on that ship. It's the only chance you've got."

Christopher wanted to argue, to refuse to leave without his brother, but deep down, he knew Michael was right. The thought of leaving Ryan behind was unbearable, but if they missed this chance, there might never be another.

"Get ready," Michael said, his voice firm. "We leave for the docks soon. We can't afford to be late."

Christopher nodded, his mind racing as he hurried to prepare himself. He tried to put on a brave face for Seamus and Rebecca, to reassure them that everything would be alright, but the truth was, he was terrified. Terrified of what lay ahead, and of the fact that they might never see Ryan again.

The time passed in a blur, and before Christopher knew it, they were making their way through the darkened streets toward the docks. The air was thick with tension, every step filled with the weight of uncertainty. When they arrived, the docks were bustling with activity, the ships creaking as they swayed gently in the water. The sight of the massive vessels filled Christopher with both awe and fear. This was it—their last chance to escape.

Michael led them to a shadowed corner of the docks, where a man stood waiting beside a small boat. "This is the man I told you about," Michael whispered to Christopher. "He'll get you on the ship without any questions. Just do as he says."

The man, a burly figure with a thick beard, nodded curtly. "Ready, lad?" he asked Christopher, his voice gruff.

Christopher swallowed hard, nodding. "I'm ready."

Michael turned to Seamus and Rebecca, kneeling down to meet their eyes. "You two need to be strong now," he said gently. "I'll take care of you, but you need to let Christopher go and make a new life for himself. He'll come back for you someday, I promise."

Seamus nodded, his eyes wide with fear, while Rebecca clung to Michael, tears streaming down her cheeks. "But what about Ryan?" she asked, her voice trembling. "We can't leave him behind..."

Michael's heart ached at her words, but he forced himself to stay strong. "I'll find Ryan," he promised, his voice firm. "I'll do whatever it takes to bring him back to you. But for now, you need to be brave and let Christopher go."

Rebecca nodded, though her tears continued to fall. Michael hugged her tightly, then turned to Christopher, his expression serious. "Remember what I said, Christopher. Stay alive. No matter what happens, you have to stay alive."

Christopher nodded, swallowing the lump in his throat. "I will, Uncle Michael. I won't let you down."

Michael placed a hand on Christopher's shoulder, his grip firm. "I know you won't, lad. I'm proud of you. Your father would be proud too."

Christopher felt a surge of emotion at Michael's words, but he forced himself to stay focused. "Thank you, Uncle Michael. For everything."

Michael nodded, his eyes filled with unspoken emotions. "Take care of yourself, Christopher."

Christopher nodded, then turned to Seamus and Rebecca, hugging them tightly. "I'll come back for you," he whispered, his voice choked with emotion. "I promise."

Seamus and Rebecca clung to him, their small hands

gripping his clothes as if they could keep him from leaving. But eventually, Michael gently pried them away, guiding them toward the dock. Christopher watched as they walked away, his heart heavy with the knowledge that this might be the last time he saw his siblings for a long time.

The burly man helped Christopher into the small boat, and they pushed off from the dock. Christopher watched as Michael, Seamus, and Rebecca faded into the distance, the dark waters of the harbour closing in around them. His heart ached with the weight of the goodbyes, but he knew there was no turning back.

When they reached the side of the ship, a rope ladder was lowered down to them. "Up you go," the man grunted, gesturing for Christopher to go first. Christopher nodded, his hands trembling slightly as he grabbed hold of the ladder and began to climb. The climb was difficult, the ladder swaying with the movement of the ship, but Christopher focused on each rung, forcing himself to keep moving.

When he finally reached the deck, he was greeted by a sailor who quickly ushered him toward the lower quarters. "Stay quiet, stay out of sight," the sailor instructed as they descended the narrow staircase. "This isn't a pleasure cruise. Keep your head down and do as you're told."

Christopher nodded, following the sailor into the cramped quarters below deck. The space was dimly lit and smelled of seawater and sweat. The constant creaking of the wooden beams filled the air, a reminder of the journey that lay ahead. Christopher found a corner where he could settle in, trying to make himself as small and unnoticeable as possible.

As the ship prepared to set sail, Christopher climbed back up to the deck, needing a moment of solitude. The cool night air whipped through his hair as he gazed out at the darkened harbour, the lights of Cork flickering in the distance. He couldn't help but feel a pang of guilt for leaving Ryan behind, but he knew that staying wasn't an option. He had to keep moving, had to make a new life for himself in America.

As the first light of dawn began to break over the horizon, Christopher stood at the ship's railing, watching as the distant shores of Ireland slowly disappeared. His heart was heavy with the weight of his promises, but he held on to the hope that someday, they would all be together again.

The vast expanse of the open sea stretched out before him, a journey filled with danger, hope, and the promise of a new life. But as the ship sailed further away from the shores of Ireland, Christopher couldn't shake the feeling that he was leaving a part of himself behind. The wind tugged at his clothes, and he felt the chill of the morning air, but it was the ache in his heart that consumed him.

He closed his eyes, letting the wind carry away his fears, if only for a moment. The journey had begun, and with it, the end of innocence. But even in the face of such overwhelming odds, Christopher held on to the hope that someday, somehow, they would all be together again.

CHAPTER 2: THE RISE OF NED KELLY

Ryan O'Donoghue's hunger gnawed at him relentlessly, a constant reminder of the desperation that had overtaken his life. Days had passed since he'd last eaten anything substantial, and his once-strong frame had become gaunt, his clothes hanging loosely on his thinning body. The streets of Cork were unforgiving, and Ryan knew he was on the edge of survival.

The market was bustling, filled with people haggling over goods, but all Ryan could focus on was the stall where loaves of bread were being sold. The vendor was distracted, deep in conversation with a customer. This was Ryan's chance—perhaps his only chance.

Ryan darted forward, snatching a loaf of bread and tucking it quickly under his shirt. But as he turned to flee, the vendor's gaze snapped back to him, eyes narrowing with suspicion.

"Thief!" the vendor shouted, his voice cutting through the noise of the market like a knife. "Stop, thief!"

Panic surged through Ryan as he heard Christopher's voice shout from somewhere behind him, "Run!" The urgency in his brother's voice sent a jolt of adrenaline through Ryan's veins. He bolted, heart pounding as he weaved through the crowd, the market erupting into chaos around him.

He could hear the heavy footsteps of the vendor behind him, the man's shouts growing louder. Ryan's lungs burned as he pushed himself to run faster, dodging carts and slipping between startled townspeople. But just as he rounded a corner, disaster struck. His foot caught on a loose cobblestone, and he went down hard, the loaf of bread tumbling from his grasp.

Pain shot through his body, but Ryan barely noticed. He scrambled to his feet, but before he could snatch up the loaf and run, the vendor was upon him. The man's hand clamped down on Ryan's collar, hauling him up with an ironclad grip.

"You filthy little thief!" the vendor snarled, shaking Ryan roughly. "You'll pay for this!"

Ryan struggled, panic surging through him, but the vendor's grip was unyielding. He could hear Christopher shouting his name, but there was nothing his brother could do. As Ryan fought to break free, he felt a cold, sinking dread settle in his stomach. The consequences of this theft were suddenly all too real.

Before Ryan could react, a constable appeared, striding purposefully through the crowd that had gathered to watch the commotion. The officer's eyes were cold and hard as he took in the scene, his hand already moving to pull Ryan away from the vendor.

"You're under arrest for theft," the constable declared, his grip on Ryan firm and unyielding.

Ryan's heart plummeted. He struggled in vain as the constable yanked him away from the vendor, dragging him toward the courthouse that loomed ominously over the square. "Christopher!" Ryan cried out, his voice filled with terror and desperation. He twisted in the constable's grasp, trying to catch one last glimpse of his brother.

Christopher was only a few paces away, his face pale with fear. He started forward, his hands outstretched as if to pull Ryan back, but another constable stepped in his path, blocking his way. "And where do you think you're going?" the constable growled, his hand clamping down on Christopher's arm with surprising force.

"Let him go! Please, let him go!" Christopher pleaded, his voice breaking with desperation. But his words fell on deaf ears as the first constable dragged Ryan through the crowd, past the gawking townspeople, and toward the courthouse steps.

As Ryan was hauled into the dimly lit courthouse, the noise of the market faded into a dull roar, replaced by the heavy silence that hung in the air. The walls seemed to close in around him as he was thrown into a cold, dark cell to await his fate. The metal door clanged shut with a finality that sent a shiver down his spine.

Time lost all meaning in the oppressive darkness of the cell. Ryan huddled in the corner, his mind racing with fear and regret. He had no idea how long he had been there—hours, days, maybe even weeks. The only sounds were the occasional distant shouts or the clank of chains, a constant reminder of the grim fate that awaited him.

He replayed the events over and over in his mind, the dread building with each passing moment. The sight of Christopher, helpless and terrified, haunted him. Christopher, who had promised to protect him, who had convinced him to steal the bread, was now out there, somewhere, alone. Ryan wondered if Christopher had managed to escape, or if he too had been caught.

When the day of his trial finally arrived, Ryan was pulled from his cell and led into the courtroom. The room was large and imposing, its wooden panelling dark and heavy, absorbing all warmth. The judge, an elderly man with deep lines etched into his face, looked down at Ryan from the bench, his expression cold and unforgiving.

"Ryan O'Donaghue," the judge intoned, his voice echoing through the silent courtroom. "You stand accused of theft. How do you plead?"

Ryan's voice was barely a whisper, his head bowed in shame. "Guilty, sir..."

"Speak up, boy," the judge demanded, his gaze sharp. "Let the court hear you."

Ryan swallowed hard, forcing himself to speak louder, though his voice trembled with fear. "Guilty, sir."

The judge nodded, his expression showing no trace of mercy. "Theft is a crime against the Crown, and in these times, with food scarce and tempers high, the law must be upheld. Do you have anything to say in your defence?"

Ryan looked up at the judge, his eyes pleading. "I was just trying to feed my family... My parents are gone, and my brothers and sister... we have nothing..."

But the judge's face remained impassive, his voice as cold as the stone walls of the courtroom. "The court is not in the business of charity, boy. You've broken the law, and you must face the consequences."

At that moment, a constable approached the bench and handed the judge a folded piece of paper. The judge's eyes darkened as he read its contents, and when he looked back at Ryan, his expression had grown even graver.

"It seems, Ryan O'Donaghue," the judge said slowly, "that you are not only here for theft. There is a warrant for your arrest on charges of murder. You, along with your brother Christopher and your mother, Ann O'Donaghue, are wanted for the murder of Major Denis Mahon."

Ryan's blood ran cold. Murder? How could this be? His mind raced, trying to comprehend what was happening. He had been part of no murder; he was just a boy trying to survive.

The judge continued, his voice unwavering. "Given the severity of your crimes, I have no choice but to impose the harshest penalty the law allows. You are hereby sentenced to life in the penal colonies of Australia. You will be transported to serve out your sentence, and may God have mercy on your soul."

The gavel came down with a resounding crack, sealing Ryan's fate. The sound echoed in Ryan's ears, final and irrevocable. His legs buckled, and he collapsed to the floor, the weight of the sentence crushing him.

In the gallery, the anguished cries of his uncle Michael and his younger siblings, Seamus and Rebecca, filled the room. They had come, hoping for a miracle, only to witness the worst possible outcome. As the constables moved to clear the courtroom, Ryan was ushered roughly toward the exit.

As he was being led out, Michael rushed toward him, his face etched with grief and desperation. Ryan looked up, his voice trembling as he asked the question that had been burning in his mind since the arrest. "Where's Christopher? Is he okay? Did they catch him too?"

Michael's heart ached as he saw the fear and confusion in Ryan's eyes. He shook his head, his voice barely above a whisper. "No, Ryan. Christopher... Christopher is gone. He's on a ship to America."

The words hit Ryan like a physical blow. Christopher was gone? On a ship to America? The shock of it all was overwhelming. His brother, who had promised to protect him, who had been his closest ally, had left him to face this nightmare alone. The disbelief quickly turned to a burning anger deep within him. Christopher had abandoned him, left him to this fate while he sailed toward a new life and a fresh start.

Ryan's world spun as the constable hauled him away, his heart pounding with a mix of fear, betrayal, and rage. The last thing he saw was the tear-streaked faces of his uncle and siblings, their cries fading as the door slammed shut behind him.

Ryan was thrown back into his cell, the door clanging shut with a finality that echoed in the empty space. Alone in the darkness, his thoughts raced. How could Christopher have left him? The brother he had trusted, who had promised to keep him safe, was now gone, free to start a new life while Ryan faced the horrors of a penal colony on the other side of the world. The anger that burned within him was all-consuming, fuelling his resolve. He would survive this, not because he had hope for the future, but because he would not let the world break him. He would endure, and one day, somehow, he would make Christopher pay for leaving him behind.

Ryan lay completely still in his small, dank prison cell. The stone walls were cold and unyielding, and the only light came from a small barred window high above. His wrists were bruised from the rough treatment, and his eyes were red from crying. The fear that had gripped him in the courtroom had not lessened; if anything, it had only grown stronger in the cold isolation of the cell.

He sat huddled in a corner, his knees drawn up to his chest, trying to make himself as small as possible. The sound of distant footsteps echoed through the corridors, sending a shiver down his spine. He could hear the low murmur of voices, the clanking of chains, the occasional scream that tore through the silence like a blade.

The cell door creaked open, and two prison guards entered, their expressions hard and emotionless. One of them held a set of heavy iron shackles, which he slapped onto Ryan's wrists and ankles. The cold metal bit into his skin, and Ryan winced, though he didn't dare protest.

"Time to go, boy," one of the guards said gruffly, pulling Ryan to his feet. "Ship's waiting for you."

Ryan didn't resist as the guards led him out of the cell. The corridor was lined with other prisoners, all of them shackled and defeated, their faces pale and gaunt. Ryan caught glimpses of their expressions—some filled with fear, others with anger, but all marked by the same sense of hopelessness.

The guards marched them through the dimly lit corridors, the walls closing in on them like a tomb. The air was thick with the stench of sweat and despair, and Ryan could feel the weight of his sentence pressing down on him, crushing the last remnants of hope.

They emerged into the cold night air, the harbour shrouded in fog. The dark waters lapped against the wooden docks, and a massive ship loomed in the distance, its sails furled and its decks crowded with prisoners being herded aboard by armed guards.

Ryan was pushed forward, his chains clinking with each step. The air was thick with the stench of salt and fear. As he approached the gangplank, he looked up at the ship, the name "H.M.S. Inferno" painted in bold letters on the bow.

A sense of dread washed over him as he realized this was the vessel that would carry him far from everything he had ever known. He whispered to himself, "I don't want to go... I don't want to go..."

But there was no escape. The guards shoved him up the gangplank, and he stumbled onto the deck, where he was immediately jostled by the other prisoners. The deck was crowded and chaotic, with men shouting, crying, and struggling against their chains.

Ryan was pushed and pulled through the crowd, his heart pounding in his chest. He caught a glimpse of the shoreline as the ship began to move, the city of Cork disappearing into the fog. He felt a lump rise in his throat as he watched the land of his birth fade into the distance, knowing he might never see it again.

The ship's hold was dark and cramped, the air thick with the smell of unwashed bodies and rotting food. The prisoners were packed tightly together, with barely enough room to move. The constant creaking of the ship's timbers and the rhythmic sloshing of the sea made it impossible to sleep.

Ryan lay curled up on the rough wooden floor, shivering from the cold and fear. He stared up at the low ceiling, his mind racing with thoughts of his lost family and the fate that awaited him in Australia.

The sound of retching filled the air as one of the prisoners nearby succumbed to seasickness. The man, a burly convict with a thick beard and weathered face, groaned in pain, clutching his stomach.

"This bloody ship... it's going to kill us all..." the man groaned, his voice rough and filled with a lifetime of hardship.

Ryan's eyes flickered to the man, who looked to be in his late forties, toughened by years of hard living. Despite his fear, Ryan felt a strange pull toward him—this was a man who had clearly seen the worst life had to offer and had survived.

The convict caught Ryan's gaze and managed a weary smile, though it didn't reach his eyes. "Hang in there, lad," he rasped. "You've got a whole life ahead of you. This voyage... it's just one more hell to endure."

Ryan nodded, too scared and overwhelmed to respond. The man's presence, though rough and intimidating, offered a strange kind of comfort. It was as if, in this nightmare, the convict's hardened resolve was something solid to hold onto.

As the hours dragged on, the man's condition worsened. His breath became laboured, and a sheen of sweat covered his brow. Ryan, watching helplessly, saw the strength ebbing out of him, the life slowly slipping away.

"Listen, boy," the convict said suddenly, his voice a strained whisper. "You get through this... you find a way to survive, no matter what. The world's a cruel place...

but you don't let it break you. Not ever."

Ryan swallowed hard, his throat tight with emotion. He didn't know why this man was telling him these things, but he felt an unspoken connection, a passing of some invisible torch.

The convict leaned back against the wall, his breaths growing shallower. "Name's Ned Kelly," he muttered, his voice fading. "Don't forget it, lad... at least someone will remember me when I'm gone."

Ryan watched as the man—Ned Kelly—closed his eyes, his chest rising and falling with effort until it finally stilled. The hold seemed to grow quieter, the oppressive darkness closing in as Ryan realized that Ned was gone.

Ned's final words lingered in Ryan's mind, reverberating through the despair that had taken hold of him. He had promised to remember, and somehow, that promise started to feel like more than just a memory. It became a part of him, a part of the new identity he was slowly, unconsciously, beginning to form.

The journey to Australia was a brutal one. The ship was tossed about by violent storms, the waves crashing against the sides as the prisoners huddled together in the hold, praying for survival. The constant motion of the ship left many of the prisoners sick and weak, their bodies unable to cope with the relentless assault.

The days blurred together, the monotony broken only by the occasional fight between prisoners, which the guards broke up with brutal efficiency. Ryan struggled to keep up, his body weakened by hunger and exhaustion. But he refused to give up, driven by a fierce determination to survive.

As the days turned into weeks, Ryan's spirit was slowly crushed by the relentless brutality of the voyage. His eyes grew harder, his face more gaunt, as he retreated further into himself. The boy who had once been Ryan O'Donaghue was slowly fading away, replaced by something harder, colder....

Weeks passed, and the ship finally sailed into calmer waters. The prisoners were allowed on deck for some fresh air, though they remained shackled and under guard. Ryan stood at the railing, staring out at the vast ocean. The moonlight reflected off the water, casting an eerie glow over the scene.

He was lost in thought, the weight of his situation pressing down on him like a physical burden. The fear and despair that had gripped him during the voyage had not lessened; if anything, they had only grown stronger. But there was something else now, something that had begun to take root in his heart—a spark of defiance, a refusal to let the world break him.

An older man with a scarred face stood beside him, glancing over at Ryan with a knowing look. The man, Meagher, had the look of someone who had seen too much and survived against the odds.

"First time out to sea, lad?" Meagher asked, his voice low and gravelly.

Ryan nodded, his voice barely above a whisper. "Aye... except on my uncle's fishing boat in Cork, but it was nothing like this."

Meagher chuckled softly, though there was no warmth

in the sound. "It's a hard life, being a convict. But you've got a fire in you, I can see it. Don't let this place break you."

Ryan looked up at Meagher, surprised by the man's words. He had expected nothing but cruelty and indifference from the other prisoners, yet here was a man offering him something akin to advice.

"How do you survive it?" Ryan asked, his voice tinged with desperation.

Meagher's expression grew serious, his eyes darkening as he spoke. "You learn to fight. You learn to adapt. And you learn to never let them see you cry."

Ryan nodded slowly, taking the words to heart. He had already learned the first two lessons—the hard way—but the third was something he had yet to master. He had cried more times than he could count during the voyage, but now, as he stood on the deck of the ship, he vowed that he would cry no more.

Meagher clapped him on the shoulder, a gesture of camaraderie in a world where trust was scarce. "Remember, lad—once we're off this ship, it's a whole new game. You've got to be ready for it."

Ryan watched as Meagher walked away, his mind churning with thoughts of the future. He gripped the railing tightly, the cold metal biting into his palms.

"I'll survive this... I have to," Ryan whispered to himself, his voice filled with a newfound determination.

As the ship sailed on into the night, the stars twinkling above like distant, unreachable dreams, Ryan knew that he was no longer the same boy who had boarded the ship in Cork. The journey had changed him, hardened him, and he was beginning to understand that the boy who had once been Ryan O'Donaghue was slowly being replaced by someone stronger, someone more dangerous.

The transformation had begun, and there was no turning back.

The Australian coastline rose on the horizon, a jagged line that grew steadily clearer as the ship drew nearer. The land was unlike anything Ryan had ever seen— wild, vast, and untamed, stretching out under a sky that seemed endlessly blue. Gone were the misty, rolling fields of Ireland; this was a harsh, unforgiving place, where survival would be fought for and earned, not given.

The prisoners were herded together on the deck, their chains rattling as they stumbled forward. The air was thick with anticipation, fear, and a sense of finality. This was the end of the world they had known and the beginning of something entirely new. For Ryan, this marked the point of no return.

The ship docked with a groan of wood and iron, the ropes creaking as they secured it to the pier. The guards, their faces hard and unfeeling, began to shout orders, and the prisoners were marched off the ship and onto the shore. Ryan's feet hit the ground with a jarring thud. The earth beneath him was dry and cracked, the sun blazing down with an intensity that made his skin prickle and burn.

The warden of the prison camp awaited them, a man as unforgiving as the land itself. He was tall and broad, with a face weathered by years of breaking men down. His cold eyes swept over the new arrivals with calculated indifference, as if assessing how long it would take to crush the spirit out of each one.

"Welcome to your new home, boys," the warden's voice boomed, gruff and laced with menace. "The law brought you here, and the law will keep you here. Step out of line, and you'll find yourself six feet under. Do I make myself clear?"

The prisoners, Ryan among them, nodded mutely. The defiance that had flared within Ryan on the ship was still there, burning in his chest, but he kept it hidden behind a mask of submission. He knew better than to challenge authority outright, especially not here, not now. Survival, he reminded himself, was a game of patience.

The warden's gaze locked onto Ryan, his eyes narrowing as if he could see the fire that Ryan tried so hard to conceal. "You've got the look of a fighter, boy," he said, leaning in close, his breath hot and foul. "But we'll see how long that fire lasts in this hellhole."

Ryan met the warden's gaze without flinching, his jaw set in a line of steely determination. He said nothing, but his silence spoke volumes. The warden smirked, amused by the silent challenge, before turning away with a flick of his coat.

"Take them to their cells," he ordered the guards. "Make sure they understand the rules."

Ryan was shoved forward, led away from the docks and into the camp. The camp was a barren, desolate place, surrounded by high wooden fences topped with barbed wire. The ground was dry and dusty, the air thick with the smell of sweat, dirt, and despair. The prisoners were divided into small groups and escorted to their cells— cramped, filthy spaces with little more than a wooden cot and a bucket for a toilet.

Ryan's cell was at the far end of the block, isolated from the others. The door slammed shut behind him with a finality that echoed through the empty corridor. He sat on the rough wooden cot, staring at the walls of his new prison, his heart heavy with the weight of his situation. But somewhere deep inside, a spark of defiance began to grow, fuelled by the fire that had been ignited on the ship.

The days at the prison camp blurred together into a monotonous, gruelling routine. From sunrise to sunset, the prisoners were forced to work under the scorching sun, their bodies pushed to the limit by the relentless labour. Ryan's hands, once smooth and unblemished, became calloused and blistered, his muscles aching with the effort of each task. But he refused to give up, driven by a determination that grew stronger with each passing day.

The guards were brutal, taking pleasure in inflicting pain on those who dared to step out of line. Ryan watched as other prisoners were beaten for minor infractions, their cries of pain echoing through the camp. But he remained stoic, learning to hide his emotions behind a mask of indifference. He knew that showing weakness was a death sentence in a place like this.

Food was scarce, and what little they were given was

barely enough to keep them alive. Hunger gnawed at Ryan's stomach, a constant reminder of his desperation. Fights often broke out among the prisoners over scraps of food, and it wasn't long before Ryan found himself caught in the middle of one such brawl.

It was over a piece of stale bread, nothing more than a crust, but to the starving men of the camp, it was worth fighting for. Ryan had managed to snatch the crust from the ground, but before he could take a bite, a burly prisoner with a mean glint in his eye lunged at him, knocking him to the ground.

The force of the blow sent Ryan sprawling in the dirt, the taste of blood filling his mouth as his head struck the ground. He blinked up at the sky, dazed, his vision swimming as the other man loomed over him, his fists clenched and ready to strike again.

Ryan's instincts kicked in, and with a surge of adrenaline, he rolled to the side, narrowly avoiding the next punch. He scrambled to his feet, his body tense and ready for a fight. The burly prisoner charged at him again, but this time, Ryan was ready. He ducked under the man's swinging fist and delivered a swift, hard kick to his stomach.

The man doubled over with a grunt, but he wasn't finished yet. He lashed out, catching Ryan across the face with a powerful backhand. The impact sent Ryan stumbling, his vision blurring as pain exploded in his cheek.

But Ryan refused to back down. He wiped the blood from his lip and charged at the man, driving his shoulder into his gut with all the force he could muster.

The two of them crashed to the ground in a tangle of limbs, grappling and wrestling in the dirt.

Ryan's mind went blank, his body moving on instinct as he fought for survival. He could hear the shouts of the other prisoners, the jeers and taunts of those who were watching the fight, but they were nothing more than background noise. All that mattered was the man in front of him, the man who wanted to take what little he had left.

The fight seemed to last forever, but in reality, it was over in seconds. Ryan, fuelled by desperation and anger, managed to pin the man to the ground, his hands wrapped around his throat. The man struggled, gasping for air, his eyes wide with fear.

"Enough!" a voice shouted, cutting through the chaos. Ryan felt rough hands grab him, pulling him away from the other prisoner. The guards had arrived, their batons at the ready.

The burly prisoner lay on the ground, coughing and gasping for breath, but Ryan didn't feel any satisfaction in his victory. He was hauled to his feet by the guards, who shoved him back toward his cell with little regard for his injuries.

"Back to your hole, O'Donaghue," one of the guards sneered. "We'll deal with you later."

Ryan didn't resist as he was thrown back into his cell, the door slamming shut behind him. He slumped against the wall, his chest heaving as he tried to catch his breath. Blood dripped from his nose and mouth, his face bruised and swollen from the fight.

But despite the pain, despite the exhaustion that

weighed him down, Ryan felt a sense of triumph. He had fought back, and he had won. It was a small victory, but it was enough to keep the fire burning inside him.

As the weeks turned into months, Ryan began to adapt to life in the prison camp. He learned the rules of survival, the unspoken code that governed the interactions between prisoners and guards. He kept his head down, worked hard, and avoided unnecessary confrontations. But he never forgot what Meagher had told him on the ship: "Don't let this place break you."

Meagher had become something of a mentor to Ryan, teaching him the skills he needed to survive in the camp. The older man was shrewd and resourceful, with a network of allies among the prisoners. He knew how to get things done, how to find small comforts in a place where comfort was a luxury.

Under Meagher's guidance, Ryan began to form alliances with other prisoners, men who were just as determined to survive as he was. They watched each other's backs, shared what little they had, and quietly planned for the day when they would no longer be prisoners.

But the camp was taking its toll on Ryan, physically and mentally. The once-innocent boy from Cork was slowly being replaced by someone harder, someone more dangerous. His body became leaner and more muscular, his face harder and more determined. The days of feeling sorry for himself were long gone; now, every day was about survival, about getting one step closer to freedom.

One night, as Ryan lay awake in his cell, his mind

racing with thoughts of escape, the door creaked open. Meagher slipped inside, his face shadowed in the dim light.

"Ryan," Meagher whispered, crouching beside the cot. "It's time."

Ryan sat up, his heart pounding with anticipation. "Time for what?"

"To make our move," Meagher said, his voice low and urgent. "We've got a plan—a way out of this hellhole. But we need you, lad. Are you in?"

Ryan's thoughts raced. The desperation of the past months, the backbreaking labour, and the constant threat of violence had shaped him into someone unrecognizable from the boy who had once been Ryan O'Donaghue. He thought of his family—his brothers, his sister—wondering if they were even alive. What would they want him to do? But deep down, he knew there was no going back. The only way out was forward.

"I'm in," Ryan whispered back, his resolve hardening. "Let's do it."

Meagher's eyes glinted with approval. "Good lad. Stick close to me, and by morning, we'll be free men."

Ryan stood, his muscles tense with anticipation. The two men slipped out of the cell, moving silently through the shadows of the camp. The night air was cool, a stark contrast to the sweltering heat of the day, and the camp was eerily quiet. Most of the guards were likely half-asleep, tired from the long shifts under the blazing sun.

They made their way to the edge of the camp, where a

group of other prisoners was already waiting, hidden in the shadows. Ryan recognized some of them—men who had shared his suffering, men who were as desperate for freedom as he was.

Meagher had explained the plan in hushed whispers over the past few weeks: overpower the guards, take their weapons, and make a break for the wilderness. It was a simple plan, but it was also incredibly risky. One wrong move, and they could all end up dead. But Ryan knew that the only thing more dangerous than trying to escape was staying in the camp.

As they approached the first guard, Ryan's heart pounded in his chest, adrenaline surging through his veins. The guard was standing with his back to them, unaware of the group of prisoners sneaking up behind him. Ryan could feel the tension in the air, the unspoken fear that this could all go horribly wrong.

But there was no time for fear. Meagher gave the signal, and Ryan sprang into action. He lunged at the guard, grabbing him from behind and wrestling him to the ground. The guard struggled, but Ryan held on with a strength he didn't know he had. Meagher followed suit, quickly disarming the guard and taking his rifle.

The other prisoners moved swiftly, subduing the remaining guards and securing their weapons. Ryan stood over the guard he had taken down, his breath coming in ragged gasps. The rifle felt foreign but powerful in his hands, a tool that could finally give him a fighting chance.

"Come on, lad!" Meagher urged, urgency lacing his voice. "We've got to move!"

Ryan nodded, shaking off the lingering fear. The group of prisoners rushed toward the fence, using the stolen weapons to cut through the wires. The sharp metal bit into their hands, but they ignored the pain, driven by the singular goal of freedom.

Suddenly, the camp's alarm rang out, a loud, shrill sound that pierced the night air. The guards were scrambling, shouting orders and firing their weapons as they tried to stop the escape. The sounds of gunfire filled the air, bullets whizzing past Ryan's head as he and the others made a break for the wilderness.

Ryan fired his rifle, the recoil jarring him, but he didn't hesitate. There was no turning back now. He was in survival mode, every instinct focused on getting out of the camp alive. He ran faster, his legs burning with the effort, the dense underbrush scratching at his skin as he pushed through it.

The group of escapees raced through the wilderness, the sounds of pursuit growing fainter as they put more distance between themselves and the camp. But Ryan knew they weren't safe yet. The Australian outback was vast and unforgiving, filled with dangers that could kill them just as easily as the guards.

They ran until their lungs burned, and their legs threatened to give out. Finally, when they could go no further, Meagher called for them to stop. They collapsed in a small clearing, panting for breath, their bodies slick with sweat and blood. Ryan's heart pounded in his ears, the adrenaline still coursing through him.

"We did it," Meagher said, a grin spreading across his face as he looked at Ryan. "We're free."

But Ryan didn't share in the jubilation. He knew their freedom was temporary, that the authorities would be hunting them down. The wilderness offered no sanctuary, only a brief respite from the relentless pursuit of the law.

"We're not done yet," Ryan said quietly, his voice carrying the weight of their situation. "We've got to keep moving. Find a place to lay low, gather supplies... and then we strike back."

Meagher looked at Ryan with newfound respect. The boy from the ship was gone, replaced by a man who had learned to survive in the harshest of conditions, a man who was willing to do whatever it took to stay alive.

"Aye," Meagher agreed, nodding. "You've got the makings of a leader, lad. You keep that fire burning, and we might just make it out of this alive."

Ryan shook his head, a small smile playing on his lips, but there was no joy in it. "Not Ryan," he said, the words slipping out before he even realized it. "Not anymore."

Meagher raised an eyebrow, curious. "Oh? And who might you be now?"

Ryan looked out at the vast wilderness before them, the sun beginning to rise in the distance, casting long shadows over the land. He thought of everything he had lost, everything that had been taken from him. The boy who had once been Ryan O'Donaghue was gone, replaced by someone harder, someone who had been forged in the fires of suffering. The memory of his first friend on the ship—the burly convict who had shared his last words and his name—surfaced in his mind.

"Ned," he said, his voice firm, unyielding. "Ned Kelly."

Meagher nodded, as if the new name fit the man who stood before him. "Well then, Ned Kelly," he said, clapping Ryan on the back. "Let's see where this new life takes us."

The group of escaped convicts disappeared into the outback, the sun setting behind them in a blaze of orange and red. It was the beginning of a new chapter, one that would be filled with hardship, danger, and the fight for survival. But for Ryan—for Ned Kelly—it was more than just a chance to reclaim the life that had been stolen from him. It was a way to honour the memory of a man who had helped him survive the voyage, a way to forge a new identity in a world that had shown him no mercy.

As the sun dipped below the horizon, casting the outback in shadow, Ryan O'Donaghue felt the weight of his past bearing down on him like the suffocating heat of the Australian sun. The name Ryan O'Donaghue no longer held any meaning for him; it was a relic of a life that had been stripped away piece by piece, leaving nothing but a hollow shell. His parents, who had once been his anchor, were gone, their memory tainted by the cruelty of a world that had shown him nothing but hardship. Their love had been his only solace, and now it was nothing more than a distant echo in the void of his heart.

And then there was Christopher—his brother, his protector—who had promised to stand by him, to keep him safe in a world that sought to tear them apart. But Christopher had left him, abandoned him to rot in a cell while he sailed toward a new life in America. The betrayal cut deeper than any wound, severing the last thread that connected Ryan to the life he once knew. The boy who had clung to the hope of his brother's loyalty was dead, buried in the cold darkness of that prison cell.

Ryan knew that to survive in this unforgiving land, he had to shed the remnants of his old self, to sever the ties that bound him to a name that had brought him nothing but pain. The name O'Donaghue was a curse, a reminder of a life marked by loss, suffering, and betrayal. It was a name that carried the weight of a murder charge, a name that would forever be hunted, feared, and reviled.

But here, in the vast wilderness of Australia, Ryan saw an opportunity to start anew, to forge a new identity free from the shadows of his past. The man who had once been Ryan O'Donaghue was gone, replaced by someone harder, colder, and more determined. Someone who would not be broken by the cruelty of the world.

And so, as the outback swallowed the last light of day, Ryan made a choice—a choice to let go of the name that had defined him, to bury Ryan O'Donaghue alongside the memories of his family and the life that had been stolen from him. In its place, he would carry the name of the only friend he had made on that cursed voyage— the name of the man who had shared his last words and his final breath.

"Ned Kelly," Ryan whispered into the encroaching darkness, the words a vow, a declaration of his rebirth. "Ned Kelly" would be the name that this new world would come to know, a name forged in the fires of suffering and survival. It was a name that carried the legacy of a man who had refused to be forgotten, and it would become a symbol of the defiance and resilience that now burned within him.

As he stood there, looking out over the endless expanse of the outback, Ned Kelly knew that he would never return to the life he had once known. The boy from Cork was dead, and in his place stood a man ready to take on whatever the world had in store for him. This harsh, unforgiving land would come to know him not as a victim of fate, but as a legend—a man who had clawed his way back from the brink of despair and had risen to carve out a new destiny in a world that had shown him no mercy.

And with the setting sun as his witness, Ned Kelly swore that he would make the name he had chosen one that would never be forgotten.

CHAPTER 3: THE OUTLAW'S GAMBIT

The searing Australian sun bore down on the vast, unforgiving expanse of the outback. Red earth stretched endlessly in every direction, broken only by clusters of dry, scraggly bushes and the occasional lonely tree that fought its way up from the cracked ground. The sky was an endless blue dome, unmarred by clouds, the horizon wavering in the heat.

A group of ragged figures trudged through this desolate landscape, their shadows long in the late afternoon sun. These were no ordinary travelers; they were men who had escaped from the depths of despair, led by a man who had become more myth than flesh in the hearts of the oppressed. This man, once known as Ryan O'Donaghue, now bore the name that would strike fear and hope into the hearts of many: Ned Kelly.

Kelly's face was hard, his eyes sharp as they scanned the horizon. The weight of his past—of his family's suffering, of the injustices they had endured—pressed down on him like the relentless sun. But he bore it without complaint, driven by a purpose that had only grown stronger with each passing year. The boy who had once crossed the ocean to this strange, brutal land was gone. In his place stood a man who had vowed to tear down the chains that had bound him and his kin for so long.

Beside him walked Meagher, a man as tough as the land they traversed. Meagher was grinning despite the heat, his rifle slung over his shoulder, as if the hardships they faced were just another challenge to be bested.

"We've come a long way, lad," Meagher said, his voice rough but full of camaraderie. "From the pits of that prison to the wilds of the outback. What's the plan now?"

Ned didn't answer immediately. He was thinking ahead, always thinking ahead. They had managed to escape, to elude the clutches of the British authorities, but he knew that their struggle was far from over. They needed a place to rest, to regroup, but also to plan their next move. For Kelly, this wasn't just about survival—it was about striking back.

"We need to find a place to lay low," Ned said finally, his voice quiet but firm. "We'll gather our strength, and when we're ready, we'll hit them where it hurts."

Meagher nodded, a glint of excitement in his eyes. "You're a natural leader, Ned. The men will follow you anywhere."

Ned allowed himself a small, grim smile. Leadership was not something he had sought, but it had found him nonetheless. The men looked to him, trusted him to lead them in this desperate fight for freedom. It was a heavy burden, but one he accepted willingly.

"We'll make them pay," Ned said, his voice low, almost to himself. "For every injustice, for every life they've taken... we'll make them pay."

As the sun dipped lower in the sky, casting long shadows across the land, the group of outlaws continued their march, disappearing into the vast wilderness.

That night, they found refuge in an abandoned homestead. The building was dilapidated, the roof sagging in places, but it provided shelter from the cold night air and the prying eyes of the British patrols that scoured the countryside for them. Inside, the men gathered around a makeshift table, the flickering light of a single lantern casting shadows across their weary faces.

Ned spread out a worn map on the table, tracing a finger over the lines that marked the roads and towns of the region. He tapped a spot on the map, his eyes narrowing in concentration.

"This is our next target—Euroa," Ned said, his voice steady. "There's a bank there, and from what I've heard, it's ripe for the picking. We'll hit it hard and fast, take the money, and disappear before they even know what's happened."

The men nodded in agreement, their eyes gleaming with anticipation. Among them was young lad, not even Ned's age when he left Ireland as Ryan O'Donaghue, Denis Bambrick, who had joined the outlaws a few years earlier. Ned had taken the young boy under his wing, finding him hungry and desolate, following the brutal death of his parents by an aboriginal tribe as a result of an incursion of sacred land. Denis looked up at his powerful figure in Ned with a mixture of admiration and determination. This gang of hardened convicts was the only family he had left.

When Denis had joined them on his first raid, the lad had been transfixed by the sheer appearance of a wad of notes; he had never even held more than a couple of coppers, let alone a fist full of notes. He was also perfect at getting into those hard to reach areas where typically the most valuable items of the heist were burrowed away. The band of men adopted Denis as a mini protégé, and affectionately nicknamed him "Cashman", reduced even further to Cash.

"We'll show them, Ned," Cash said, his voice filled with youthful fervor. "We'll show them they can't push us around anymore."

Ned placed a hand on his "adopted" brother's shoulder, a rare moment of warmth breaking through his hardened exterior. "Aye, Cash. We'll show them."

Meagher leaned forward, his expression serious. "We'll need to be careful, though. The British are stepping up their patrols. They know we're out here, and they're getting desperate to catch us."

Ned nodded, his mind already working through the details of the plan. "We'll need to split up after the job," he said. "Regroup in the hills and wait for things to cool down. If we stick to the plan, we'll be fine."

The men murmured in agreement, their confidence in Ned unwavering. He had led them this far, and they trusted him to lead them to victory. Ned rolled up the map, his expression set with determination.

"Get some rest, lads," he said. "Tomorrow, we strike."

As the men dispersed, finding places to sleep within the homestead, Ned remained at the table, staring at the map, his thoughts racing. He could feel the weight of their expectations pressing down on him, but he welcomed it. He had chosen this path, and he would see it through to the end.

Rising from the table, he walked to the window, looking out at the moonlit landscape. The night was still, the only sound the distant call of a night bird. For a moment, Ned allowed himself to think of Ireland, of the green hills and misty mornings he had left behind. But that was a lifetime ago, in another world. Now, his battle was here, in this harsh, unforgiving land.

"For Ireland... for my family..." Ned whispered to himself. "I won't let them down."

The following morning, the town of Euroa bustled with activity, the townspeople going about their daily business, unaware of the storm that was about to descend upon them. The bank, a modest building in the center of town, was busy with customers, the clink of coins and the murmur of voices filling the air.

On a side street, just out of sight, Ned and his gang were making their final preparations. They were dressed in long coats and wide-brimmed hats, their faces partially obscured by scarves. The tension was palpable as they checked their weapons and went over the plan one last time.

"Remember," Ned whispered, his voice carrying the weight of command. "No unnecessary violence. We're here for the money, not bloodshed. Get in, get out, and don't let them catch you."

The men nodded, their faces set with determination. Ned took a deep breath, steadying his nerves. This was the moment of truth. Everything they had planned for led to this.

"Alright, lads," Ned said. "Let's go."

The gang moved out, splitting up as they approached the bank from different directions. Ned and Meagher led the way, their movements quick and efficient. They burst into the bank, weapons drawn, catching the customers and staff off guard.

"Everyone down! Now!" Ned shouted, his voice cutting

through the air like a whip.

The customers screamed and dropped to the floor, while the bank staff raised their hands in surrender. Ned and the others moved swiftly, rounding up the staff and forcing them to open the vault. The tension in the air was thick as the seconds ticked by, every moment bringing them closer to discovery.

At the doors, Cash and Joe Byrne kept watch, their eyes scanning the street for any signs of trouble. Joe, always the cautious one, whispered to his young accomplice, his voice tight with anticipation.

"We've got to be quick boy," Joe said. "The law could show up any minute."

Cashman nodded, his grip tightening on his rifle. Inside, Ned and Meagher worked quickly, emptying the vault and stuffing the money into sacks. The haul was substantial, more than they had dared to hope for. Enough to keep them supplied for months, maybe longer.

Ned glanced at the bank manager, who was cowering behind the counter, his face pale with fear.

"Don't do anything stupid," Ned said calmly. "And you'll live to see another day. Understand?"

The manager nodded frantically, too terrified to speak. Satisfied, Ned gave a signal to the others, and they began to move out, the money in tow. But just as they stepped outside, a shot rang out, shattering the tense silence.

One of the outlaws cried out, clutching his arm as blood seeped through his fingers. Ned whirled around, his eyes narrowing as he spotted a group of British soldiers emerging from a nearby alley, their rifles raised and ready.

"Surrender, Kelly!" the British officer shouted, his voice ringing out across the square. "You're surrounded!"

Ned's mind raced. They were outnumbered, but they weren't outgunned. Without hesitation, he raised his rifle and fired, the shot hitting one of the soldiers square in the chest. The gang quickly followed suit, a fierce firefight erupting in the middle of the town.

The townspeople scattered, diving for cover as bullets flew through the air. Ned and his gang fought with the desperation of men who knew they had no other choice. Each movement was precise, each shot fired with deadly intent. The bank heist had suddenly turned into a full-blown battle, and the streets of Euroa were now a battlefield.

Ned's sharp eyes took in the situation with rapid calculation. They were in a precarious position. The British soldiers were well-trained and disciplined, their movements coordinated as they advanced on the gang. The narrow streets of the town provided little cover, and Ned knew that they couldn't hold out for long.

Denis a.k.a. Cashman, just a few paces away, was exchanging fire with a group of soldiers who had taken cover behind a horse-drawn cart. Joe Byrne was beside him, his rifle steady as he squeezed off shots, his face set in a mask of concentration. Despite the chaos, Ned felt a surge of pride in his young protégé's resolve and in the loyalty of his men. They were outnumbered, but they were not outmatched.

"We need to retreat!" Meagher shouted over the din of

gunfire, his voice urgent. He had taken cover behind a stack of barrels, his rifle trained on the soldiers advancing from the opposite side of the street. "We can't hold them off here!"

Ned nodded sharply. He knew Meagher was right. They were running out of time, and the longer they stayed, the greater the risk of being captured or killed.

"To the horses!" Ned yelled, his voice cutting through the clamor. "Fall back!"

The gang began to move, firing as they went, covering each other as they made their way toward the alley where their horses were tied. Cashman took a step back, still firing, but a bullet whizzed past his ear, narrowly missing him. The sound of metal striking wood was followed by a shout of pain as one of the soldiers fell, clutching his side.

Ned reached his horse first, swinging into the saddle with practiced ease. He turned and fired one last shot, his gaze sweeping over the battlefield. His eyes locked on the British officer who had called for his surrender. The officer's face was a mask of determination, but there was also a flicker of something else—frustration, perhaps even fear.

Ned fired at the officer, the bullet grazing the man's arm, causing him to flinch and duck behind a nearby wagon. It wasn't a fatal shot, but it was enough to buy Ned and his men a few more precious seconds.

"Ride!" Ned shouted, spurring his horse into a gallop. The gang followed suit, their horses surging forward, hooves pounding against the dirt as they raced out of the town. Behind them, the soldiers gave chase, but the outlaws had a head start, and they knew the terrain better than their pursuers.

The gang galloped down the narrow streets, the wind whipping at their faces as they fled toward the outskirts of town. The sound of gunfire faded into the distance as they put more ground between themselves and the soldiers. But the danger was far from over. The British would not give up the chase so easily, and Ned knew that they would need to outmaneuver their enemies if they were to survive.

The landscape around them began to change as they left the town behind, the buildings giving way to the rugged wilderness of the Australian outback. The terrain was harsh and unforgiving, but it was also familiar to Ned and his gang. They had spent months hiding in these hills, learning every twist and turn of the land, every hidden ravine and treacherous path.

Ned led the way, his eyes scanning the terrain ahead. He knew that they couldn't outrun the soldiers forever; they needed a plan. As they approached a narrow pass between two cliffs, an idea began to form in his mind. It was risky, but it might just give them the edge they needed.

"Through the pass!" Ned called out, his voice carrying over the thunder of hooves. "Keep going, and don't stop until we're through!"

The gang obeyed without question, following Ned into the pass. The walls of the cliffs rose high on either side, the narrow path winding through the rocky terrain. The soldiers were still in pursuit, but the pass forced them to slow down, giving the gang a crucial advantage.

As they neared the end of the pass, Ned pulled a small revolver from his coat. His eyes locked onto a precariously balanced boulder high above the pass, its weight resting on a thin ledge. It was a long shot, but if he could dislodge it, it might block the pass and stop the soldiers in their tracks.

Ned took a deep breath, steadying his aim as the horses galloped beneath him. The sound of the soldiers' shouts echoed through the pass, growing louder as they closed the distance. Ned's finger tightened on the trigger, and he fired.

The shot rang out, the sound bouncing off the cliff walls. For a moment, nothing happened, and then, with a low rumble, the boulder began to shift. It teetered on the edge, and then, as if in slow motion, it tumbled down the cliffside, crashing onto the path below. The impact triggered a small landslide, rocks and debris cascading down, filling the narrow pass with a wall of rubble.

The soldiers pulled up short, their horses rearing as the path was blocked. The British officer cursed loudly, his face twisted in frustration as he realized that the outlaws had once again eluded him.

"Damn you, Kelly!" the officer shouted, his voice filled with rage. "You won't get away with this!"

But Ned was already far ahead, his mind focused on the next step of their plan. The gang rode hard, pushing their horses to the limit as they put more distance between themselves and their pursuers. The sun was beginning to set, casting long shadows across the land, and Ned knew that they needed to find a place to rest before nightfall.

As they rode, Ned's thoughts turned to their next move. The heist had been successful, but it had also been a close call. They had the money they needed, but they were now more wanted than ever. The British would stop at nothing to hunt them down, and Ned knew that they couldn't keep running forever.

They needed a safe place to hide, a place where they could regroup and plan their next move. And as the sun dipped below the horizon, bathing the outback in the soft glow of twilight, Ned began to form a new plan—one that would take them deeper into the wilderness, where the British would be hard-pressed to follow.

The gang rode through the night, the cool air a welcome relief after the blistering heat of the day. The land around them was a vast, empty expanse, the only sound the rhythmic pounding of hooves on the hard earth. The moon rose high in the sky, casting a silver light over the landscape, guiding them as they made their way deeper into the outback.

Finally, as the first light of dawn began to creep over the horizon, they reached their destination—a hidden cave nestled deep within the hills. The entrance was concealed by thick underbrush, and the cave itself was cool and dark, a perfect refuge from the dangers that lurked outside.

The gang dismounted, leading their horses into the cave. Inside, the men moved quickly to set up camp, their movements efficient despite their exhaustion. They tended to their wounds, dividing the spoils of the heist and sharing what little food they had left. Despite the hardships they had endured, there was a sense of camaraderie among the men, a bond forged in the fires of rebellion.

Ned Kelly sat by the fire in the hidden cave, staring into the flickering flames as the weight of the world pressed down on him. The escape from Euroa had been a success, and for a moment, it felt like a victory. But Ned knew better. The firelight cast shadows on the rough walls of the cave, making the figures of his men seem larger than life. They had divided the spoils of the heist, their spirits lifted by the weight of gold and the promise of survival. Yet, beneath the surface, the fear of what lay ahead gnawed at their resolve.

Denis "Cashman", his leg hastily bandaged, limped over to sit beside his brother. The young man's face, lined with exhaustion, bore a look of triumph that only youth could muster after such a harrowing ordeal.

"We did it, Ned," Cash said softly, a hint of pride in his voice. "We got away."

Ned nodded, though his expression was distant. "Aye, we did. But this is only the beginning, Cash. The British won't stop until they've hunted us down. We've got to be smarter, faster... more ruthless."

Cashman looked at his leader, sensing the heavy burden Ned carried. Ned had become more than just an outlaw leader; he was now a symbol, a beacon for those who had been wronged by the Empire. And with that symbolism came a responsibility that Cash knew weighed heavily on his Ned's shoulders. "Whatever happens, I'm with you, Ned. I'll follow you to the end."

Ned placed a hand on the young lad's shoulder, a rare

moment of tenderness breaking through his hardened exterior. "I know you will, Denis", using his birth name, acknowledging the significance of Cash's loyalty: "And I'll do whatever it takes to keep you safe."

The fire crackled softly, the warmth of the flames a welcome comfort in the cool night air. The gang sat around the fire, their faces illuminated by the flickering light, their spirits lifted by the successful escape. But even as they rested, Ned's mind was already working, planning their next move.

He knew that their fight was far from over. The British Empire was a powerful enemy, and they would stop at nothing to crush the rebellion. But Ned was determined to stand his ground, to fight for the freedom that had been denied to him and his family for so long.

As the first light of dawn began to break, casting a pale glow over the land, Ned rose from his place by the fire. He walked to the entrance of the cave, looking out at the vast expanse of the outback. The land was harsh and unforgiving, but it was also a place of freedom, a place where a man could make his own way, far from the reach of the British authorities.

Ned took a deep breath, the cool morning air filling his lungs. He knew that the path he had chosen was a dangerous one, but it was a path he was willing to walk.

As the sun rose higher in the sky, casting long shadows across the land, Ned turned back to the cave. His men were waiting, ready to follow him into the next battle. And Ned knew that, whatever lay ahead, he would face it with courage and determination.

The fight was far from over, but Ned Kelly was ready.

And with his men by his side, he knew that they would not go down without a fight.

As the days turned into weeks, Ned Kelly and his gang continued their campaign against the British. They were no longer just outlaws; they had become folk heroes, symbols of defiance against the crushing force of the British Empire. Each raid, each heist, brought them closer to the edge, but also deeper into the hearts of the oppressed. The Irish immigrants, who had come to Australia in search of a better life, saw in Ned Kelly a reflection of their own struggles. His actions resonated with them, his rebellion an echo of their own fight against centuries of tyranny.

The gang's attacks grew bolder, more daring. They robbed banks with precision, stole horses under the cover of darkness, and disrupted British supply lines, leaving chaos in their wake. The authorities were humiliated, their every attempt to capture Kelly thwarted by his cunning and audacity. The bounty on his head increased with each passing day, the manhunt becoming more desperate, more intense. Yet, no matter how many soldiers were sent, no matter how many traps were laid, Ned and his men remained elusive, always one step ahead.

In the remote recesses of the outback, away from the prying eyes of the British, Ned worked on a project that would come to define his legacy. His homemade armor, crafted from rough, unpolished metal plates, was a far cry from the sleek armor of knights. It was heavy, cumbersome, and crudely made, but it was functional. Each piece was designed to protect him from the bullets of the British soldiers. He tested the armor in secret, refining it with each trial, until it became more than just protection—it became a symbol of his unyielding spirit, his refusal to bow to the forces that sought to destroy him.

The tension within the gang built alongside their reputation. They knew the end was near, that the British would eventually corner them. But they were ready, prepared to face whatever came with the same defiance that had carried them this far. The days leading up to their final stand were marked by a grim determination, an unspoken understanding that they were walking into history.

As they prepared for their last battle, the gang took refuge in the small town of Glenrowan. The town was quiet, the streets deserted under the cover of night. But there was a sense of anticipation in the air, as if the town itself knew that something monumental was about to happen. The residents were asleep, unaware of the storm brewing on their doorstep.

Ned and his gang fortified the Glenrowan Inn, turning it into their final stronghold. The inn was dimly lit, the windows covered to keep out prying eyes. Inside, the men prepared for what they all knew could be their last stand. Weapons were laid out on tables, and the air was thick with tension and determination. This was it— the culmination of their fight, the moment that would define their legacy.

Ned stood at the center of the room, his armor clinging to his body like a second skin. The metal plates, though rough and unpolished, covered his chest, back, and limbs, leaving only his face exposed. The armor was heavy, but Ned wore it with ease, his movements deliberate and controlled. He knew that this armor was his best chance of surviving what was to come, but it was more than that. It was a statement, a challenge to the British forces: Come and get me.

Cashman approached him, his eyes wide with awe as he took in the sight of his leader in the armor. "Ned... you look like a bloody knight."

Ned smiled faintly, adjusting the straps of the armor. "This armor isn't just for show, Cash. It's our best chance of surviving what's coming."

Cash nodded, his expression serious. "The British are coming, aren't they? They're going to try and take us down."

Ned's smile faded, replaced by a look of steely resolve. "Aye, they're coming. And they'll come at us with everything they've got. But we won't go down without a fight."

Meagher, one of Ned's closest allies, stepped up beside him, his weapon at the ready. "We're with you, Ned. To the end."

Ned nodded, grateful for the loyalty of his men. These were the men who had stood by him through thick and thin, who had fought and bled alongside him. They were more than just followers—they were his brothers in arms, bound by a shared cause, a shared destiny.

"Then let's make them remember the name Kelly," Ned said, his voice filled with determination. "No matter what happens, they'll know we didn't go quietly."

The sound of hoofbeats in the distance grew louder, the unmistakable sign that the British forces had arrived.

The men inside the inn exchanged tense glances, their grip tightening on their weapons. This was it—the final showdown.

The British soldiers rode into Glenrowan with a thundering of hooves, their horses kicking up dust as they galloped through the deserted streets. The soldiers dismounted, their rifles at the ready, as they surrounded the inn. The officer in charge stepped forward, his voice cutting through the still night air.

"Ned Kelly! This is your last chance! Surrender now, and we'll spare your lives!"

Inside the inn, Ned exchanged a look with his men. They all knew there would be no surrender, no mercy to be found in the hands of the British. This was a fight to the death, and they were prepared to give their lives for the cause they believed in.

Ned stepped to the door, raising his rifle with a steady hand. His voice was low, almost a whisper, but the words carried the weight of a lifetime of defiance. "Come and get me."

With those words, the door to the inn burst open, and chaos erupted. Gunfire filled the air, bullets flying in all directions as the British soldiers charged. Ned and his gang fought with the desperation of men who had nothing left to lose. Every shot was fired with precision, every movement a calculated act of defiance. They were outnumbered, but they were not outmatched.

Ned's armor took hit after hit, the bullets ricocheting off the metal with a deafening clang. He kept moving, kept fighting, refusing to go down even as his men fell around him. Each shot he fired found its mark, each movement a testament to the skill and determination that had kept him alive for so long.

The battle raged with unrelenting fury, the air thick with smoke and the acrid stench of gunpowder. Ned's eyes burned with the intensity of a man facing his destiny, yet unwilling to surrender to it. He fought with everything he had, every ounce of strength and determination channeled into a singular goal: to endure, to survive.

But the British forces pressed in from all sides, their numbers overwhelming, their resolve unyielding. One by one, the members of Ned's gang were cut down. Young Cashman, who had stood fearlessly beside Ned through every trial, almost like a brother, fell with a cry, his body riddled with bullets. Nearby, Meagher, Ned's closest friend, took a hit to the shoulder and crumpled to the ground, his voice twisted in pain.

Seeing his young protégé fall, something inside Ned broke. A raw, burning rage surged through him, blurring the edges of his vision with red. He fought with a ferocity that defied reason, his every movement fueled by grief and defiance. But even his iron will could not hold back the advancing tide, and the weight of the soldiers bore him down at last. He crumpled to his knees, his armor battered and his limbs heavy from the relentless assault.

A British officer approached, his rifle leveled at Ned's chest, his expression as cold as the dawn air. Ned looked up, bloodied but unbroken, his breath coming in ragged gasps. "You can kill me... but you'll never kill what I stand for," he managed, his voice carrying a defiance that pierced the morning stillness.

For a moment, the officer hesitated, the gravity of Ned's words lingering between them. There was something in Ned's eyes—a fire, an unyielding determination that seemed almost beyond the grasp of mortal men. The officer's grip faltered on the trigger as doubt flickered in his mind. But then duty overtook hesitation, and he squeezed the trigger. The gunshot echoed through the air, and Ned's body fell back, motionless, into the dust.

Yet, as his body lay still, there was no sense of finality. His face, framed by the early light, bore a small, enigmatic smile, his eyes half-closed as if he lingered somewhere between life and death. Blood pooled beneath him, staining the earth, yet something about the scene resisted closure—something that suggested the man who lay there might yet have a final card to play.

As dawn broke over Glenrowan, the battlefield fell silent. Smoke curled into the sky above the ruins of the inn, mingling with the rising sun. The British soldiers stood around the fallen figures, their expressions a mixture of triumph and unease. They had won, but as they looked down at the still form of Ned Kelly, an unsettling thought gnawed at the edges of their victory: perhaps they had not truly defeated him after all.

The officer, his face shadowed with doubt, gazed down at Ned's body. He had done his duty, but he couldn't shake the sense that, in some unfathomable way, they had been outplayed. Ned Kelly—the outlaw, the legend —had fallen, but his death felt more like a question mark than an end.

As the sun crested the horizon, casting its golden light across Glenrowan, the story of Ned Kelly began to take root, whispered in hushed tones among those who had witnessed the battle. His name would echo through the hills, a reminder that defiance cannot be buried as easily as a body. And as they turned away from the scene, none noticed the faint flutter of breath on the breeze, the subtle shifting of shadows beneath the mask.

For Glenrowan, and the world, it seemed that Ned Kelly had died that morning. But perhaps, just perhaps, his story was not yet over.

CHAPTER 4: TAMMANY'S GRASP

The stench of death and sickness clung to the air, thick and unrelenting. Christopher O'Donaghue stood on the deck of the ship, his legs unsteady from the weeks spent at sea. The "Coffin ship," as the passengers had come to call it, had lived up to its grim reputation. They had left Ireland with over three hundred souls crammed into the hold, but now, with land finally in sight, it was clear that not all of them would step foot on American soil. Some had been buried at sea, their bodies wrapped in cloth and lowered into the cold depths, while others lay below deck, too weak to stand.

Christopher's grip tightened on the rail, his knuckles white against the rough wood. His body was sore, his muscles stiff from days spent in the cramped, disease-ridden quarters below. The smell of sweat, vomit, and rotting food had become so constant that he barely noticed it anymore. It was the smell of survival—of those who had endured the journey across the Atlantic, but barely.

The wind whipped across the deck, carrying with it the faint promise of land, but Christopher could barely muster the energy to care. His clothes hung loose on his body, the weight he had lost during the journey evident in the hollow look of his face. The sun, when it peeked through the clouds, did little to warm him. It had been a grueling voyage, filled with death and despair. And though New York's skyline loomed in the distance, the weight of what they had left behind still hung over him like a shadow.

He thought of Seamus and Rebecca back in Cork, of Uncle Michael's shop where he had spent his last days before leaving Ireland. They had all been so hopeful when he boarded the ship, believing that America would offer something better, something more than the hunger and despair that had swallowed their home. But the journey had been harder than he had imagined. People had died—more than anyone had anticipated. It wasn't the promise of freedom that awaited them; it was the bitter reality of survival.

Christopher turned, his eyes sweeping over the other passengers huddled on the deck. They were all Irish, all fleeing the famine that had ravaged their homeland. Mothers clutched their children close, their faces pale and gaunt from the long weeks at sea. Men leaned against the rails, coughing into their hands, their eyes hollow with exhaustion. The children, those who had survived, were quiet, their eyes wide with fear.

Christopher had tried to stay strong during the journey. He had kept to himself, helping where he could, but there was no escaping the sickness that spread like wildfire below deck. He had seen families torn apart as fathers and mothers succumbed to fever, leaving their children orphaned in a foreign land before they had even set foot on it. The cries of the dying had become a constant chorus, a reminder that not everyone would survive this journey.

He swallowed hard, his throat dry and raw. The thought of food made his stomach turn. The rations they had been given were barely edible—moldy bread, salted meat that tasted like rot, and water that was brackish at best. He had forced himself to eat, knowing that if he didn't, he might not make it to America. But now, standing here on the deck with the city in sight, he wondered if he had made the right choice.

The ship finally docked with a jarring thud, and the passengers slowly began to disembark. There was no rush. No one had the strength to push forward. Christopher watched as the people around him stumbled down the gangplank, their feet unsteady on the solid ground. He waited his turn, his body swaying as the ship rocked gently in the harbor. When he finally stepped onto the dock, the world spun around him, and he had to steady himself against a nearby crate.

The air here was different—fresher, though still filled with the sounds and smells of the city. But after weeks at sea, it was almost a relief. Almost.

Christopher took a deep breath, trying to clear his head. He felt light-headed, his legs weak from the journey, but there was no time to rest. The immigration officers were already shouting at the passengers to line up, barking orders as they prepared to process the newcomers. He wiped a hand across his forehead, wiping away the sweat that had gathered there. The ship had taken so much from them, but now came the real test.

He shuffled forward with the others, his bag slung over one shoulder. It was a small bag—everything he owned, packed into one worn leather satchel. He could feel the weight of Uncle Michael's letter inside, though he hadn't read it in days. He hadn't had the heart.

As he approached the line, his eyes flicked over the faces of the other Irish immigrants, each one etched with the same exhaustion and desperation he felt. The officer in front of him looked bored, his mustache twitching as he scanned the crowd.

"Papers!" the officer shouted.

Christopher reached into his coat and pulled out the crumpled documents, handing them over with a trembling hand. The officer glanced at them briefly before stamping them with a loud thud.

"Move along."

Christopher nodded, stuffing the papers back into his coat as he moved past the officer. He could barely keep his eyes open. The journey had drained him of everything—his strength, his hope, even his sense of purpose. He wanted to collapse right there on the dock, to lay down and sleep for days. But he knew he couldn't. Not yet.

The streets of New York were a blur. As Christopher made his way through the city, he couldn't take it all in. The towering buildings, the noise, the people moving in every direction—it was too much, too fast. He stumbled down a narrow alley, his vision swimming. The smells of the city—coal smoke, garbage, and something he couldn't quite place—mixed with the nausea that had been his constant companion on the ship.

He found a small, dark corner at the edge of the alley and collapsed against the wall, his breath coming in ragged gasps. The exhaustion hit him like a wave, pulling him under. He had survived the journey, but now he was here, alone in a city that felt just as foreign and hostile as the Atlantic.

He closed his eyes, the weight of everything pressing down on him. The ship, the famine, the dying faces of those who hadn't made it... all of it came crashing down. He had come to America for a fresh start, but now, sitting here in the shadows, he wasn't sure if he had the strength to carry on.

Hours passed. Christopher wasn't sure how long he sat there, slumped against the wall. The noise of the city faded into the background, a dull hum that he barely noticed. At some point, the sun had begun to set, casting long shadows across the street. His body ached, his head throbbed, and his stomach growled with hunger, but he couldn't bring himself to move.

Eventually, the sound of footsteps pulled him from his stupor. He looked up, squinting through the dim light as a figure approached. For a moment, he thought it might be one of the immigration officers, come to drag him back to the ship. But as the figure drew closer, Christopher realized it was just a man—an Irishman, by the look of him.

The man stopped a few feet away, his eyes narrowing as he took in the sight of Christopher slumped against the wall. "You alright, lad?"

Christopher blinked, trying to focus. His throat was dry, his voice barely a whisper. "I…I think so."

The man crouched down, looking him over with a mixture of curiosity and concern. "You look like you've been through hell."

Christopher let out a bitter laugh. "Aye. You could say that."

The man nodded, his expression softening. "Came over on the Coffin ships, did you?"

"Aye."

The man stood and offered Christopher a hand. "Come on, then. You can't stay here all night. Let's get you sorted."

Christopher hesitated for a moment, then reached up and took the man's hand. His legs wobbled as he stood, but the man held him steady. "Thank you," he muttered.

"Don't mention it. Name's Sullivan, by the way."

"Christopher O'Donaghue."

Sullivan gave him a once-over, then clapped him on the back. "Well, Christopher O'Donaghue, welcome to New York. It's a tough place, but you'll find your way. Just need a bit of rest first."

Christopher nodded weakly, grateful for the help. The journey wasn't over, but for the first time since leaving Ireland, he felt a flicker of hope.

Christopher woke the next morning with the dull ache of hunger gnawing at his stomach. The hard floor beneath him offered no comfort, but the rough wool blanket draped across his body was a welcome surprise. It took him a moment to remember where he was— the dark, cramped room at the back of the tenement building that Sullivan had led him to the night before. The walls were damp, the air thick with the smell of mold, but it was a roof over his head, and for now, that was enough.

Sitting up, he glanced around the room. There was a small, rickety table near the window, a chair with one leg shorter than the others, and a half-empty pitcher of water. His bag lay in the corner, untouched. For a moment, Christopher allowed himself to feel a sliver of relief. He had made it through the first night.

But as he stood, his legs weak and unsteady, the reality

of his situation hit him like a wave. He had nothing—no money, no family, and no prospects. He had come to America with the hope of building a new life, but the journey had stripped him of everything. He felt hollow, like a shell of the man who had left Ireland months ago.

A knock at the door startled him. Before he could answer, the door creaked open, and Sullivan stepped inside, a grin on his face.

"Morning, lad," Sullivan said, tossing a small loaf of bread onto the table. "Thought you could use something to eat."

Christopher's stomach growled at the sight of the bread, and he quickly tore off a piece, shoving it into his mouth. It was stale, but it was food. After weeks of near starvation on the ship, he wasn't about to complain.

"Thank you," Christopher muttered between bites.

Sullivan waved a hand dismissively. "Don't mention it. You'll find that us Irish have to stick together in this city. It's not kind to those who come here with nothing."

Christopher nodded, his mouth too full to respond.

Sullivan pulled up the rickety chair and sat down, leaning back with a casual ease. "You've got the look of a man who's been through it. What's your story, then?"

Christopher swallowed hard, the lump of bread catching in his throat. He hadn't thought about telling anyone his story—hadn't even thought about the words he would use to describe everything that had happened. His thoughts flickered back to Ireland, to the famine, to Seamus and Rebecca. It all felt so far away now, like another life.

"I left Ireland to escape the famine," Christopher said slowly, the words heavy in his mouth. "My family... they're still there. Seamus and Rebecca, my younger siblings, they're with my Uncle Michael in Cork. I came here to..."

He trailed off, unsure how to finish the sentence. What had he come here to do? Survive? Build a new life? It all seemed so distant now, after everything he had endured.

Sullivan nodded, his expression serious. "I understand. A lot of us came here for the same reason. Ireland's been bleeding for years, and America seemed like the answer. But this city—it's a hard place, lad. You'll find that out soon enough."

Christopher frowned, looking down at the loaf of bread in his hands. "I thought... I thought it would be different. I thought there would be work, opportunities. But all I see is more struggle."

Sullivan sighed, rubbing a hand over his unshaven face. "Aye, that's the truth of it. You'll get by, but it won't be easy. The Irish aren't exactly welcomed with open arms here. The Americans don't want us, and the ones with power—they don't care about us. You'll need to find a way to survive, and that means doing things you might not be proud of."

Christopher's stomach twisted at the implication. "What do you mean?"

Sullivan shrugged, leaning forward. "There's work, aye. But it's not the kind of work you might've imagined. This city runs on deals, and those deals aren't always clean. If you want to make a life for yourself, you'll need friends. Connections. And those connections... well, they come with a price."

Christopher's heart sank. He had known, deep down, that this would be the case. He had heard stories about the gangs and political machines that controlled New York, about Tammany Hall and the corruption that ran through the city like a dark vein. But he had hoped— hoped that there might be a way to make it on his own, without falling into that world.

Sullivan watched him carefully, his eyes narrowing. "You've got that look about you—the look of a man who thinks he can make it without getting his hands dirty. Let me tell you something, lad. No one makes it in this city without getting a little mud on their boots."

Christopher didn't respond. He couldn't. The weight of his exhaustion, both physical and emotional, pressed down on him like a lead blanket. He wanted to believe that there was still a way out, still a way to make something of himself without giving in to the darkness that seemed to loom over every corner of the city. But the truth was, he didn't know if he had the strength to fight anymore.

"I'll think about it," Christopher muttered finally, though the words felt hollow in his mouth.

Sullivan nodded, standing up and dusting off his coat. "You do that. But don't think too long. This city doesn't wait for anyone."

He turned to leave, but paused at the door, glancing back over his shoulder. "If you need work, real work, come find me at O'Grady's Tavern down on the Bowery. We've got connections. People who can help you get on your feet. But like I said—it won't be clean."

With that, he left, closing the door behind him with a soft thud.

Christopher sat in silence for a long time, staring at the loaf of bread on the table. His body was still sore from the journey, his mind foggy with exhaustion. But Sullivan's words echoed in his head, refusing to leave him in peace.

The city doesn't wait for anyone.

He knew that Sullivan was right. The few hours he had spent wandering the streets after arriving had shown him that much. New York was a place of constant movement, of ambition and desperation. No one would stop to help him. No one would offer him a hand unless they had something to gain from it.

His thoughts drifted back to Ireland, to Seamus and Rebecca. They were counting on him. Uncle Michael had trusted him to make a better life for their family, to send money back home so they could survive. Christopher couldn't fail them—not after everything they had been through. But the path that lay ahead of him was dark and uncertain, and he wasn't sure if he could walk it without losing himself along the way.

Pushing himself up from the table, Christopher crossed the room to the small, cracked window. Outside, the city was waking up, the streets coming alive with the sound of carriages and vendors setting up their stalls. He watched as people moved past, their faces a blur of determination and exhaustion. They all had their own stories, their own struggles, but none of them would stop to help him. This was New York. Everyone was on their own.

Taking a deep breath, Christopher turned away from the window and grabbed his coat. His legs wobbled as he stood, but he forced himself to keep moving. He couldn't stay here, waiting for a miracle. He had to find work, and fast.

As he stepped out onto the street, the cold morning air bit into his skin, waking him up fully for the first time in days. He pulled his coat tighter around him and began walking, his mind already churning with thoughts of what lay ahead. Sullivan had offered him a way in—a chance to make connections, to find a foothold in the city. But at what cost? And was it a price he was willing to pay?

The day passed in a blur of exhaustion and frustration. Christopher knocked on doors, spoke to shopkeepers, and even tried his luck at the docks, but everywhere he went, the answer was the same—no work for an Irishman. The Americans wanted nothing to do with him, and even the few Irish shopkeepers he found were barely scraping by themselves.

By the time the sun began to set, Christopher's legs were aching, and his stomach was growling with hunger. He hadn't eaten since the small loaf of bread that morning, and the exhaustion from the journey still weighed heavily on him. But he couldn't stop. Not yet.

As he made his way down a narrow street in the Bowery, his thoughts turned back to Sullivan's offer. O'Grady's Tavern wasn't far from here. He could find Sullivan, see what kind of work he was talking about. It wouldn't be clean, but maybe—just maybe—it would be enough to get him through the next few days. And after that? He didn't know. But right now, survival was all that mattered.

Taking a deep breath, Christopher turned toward the tavern, the flickering light from its windows casting long shadows on the street.

The days blurred into weeks, and the weeks into months. Christopher had become a familiar face at O'Grady's Tavern, running errands for Tammany men, delivering messages and packages that grew heavier with meaning. The small tasks had given way to more serious responsibilities—intimidating local business owners who hadn't paid their dues, ensuring political rivals kept their distance. Every task solidified his place in the web of Tammany Hall, and every time he returned to Sullivan, the man's smile grew wider.

But with each step deeper into Tammany's world, Christopher's sense of unease grew. The hunger for power he saw in the men around him, the cold, calculating way they dealt with problems—it wasn't the life he had imagined when he'd arrived in New York. And yet, he couldn't deny the opportunities that had opened up for him since he'd thrown in his lot with Tammany. The streets, once hostile and indifferent, now bent to his will. Where there had once been closed doors, there were now nods of recognition, doors that opened without question.

It was Sullivan who first suggested the idea. They had been sitting in the corner of O'Grady's, the familiar haze of smoke hanging in the air, when Sullivan leaned forward, his voice low.

"You ever thought about joining the police, O'Donaghue?"

Christopher had blinked, unsure if he'd heard him correctly. "The police?"

Sullivan nodded, taking a long drag from his cigarette. "Tammany's got a lot of influence with the force. You've proven yourself to be reliable, and we could use a man like you on the inside. It'd be good for you, too. Get some protection. Rise through the ranks. Hell, you might even make captain one day."

Christopher had scoffed at the idea at first. Him? A policeman? After everything he'd done, all the lines he had crossed, the idea seemed laughable. But Sullivan's tone was serious, and as the days passed, Christopher found himself considering it more and more. It wasn't just about survival anymore. It was about control— control over his own fate, over the city that had once threatened to swallow him whole.

The decision had been made in a moment of clarity, or perhaps desperation. Christopher had stood in front of the mirror in his small room, his eyes hollow from sleepless nights, his hands shaking with the weight of the choices he had made. He didn't recognize the man staring back at him. But maybe, just maybe, this was a way to regain some of the dignity he had lost. A way to build something real.

Christopher's initiation into the New York City police force was swift. The uniform they gave him was a little too large, the boots stiff and unyielding, but it carried with it an undeniable sense of authority. As he walked the streets of New York in his new role, Christopher felt the eyes of the people on him—some filled with hope, others with suspicion or resentment. The badge on his chest marked him as a figure of power, but it also made him a target.

The city was a maze of contrasts. One moment, Christopher would be patrolling past grand townhouses and bustling businesses, and the next, he would find himself in the narrow, filthy alleys of the slums. Poverty and wealth existed side by side here, and it was his job to keep the peace between these disparate worlds.

But Christopher quickly learned that being a cop in New York was not just about enforcing the law. It was about navigating the complex web of politics, crime, and loyalty that defined the city. Every decision he made, every action he took, was scrutinized—not just by his superiors, but by the powerful men of Tammany Hall who had placed him here.

One day, as Christopher was patrolling his beat, he was approached by Michael Flanagan, the quick-talking enforcer who had been with Liam when Christopher first went to O'Grady's. Flanagan was a shrewd man, always with a smile on his face that didn't quite reach his eyes. Christopher had learned to be cautious around him, knowing that Flanagan's interests were always aligned with Tammany's, not his own.

"O'Donaghue," Flanagan called out, his voice cheerful as he approached. "Just the man I was looking for."

Christopher stopped and turned to face him, his expression guarded. He had a feeling that whatever Flanagan wanted, it wasn't going to be good for him.

"There's a little situation down by the docks," Flanagan continued, his tone casual but with an edge of urgency. "Some of our friends are having trouble with the authorities. Thought you might be able to lend a hand."

Christopher knew immediately what Flanagan meant by "friends." He was referring to the smugglers who operated under Tammany's protection, bringing in contraband and goods that were sold on the black market. It was a lucrative business, and one that Christopher had been warned to steer clear of.

"What kind of help are you looking for?" Christopher asked, his voice flat.

"Just a bit of discretion, officer," Flanagan said with a grin. "Maybe look the other way while our boys unload some goods. Nothing too serious."

Christopher felt a wave of discomfort wash over him. He knew that getting involved in this could put him at odds with everything he stood for, but he also knew that refusing could make him an enemy of Tammany Hall. He was already too deep to back out now, and the thought of what Tammany could do to him if he crossed them sent a chill down his spine.

"I'll see what I can do," Christopher said finally, his tone grudging. "But remember, I'm not here to break the law."

Flanagan clapped him on the back, a satisfied grin on his face. "That's the spirit, O'Donaghue. We knew we could count on you."

As Flanagan walked away, Christopher stood there, the weight of the decision he had just made pressing down on him like a physical burden. He had come to this city to build a new life, to leave behind the poverty and despair of his past, but now he was caught in a web of corruption and deceit that threatened to destroy everything he had worked for.

Becoming a policeman hadn't been as difficult as Christopher had expected.

The streets took on a different feel now. Walking his beat, dressed in his new uniform, Christopher felt the weight of authority settle on his shoulders. The power that came with the badge was intoxicating, and for a time, it allowed him to push aside the nagging doubts that had been gnawing at him.

He began to climb the ranks quickly. The small favors he did for Tammany didn't go unnoticed, and soon, he was more than just another Irish immigrant on the force. He became known as the man who could get things done, the officer who looked the other way when needed and enforced the law when it suited the powers behind the scenes.

But with every promotion, the weight of Tammany's grip on him tightened. The favors became bigger, the expectations more dangerous. There were nights when Christopher lay awake in his small apartment, staring at the ceiling, wondering how far he was willing to go. The money was good, the power even better, but the price was his soul, and he could feel it slipping further away with each passing day.

By 1855, Christopher had risen to the rank of captain.

His uniform was crisp, his badge polished, and when he walked the streets, people stepped aside. But with his newfound status came new responsibilities. He was no longer just a pawn in Tammany's game—he was a player, and that came with its own dangers. Political favors, backroom deals, and the occasional "enforcement" were all part of the job now. And every time he thought about walking away, Sullivan was there, reminding him of everything Tammany had done for him.

"You're one of us now, O'Donaghue," Sullivan had said one night, clapping him on the shoulder. "There's no going back."

The morning sun poured into the narrow alleyways of the city, casting long shadows on the cobblestone streets. Christopher O'Donaghue stood at the precinct window, his uniform freshly pressed, his captain's badge shining on his chest. The rise to captain had come quicker than he expected—Tammany's influence, their subtle maneuvering behind the scenes, had cleared the way for his promotion. But with every step he climbed, the weight on his shoulders grew heavier.

It was strange, Christopher thought, how success had begun to taste bitter. He turned away from the window, his mind buzzing with thoughts of the favors he owed to men like Sullivan, of the whispered deals made in smoke-filled rooms. His grip tightened on the morning paper in his hand, the ink smudging slightly under his fingers. He had been reading it absently, scanning through the usual reports, when a single name caught his eye.

Kelly. Ned Kelly.

His heart skipped a beat as he read further.

"Outlaw Ned Kelly Killed in Australia," the headline blared. His breath hitched, the words blurring for a moment as he stared at the page. For most, the name meant nothing more than the tale of a notorious Australian criminal finally meeting his end. But for Christopher, the name rang out with personal pain and recognition.

Ned Kelly... His brother.

It felt like the air had been sucked from the room. Years ago, not long after he had set foot in New York, before the corruption of Tammany Hall had taken its toll on his soul, Christopher had received a letter from Uncle Michael. A letter that revealed Ryan—his younger brother—had escaped the penal colony in Australia and taken on the name of Ned Kelly. The letter had been brief, filled with hope that Ryan had forged a new life for himself, far away from the British and their tyranny.

Now, that hope was gone.

Christopher read the details of the article, his mind spinning. The man described in the article—an outlaw, a rebel, a fugitive—was not the brother he remembered. It was hard to reconcile the boy from Cork, the boy who had stolen bread to survive, with the legend of Ned Kelly, a man who had fought against the colonial authorities and been killed in a final stand.

For a moment, Christopher felt the world tilt. The corruption he had allowed to fester in his own life, the compromises he had made to survive, suddenly seemed too much. What had he become? What would Ryan—

Ned—think of him now? Had he turned into something worse than the enemies they had once fought against?

His hands trembled as he set the newspaper down on the desk, the room seeming to close in on him. Memories of Ireland flooded back—the famine, the hunger, the promises he had made to protect his family. He had promised Ryan that he would find a way for them to survive, to escape the poverty and oppression that had destroyed their homeland. But here he was, alive, wearing the uniform of a captain in New York's police force, but feeling hollow, tainted by the very power he had sought.

It was a bitter realization, and for the first time, Christopher wondered if his soul could still be saved.

The day wore on, but the thoughts gnawed at him relentlessly. He couldn't shake the image of his brother's face—the way Ryan had looked at him before they were separated, before Christopher had boarded that ship to America, leaving Ryan to face his fate in Ireland. The guilt simmered beneath the surface, a dark weight that had followed him ever since.

Now, reading about Ryan's death, it all came rushing back.

By the afternoon, Christopher couldn't stand the suffocating silence of the precinct any longer. He grabbed his coat and left, walking the streets of New York, his mind buzzing with thoughts of Ireland, of Ryan, of the choices he had made. The city pulsed around him—the noise of carriages, the calls of vendors, the distant hum of factory bells—but Christopher felt detached, as though he were walking through a fog.

Eventually, he found himself back at O'Grady's Tavern. It was a place he had come to associate with deals, power, and the ever-watchful eye of Tammany Hall. But now, it felt different—like a cage.

Sullivan was there, as always, nursing a pint at the bar. His sharp eyes flicked up as Christopher entered, and he gave a slow smile.

"Captain O'Donaghue," he said, his voice low and smooth. "Looking sharp as ever."

Christopher didn't respond at first. He simply sat at the bar, his mind still spinning from the morning's news. He stared at his reflection in the glass of the whiskey bottle, wondering how it had come to this.

"What's on your mind, lad?" Sullivan asked, his tone a mixture of curiosity and amusement. "You look like you've seen a ghost."

Christopher's jaw tightened. "I read about my brother today," he said, his voice rough. "Ryan. He's dead."

Sullivan raised an eyebrow, but said nothing.

"He went by the name Ned Kelly in Australia," Christopher continued, the words tumbling out before he could stop them. "He was an outlaw. Killed in a shootout. And I... I didn't even know."

There was a silence between them, the weight of it heavy in the air. Sullivan took a long drink, his eyes never leaving Christopher's face.

"Well, that's the way of the world, isn't it?" Sullivan said finally, his tone calm, almost indifferent. "We all make our choices. Your brother chose his path. You chose yours."

Christopher's hands clenched into fists. "But what kind of path is this? What have I become?"

Sullivan's smile faded slightly, his eyes narrowing. "You've become a captain in the New York police, backed by men with real power. You've made something of yourself in this city, O'Donaghue. Don't go soft on me now."

But Christopher wasn't listening. His mind was far away, back in Cork, back in the fields where he and Ryan had run as children. He could still hear Ryan's voice, laughing, full of life and hope. And now that voice was silenced forever.

"I need to think," Christopher muttered, standing abruptly.

Sullivan watched him go, his expression unreadable.

As the months turned into years, Christopher found himself sinking deeper into the murky waters of New York politics. Tammany Hall had its tentacles in every aspect of the city, and Christopher was no exception. He learned quickly that in order to survive, he had to navigate the delicate balance between enforcing the law and maintaining his loyalty to the powerful organization that had helped him rise.

Christopher turned a blind eye to minor infractions, allowing certain activities to go unpunished in exchange for the promise of protection and Favor from Tammany. It was a slippery slope, one that Christopher struggled to reconcile with his own sense of integrity. He knew that he was compromising, but he told himself that it was necessary—that he had to play the game in order to survive.

Despite the compromises, Christopher's reputation grew. He was known as a tough but fair captain, a man who could be relied on to get the job done. He rose through the ranks of the police force, his influence expanding with each promotion. But with each step up, Tammany Hall's hold on him tightened.

Christopher was invited to lavish parties thrown by Tammany Hall, where he rubbed shoulders with politicians, businessmen, and criminals alike. These gatherings were a display of wealth and power, a stark contrast to the poverty and desperation that filled the streets of the city. Christopher moved through these circles with caution, aware that every word he spoke, every gesture he made, was being observed and evaluated.

At night, when the city was quiet and the weight of his choices pressed down on him, Christopher would stand at his office window, staring out over the city he had come to call home. The lights of New York stretched out before him, a glittering expanse of opportunity and danger. He had achieved a level of success that he had once only dreamed of, but it had come at a cost.

Christopher knew that he was standing on the edge of a precipice. One wrong move, one misstep, and everything he had built could come crashing down. He was playing a dangerous game, and the stakes were higher than ever.

One night, Christopher was called to the docks by Flanagan. The moon hung low in the sky, casting an eerie glow over the water. The air was thick with the smell of salt and the faint stench of rotting fish. Christopher had a bad feeling about this, but he had learned to hide his unease behind a mask of calm.

When he arrived, Flanagan was waiting for him, his expression serious. "This is a big one, O'Donaghue," Flanagan said, his tone lacking its usual cheerfulness. "We need you to keep things quiet—make sure nothing goes wrong."

Christopher nodded, though his stomach churned with the implications of what he was about to do. He had been involved in minor operations before, but this felt different—bigger, more dangerous.

"I'll take care of it," Christopher said, his voice grim.

As the shipment arrived, Christopher oversaw the operation, ensuring that the goods were unloaded without interference. The night was quiet, too quiet, and Christopher couldn't shake the feeling that something was about to go wrong.

His instincts proved correct. Just as everything seemed to be going smoothly, a rival gang ambushed the operation. The night exploded into chaos as bullets flew through the air, men shouting and scrambling for cover. Christopher found himself in the middle of the firefight, his heart pounding as he fought to protect himself and the shipment.

The violence was brutal and swift. Christopher managed to hold his ground, but the experience left him shaken. As the last of the rival gang members fled into the darkness, Christopher surveyed the damage. Men lay dead or wounded on the ground, the shipment scattered across the dock.

Christopher had survived, but he knew that this was only the beginning. He had been dragged into something much bigger than himself, something that threatened to consume him. And as he stood there, the smoke of gunfire still lingering in the air, Christopher made a decision.

He couldn't continue down this path. He had to find a way out of Tammany Hall's grasp before it destroyed him.

The next morning, Christopher was summoned to Tammany Hall's headquarters. The mood was tense as he entered the grand office where Boss Tweed and Liam O'Sullivan were waiting. The air was thick with unspoken accusations, and Christopher could feel the weight of their disappointment.

"That was a close call, O'Donaghue," Boss Tweed said, his voice dripping with anger. "We can't afford any more mistakes. You're valuable to us, but don't think for a second that you're untouchable."

Christopher met Tweed's gaze, his own anger simmering beneath the surface. He had done his job, had risked his life to protect the shipment, and yet here he was, being chastised like a child.

"I did my job," Christopher replied, his voice firm. "But I won't be dragged into any more of your schemes. I'm here to protect this city, not to be your puppet."

Tweed's eyes narrowed, and for a moment, the tension in the room was palpable. But before things could escalate further, Liam stepped in, his tone smooth and conciliatory.

"Now, now, gentlemen," Liam said, his voice a soothing balm on the frayed nerves in the room. "Let's not lose sight of what's important. We're all working toward the same goal, aren't we? A prosperous New York for all of us."

Christopher nodded, though his resolve was firm. He knew that he couldn't continue down this path. He had to find a way out before Tammany Hall's grasp tightened even further.

"I'm not your errand boy, Tweed," Christopher said, his voice steady. "I'll do my duty, but I'm not compromising my integrity any further."

Boss Tweed leaned back in his chair, a calculating look in his eyes. "We'll see how long that lasts," he said, his tone dismissive.

Christopher left the meeting with a sense of determination. He knew that breaking free from Tammany Hall wouldn't be easy, but he was willing to do whatever it took to reclaim his integrity and his future.

As Christopher walked the streets of New York, his mind raced with thoughts of how to escape the stranglehold that Tammany Hall had on him. He knew that the consequences of defying them could be severe, but he also knew that he couldn't continue to live this way. He had come to this city to build a better life, and he was determined to do so on his own terms.

As he passed by a recruitment poster for the Union Army, Christopher stopped in his tracks. The bold lettering called for men to fight for the preservation of the Union. The Civil War was raging, and the country was in desperate need of soldiers.

Christopher stared at the poster, the wheels turning in his mind. Joining the army would be a way out —a way to escape Tammany Hall's grasp and to fight for something he believed in. It would be a chance to prove himself, to make a difference, and to reclaim his honour.

With a renewed sense of purpose, Christopher made his way to the recruitment office. The building was bustling with activity, filled with men signing up to fight in the war. Christopher approached the desk, where a recruiting officer sat, eyeing him curiously.

"What can I do for you, Captain?" the officer asked, his tone respectful.

"I'm here to enlist," Christopher said, his voice resolute. "I want to fight for the Union."

The recruiting officer raised an eyebrow, surprised by the decision of a police captain to join the ranks of the infantry. "You sure about this?" he asked, his voice laced with concern. "War's no place for a man like you."

"I'm sure," Christopher replied, his expression determined. "I need to do this."

The officer nodded, handing Christopher the enlistment papers. Christopher signed his name, sealing his fate as a soldier in the Union Army.

As he walked out of the office, Christopher felt a sense of relief wash over him. He had made his choice. He was no longer a pawn in Tammany Hall's game. He was a soldier, ready to fight for a cause he believed in, and to forge a new path for himself in this vast, unpredictable world.

But even as he prepared to leave New York behind, Christopher knew that the shadows of his past would not be so easily shaken. Tammany Hall was a powerful force, and its reach extended far beyond the city's borders. Christopher had made enemies, and he would have to stay vigilant if he was to survive the trials that lay ahead.

As he boarded the train that would take him to the Union camp, Christopher took one last look at the city that had been his home for the past few years. He had come here seeking a new life, and while he had found success, it had come at a cost. But now, as the train pulled away from the station, Christopher felt a renewed sense of hope. He was leaving behind the corruption and deceit, and heading toward a new beginning—a beginning that would test his courage, his resolve, and his very soul.

And as the city faded into the distance, Christopher made a silent vow. He would return to New York one day, but not as a man under Tammany Hall's thumb. He would return on his own terms, with his integrity intact and his head held high.

For Christopher O'Donaghue, the journey was just beginning.

Christopher's decision to enlist in the Union Army marked a turning point, not only in his life but in the ongoing struggle within his soul. The decision had come after months of wrestling with the corruption that surrounded him, his conscience, and the unspoken threats from Tammany Hall. The army offered him a way out—a way to cleanse himself from the filth that had clung to him since his arrival in New York. But it was also a way to atone for the compromises he had made, to fight for something that felt just and righteous in a world that had shown him so little mercy.

When Christopher entered the recruitment office, he felt the weight of his choice bearing down on him, but it was a weight he carried gladly. The old Christopher, the immigrant boy who had walked off the boat in New York with nothing but hope and hunger in his heart, had been slowly eroded by the city. He had become someone else—a man shaped by the harsh realities of survival in a city where power corrupted absolutely. But this enlistment, this new uniform, would forge him anew.

The drill sergeants were merciless, barking orders as Christopher and the other recruits drilled endlessly. But Christopher thrived under the harsh conditions, pushing his body and mind to their limits. The physical exertion was a balm for his troubled mind; it kept the demons of his past at bay, at least for the moment. The days bled into nights of aching muscles and dreamless sleep, and slowly, Christopher began to feel the change within himself. The city's corruption seemed like a distant memory as he became a soldier, a man of discipline and duty, fighting for a cause greater than himself.

He was assigned to the 37th New York Infantry, known as the "Irish Rifles," a regiment comprised largely of

Irish immigrants like himself. Here, among these men who shared his heritage and his struggle, Christopher found a camaraderie he had not known since leaving Ireland. They were soldiers now, but they had once been labourers, farmers, and sons of famine-ravaged lands. The bond they shared was forged in their collective hardship, in the knowledge that they fought not just for the Union, but for their own place in a world that had cast them aside.

Christopher quickly distinguished himself in training, his previous experience as a police captain giving him an edge in leadership and tactics. His superiors took notice, and it wasn't long before Christopher was promoted to the rank of major, and later, to colonel. His rise through the ranks was not just a testament to his abilities, but to his unwavering determination to succeed in this new life he had chosen for himself.

The battles were brutal and relentless, each one a test of endurance and will. Christopher led his men into the fray with the courage of a seasoned warrior, his voice a steadying presence amid the chaos of war. The battlefield was a hellscape of smoke and fire, the deafening roar of cannons and the screams of the dying filling the air. But Christopher never faltered, his resolve hardened by the knowledge that this was the price of freedom—the price of redemption.

The war took its toll on all of them. Christopher saw men he had come to consider brothers fall beside him, their lifeblood soaking into the earth. Each loss was a wound to his soul, a reminder of the fragility of life and the futility of war. But Christopher pushed these thoughts aside, focusing on the mission, on the next battle, on the next step forward. There was no room for doubt or hesitation, not when so much was at stake.

And yet, despite the horrors of the battlefield, Christopher found a sense of purpose in the war. The cause of the Union, the fight to preserve a nation divided by hatred and greed, gave him a sense of belonging, of being part of something larger than himself. He was no longer just a pawn in Tammany Hall's game—he was a soldier, a leader, a man fighting for a better future.

But the war was not just a physical battle. It was a mental one as well, and as the months wore on, Christopher felt the weight of the conflict pressing down on him. The carnage he witnessed day after day began to take its toll, eroding the walls he had built around his heart. He found himself haunted by the faces of the men he had lost, by the memories of the lives he had taken in the heat of battle. Sleep became a luxury, and when it did come, it brought with it nightmares of blood and death.

Yet, Christopher knew he could not allow himself to be consumed by the darkness. He had seen too many men fall victim to despair, their minds broken by the horrors they had witnessed. Christopher had come too far, fought too hard, to allow himself to be lost in the same way. So he held onto his sense of duty, to the knowledge that his fight was just, and that in the end, it would be worth the cost.

And then came the news that shook the very foundations of the Union.

It was after a particularly brutal battle, the dead and

wounded scattered across the field like broken dolls. The survivors, battered and bloodied, stood in silence, the weight of their victory heavy on their shoulders. Christopher was among them, his uniform stained with dirt and blood, his face a mask of exhaustion and grief.

As he surveyed the battlefield, trying to make sense of the senseless violence that surrounded him, a Union officer approached, his expression grim.

"Colonel O'Donaghue," the officer said, his voice heavy with the burden of the news he carried. "We've received orders."

Christopher turned to face the man, sensing that whatever he was about to hear would change everything.

"There's been an assassination," the officer continued, his tone grave. "President Lincoln is dead."

The words hit Christopher like a physical blow, the breath leaving his lungs in a rush. He stared at the officer, unable to fully comprehend what he had just heard.

"Lincoln... dead?" he echoed, the disbelief evident in his voice. "How?"

"John Wilkes Booth," the officer replied, his voice tinged with disgust. "An actor. He shot the president at Ford's Theatre. The country's in chaos, and they need someone to lead the manhunt. They're calling on you, Colonel."

Christopher felt the weight of the responsibility settle on his shoulders like a heavy cloak. This mission, this hunt for the man who had taken the life of the president, would be unlike anything he had faced before. It was not just a matter of finding and bringing a criminal to justice—it was a matter of restoring order to a nation on the brink of collapse.

"I'll do it," Christopher said, his voice resolute. "We'll find him and bring him to justice."

The officer nodded, a look of relief crossing his features. "Thank you, Colonel," he said. "I know we can count on you."

As the officer walked away, Christopher stood alone on the battlefield, the weight of his new mission pressing down on him. He knew that this task would test everything he had learned, every skill he had honed, and every principle he held dear. But he also knew that he could not turn away from it. This was his chance to prove himself, to show that he was more than just a soldier, more than just a man trying to escape his past. This was his chance to make a difference, to fight for something that truly mattered.

Christopher's thoughts turned to Lincoln, the man who had led the nation through its darkest hour, who had fought to preserve the Union against all odds. Lincoln had been more than just a president—he had been a symbol of hope, of unity, of the belief that a nation torn apart by hatred and division could be healed.

But now that symbol was gone, snuffed out by a single act of violence. And in the wake of that loss, the nation teetered on the edge of chaos. It would be up to men like Christopher to restore order, to bring the nation back from the brink.

Christopher's resolve hardened as he thought of the task ahead. He would not allow Lincoln's death to be in vain. He would find Booth, and he would bring him to justice. And in doing so, he would honour the memory of the man who had given everything for the Union.

The hunt for Booth would take Christopher across the war-torn country, through cities and towns ravaged by the conflict, through forests and fields that had seen the blood of countless men spilled. It would be a journey fraught with danger, with the constant threat of violence lurking around every corner. But Christopher was ready. He had been preparing for this his entire life, though he had never known it until now.

As Christopher began to make preparations for the hunt, gathering his men and planning their route, he felt a sense of purpose settle over him. This was what he had been searching for, ever since he had left Ireland all those years ago. A cause worth fighting for, a battle worth waging. And now, he would see it through to the end.

Christopher's thoughts returned to Tammany Hall, to the corrupt men who had tried to pull him down into the muck of their world. He had escaped them, had found a way out of their grasp, and now he was on a path that was entirely his own. The shadows of his past still lingered, but they no longer held any power over him. He had forged a new life for himself, a life built on principles and honour, and he would not allow anything to take that away from him.

As Christopher mounted his horse, ready to lead his men on the most important mission of his life, he looked out over the horizon. The sun was beginning to rise, casting a golden glow over the landscape. It was a new day, a new beginning, and Christopher was ready to face whatever challenges lay ahead.

He would find Booth, he would bring him to justice, and he would do it not just for the Union, but for himself. For the man he had become, and for the man he would continue to be.

With a final glance at the battlefield behind him, Christopher urged his horse forward, the sound of hoofbeats echoing across the land. The hunt had begun.

CHAPTER 5: A BROTHER'S WAR

The streets of Cork were a world unto themselves, teeming with life yet shrouded in a pervasive gloom that clung to every corner. Seamus O'Donaghue, now a wiry youth of twelve, navigated the alleys with the confidence of someone who had spent their entire short life threading through its narrow, labyrinthine passages. He held his young sister, Rebecca, close, shielding her from the cold wind that swept in from the harbour. Their destination was Uncle Michael's small, weather-beaten shop, a place that had become their fragile refuge in a city struggling to survive.

The shop, a dim and cramped space filled with basic goods, was where Uncle Michael, a man who seemed older than his years, tried to eke out a living. Michael was a man hardened by life's relentless blows—first, the famine that had decimated his family, and then the brutal hand of British rule that seemed determined to crush whatever spirit remained in the Irish people. He was all that Seamus and Rebecca had left in the world, and he bore that burden with quiet resilience.

Seamus pushed open the door, the bell above it jingling softly, a sound that had once been a comforting welcome but now felt like a reminder of their precarious existence. Inside, the smell of stale bread and damp wood hung in the air. Uncle Michael was behind the counter, struggling with a sack of flour. His hands, gnarled and calloused, bore the marks of a life spent in toil.

"Let me help," Seamus offered, his voice strong despite his youth. Together, they lifted the sack onto the counter. Michael wiped his brow and gave Seamus a tired smile, a rare expression of warmth in a life filled with hardship.

"Thank you, lad," Michael said softly. "You've got a strong back. I don't know what I'd do without you."

Seamus nodded solemnly, his mind drifting to memories of his parents, whose sacrifices had left deep scars on his heart. They had given everything to keep their children alive, only to be taken by the famine and the cruel indifference of those who ruled over them.

"It's the British who've made our lives this way," Seamus said, bitterness seeping into his voice. "They've taken everything from us, and I'll never forgive them."

Michael looked at his nephew, concern etching lines deeper into his already worn face. "Hatred is a heavy burden, Seamus. Don't let it consume you. Focus on what you can do here and now."

But Seamus's young heart was already burning with the fire of rebellion. It was a fire that would only grow, fed by the injustices he had witnessed and the loss that had shaped his life. As he helped his uncle with the shop's daily tasks, the seed of defiance took root within him, nurtured by the harsh realities of their existence.

The docks of Cork were a place of constant activity, even in the dead of night. Lanterns swayed in the cold wind, casting long shadows across the wooden planks. Ships loomed in the darkness, their masts slicing through the night sky like the fingers of giants. British soldiers patrolled the area, their boots echoing off the docks, a constant reminder of the oppression that hung over the city like a shroud.

Uncle Michael moved among the workers, his movements slow and laboured. His eyes, once sharp and full of life, were now clouded with desperation. He had seen too many hard winters, too many empty fields, and too many hungry mouths to feed. As he watched a sack of wheat being unloaded from one of the ships, something inside him snapped. The hunger, the desperation—it all came crashing down, overwhelming the caution that had kept him alive all these years.

Michael waited for the right moment, for the soldiers to be distracted, before making his move. He grabbed the sack, its weight a reminder of the life he had once known, and slipped into the shadows. But escape was a fleeting hope. A group of British soldiers, led by a sergeant with cold eyes and a cruel smile, spotted him almost immediately. They gave chase, their heavy boots pounding on the wooden planks as they pursued him through the narrow alleyways that lined the docks. Michael ran as fast as he could, but he was no match for the younger, fitter soldiers. They cornered him in a narrow alley, where the shadows seemed to close in around him.

He dropped the sack and raised his hands, his voice trembling as he pleaded with the soldiers. "Please... I've a family to feed... just let me go..."

The sergeant sneered, his club raised. "You should've thought of that before you stole from the Crown."

With a vicious swing, the sergeant struck Michael across the face, sending him crashing to the ground. The other soldiers joined in, their boots and fists raining down on him with brutal force. Michael lay there, his body absorbing each blow, until the pain became distant, replaced by a numbness that spread through his limbs.

As the soldiers walked away, their laughter echoing in the night, Michael's world faded into darkness. The last sound he heard was the distant hum of the harbour, a reminder of the life he had fought so hard to protect but could not save.

Seamus sat alone in the shop, the flickering candle casting a dim light across the room. Rebecca slept nearby, her small form curled up under a worn blanket. The shop was eerily quiet, the usual hustle and bustle of the town muted by the late hour. Suddenly, the door burst open, and a neighbour rushed in, her face pale, her eyes wide with fear.

"Seamus! Seamus, it's your uncle... he's been killed at the docks!"

The news hit Seamus like a physical blow. His heart pounded in his chest as the neighbour grabbed his arm, trying to steady him. "I'm so sorry, lad. They say he was caught stealing... the soldiers beat him to death."

Seamus's eyes filled with tears, his breath coming in ragged gasps. He shook off the neighbour's grip and bolted out of the shop, racing towards the docks.

The docks were a maze of shadows and flickering lights as Seamus sprinted through the darkened streets. His feet pounded the cobblestones, his heart racing as he searched for any sign of his uncle. When he finally found him, lying lifeless in the alley, the sight was more than he could bear. Seamus dropped to his knees beside Michael, tears streaming down his face. His hands trembled as he reached out to touch his uncle's cold, bloodied face.

"Uncle Michael... I'm so sorry... I couldn't protect you..."

The weight of his loss crashed down on him, and for a moment, all he could feel was the overwhelming grief that threatened to consume him. But as the tears flowed, that grief slowly transformed into something else—something stronger, more powerful.

"I'll make them pay, Uncle," Seamus whispered through his tears. "I swear it... I'll make them all pay."

The resolve that had taken root in his heart earlier now bloomed into a fierce determination. He rose to his feet, his fists clenched, his face hardening with anger. He walked away from the scene, his silhouette a dark figure against the night sky, a shadow that would soon cast its influence far beyond the streets of Cork.

In the dim light of a small, hidden room, a group of young Irish men had gathered. The room was filled with the low murmur of voices, the scrape of chairs against the wooden floor. At the head of the table stood Seamus, now a strong young adult himself, his face set with determination. The fire that had been ignited in him that night at the docks had grown into an inferno, one that now fuelled his every action. On the wall behind him hung a banner with the words "Phoenix National and Literary Society" boldly written across it. It was a name that carried with it the promise of renewal, of a cause that would rise from the ashes of their oppression.

Seamus's voice was fierce as he addressed the group. "The British have taken everything from us—our families, our homes, our dignity. But we won't be silent any longer. The Phoenix Society will be the spark that ignites the fire of revolution in Ireland!"

The room erupted in cheers, the young men's voices rising in unison. They spoke of their plans to arm themselves, to recruit more members, to strike at the British forces with the fury of a people who had been pushed to the brink. As the meeting came to an end, one of Seamus's close friends, Sean, pulled him aside.

"Seamus, we've heard news from America," Sean said urgently. "The war there has begun, and the Irish Brigade is fighting for the Union. They've got weapons, supplies... things we could use here."

Seamus's eyes narrowed as he considered the possibility. "Then that's where I need to be. If I can secure weapons for our cause, we'll have a real chance at winning this fight."

Sean nodded, his expression serious. "You're taking a big risk, Seamus. But if anyone can pull it off, it's you."

Seamus's resolve was firm. "For Uncle Michael... and for Ireland."

As he left the meeting room, his mind was set on the dangerous mission that lay ahead. He would go to America, join the fight, and bring back the tools they needed to strike at the heart of British rule. It was a mission born out of loss, fuelled by anger, and driven by a desire for justice.

The streets of New York were a world away from the narrow alleys of Cork, yet they were just as alive with the energy of a people struggling to survive. Soldiers marched in formation, their uniforms crisp, their faces set with determination. The city was a melting pot of cultures and ideas, a place where the old world and the new collided in a cacophony of sights and sounds. Seamus arrived in the city with nothing but the clothes on his back and the fire in his heart. He blended in with the throngs of Irish immigrants who had come to America seeking a better life, but his purpose was different. He was here to fight, not just for the Union, but for the cause that had driven him across the ocean.

His face set with determination as he made his way to the enlistment office. The building was crowded with men eager to join the fight, the tension and excitement in the air palpable. The senior officer eyed Seamus with a mix of curiosity and respect. "Name?"

"Seamus O'Donaghue," Seamus replied, his voice steady, his resolve unshaken.

The officer scribbled the name down on a list, then looked up at Seamus with a discerning eye and even a familiarity. "You look young, but I've seen younger. The Irish Brigade could use a man with fire in his belly. You ready to fight?"

Seamus nodded, his expression resolute. "I'm ready, sir. For the Union—and for Ireland."

The officer handed Seamus a pen and motioned for him to sign the enlistment papers. Seamus scrawled his name with a firm hand, sealing his commitment. The officer nodded approvingly. "Welcome to the Union Army, Corporal O'Donaghue. Report to the barracks for your gear."

Seamus left the office, his heart pounding with a mix of anticipation and fear. The road ahead was fraught with danger, but he knew that this was where he needed to be. The war in America was not just a fight for the Union; it was a fight for the soul of his people, for the freedom that had been denied them for so long.

The moment Seamus spoke his name, something flickered in Thomas Meagher's mind. It was impossible to ignore the familiarity in the young man's features— the fire in his eyes, the sharpness in his jawline. He had seen that same look before, in the face of a man who had been like a brother to him. Ryan O'Donaghue. Or rather, Ned Kelly, as he had come to call himself during their time together in Australia.

Meagher's grip tightened on the pen in his hand, but he kept his face impassive, forcing the memories to stay buried. He had shared many battles with Ryan —against the British, against the crushing weight of their imprisonment, and against the bleakness of exile in Australia. Together, they had fought side by side, not just as outlaws, but as men determined to defy the chains of tyranny. Ryan had been a leader among them, fiercer and braver than any other. But with that fierceness came a darkness, a recklessness that had ultimately led to his demise.

Meagher had witnessed Ryan fall in battle, gunned down by British soldiers. It had been the moment that broke him. After Ryan's death, Meagher had known he could no longer remain in Australia, fighting a war he felt they could no longer win. The guilt had weighed on him for years—their choices as outlaws, the brutality they had been forced into. And now, here stood Ryan's younger brother, Seamus, completely unaware of the bond that had once existed between Meagher and his family.

He could have told Seamus right then—about Ryan, about their past. But something stopped him. Maybe it was the look in Seamus's eyes, the fire of a man focused solely on his mission. Meagher had no desire to dredge up the ghosts of the past. There were parts of his time with Ryan that he wished to forget, parts of it that still haunted him. Telling Seamus the truth wouldn't bring his brother back, nor would it help him in the fight that lay ahead.

Besides, it wasn't just Seamus that Meagher felt responsible for. Christopher O'Donaghue—Ryan's other brother—was already making a name for himself in the Union Army. A rising officer in the 37th New York Infantry, "The Irish Rifles," Christopher had already earned a reputation for bravery. Meagher had heard reports of his exploits on the battlefield, and while Christopher and Seamus likely didn't realize it yet, they would soon fight side by side.

Meagher took a deep breath and handed the enlistment papers to Seamus, but not before making a silent vow. He had failed to protect Ryan. He wouldn't fail again. Both Seamus and Christopher were now under his watch, even if they never knew it. Meagher would ensure they survived this war, whatever it took.

As Seamus signed his name and handed the papers back, Meagher forced a small smile, though his heart was heavy with memories. Watching the young man before him, so full of determination, reminded him too much of Ryan—of the hope, the passion, and the devastation that had come with it.

"Report to the barracks for your gear, Corporal O'Donaghue," Meagher said, his voice steady, but his mind racing with thoughts of the past. "And good luck."

As Seamus turned to leave, Meagher watched him go, feeling the weight of his old friend's memory hanging over him. He had sworn to protect these brothers, even if that meant keeping the past buried. Ryan's death was a secret he would take to his grave.

The days that followed were gruelling, as Seamus underwent training with the Irish Brigade. The scenes were intense, with drill instructors barking orders, soldiers practicing manoeuvres under the sweltering sun. Every muscle in Seamus's body ached, but he pushed through the pain, driven by the same fire that had brought him here.

He quickly proved himself in combat, showing both courage and tactical skill. His fellow soldiers respected him, his superiors took notice, and his reputation as a fierce and dedicated fighter grew with each passing day. But even as he fought for the Union, his mind remained focused on his mission—the mission that had brought him to this foreign land.

Seamus carefully cultivated connections with key figures who might aid him in his goal. He spoke with other Irishmen who had come to America with similar intentions, men who shared his anger, his resolve, his burning desire for justice. Together, they formed a network, one that stretched from the battlefields of the Civil War to the darkened alleys of Cork.

The day dawned cold and grey, the air thick with the promise of rain. The Irish Brigade marched across a war-torn landscape, the ground beneath their boots scarred by the ravages of battle. The thunder of artillery echoed through the air, the shouts of officers trying to maintain order amidst the chaos. Seamus was in the thick of it, leading his unit with a mixture of bravery and tactical acumen. The sounds of battle were deafening, but Seamus's focus was unbreakable. He moved through the battlefield with the confidence of a man who had faced death before and had no fear of facing it again.

As the battle raged, Seamus's eyes were drawn to a familiar figure fighting in the distance. A Union officer commanding his troops with the authority and presence of a seasoned leader. The sight of him stopped Seamus in his tracks, his heart skipping a beat. It was Christopher.

His brother, whom he had not seen in years, was here, on this battlefield, leading men into battle with the same fire that burned within Seamus's own heart. The moment was surreal, a collision of past and present, of family and war.

But there was no time for reunion. A Confederate soldier charged at Christopher, bayonet raised, his intent clear. Without thinking, Seamus sprinted across the battlefield, his feet moving before his mind could catch up. He barreled into the Confederate soldier, knocking him to the ground just as Christopher turned to see what had happened.

Their eyes met, and for a moment, the battlefield faded away. The noise, the chaos, the war—it all disappeared, leaving only the two brothers standing in the midst of it all.

"Seamus?" Christopher shouted, his voice filled with shock and disbelief. "Is that really you?"

Seamus helped Christopher to his feet, their eyes locking in a moment of intense emotion. But before they could speak, the battle surged around them, forcing them to fight side by side, as brothers once more.

The sun hung low in the sky, casting long shadows over the blood-soaked earth. Seamus and Christopher fought back-to-back, their bond as brothers reawakened in the heat of battle. For Seamus, the anger he once harbored toward Christopher had dissipated, replaced by the overwhelming need to protect the brother he had thought he had lost forever.

The battlefield was a whirlwind of smoke and blood. Musket fire cracked through the air, cannons roared, and men fell, their cries lost in the cacophony. Seamus's rifle was hot in his hands, the recoil becoming a familiar sensation. He fired again, dropping a Confederate soldier who had been charging toward their position. Christopher, with the authority of a seasoned officer, rallied his men.

"Hold the line!" he shouted, his voice carrying over the din of battle. "For the Union!"

Seamus moved beside him, his eyes scanning the battlefield. It was a scene of chaos, but amidst the disorder, he could see patterns, weaknesses in the Confederate lines. His experience, his tactical mind, guided his every move. He had learned much during his time in the Irish Brigade, but now, standing beside Christopher, he realized something deeper—their fates had always been intertwined. The battlefield was merely the stage upon which they would once again become brothers.

But fate, as always, was cruel. In the midst of the battle, Seamus saw it happen—saw the Confederate rifleman raise his musket, saw the glint of steel in the late afternoon sun, saw the puff of smoke as the trigger was pulled. Time slowed, and Seamus's heart leaped into his throat.

"Christopher!" Seamus shouted, lunging forward, but it was too late.

The bullet found its mark, slamming into Christopher's chest with brutal precision. Christopher staggered backward, his hand instinctively going to the wound. The world seemed to pause around them as Christopher collapsed to the ground, blood spreading across his uniform.

"No!" Seamus's voice was raw with emotion as he dropped to his knees beside his brother.

Seamus cradled Christopher's head in his arms, his hands trembling as he tried to stem the flow of blood. The sounds of battle faded into the background, replaced by the deafening roar of his own heartbeat. Christopher coughed, blood staining his lips, but he managed a weak smile, his eyes filled with a mixture of pain and relief.

"Seamus..." Christopher's voice was barely a whisper, his strength waning with each passing second. "I'm sorry... I left... but I never stopped fighting... for you... for Rebecca..."

Tears welled in Seamus's eyes as he tightened his grip on his brother, the anger and resentment he had carried for so long dissolving into an overwhelming wave of love and grief. "Don't talk, Christopher. Save your strength.

We'll get you out of here. You're going to be fine."

But even as he spoke, Seamus knew the truth. He could feel it in the way Christopher's body grew heavier in his arms, in the way his breathing grew shallower. There was nothing he could do, nothing but hold his brother and try to ease his suffering.

Christopher's hand found Seamus's, his grip weak but determined. "Take care... of Rebecca... promise me..."

Seamus nodded, his voice choked with emotion. "I promise, Christopher. I'll take care of her. I'll take care of everything."

Christopher's eyes fluttered closed, his breath hitching as he struggled to hold on. "Together, Seamus... we'll fight... together..."

Seamus felt a surge of desperation. He couldn't let Christopher die, not like this, not after everything they had endured. He looked around the battlefield, his mind racing for a solution, for anything that could save his brother. But all he saw was chaos, the brutal reality of war, and the faces of soldiers locked in a life-and-death struggle.

Refusing to give up, Seamus gathered his strength and heaved Christopher over his shoulder, staggering under the weight of his brother's limp body. He stumbled forward, his legs trembling with exhaustion, his vision blurred by tears and sweat. The sounds of battle were distant now, muted by the singular focus of getting Christopher to safety.

Seamus pushed through the pain, through the burning in his muscles, driven by the knowledge that he couldn't let Christopher die on this forsaken battlefield. He navigated the chaos, dodging bullets and fallen soldiers, every step an agonizing reminder of the fragility of life.

Finally, Seamus spotted a group of Union soldiers taking cover behind a barricade. With a final burst of strength, he reached them, collapsing to his knees as he carefully laid Christopher down on the ground. The soldiers immediately recognized the severity of Christopher's condition and rushed to provide aid.

A field medic arrived, his hands moving quickly to assess Christopher's injuries. Seamus hovered over them, his breath ragged, watching every movement with a mix of hope and dread. The medic's face was tense as he worked, but there was a determined focus in his eyes that gave Seamus a sliver of hope.

"This is bad," the medic muttered, more to himself than to Seamus, as he cut away the fabric around Christopher's wound. Blood pooled beneath Christopher, soaking into the earth, but the medic remained calm, applying pressure to the wound, trying to stem the bleeding.

Seamus knelt beside his brother, gripping his hand. "Christopher, you stay with me, you hear? You're not going anywhere."

Christopher's eyelids fluttered, his breathing shallow, but he managed a faint smile. "I'm... not done fighting, Seamus," he whispered, his voice barely audible over the din of the battlefield.

The medic worked swiftly, packing the wound with gauze, doing everything he could to stabilize Christopher. "We need to get him to the field hospital," he said, his tone urgent but controlled. "He's lost a lot of blood, but if we can get him back to the surgeons, he has a chance."

Seamus nodded, his jaw clenched with determination. "Then let's go."

With the help of the medic and a few other soldiers, Seamus carefully lifted Christopher onto a makeshift stretcher. The battlefield seemed to stretch on forever as they carried him toward the rear lines, where the field hospital had been set up. Every step felt like a lifetime, the weight of the situation pressing down on Seamus's shoulders.

They finally reached the field hospital, a hastily assembled collection of tents filled with wounded soldiers. The groans of the injured and the frantic calls of medics filled the air, creating a symphony of suffering that Seamus would never forget. They brought Christopher into one of the tents, where a surgeon took over, his face grim as he examined the wound.

"You did well to get him here," the surgeon said to Seamus, his voice steady. "Now let us do our job."

Seamus nodded, stepping back reluctantly as the surgeon and his team began their work. He felt an overwhelming sense of helplessness wash over him. The fight was out of his hands now. All he could do was wait.

The hours dragged on, each minute feeling like an eternity. Seamus paced outside the tent, his thoughts racing, his heart heavy with fear. He couldn't lose Christopher—not after they had found each other again, not after everything they had been through. The idea of returning to the battlefield without his brother by his side was unthinkable.

Finally, after what felt like an eternity, the surgeon emerged from the tent, wiping his hands on a bloodstained cloth. His expression was tired but not without hope.

"Your brother is strong," the surgeon said, meeting Seamus's anxious gaze. "He's lost a lot of blood, but we've managed to stabilize him. He's not out of the woods yet, but if he makes it through the night, he has a good chance of surviving."

Seamus felt a wave of relief wash over him, so intense it nearly brought him to his knees. "Thank you," he whispered, his voice thick with emotion.

The surgeon nodded, placing a reassuring hand on Seamus's shoulder. "He's a fighter, just like you. Keep faith, and he'll pull through."

Seamus watched as the surgeon returned to his work, tending to the endless stream of wounded soldiers. The tent where Christopher lay was quiet now, the only sound the steady rhythm of his breathing. Seamus stepped inside, his eyes immediately finding his brother lying on a cot, pale but alive.

He pulled up a stool beside Christopher's cot and sat down, exhaustion finally catching up with him. He reached out, taking Christopher's hand in his own, holding it tightly as if to tether him to life.

"You're going to make it, Christopher," Seamus said softly, more to himself than to his unconscious brother. "We've got too much left to do for you to leave me now."

As the night wore on, Seamus stayed by Christopher's side, refusing to leave. The battlefield outside had quieted, the sounds of battle replaced by the eerie stillness of night. The sky was clear, the stars shining down like distant, indifferent witnesses to the suffering below.

Seamus felt the weight of everything that had happened pressing down on him, but he refused to let it crush him. He had made a promise to Christopher, and he intended to keep it. They would get through this—together.

When dawn finally broke, the first light of day creeping into the tent, Christopher stirred. His eyes fluttered open, and he looked around in confusion before his gaze settled on Seamus.

"Seamus..." he murmured, his voice hoarse but filled with relief. "You stayed."

"Of course I did," Seamus replied, a smile breaking through the exhaustion on his face. "I wasn't going to let you get away that easily."

Christopher managed a weak chuckle, though it quickly turned into a wince of pain. "I thought I was done for..."

"You're tougher than you look," Seamus said, his tone light but his eyes filled with emotion. "And I'm not done fighting this war with you."

Christopher squeezed his brother's hand, a silent acknowledgment of the bond that had saved his life. "Together," he whispered, echoing the promise they had made to each other on the battlefield.

As the day wore on, Christopher's condition improved,

though he remained weak and bedridden. The surgeons and medics checked on him regularly, their expressions becoming more optimistic with each passing hour. Seamus never left his side, keeping watch over his brother as he slept, recovering from the ordeal that had nearly claimed his life.

The brothers spoke in quiet moments, sharing stories of their time apart, of the battles they had fought both on the battlefield and within themselves. Seamus told Christopher about Uncle Michael's murder, about the Phoenix Society, and about his burning desire to return to Ireland and continue the fight for their homeland. Christopher listened, his eyes reflecting a deep understanding of the pain and anger that had driven Seamus to America.

"We've both been fighting our own wars," Christopher said softly, his gaze distant as he recalled the years they had spent apart. "But now we have a chance to fight together again."

Seamus nodded, his resolve stronger than ever. "We'll finish this war, Christopher. And then we'll go back to Ireland. We'll make things right."

The days turned into weeks, and Christopher's strength slowly returned. The bond between the brothers grew stronger, forged in the fire of battle and tempered by the shared experiences of loss and survival. They knew that the road ahead would be long and filled with challenges, but they were ready to face it—together.

When Christopher was finally strong enough to leave the field hospital, the brothers returned to their regiment, greeted by the cheers and relief of their fellow soldiers. They had become legends in the ranks of the Irish Brigade, their story one of resilience, brotherhood, and the unbreakable spirit of the Irish people.

As they prepared to rejoin the fight, Seamus and Christopher stood side by side, their hearts filled with determination. The war was far from over, but they knew that as long as they had each other, they could face whatever came their way.

The battlefield stretched out before them, a landscape of destruction and hope. The Union Army was on the move, the tide of war beginning to turn in their favor. But Seamus's thoughts were already turning to the future, to the fight that still awaited them across the ocean.

"We'll finish what we started, Christopher," Seamus said, his voice resolute. "For Ireland. For our family. For everything we've lost."

Christopher nodded, his eyes burning with the same fire that had driven them both for so long. "For everything."

And with that, the brothers marched forward, ready to face whatever battles lay ahead, knowing that as long as they stood together, there was nothing they couldn't overcome.

The war would test them, would push them to their limits, but it would never break them. For in each other, they had found the strength to keep fighting, to keep moving forward, no matter the cost.

And in the end, that was what would carry them through—brotherhood, loyalty, and the unshakable belief that together, they could change the world.

As they disappeared into the ranks of the Union Army, the sun began to rise, casting a golden light over the battlefield. It was a new day, a new chance to fight, to survive, and to win.

Seamus and Christopher O'Donaghue were ready to meet it head-on, side by side, as brothers once more.

As the war drew to its close in 1865, the brothers faced the prospect of a world beyond the battlefield. The Union victory had turned the tide, bringing the Confederacy to its knees. The Irish Brigade, battered but proud, disbanded, and Christopher and Seamus parted ways with promises to stay connected, their bond stronger than ever. But while Christopher's recovery took him back to New York, where he would rebuild a life shaped by his time in the ranks, Seamus felt a pull toward another kind of fight—a struggle that had lingered in his heart even as he fought in America.

For Seamus, the end of the Civil War was not the end of his battles. It was a turning point, a shift from fighting on American soil to reigniting the dream of freedom for Ireland. The cause of Irish independence had been his driving force long before he joined the Union Army, and now, with the war over, he found himself seeking the remnants of the Fenian Brotherhood. The Irish nationalists who had fled to America had long spoken of returning to free their homeland, and Seamus, like many of them, believed that the time had come.

Philadelphia became his base—a city that had become a refuge for Irish immigrants seeking work and opportunity, but also a hotbed for revolutionary fervor. Here, among the narrow streets and bustling docks,

Seamus found kindred spirits, men who had fought with him in the Civil War and now looked to Ireland with a restless determination. It was a city where the whispers of rebellion traveled quickly, carried on the wind through taverns and back alleys. And it was here that Seamus threw himself into the cause, ready to trade his Union blue for the green banner of Ireland.

Seamus O'Donaghue moved through the narrow, fog-filled streets of Philadelphia with purpose, the cold wind biting at his skin. Although the American Civil War had ended, the fight for Ireland had only just begun. The divided Fenian Brotherhood was at a crossroads, and tonight's gathering would determine the course of action. Seamus felt the weight of his brotherhood's future pressing down on his shoulders.

In his coat pocket, the letters from John O'Mahony rustled with every step. O'Mahony, leader of the Fenian Brotherhood faction that sought to wage the fight on Irish soil, had sent word that the meeting would decide everything. William R. Roberts, the leader of the other faction, had his supporters rallying for a bold invasion of British-controlled Canada. Seamus knew which side he stood on, but convincing the others would be no easy task.

As he reached the hall, the murmur of voices greeted him even before he entered. Men, many of whom had fought alongside him in the Civil War, filled the room. Their faces were set with determination, their eyes glinting with the promise of action. Seamus pushed the heavy wooden doors open and stepped inside, his gaze immediately seeking out Roberts.

Roberts stood at the center of the room, his voice booming as he laid out his plan with conviction. "We have fifty thousand Irish-American volunteers ready to fight, six thousand rifles, and the tacit approval of President Andrew Johnson! We take Canada, and we force the British to the table. They'll have no choice but to negotiate for Ireland's freedom!"

Cheers erupted from the men around him, their fists raised in agreement. Seamus, however, remained silent, his jaw clenched. He understood the allure of Roberts's plan—it was bold, immediate, and offered the promise of striking back at the British. But Seamus had seen too many men die for promises that never materialized. His mind drifted to his brother Christopher, who had nearly died in 1862 after being shot in the lung. That war had changed them both, but Seamus had emerged with a singular focus: Ireland's freedom. Not through symbolic gestures, but through real, tangible action on Irish soil.

Seamus's eyes found John O'Mahony at the back of the room. The older man stood quietly, his presence commanding without the need for grand speeches. While Roberts riled up the men with visions of glory in Canada, O'Mahony represented a steadier, more calculated approach—one that focused on Ireland, not a faraway British colony. Seamus made his way through the throngs of men until he reached O'Mahony's side.

"O'Mahony," Seamus greeted him with a nod. "Roberts has them fired up. They're ready to follow him to Canada."

O'Mahony sighed, his face lined with weariness. "They want action, Seamus. They've waited so long, and

Roberts is giving them something to grasp. But Canada is a distraction. The British won't trade one colony for another. We need to focus on Ireland."

Seamus folded his arms, glancing back at Roberts, who was still holding the room's attention. "Then why are they listening to him?"

O'Mahony's voice lowered. "Because Roberts promises them something immediate. But Ireland's freedom won't come from quick victories abroad. It requires patience, planning. That's what they've run out of."

Seamus understood the frustration. The men in the room had fought for years in a war that wasn't theirs, and now they wanted to bring that fight home. But the path Roberts offered felt like a dangerous gamble. If they diverted their efforts to Canada, they risked losing sight of their true goal.

"What do you need me to do?" Seamus asked, his voice steady.

O'Mahony's gaze sharpened. "The weapons we've gathered for the Canadian invasion—they need to be sent to Ireland. We've arranged for a ship in New York Harbor, but it has to be done quietly. If Roberts finds out, it'll tear the Brotherhood apart."

Seamus raised an eyebrow. "You want me to smuggle the weapons out under Roberts's nose?"

O'Mahony's eyes narrowed. "Not smuggle. Reallocate. These weapons were always meant for Ireland, not Canada."

Seamus let out a short laugh, though the gravity of the task was not lost on him. "That's a fine line, O'Mahony.

If we're caught, it'll be more than just a division in the Brotherhood. It could end the whole movement."

O'Mahony nodded gravely. "I know the risk, but we don't have a choice. Ireland needs those weapons, not some far-off colony. Can I count on you?"

Seamus looked around the room, at the faces of the men who had bled for the same cause. He knew O'Mahony was right. The real fight was in Ireland, and they couldn't afford to waste their resources on a symbolic victory in Canada.

"I'll do it," Seamus said firmly. "But we need to move fast. Roberts has eyes everywhere."

O'Mahony clasped Seamus's shoulder, relief flooding his expression. "Thank you. I'll make the necessary arrangements. You and your men need to be in New York by week's end."

Over the next few days, Seamus and his trusted ally, O'Malley, worked tirelessly to prepare for the mission. Every crate had to be accounted for, every step of the plan meticulously crafted to avoid suspicion. They met in dimly lit taverns, whispering their plans as they loaded the weapons meant for Canada onto carts bound for New York.

"You ever think we'd end up stealing from our own?" O'Malley asked one night as they hefted a crate of rifles onto a cart.

Seamus wiped the sweat from his brow. "It's not stealing, O'Malley. It's setting things right."

O'Malley chuckled, but his eyes were serious. "Call it what you want, but Roberts isn't going to see it that way when he finds out."

"That's why he can't find out," Seamus replied, tightening the ropes securing the crate. "We have to be in and out before anyone notices."

The night before they were set to leave for New York, Seamus found himself sitting in a quiet corner of a tavern, a glass of whiskey in hand. O'Malley sat across from him, his usual jovial demeanor replaced by a rare moment of silence.

"You ever think about how this ends?" O'Malley asked, swirling the amber liquid in his glass. "All this fighting, the Brotherhood, Ireland. You think we'll ever see it free?"

Seamus stared into his drink, the weight of the question settling over him. "I have to believe we will. Otherwise, what the hell are we doing this for?"

O'Malley nodded, though his expression remained somber. "Aye, I suppose you're right. But sometimes... it feels like we're just running in circles."

Seamus didn't have an answer for that. He had asked himself the same question many times over the years. But every time he thought of his brother lying in that field hospital, clinging to life, he was reminded of why he couldn't stop. The fight for Ireland was all they had left.

The next morning, they set off for New York with the cart of weapons, the dawn just beginning to break over the horizon. Seamus and O'Malley rode at the front, their eyes scanning the darkened streets for any sign of trouble. British spies were everywhere, and Roberts's men could be watching. One wrong move, and the entire operation would be in jeopardy.

As they neared New York Harbor, Seamus felt his pulse quicken. The ship was waiting, its crew loyal to O'Mahony and ready to sail. But they still had to load the weapons without drawing attention.

"Everything's in place," O'Malley whispered as they approached the dock.

Seamus nodded, his heart pounding. "Let's get this done."

The men worked quickly, lifting the crates onto the ship as quietly as possible. Every creak of the boards, every thud of a crate landing in the ship's hold felt like a gunshot in the silence of the harbor. But the work went smoothly, and within the hour, the ship was ready to sail.

Seamus stood on the dock, watching as the ship began to pull away, the weapons on board and bound for Ireland. Relief washed over him, but it was tempered by the knowledge that this was only the beginning. The road ahead was long, and the fight for Ireland's freedom was far from over.

"We did it," O'Malley said, clapping him on the back. "Roberts will never know what hit him."

Seamus nodded, though his thoughts were already on the next steps. "This is just the start. There's a lot more to do before we can call this a victory."

O'Malley grinned. "Aye, but it's a damn good start."

Seamus watched as the ship disappeared into the distance, the future of their cause carried on the waves. The fight for Ireland had begun in earnest, and Seamus knew that whatever came next, he would face it head-on.

The cold wind whipped across the harbor as Seamus stood on the dock, his gaze fixed on the ship as it slowly disappeared into the early morning fog. He felt the weight of what they had just accomplished settle on his shoulders. They had done it—they had smuggled the weapons meant for Roberts' doomed Canadian invasion and sent them to where they truly belonged. But the gravity of the situation still lingered. He knew that if Roberts ever found out, the Fenian Brotherhood could fracture beyond repair.

O'Malley, standing beside him, broke the silence. "What now, Seamus? We've got the weapons on their way, but what's the next move? We can't just sit back and hope for the best."

Seamus took a deep breath, the chill in the air filling his lungs and grounding him in the present moment. "Now? Now we get to Ireland. There's more work to be done. Weapons are one thing, but without leadership, strategy, and men on the ground, they won't get us far. O'Mahony's plan is solid, but we need to make sure it gets executed properly."

O'Malley's grin returned, though it was tempered by the knowledge of the risks ahead. "I suppose a quiet trip across the Atlantic isn't in the cards, then?"

Seamus shot him a look, though there was a hint of amusement in his eyes. "Quiet trips aren't for us, O'Malley. You know that. We'll be in the thick of it soon enough."

The two men walked away from the dock, the weight of their next steps heavy on their minds. They needed to regroup with O'Mahony and plan their journey to Ireland. The fight wasn't just about smuggling weapons —it was about the hearts and minds of the Irish people. They needed to reignite the fire of rebellion, to show their countrymen that the time for talk was over, and the time for action had begun.

As they made their way back through the narrow streets of New York, Seamus's mind raced. The challenges ahead were monumental, and the odds were against them. But he had seen the determination in O'Mahony's eyes, the unyielding belief that they could free Ireland from British rule. It was that belief that had brought Seamus here, that had kept him fighting all these years. And now, it would carry him across the ocean to the land he had always called home.

They arrived at the safe house where O'Mahony was waiting, a modest building tucked away in the quieter part of the city. The leader of the Brotherhood looked up as they entered, his expression unreadable.

"It's done," Seamus said, his voice steady. "The weapons are on their way."

O'Mahony gave a single nod, though his face remained solemn. "Good. But the real work starts now. Roberts will catch wind of this soon enough, and when he does, he'll come for answers."

"We'll be long gone by then," O'Malley interjected, leaning against the doorframe with his usual air of nonchalance. "Roberts won't know what hit him."

O'Mahony's lips pressed into a thin line. "Don't

underestimate him. Roberts has power, influence. If he discovers what we've done, it won't just be the Brotherhood that's at risk—it'll be every man who's aligned with us. We can't afford to get sloppy."

Seamus nodded in agreement. "We'll leave as soon as possible. O'Malley and I can board a ship tomorrow, get to Ireland before the weapons arrive on the slow boat, and start organizing on the ground. We can't let this momentum slip away."

O'Mahony studied them both, his gaze lingering on Seamus. "I trust you to do what's necessary, but understand this: when you get to Ireland, you're not just fighting the British anymore. You're fighting time, politics, and the will of the people. They're weary, Seamus. They've seen rebellions rise and fall. You need to convince them that this is different."

Seamus met his gaze, the fire in his own eyes unmistakable. "This is different. We have the weapons, the men, and the will. It's time to finish what we started."

O'Mahony's expression softened slightly, though the weight of leadership still hung heavy on his shoulders. "Godspeed, Seamus. You know what's at stake."

The journey across the Atlantic was long and grueling, the seas unforgiving as Seamus and O'Malley made their way to Ireland. Each day brought with it a new wave of challenges—both physical and mental. The closer they got to their homeland, the more Seamus felt the burden of what lay ahead. He wasn't just returning to Ireland as a soldier. He was returning as a leader, a man who would have to inspire others to rise up, to believe that freedom was possible after so many years of oppression.

O'Malley, ever the optimist, tried to lighten the mood as they stood on the deck, watching the Irish coastline slowly come into view. "So, Seamus, you think they'll roll out the red carpet for us when we get there? Maybe throw a parade in our honor?"

Seamus smirked, though his thoughts were far from jovial. "More like we'll be met with skepticism and suspicion. The people are tired, O'Malley. They've heard promises before, seen men rise up only to be crushed. We'll have to prove ourselves before they'll follow."

O'Malley shrugged, his eyes twinkling with mischief. "Well, I've always been good at making friends. I'm sure we'll win them over."

The ship docked quietly in the dead of night, and the two men disembarked with little fanfare. The Irish countryside stretched out before them, dark and silent, as they made their way toward the rendezvous point where they would meet with local leaders. The weapons would arrive in a matter of days, but there was much to do before then.

As they approached the small village where their allies were waiting, Seamus felt a strange mix of anticipation and dread. Ireland was his home, but it had changed since he had last set foot on its soil. The British presence was stronger than ever, and the scars of previous uprisings were still fresh. But now, with weapons and men at their disposal, they had a real chance to make a difference.

The meeting with the local leaders was tense. These men had seen too many failed rebellions to put their faith in another one easily. But Seamus spoke with the fire of conviction, laying out their plan with precision and passion. He told them of the weapons on their way, of the men willing to fight, and of O'Mahony's vision for a free Ireland.

For hours, the men argued, debated, and questioned, but Seamus never wavered. He knew what was at stake, and he knew that this was their best chance.

Finally, one of the older men, a grizzled veteran of past rebellions, stood and addressed the room. "We've seen men like you come and go, Seamus. Men with grand ideas and plans for freedom. But they all fell, and we were the ones left to pick up the pieces. Why should we believe that this time will be any different?"

Seamus met the man's gaze, his voice steady but filled with emotion. "Because this time, we're ready. We have the weapons, the men, and the resolve. We've learned from our mistakes. And most importantly, we have something the British can't take from us—hope. Hope for a future where Ireland is free. This is our time, and I promise you, we won't fail."

The room fell silent as the weight of Seamus's words hung in the air. Slowly, one by one, the men nodded their agreement. The rebellion had begun.

CHAPTER 6: THE HUNT FOR JUSTICE

Christopher O'Donaghue stood in the quiet streets of Washington, D.C., his eyes tracing the path ahead, but his thoughts lingered in the past. The nation was in mourning, and the city reflected its grief—black crepe hung from windows, and flags fluttered at half-mast, their colors muted against the somber sky. But it wasn't just the city that weighed heavy on his mind. Christopher's hand instinctively moved to the medal that hung around his neck, the Medal of Honor awarded to him by President Abraham Lincoln himself.

He remembered the day clearly, a day that had both honored him and sealed his fate as a man forever changed by the war. It was after the Battle of Fair Oaks on June 1, 1862, a brutal clash that had tested every ounce of strength and courage he possessed. He had fought valiantly, leading his men through the chaos, and it was during that battle that he had been reunited with his brother, Seamus, after years of separation.

Seamus had been a fierce fighter, his resolve hardened by years of struggle and loss. When Christopher saw him on the battlefield, it was as if time had stopped. In the midst of war, surrounded by the cacophony of gunfire and the cries of the wounded, they had locked eyes, and in that moment, the years of anger and abandonment had melted away. They had fought side by side, just as they had in their youth, defending each other with a bond that no bullet could break.

But the battle had not spared them. Christopher had taken a bullet to the lung, a wound that nearly ended his life. The pain had been excruciating, each breath a struggle as the chaos of battle raged around him. He remembered Seamus's voice, urgent and desperate, calling out to him, dragging him to safety despite the hail of bullets. It was Seamus's determination, his refusal to let Christopher slip away, that had kept him alive.

After the battle, as Christopher lay in a field hospital, gasping for breath and clinging to life, President Lincoln himself had visited the wounded. The President's presence had been a balm to the soldiers, his calm demeanor a stark contrast to the horrors they had faced. When Lincoln approached Christopher's cot, his eyes filled with the sorrow of a man who had seen too much death, he had paused, recognizing the young officer who had fought so bravely.

"You've done your country proud, Major O'Donaghue," Lincoln had said, his voice tinged with sadness. "Your bravery on the battlefield has not gone unnoticed, and for that, I am honored to present you with this Medal of Honor."

Christopher had struggled to sit up, wincing at the pain in his chest, but Lincoln had placed a hand on his shoulder, gently urging him to stay down. The President had pinned the medal to Christopher's uniform, his touch light but firm, as if bestowing a piece of his own strength upon the wounded soldier. "This nation owes you a great debt, Major," Lincoln had said, his eyes meeting Christopher's with a solemn intensity. "You have given so much, and yet I must ask you to give more. The Union needs men like you, men who will fight not just for victory, but for justice."

Those words had stayed with Christopher, driving him forward through the darkest days of the war and into the present moment three years later, where the weight of that medal seemed heavier than ever. Lincoln was gone, taken by an assassin's bullet, and now it was up to Christopher to fulfill the promise he had made to the President on that day—to fight for justice, no matter the cost.

As Christopher ascended the steps of the War Department, his hand fell away from the medal, and he straightened his shoulders, the resolve of a soldier settling over him like a mantle. This was more than just another mission. It was a continuation of the fight he had begun on the battlefield, a fight that would not end until justice was served for the man who had believed in him when he was at his lowest.

Inside the War Department, the tension was palpable. The air was thick with the scent of tobacco smoke and the low hum of voices, punctuated by the occasional crackle of a telegraph machine. A large map of the Eastern United States dominated the room, its surface marked with red lines that traced the possible escape routes of John Wilkes Booth, the man who had plunged the nation into mourning by taking the life of its beloved President.

General Winfield Scott Hancock stood at the head of the table, his presence commanding and authoritative. He was a man who had seen the worst of the war, who had led men into battles that would be remembered for generations. But today, his face was set in grim determination, his eyes reflecting the weight of the task before them.

"Colonel O'Donaghue," Hancock began, his voice carrying the authority of a man who knew what needed to be done, "thank you for coming on such short notice. We have a situation that requires your immediate attention."

Christopher stepped forward, his expression unreadable but his mind sharp and alert. "I'm at your service, General. What's the situation?"

Hancock gestured toward the map, where several routes were marked in bold red lines, each representing a possible escape path for Booth. "Booth is on the run. We have reason to believe he's headed south, possibly toward Virginia. We need someone with your skills and experience to lead the manhunt."

Christopher studied the map closely, the lines and markers forming a mental web of possibilities. The task was enormous—Booth had a head start, and the terrain they needed to cover was vast and varied. The assassin was desperate, and the longer he remained at large, the greater the risk of further instability in an already fragile nation.

"I'll do whatever it takes to bring him to justice, sir," Christopher replied, his voice steady and resolute, though he understood the magnitude of what was being asked of him.

Hancock's expression remained serious, but there was a flicker of trust in his eyes. "This mission is of the utmost importance, Colonel. Booth is dangerous and desperate. He knows the terrain, and he's not working alone. You'll need to be prepared for anything."

Christopher glanced around the room, reading the faces of the men who would support this operation. These were officers who had seen the worst of the war, who had led men into battles that would be etched in the annals of history, and yet the tension in the room was palpable. The fear of failure hung over them like a cloud.

"We'll find him, General," Christopher said with quiet conviction. "He won't escape justice."

Hancock stepped closer, his tone dropping to a more personal level. "Christopher, you've proven yourself time and again on the battlefield. You've led men through hell and back, and now, this mission will be your most important yet. Succeed, and I'll see to it that you earn a star on your shoulder." Hancock's hand briefly touched Christopher's shoulder, where the new insignia would sit if he succeeded. "We need this done, and we need it done right."

Christopher met Hancock's gaze, the promise of a General's star adding a new dimension to his mission. The significance of such an offer wasn't lost on him— it was an honor that could solidify his place in history, but more importantly, it was a recognition of his capabilities and dedication to the Union.

As Christopher exited the War Department, the enormity of the mission settled in. The fate of the nation, justice for a fallen leader, and the future of the Union were all at stake. But there was also a personal weight that Christopher carried—this was a chance to prove himself not just as a soldier, but as a leader of men, a man who could be counted on when the nation needed him most.

Joining Christopher on this critical mission was Captain Edward Doherty, a fellow Irishman whose history was as storied as Christopher's own. Born Éadbhard Ó Dochartaigh in Canada to parents from County Sligo, Doherty had immigrated to New York City, where he quickly made a name for himself in the vibrant, often tumultuous Irish-American community. He had served with distinction in General Michael Corcoran's Irish Legion, a unit renowned for its bravery and fierce loyalty to the Union cause. Corcoran himself, a native of County Sligo, had been court-martialed before the war for refusing to allow his 69th New York Regiment to march in a parade honoring the visiting Prince of Wales —an act of defiance that endeared him to his men and to the broader Irish-American community.

Doherty had survived the bloodiest battles of the war, and his reputation as a relentless and determined officer had earned him a place on this mission. As he fell into step beside Christopher, the two men shared a silent understanding—this was a mission that transcended their personal histories, one that would test their resolve and their loyalty to the country they had fought to preserve.

"Christopher," Doherty said, his voice carrying the unmistakable cadence of his Irish roots, "it's an honor to be working with you on this. Booth's a slippery one, but together we'll bring him in."

Christopher nodded, appreciating the camaraderie. "We've faced worse odds before," he replied. "We'll get him."

The two men mounted their horses, joining the convoy of soldiers and detectives that would form the backbone of the manhunt. The journey southward was fraught with tension, every mile bringing them closer to the fugitive they sought. The landscape around them shifted from the orderly streets of Washington to the wild and unpredictable terrain of the Maryland countryside, a land that had seen its share of bloodshed and sorrow during the war.

As they rode, Christopher's thoughts drifted back to the Battle of Fair Oaks, the moment when his path had crossed once again with his brother Seamus'. It had been a brutal day, the air thick with the smell of gunpowder and the cries of the wounded. The sight of Seamus, leading his men with the same fire and determination that had always defined him, had filled Christopher with a mix of pride and regret. They had fought side by side, just as they had when they were boys, their bond forged in the crucible of war.

But that day had also marked the moment when Christopher's life had nearly ended. The bullet that tore through his lung had been meant to kill him, and it was only through Seamus's quick thinking and sheer force of will that Christopher had survived. The memory of that pain, of the desperate struggle to breathe, was something that had stayed with Christopher, a reminder of the fragility of life and the strength of the ties that bound him to his brother.

Now, as he rode toward the farmhouse where Booth was believed to be hiding, Christopher felt that same determination surge within him. This mission was not just about bringing a murderer to justice—it was about honoring the memory of the man who had believed in him, who had entrusted him with the task of protecting the Union. It was about proving to himself and to those who depended on him that he was worthy of the trust that had been placed in him.

The farmhouse came into view as the sun dipped below the horizon, its light casting long shadows across the landscape. The structure was a decrepit relic of another time, its walls weathered by years of neglect, its windows dark and empty. The air around it was heavy with anticipation, as if the very land was holding its breath, waiting for the inevitable confrontation.

Christopher signaled for the men to dismount, and they did so with the practiced precision of seasoned soldiers. The stillness of the night was broken only by the soft rustle of leaves and the distant call of a night bird. Christopher could feel the tension in the air, a palpable energy that hummed beneath the surface as they approached the farmhouse, weapons at the ready.

Doherty moved alongside Christopher, his eyes scanning the surroundings with the practiced vigilance of a man who had seen too much death. "He's in there," Doherty said quietly, his voice steady. "I can feel it."

Christopher nodded, his focus sharpening. "We'll take him together," he replied. "No mistakes."

As they reached the front door, Christopher paused, his hand tightening on his revolver. He could feel the weight of the mission, the responsibility that rested on his shoulders, but he also felt the strength that came from knowing he was not alone. Doherty was with him, as were the men who had followed him through the fires of war. They were ready, and so was he.

With a swift, decisive kick, Christopher forced the door open, the sound echoing through the silent house. The soldiers behind him moved with the same precision, their weapons raised, their eyes sharp. Inside, the air was thick with the scent of mildew and decay, the floorboards creaking under the weight of their steps. The only light came from a single oil lamp, casting long, flickering shadows on the walls.

Christopher's senses were on high alert as he led the search through the farmhouse. Each room they entered was empty, the furniture covered in dust and cobwebs, but Christopher knew that Booth was close. The man was desperate, cornered, and that made him dangerous.

Finally, as they approached the back of the house, Christopher heard a faint sound—a shuffling, almost imperceptible, coming from behind a closed door. He motioned for the men to hold their positions and approached the door cautiously, his heart pounding in his chest.

His hand tightened on his revolver as he nudged the door open with his foot, revealing a small room dimly lit by the flickering lamp. In the corner, huddled and wounded, was John Wilkes Booth, the man who had changed the course of history with a single bullet.

Booth's eyes were wild, a mix of fear and defiance etched across his face. His hand clutched a revolver, trembling but ready to fire. "Stay back!" he snarled, his voice filled with desperation. "I won't be taken alive!"

He scuttled behind a closet—a desperate shuffle. Booth's silhouette appeared through the gaps in the slats, his form illuminated by the growing inferno with all the buildings set alight by the soldiers snuffing out the bandist.

A moment passed, brief but heavy.

Then—a gunshot.

Booth lurched, his body twisting in pain before crumpling to the ground.

Christopher spun, his gaze locking onto Sergeant

Boston Corbett, still holding his smoking revolver.

"Who gave that order?" Christopher barked.

Corbett didn't flinch. "He raised his pistol. I fired before he could shoot."

Christopher's jaw tightened. Booth had been seconds from surrendering, his stance faltering. Had he truly raised his weapon, or had Corbett simply ensured he never had the chance to speak?

Inside the barn, the fire crackled, its heat unbearable. Soldiers rushed forward, dragging Booth's body into the cool night air. His breath came in ragged, gasping shudders. The bullet had ripped through his neck, shattering vertebrae and leaving him paralyzed.

Christopher knelt beside him, watching as the assassin's life drained away. Booth's lips moved, forming faint words.

"Tell my mother I died for my country."

His fingers twitched as if grasping at something unseen. His mouth parted once more.

"Useless... useless."

Then—silence.

The fire roared behind them, devouring the barn close by as dawn's first light crept over the horizon. Christopher remained still, his mind churning. Booth's final words hung in the air like an unfinished sentence, a puzzle without a missing piece.

Doherty knelt beside him. "It's over."

Christopher wasn't so sure. His eyes flicked toward Corbett, standing eerily still. The sergeant had fired too quickly, too cleanly. And Booth—he had been seconds away from saying something more.

Something he had taken to his grave.

Christopher rose slowly, his gaze shifting to the road ahead. The assassin was dead, but the questions were only beginning.

Before leaving, Christopher took a moment to step outside into the cool night air. He leaned against the wall of the farmhouse, taking a deep breath as he processed what had just happened. The stars were barely visible through the heavy clouds that hung low over the countryside, and the night felt eerily still after the tense confrontation.

As Christopher stood there, he couldn't help but think about the offer Hancock had made—the promise of a General's star if he succeeded. He had succeeded, but at what cost? The man responsible for the nation's grief was now dead but the wounds of this war, both physical and emotional, would take far longer to heal.

The gravity of his accomplishment settled over him. He had led his men successfully, killed the most wanted man in America, and secured his place in history. But the victory was bittersweet, tinged with the knowledge that even this success could not bring Lincoln back, nor could it fully mend the broken heart of a nation.

Christopher pushed off the wall, straightened his uniform, and rejoined his men. The journey back to Washington would be long, but it was a journey that marked the beginning of a new chapter in his life— a chapter where he would wear the star of a General, earned not just through valor on the battlefield, but through a relentless pursuit of justice in the face of adversity.

Christopher O'Donaghue returned to Washington, D.C., the weight of his mission completed but the burdens of leadership still pressing heavily upon him. The city was draped in mourning, black crepe hanging from buildings, and the flags at half-mast a stark reminder of the nation's profound grief. Lincoln's assassination had not only stolen a leader but also struck at the heart of the hope that had sustained the Union through the Civil War.

As Christopher rode through the capital's streets, he felt a mixture of emotions—relief at the capture and subsequent death of Booth, and sorrow for the President who had placed his trust in him. The memory of President Lincoln awarding him the Medal of Honor was vivid in Christopher's mind, and his hand instinctively moved to touch the medal that now hung around his neck. It was during the Battle of Fair Oaks, where he had fought alongside his brother Seamus, that Christopher had earned this honor. He remembered the ferocity of the battle, the blood, the pain of the bullet that had torn through his lung, and the moment when Lincoln had pinned the medal to his chest. The President's words echoed in his mind: "The true measure of a man is not just in his bravery on the battlefield, but in what he does after the war is over."

Christopher dismounted and handed his horse's reins to a young soldier standing by the entrance of the War Department. The building loomed before him, austere and solemn, reflecting the gravity of the events that had unfolded in the nation. As Christopher walked up the steps, he knew that his journey was far from over. The mission had been completed, but the task of healing the nation—and ensuring that the sacrifices made were not in vain—had only just begun.

Inside, the War Department was a hive of activity, but the usual buzz was muted by the weight of the collective grief. Christopher made his way to the office where General Winfield Scott Hancock awaited him. Hancock had been one of the first to understand the gravity of the situation when Lincoln was shot, and he had entrusted Christopher with the most crucial mission of his life—bringing the assassin to justice.

As Christopher entered the room, General Hancock rose to greet him, his eyes reflecting both relief and respect. The general's demeanor was one of stern pride, and he extended his hand to Christopher, who took it with a firm grip.

"You did the nation a great service, General O'Donaghue," Hancock said, emphasizing the new rank that Christopher now held. He gestured to the velvet case on his desk, already opened and empty, the two silver stars that had once lain inside now affixed to Christopher's shoulders.

Christopher nodded, his expression somber. "Thank you, sir. It was an honor to serve, but this victory feels hollow given the loss we've all suffered."

Hancock sighed, his gaze shifting to the window as if looking out at the city could somehow bring back the fallen President. "Lincoln was a great man, and his loss is incalculable. But we must move forward. The stars on your shoulders are not just a reward, Christopher; they're a reminder of the responsibility you now bear."

Christopher understood the weight of the general's words. The stars represented more than rank—they symbolized the trust the nation had placed in him, the expectation that he would continue to serve with honor and integrity, even as the nation struggled to find its footing after the war.

"There's still much to be done," Hancock continued, his tone softening slightly. "The country is fragile, and the peace we've fought for is precarious. You've shown you can lead in battle, but now we need leaders who can guide us through the reconstruction of our nation. Take some time to rest, but know that your service is far from over."

Christopher nodded, his resolve firm. "I understand, General. I'll be ready when the time comes."

Hancock gave him a measured nod, then added almost as an afterthought:

"Good. The country will need strong hands in the years ahead. And not just in war. The world is changing, and those who understand the balance of power... they will shape what comes next."

There was nothing overtly unusual about Hancock's words—at the time, Christopher took them as a simple acknowledgment of his leadership and potential role in rebuilding a fractured nation.

It wasn't just war leaders they needed. It wasn't just military men.

It was men like him. Men with experience, loyalty,

and—most importantly—a sense of duty that could be harnessed before they even realized it.

Christopher left the office, his mind occupied with thoughts of home and the next steps in his life. Yet something gnawed at him.

Hancock had wanted Booth alive. Had been adamant about it. And yet—Booth had been silenced.

Christopher clenched his fists. Maybe it was nothing. Maybe Corbett had acted on impulse.

Or maybe Lincoln's murder had never been about one man.

Maybe it had always been bigger than that. Or maybe this will be something that will remain buried with Booth.

The streets of Washington were still bustling with life, the general's words still echoing in his mind, but the atmosphere around him was heavy with sorrow. As Christopher rode through the city, his thoughts turned to his next challenge—returning to New York City, a place that had changed dramatically during the years he had been away fighting.

New York was not just the city he had once called home; it was now a battleground of a different kind. The influence of Tammany Hall, the powerful political machine, had grown unchecked during the war, and Christopher knew that if he wanted to serve the people of New York, he would have to confront the corruption and exploitation that Tammany represented.

His thoughts drifted back to Tammany Hall and its notorious leader, William "Boss" Tweed. Christopher had heard of Tweed's rise to power, his ability to manipulate the city's political landscape to his advantage, and the iron grip he held over the city's resources. Tammany Hall had once been an organization that represented the interests of the working-class immigrants, but under Tweed, it had become synonymous with corruption and greed.

As Christopher approached New York, he prepared himself for the confrontation he knew was inevitable. He had no illusions about the difficulty of the task ahead—taking on Tammany Hall would be like going to war all over again, but this time, the enemy was entrenched within the very fabric of the city.

Upon arriving in New York, Christopher was immediately summoned to Tammany Hall. The imposing building was as much a symbol of power as it was of corruption, and as Christopher entered its grand halls, he could feel the tension in the air. The men who worked for Tammany were sharp-eyed and calculating, their loyalties bought and paid for by the power brokers who controlled the city.

Christopher was led to a large, ornately decorated room where Liam O'Sullivan and several other key figures of Tammany were gathered. Liam, who had once been an ally, now looked at Christopher with a mixture of wariness and expectation. The men fell silent as Christopher entered, their eyes following his every move.

Liam rose from his chair, forcing a smile onto his face as he extended a hand to Christopher.

"General O'Donaghue," he greeted, using the title that Christopher had recently earned. "You've done the city proud, lad. With your reputation and influence, we can accomplish great things here. Tammany Hall is ready to support you in whatever endeavors you choose."

Christopher took Liam's hand but did not return the smile. He had faced death on the battlefield; the political games of Tammany Hall no longer intimidated him. "I didn't fight and bleed for this country to become a pawn in anyone's schemes, Liam," Christopher said, his voice cold and firm. "I'm done with Tammany Hall. I'm done being used."

A murmur spread through the room as the men exchanged uneasy glances. Liam's smile faltered, and he narrowed his eyes, his tone turning more serious. "You don't just walk away from Tammany, Christopher. You owe us, and we expect loyalty in return for everything we've done for you."

Christopher met Liam's gaze head-on, his voice unwavering. "I've paid my debt, Liam. And I'll continue to serve this city, but I won't be controlled by Tammany or anyone else. I'm my own man now."

Before Liam could respond, the door to the room swung open with a creak, and the atmosphere grew even tenser. The men turned as William "Boss" Tweed entered the room, his presence immediately commanding attention. Tweed was a large, formidable man, his reputation as the most powerful and feared figure in New York preceding him.

Tweed's eyes locked onto Christopher, and a slow, calculated smile spread across his face. "General

O'Donaghue," Tweed said, his voice a low, rumbling drawl. "I've heard much about you. A war hero, a man of principle. Just the kind of man we could use here in New York."

Christopher stood his ground, unflinching under Tweed's gaze. "I'm here to serve the people of New York, not to further anyone's ambitions, Mr. Tweed."

Tweed's smile did not waver, but there was a glint in his eyes that spoke of a man unaccustomed to being challenged. "You misunderstand me, General. Tammany Hall is the people of New York. We provide jobs, services, protection. We make sure this city runs smoothly. Surely, a man of your experience understands the importance of maintaining order."

Christopher saw through the veneer of Tweed's words, recognizing the underlying threat. "Order is important," Christopher agreed, his tone measured. "But not at the expense of justice. The kind of order you're talking about sounds more like control."

Tweed's expression darkened slightly, and the tension in the room thickened. "Careful, General," he warned, his voice dripping with menace. "You're treading on dangerous ground. Tammany has a long reach and an even longer memory."

Christopher did not back down. He had faced enemies on the battlefield that could kill him with a bullet; he would not be cowed by a man who wielded power through corruption and fear. "And so do I," Christopher replied, his tone resolute.

The silence that followed was heavy, the air thick with unspoken threats. Christopher knew that he had made a powerful enemy in Tweed, but he also knew that he could not allow himself to be intimidated or swayed from his principles. He had fought too hard and lost too much to let fear dictate his actions now.

Tweed's eyes bore into Christopher's, the two men locked in a silent battle of wills. Finally, Tweed broke the silence, his voice softer but no less dangerous. "You're a brave man, O'Donaghue. But bravery alone won't save you in this city. Remember that."

With those parting words, Tweed turned and left the room, his departure leaving a palpable void in his wake. The men of Tammany Hall looked at each other, the unease evident in their expressions. Liam O'Sullivan, however, seemed more resolved than before, his gaze hardening as he turned back to Christopher.

"You've made a powerful enemy today, Christopher," Liam said, his voice filled with a mix of warning and regret. "I hope you know what you're doing."

Christopher met Liam's gaze, his own filled with determination. "I do, Liam. And I won't back down."

Without another word, Christopher turned and walked out of the room, leaving the men of Tammany Hall to ponder the implications of what had just transpired. As he stepped out into the bustling streets of New York, Christopher knew that the battle he was about to fight would be unlike any he had faced before. It was a battle not just for the soul of the city, but for the future of a nation still healing from the scars of war.

Christopher walked through the city, his mind racing with the possibilities and the dangers that lay ahead. He knew that confronting Tweed and Tammany Hall would be a long and difficult struggle, but he was determined to see it through. He had fought for justice on the battlefield, and now he would fight for it in the streets of New York.

He stopped at a newsstand, where a paper with the headline "BOOTH CAPTURED!" was on display. Christopher picked it up, scanning the article briefly before folding it under his arm. As he continued walking, the camera of his mind pulled back to reveal the towering buildings and the throngs of people, each with their own story, each with their own battles to fight.

Christopher had risen from the streets of New York to the battlefields of the Civil War and now found himself facing the most powerful man in the city. But he was determined to forge his destiny on his own terms, to fight for the principles that had guided him through the darkest days of the war.

As he walked through Central Park later that day, Christopher found a rare moment of peace amidst the chaos of the city. He sat on a bench, watching the people around him—families, children, couples enjoying the sunny day. The contrast between this serene scene and the battles he had fought was stark, but it was a reminder of what he was fighting for.

An old friend and fellow officer from the NYPD, Officer James McGuire, approached and sat down beside Christopher with a knowing smile.

"Heard you had quite an adventure down in D.C., General," McGuire said, his tone light but respectful. "The city's buzzing with talk of your exploits."

Christopher chuckled, shaking his head. "Seems like a lifetime ago already. How've you been, James?"

McGuire shrugged, his expression thoughtful. "Same old, same old. The city never changes, does it? But you… you've changed. I can see it."

Christopher looked out over the park, his eyes distant. "War does that to a man. But I'm trying to figure out what comes next. The city's still standing, and so am I. I've got to decide how to make the most of that."

McGuire nodded, understanding the weight of Christopher's words. "You've got a lot of influence now, Christopher. People respect you. If anyone can make a difference in this city, it's you."

Christopher turned to McGuire, a determined glint in his eye. "That's the plan, James. I'm going to use everything I've learned, everything I've fought for, to make this city better. On my terms."

McGuire grinned, clapping Christopher on the back. "That's the spirit, General. Whatever you decide to do, you've got my support."

Christopher nodded, grateful for the friendship and loyalty of those who had stood by him. The challenges ahead were daunting, but he was ready to face them. He had fought for his country, and now he would fight for his city.

Christopher stood on the steps of New York City Hall, looking out over the bustling streets below. The sun was setting, casting a warm glow over the city. Christopher's expression was one of determination and resolve, knowing that his journey was far from over. The future was wide open before him, and he was ready to face whatever challenges came his way.

Christopher O'Donaghue had faced down the shadows of his past and emerged stronger, a man who had fought for justice both on the battlefield and in the streets of New York. His journey was far from over, but now, he walked it as his own man.

CHAPTER 7: REBECCA'S ASCENT, PART 1

The rugged hills of Cork, Ireland, bore witness to the harshness of life in the aftermath of the Great Famine, but in the midst of this, a young girl named Rebecca O'Donaghue was beginning to make her mark on the world. The year was 1858, and Rebecca was fourteen years old, living under the care of her older brother Seamus, who had taken on the responsibility of looking after her after the death of their Uncle Michael five years earlier. The memory of their uncle's passing still lingered, but it was Seamus's resilience and love that had seen them through the dark days that followed.

Rebecca had always been a spirited child, with a voice that seemed to carry the very soul of Ireland within it. Even as a young girl, her singing had captured the hearts of those around her. The people of Cork spoke of her with a kind of reverence, as if she were a gift from the heavens sent to bring a little light into their lives.

Seamus, who had taken over the running of Uncle Michael's shop, encouraged Rebecca to pursue her singing. He had seen the way people's faces lit up when she sang, how their burdens seemed to lift, if only for a moment. Despite the hardships they faced, Seamus was determined that Rebecca would have a chance to make something of herself, even if it meant letting go of the only family he had left.

One crisp autumn day, as Rebecca walked through the streets of Cork, her voice filled the air with a haunting Irish ballad. The sound was pure and clear, carrying on the wind and drawing the attention of those who passed by. It was on this day that her life would change forever.

As Rebecca sang, she caught the attention of a well-dressed Englishman who was traveling through Cork on business. Sir Reginald Townsend, a man of wealth and influence, was instantly captivated by the beauty and power of her voice. He was a tall, distinguished gentleman, with a neatly trimmed beard and eyes that spoke of a life well-lived. As soon as he heard Rebecca's voice, he knew he had found something extraordinary.

Sir Reginald ordered his carriage to stop, and he stepped out onto the cobblestone street, his eyes fixed on the young girl who had enchanted him with her singing. He approached her with a kind smile, his manner respectful and warm.

"Young lady," he began, his voice carrying the refined tones of the English upper class, "your voice is truly remarkable. I have traveled far and wide, and I have never heard anything quite like it."

Rebecca blushed, not accustomed to receiving such praise from a stranger, especially one who looked as important as Sir Reginald. "Thank you, sir," she replied shyly. "I sing because it brings me joy. I never thought anyone else would take much notice."

Sir Reginald chuckled softly. "Well, I can assure you, I have taken notice. And I believe that with a voice like yours, you could do more than just bring joy to yourself. You could bring joy to the world. Have you ever considered where your singing might take you?"

Rebecca looked up at him, her heart suddenly pounding in her chest. "Take me?" she echoed, unsure of what he meant.

"Yes," Sir Reginald said, his tone serious now. "I believe that you have the potential to sing on the grandest stages of Europe, to perform before kings and queens. If you are willing to take a chance, I would like to help you make that a reality."

Rebecca was stunned. The idea of leaving Cork, of traveling to places she had only ever read about in books, was both exhilarating and terrifying. She had never thought of herself as anything more than a simple girl from Cork, someone whose life would be spent in the shadow of the great famine that had ravaged her country. But now, standing before this kind and generous stranger, she could see a different future —a future filled with possibilities she had never dared to dream of.

"I... I don't know what to say," she stammered, her mind racing.

"You don't have to decide right now," Sir Reginald said gently. "But I urge you to think about it. I will be staying at the Imperial Hotel for the next few days. If you decide you would like to take this opportunity, come and find me there."

With that, he tipped his hat to her and returned to his carriage, leaving Rebecca standing on the street, her heart and mind swirling with thoughts of what could be.

That evening, Rebecca returned to the shop where Seamus was busy with the day's work. The smell of freshly baked bread filled the air, and the shelves were stocked with goods that had come from far and wide. Seamus had done well to keep the business going after Uncle Michael's death, and Rebecca knew how much he had sacrificed to give her a chance at a better life.

She told Seamus about her encounter with Sir Reginald, her voice trembling with a mix of excitement and fear. Seamus listened carefully, his brow furrowing as he considered the implications of what she was saying.

"So, this man thinks you could be a famous singer?" Seamus asked, his tone measured.

Rebecca nodded. "He said he could help me. That I could sing in Dublin, maybe even in Paris."

Seamus was silent for a moment, his thoughts clearly racing. He had always known that Rebecca was special, that she was destined for more than the life they were living. But the thought of her leaving, of her going out into the world alone, filled him with a deep sense of dread.

"Rebecca," he began, his voice soft, "this is a big decision. It's not something you can take lightly. The world out there... it's not always kind, especially to someone as young and innocent as you."

Rebecca looked at him, her eyes wide with a mix of hope and fear. "I know, Seamus. But I feel like... I feel like this is my chance to do something with my life. Something that matters."

Seamus sighed, rubbing his hand over his face. He had always tried to protect Rebecca, to shield her from the harsh realities of life. But he also knew that he couldn't hold her back, that she had to make her own choices, even if those choices took her far away from him.

"If this is what you want, Rebecca, then I'll support you," he said finally, his voice thick with emotion. "But you have to promise me that you'll be careful. That you'll remember who you are, where you come from."

Tears welled up in Rebecca's eyes as she nodded. "I promise, Seamus. I'll never forget."

The decision made, Rebecca felt a strange mixture of excitement and fear. She knew that her life was about to change forever, but she also knew that she was ready for whatever lay ahead.

The days leading up to her departure were filled with a flurry of preparations. Seamus helped her pack, offering advice and words of encouragement as they folded her few belongings into a small trunk. They spent their evenings talking by the fire, sharing stories and memories, knowing that their time together was growing short.

The night before Rebecca was to leave for Dublin, they sat in silence, the weight of the impending separation heavy in the air. Seamus took Rebecca's hand in his, his grip firm but gentle.

"Rebecca," he said quietly, "you're going to do great things. I know it. But never forget where you come from. Never forget your family, and never forget the people who love you."

Tears welled up in Rebecca's eyes as she nodded. "I won't, Seamus. I promise."

The next morning, they said their goodbyes at the coach station. Seamus embraced Rebecca tightly, holding her close as if he could somehow protect her from the world she was about to enter.

"Take care of yourself, Rebecca," he whispered, his voice choked with emotion. "And remember, I'll always be here if you need me."

Rebecca clung to him for a moment longer before finally pulling away. She wiped her tears and forced herself to smile. "I'll write to you as soon as I get to Dublin," she promised.

Seamus nodded, his own eyes brimming with unshed tears. "I'll be waiting."

With one last look at her brother, Rebecca boarded the coach that would take her to Dublin and to the future that awaited her.

As the coach pulled away, Rebecca felt a mixture of excitement and fear welling up inside her. She was leaving everything she had ever known, stepping into a world that was entirely unfamiliar. But she was also filled with a sense of purpose, a determination to make something of herself, to honor the sacrifices her family had made for her.

The journey to Dublin was long and tiring, but Rebecca's spirits were high. She watched the landscape change as they traveled, the rolling hills of Cork giving way to the bustling streets of the city. By the time they arrived in Dublin, it was evening, and the city was alive with the sounds of people going about their business.

Rebecca stepped off the coach and took a deep breath, the scent of the city filling her senses. She had never been anywhere like this before, and the sheer size and energy of Dublin were both exhilarating and overwhelming.

She found her way to the address Sir Reginald had given her, a small but comfortable boarding house in the heart of the city. The landlady, a kindly woman named Mrs. O'Leary, welcomed her with a warm smile and showed her to her room.

The room was small but cozy, with a comfortable bed, a writing desk, and a window that looked out over the bustling street below. Rebecca set her trunk down and sat on the edge of the bed, taking a moment to collect her thoughts. This was the beginning of her new life, and she was determined to make the most of it.

The next day, Rebecca met with Sir Reginald at the Imperial Hotel. He greeted her warmly, his eyes gleaming with excitement.

"Welcome to Dublin, my dear," he said, taking her hand in his. "I trust your journey was pleasant?"

Rebecca smiled and nodded. "Yes, sir. It was long, but I'm glad to be here."

Sir Reginald led her to a sitting room, where they sat down to discuss her future. He had arranged for her to meet with one of the city's most respected vocal teachers, Madame Dubois, who would assess her voice and begin her formal training.

"Madame Dubois is a strict teacher, but she is also one of the best," Sir Reginald explained. "If you can impress her, there's no telling how far you can go."

Rebecca's heart raced at the thought. This was the opportunity she had been waiting for, the chance to prove herself and take the first steps toward achieving her dreams.

The meeting with Madame Dubois took place the following day. Rebecca was nervous as she entered the small, elegant studio, her hands trembling slightly as she clutched her sheet music. But when she began to sing, all of her fears melted away.

Madame Dubois listened intently, her sharp eyes never leaving Rebecca's face as she sang. When Rebecca finished, there was a moment of silence before the older woman nodded approvingly.

"You have a remarkable voice, Mademoiselle O'Donaghue," she said, her tone thoughtful. "But there is much work to be done. You have raw talent, but it must be honed and refined if you are to succeed in this world."

Rebecca nodded, her heart swelling with pride and determination. "I'm ready to work hard, Madame," she said, her voice steady. "I'm ready to do whatever it takes."

And so, Rebecca's training began. The days were long and grueling, filled with vocal exercises, breathing techniques, and hours of practice. Madame Dubois was a demanding teacher, but Rebecca thrived under her guidance. She pushed herself to her limits, determined to make the most of this opportunity.

As the weeks passed, Rebecca's voice grew stronger, more controlled. She learned to channel her emotions into her singing, to convey the depth of feeling that had always been present in her music. She began to see herself not just as a singer, but as an artist, someone who could touch the hearts of those who listened to her.

Her hard work did not go unnoticed. Sir Reginald was pleased with her progress, and he arranged for her to perform at a small recital in front of some of Dublin's most influential patrons of the arts. It was a nerve-wracking experience, but Rebecca was determined to succeed.

The night of the recital arrived, and Rebecca found herself standing backstage, her heart pounding in her chest. She could hear the murmur of the audience as they took their seats, the rustle of programs, the soft clearing of throats. It was a small, intimate venue, but to Rebecca, it felt as grand as any opera house.

She closed her eyes and took a deep breath, reminding herself of all the hours of practice, all the sacrifices that had brought her to this moment. When she stepped onto the stage, she felt a calmness settle over her, a sense of purpose that guided her every move.

The music began, and Rebecca sang with a passion and intensity that surprised even herself. She poured her heart into every note, every phrase, her voice soaring and dipping with a grace that captivated the audience. She sang not just for herself, but for her family, for the people of Cork, for everyone who had believed in her.

When the final note faded, there was a moment of stunned silence before the room erupted into applause. Rebecca stood there, breathless and overwhelmed, as the audience rose to their feet in a standing ovation.

Sir Reginald beamed with pride as he watched her, knowing that this was only the beginning of her journey. He approached her after the performance, his eyes shining with excitement.

"You were magnificent, Rebecca," he said, taking her hands in his. "There's no doubt in my mind now. You're ready for the next step."

Rebecca's heart raced as she looked up at him. "The next step?"

Sir Reginald nodded, his expression serious. "Paris," he said simply. "It's time for you to go to Paris, to study with the best and perform on the grandest stages. I have no doubt that you will succeed."

The word "Paris" hung in the air between them, full of promise and possibility. Rebecca had never imagined that her journey would take her this far, but now that the opportunity was before her, she knew that she had to take it.

"I'll go," she said, her voice filled with determination. "I'll go to Paris and make the most of this chance."

Sir Reginald smiled, knowing that Rebecca was ready for whatever lay ahead. "Then it's settled," he said. "We'll make the arrangements, and soon you'll be on your way to Paris."

As they left the recital hall, Rebecca felt a sense of exhilaration and anticipation. The road ahead was uncertain, but she knew that she was ready to face whatever challenges came her way. She had come so far from the streets of Cork, and now, she was on the brink of something extraordinary.

Rebecca couldn't help but feel a pang of sadness as she thought of Seamus and the life she was leaving behind. But she also knew that this was her path, her destiny. And she was determined to walk it, no matter where it led.

As Rebecca settled into her new life in Paris, she quickly realized that this city was unlike any place she had ever known. Paris in the mid-19th century was a hub of artistic brilliance, a place where the old world met the new in a constant swirl of innovation and grandeur. For Rebecca, it was as if she had stepped into a dream— one filled with the promise of fame, fortune, and a life beyond anything she had ever imagined.

From the moment she arrived, it was clear that Paris was ready to embrace her. She was introduced to Manuel Garcia, a vocal teacher of unparalleled reputation. Garcia had trained some of the most illustrious singers of the time, and he quickly recognized that Rebecca possessed a rare and extraordinary talent. He knew that with the right training, she could surpass even the greatest sopranos of the age.

Garcia's training regimen was not for the faint of heart. He was demanding, exacting in his expectations, and relentless in his pursuit of perfection. Each day began before dawn and ended long after the sun had set. Rebecca would spend hours working on scales, arias, and the intricacies of breath control. Garcia pushed her to expand her vocal range, to hone her technique, and to pour every ounce of emotion into her performances. The days were grueling, the physical and mental toll immense, but Rebecca was undeterred. She understood that this was the path to greatness, and she embraced it with the same determination that had driven her through the hardships of her early life in Cork.

Within a year, Rebecca made her debut on the Parisian stage. The performance took place at the Opéra-Comique, one of the city's most prestigious venues. The theater was packed, every seat filled with an audience eager to witness the debut of the young soprano who had been the subject of so much speculation. As the orchestra began to play and Rebecca stepped into the spotlight, the room fell silent. Then, her voice—rich, powerful, and filled with emotion—filled the theater, captivating everyone present.

Rebecca's performance was nothing short of a triumph. The audience was entranced by her voice, which had grown more powerful and expressive under Garcia's tutelage. It wasn't just her technical skill that drew them in—it was the depth of feeling she conveyed with every note, the way she seemed to live and breathe the music. When the final note of her aria hung in the air, the theater erupted in applause, the audience rising to their feet in a thunderous standing ovation. Paris, known for its discerning and often harsh critics, had found its new star.

Word of Rebecca's talent spread quickly. Her name became the talk of the town, whispered in salons, cafés, and theaters across the city. Critics hailed her as the next great soprano, comparing her to the likes of Jenny Lind and Pauline Viardot. Invitations to perform at other prestigious venues across Europe soon followed. Vienna, Milan, London—each city welcomed her with open arms, and each performance was met with accolades and praise.

In Vienna, she performed before the Emperor himself, who was so moved by her rendition of Mozart's "Queen of the Night" aria that he presented her with a diamond-studded brooch—a symbol of the imperial favor. In Milan, she graced the stage of La Scala, where her performance of Verdi's "La Traviata" was met with such enthusiastic applause that she was called back for encore after encore. In London, she was the guest of honor at a grand ball hosted by the Duke of Wellington, where she was introduced to the most influential figures in British society, all eager to meet the soprano whose voice had captured the hearts of Europe.

But even as her fame grew, Rebecca remained grounded. She never forgot where she came from, the hardships she had endured, or the promise she had made to herself to honor her family's legacy. She wrote regularly to Seamus, sharing her experiences and sending money back to Cork, ensuring that the O'Donaghue name would be remembered not just for its struggles but for its triumphs. She knew that her success was not just her own—it was for her family, for her brother who had sacrificed so much to give her this chance.

Rebecca's success brought her into contact with many influential figures. Among them were Joseph Oller and Charles Zidler, two ambitious entrepreneurs who were planning to create something entirely new in the world of entertainment. They envisioned a venue that would combine the high art of opera with the vibrant, energetic dance culture that was sweeping through Paris—a place where the boundaries between high society and the bohemian underworld would blur. This venue would become the Moulin Rouge.

Oller and Zidler had heard of Rebecca's talents long before they met her. They had seen her perform at the Théâtre des Italiens, and they knew immediately that she was the star they needed to bring their vision to life. After the performance, they arranged a private meeting with her to present their proposition.

Rebecca was intrigued by their offer. The idea of blending her operatic skills with something as daring as the can-can was both thrilling and daunting. But Rebecca had never been one to shy away from a challenge, and the prospect of redefining entertainment in Paris was too exciting to pass up.

"What you're proposing is... unlike anything I've ever done," Rebecca admitted during their first meeting, her voice tinged with both excitement and caution.

Oller leaned forward, his eyes alight with passion. "Exactly! That's what will make it extraordinary. You have the voice, the presence—everything we need to create a spectacle that will take Paris by storm. With you as our star, the Moulin Rouge will be the most talked-about venue in Europe."

Zidler, ever the showman, added with a flourish, "Imagine it, Mademoiselle O'Donaghue. Your name in lights, your face on posters all over the city. You won't just be a singer—you'll be a legend."

The offer was impossible to resist. Rebecca had already achieved so much, but this was a chance to take her career to an entirely new level, to transcend the boundaries of opera and become a cultural icon. After careful consideration, Rebecca agreed. She would become the star of the Moulin Rouge, helping to create a show that would redefine entertainment in Paris.

Preparations for the grand opening of the Moulin Rouge began immediately. The venue itself was a marvel of design, with its iconic red windmill and lavish interior that combined the elegance of a theater with the lively energy of a dance hall. It was a place where the rigid boundaries of society could dissolve, where aristocrats could mingle with artists, writers, and the everyday people of Paris.

Rebecca threw herself into the preparations with her characteristic determination. She worked closely with choreographers, costume designers, and musicians to create a show that would not only showcase her vocal talents but also introduce something entirely new to the Parisian stage. The show would be a blend of operatic arias, lively can-can dances, and moments of pure theatricality that would leave the audience breathless.

As opening night approached, the buzz in Paris reached a fever pitch. The Moulin Rouge was the talk of the town, and everyone who was anyone wanted to be there for the grand opening. The guest list included not just the wealthy and powerful but also the artists and intellectuals who shaped the cultural life of the city. Everyone was eager to see the new spectacle that promised to break down barriers and set new standards for entertainment.

On the night of the grand opening, Rebecca stood backstage, her heart pounding with a mixture of nerves and excitement. She was dressed in a costume that was both elegant and provocative, a reflection of the show's unique blend of high art and popular culture. The audience was already in their seats, the air thick with anticipation as they waited for the curtain to rise.

Rebecca took a deep breath, reminding herself of the journey that had led her to this moment. She thought of Seamus, of the streets of Cork, and of the promise she had made to herself all those years ago. This was her moment, and she was ready to seize it.

As the curtain rose, Rebecca stepped onto the stage, her voice filling the theater with a hauntingly beautiful melody. The audience was instantly captivated. They had come expecting a spectacle, but what they received was something much more—a performance that was as much about emotion and artistry as it was about entertainment.

Rebecca's performance was unlike anything Paris had ever seen. She moved with grace and power, blending the elegance of opera with the exuberance of the can-can. She was a vision on stage, commanding the attention of everyone in the room. Her voice soared through the theater, carrying with it all the emotion and passion she had poured into her training. The audience was entranced, their applause growing louder with each passing moment.

Among those in the audience was Emperor Napoleon III, who had come to see the show that everyone was talking about. He watched Rebecca with a mixture of admiration and desire, drawn to her not just by her beauty but by the undeniable power of her performance.

As the performance reached its climax, Rebecca spotted Napoleon in the crowd. With a playful smile, she sauntered over to his table, her voice lowering to a sultry purr as she teased, "Hey, Emperor, the champagne's on you!"

The audience erupted in laughter and applause, delighted by Rebecca's audacity. Napoleon, far from offended, laughed heartily, his eyes twinkling with amusement and admiration.

"Indeed it is, Mademoiselle. And I must say, it's the finest I've ever had," he replied, raising his glass to her.

The connection between Rebecca and Napoleon was electric, a spark that would soon ignite into something much more. But for now, it was enough to know that she had captured the heart of not just the audience, but the most powerful man in France.

As the final notes of the performance echoed through the theater, the audience rose to their feet in a thunderous standing ovation. Rebecca stood in the spotlight, her heart swelling with pride and triumph. She had done it—she had taken a leap of faith, and it had paid off in ways she had never imagined.

The Moulin Rouge was an instant success, and Rebecca's fame reached new heights. She was no longer just a celebrated soprano—she was a legend, a symbol of Parisian culture and the embodiment of the city's spirit of innovation and daring. The show's success was not just in its entertainment value but in how it pushed the boundaries of what performance could be. It was a testament to the power of blending art forms, of daring to do something different and succeeding beyond all expectations.

After the show, the night continued with a grand celebration. The champagne flowed freely as guests mingled, congratulating Rebecca on her stunning performance. Napoleon himself came to her side, his eyes alight with admiration.

"You were magnificent, Mademoiselle O'Donaghue," he said, his voice low and sincere. "Paris has never seen anything like you."

Rebecca smiled, her heart racing with the thrill of the night's success. "Thank you, Your Majesty. I'm honored that you were here to see it."

Napoleon took her hand, his touch sending a shiver down her spine. "This is just the beginning, Rebecca. I have no doubt that you will achieve even greater things."

As the night wore on, Rebecca found herself reflecting on her journey—the twists and turns, the highs and lows that had brought her to this moment. She thought of Seamus, of her family, and of the promise she had made to herself all those years ago. She had fulfilled that promise, but she knew that there was still so much more to achieve.

With the Moulin Rouge behind her and the world at her feet, Rebecca was ready to embrace whatever came next. The future was bright, and she was determined to make the most of every opportunity that came her way. The lights of the Moulin Rouge glittered like stars in the Parisian night, a symbol of the new world Rebecca had found herself in—one where she was free to shine as brightly as she dared.

In the weeks and months that followed, Rebecca's reputation only grew. She became the face of the Moulin Rouge, her image appearing on posters and in newspapers across Europe. Her performances were the hottest ticket in town, and her name became synonymous with the glamour and excitement of Parisian nightlife. But more than that, she became a symbol of change—a woman who had dared to break the mold and create something entirely new.

Yet despite all her success, Rebecca never forgot her roots. She continued to send money home to Seamus, to support the family that had made her dreams possible. She wrote letters filled with stories of her adventures, always mindful of the promise she had made to herself. And as she looked out at the world she had created, she knew that she was ready for whatever challenges lay ahead.

The Moulin Rouge was just the beginning. Rebecca O'Donaghue was destined for greatness, and she was determined to make the most of every opportunity that came her way. The world was hers for the taking, and she was ready to shine brighter than ever before.

CHAPTER 8: A BEACON OF HOPE

As the sun rose over the sprawling metropolis of New York City in the late 1870s, the morning light cast a golden hue over the buildings and streets, painting a picture of a city brimming with promise. The city was alive with the bustle of commerce, its streets filled with the clatter of horse-drawn carriages, the shouts of vendors, and the chatter of people going about their daily lives. Yet beneath the surface, New York was a city in turmoil, where corruption festered in the halls of power, and the struggles of the common people often went unheard.

General Christopher O'Donaghue walked with purpose through the crowded streets, his stride confident and determined. His years of service to the Union had earned him respect and recognition, but the war had also left him with a burning desire to fight another kind of battle—a battle for the soul of his adopted city. As he passed by the throngs of people, many of whom were immigrants like himself, Christopher felt a deep connection to the city and its inhabitants. He had risen from humble beginnings, and now he was determined to use his influence to bring about the change that New York so desperately needed.

Christopher approached a grand building, the headquarters of his newly established shipping company, R. P. O'Donaghue & Company. The name, chosen in honor of his late brother Ryan, was a reminder of the sacrifices that had shaped his life and his resolve to create something meaningful in their memory. The company had grown rapidly, its ships now traversing the globe, carrying goods to and from far-flung destinations. As Christopher entered the bustling offices, he was greeted by the sight of clerks busy with ledgers, telegraphs humming with the latest business news, and maps of trade routes adorning the walls.

John Muldoon, Christopher's trusted business partner and a fellow Irish immigrant, approached him with a smile, holding a document that contained the latest financial figures. John had been with Christopher from the beginning, helping to build the company from the ground up. His loyalty and hard work had been instrumental in their success.

"General, the latest figures are in," John said, his voice tinged with excitement. "We're on track to double our profits this quarter. The expansion into South America is paying off handsomely."

Christopher took the document, glancing over the numbers with satisfaction. The success of the company was a testament to the hard work and determination of everyone involved, but Christopher knew that their work was far from over. There were greater challenges ahead, challenges that went beyond the world of commerce.

"Good work, John," Christopher replied, his tone serious. "We've come a long way since our first ship set sail. But there's more to be done—this city needs leaders who aren't afraid to stand up to the likes of Tammany Hall."

John nodded, understanding Christopher's determination to reform the city he had once served in uniform. Tammany Hall, the political machine that had controlled New York for decades, was notorious for its corruption and influence over city politics. Christopher had seen firsthand the impact of their greed and dishonesty, and he was determined to put an end to it.

"You've got the influence, Christopher," John said, his

voice filled with conviction. "And more importantly, the people respect you. If anyone can challenge Tammany, it's you."

Christopher's expression hardened as he thought of the corruption and vice that still plagued New York. He had fought for freedom and justice on the battlefield, and now he was ready to take that fight to the political arena.

"I owe it to this city, John," Christopher said, his voice resolute. "And to the people who believed in me. We're going to make New York a place where justice isn't for sale."

With those words, Christopher handed the document back to John, his mind already turning to the political challenges ahead. The road would be difficult, but Christopher had never been one to back down from a fight. He had faced adversity before, and he knew that with determination and the support of the people, they could overcome any obstacle.

As Christopher left the office and walked through the diverse neighborhoods of New York, he was reminded of the city's incredible vitality and resilience. From the bustling markets of the Lower East Side, where immigrants from all corners of the globe struggled to make a living, to the stately mansions of Fifth Avenue, where the city's elite enjoyed the fruits of their wealth, New York was a city of contrasts. But despite these differences, there was a shared sense of hope and ambition that united the people.

Christopher took the time to meet with people from all walks of life—business owners, laborers, immigrants

—listening to their stories and concerns. Many spoke of the challenges they faced, the difficulties of making ends meet in a city where the powerful often seemed to care little for the plight of the common man. Christopher listened with empathy, his resolve to bring reform to the city growing stronger with each conversation.

The respect and admiration in the eyes of the people he met was evident. They saw in Christopher a man who understood their struggles, who had walked in their shoes, and who was committed to making a difference. Christopher knew that the trust they placed in him was both a privilege and a responsibility, one that he would not take lightly.

That evening, Christopher found himself at an upscale political club, a place where New York's elite gathered to discuss the future of the city. The room was filled with the scent of cigars and the murmur of conversation, as powerful men from the worlds of politics and business exchanged ideas and made deals. Christopher was no stranger to these gatherings, but tonight was different —tonight, he was here with a purpose.

As he entered the room, Christopher was greeted by Liam O'Sullivan, now a prominent figure in Tammany Hall but whose influence was beginning to wane in the face of growing public discontent with the organization's corruption. Liam was a man who had always known how to navigate the treacherous waters of New York politics, but even he could see that the tide was turning.

"General O'Donaghue, always a pleasure," Liam said with a pleasant smile, though there was a hint of something else in his eyes. "I've been hearing about your... endeavors. It seems you're making quite a name for yourself outside the usual channels."

Christopher shook Liam's hand, his smile cordial but his eyes steely. He knew that Liam was not to be trusted, that his words were always laced with ulterior motives.

"I'm doing what I can for the city, Liam," Christopher replied coolly. "Someone has to clean up the mess Tammany's made."

Liam's smile tightened, but he maintained his composure. "You've always been a man of principle, Christopher. But politics is a different game. It's not as simple as leading a charge on the battlefield."

Christopher's expression hardened, his voice firm as he responded. "Maybe not. But that doesn't mean we should ignore what's right. I'm not afraid to stand up for what I believe in, Liam. And I'm not afraid of Tammany Hall."

Liam's eyes narrowed slightly, but he quickly recovered, his tone becoming more conciliatory. "We're all on the same side here, Christopher. New York needs strong leaders, men like you. There's no reason we can't work together to achieve our goals."

Christopher nodded politely, though he remained cautious. He knew better than to trust Liam or the promises of Tammany Hall. "We'll see, Liam. We'll see."

With that, Christopher turned and walked away, leaving Liam watching him with a calculating expression. Christopher knew that Liam was sizing him up, trying to determine how best to manipulate or neutralize this new threat to Tammany's power. But

Christopher was not a man to be easily swayed or intimidated. He had faced far worse on the battlefield, and he was prepared to fight for what was right, no matter the cost.

As Christopher navigated through the club, he made connections with reform-minded individuals who shared his vision for a cleaner, more just city. They spoke in hushed tones, their conversations filled with the hope and determination that change was possible. Christopher could feel the momentum building, the sense that they were on the cusp of something significant.

In the weeks that followed, Christopher launched his political campaign with a fervor that matched his military zeal. He gave speeches in packed halls, his words filled with passion and a clear vision for New York's future. He spoke out against Tammany Hall's corruption, promising to bring accountability and integrity to city government. The people listened, their hopes rekindled by the possibility of real change.

Christopher met with business leaders, gaining their support for his campaign. He emphasized the need for honest governance and the importance of reducing taxes and cutting wasteful spending. His message resonated with those who were tired of seeing their hard-earned money squandered by corrupt officials.

Christopher also held rallies in the city's neighborhoods, connecting with working-class voters and immigrants. He listened to their concerns and pledged to fight for their interests, not the interests of political machines. The people responded with enthusiasm, their belief in Christopher growing stronger with each passing day.

General Christopher O'Donaghue stood at the window of his expansive office, overlooking the bustling docks of New York City. The sun had just begun its descent, casting a warm, golden hue over the city that never slept. Ships bearing the name of his company, R. P. O'Donaghue & Company, bobbed gently in the harbor, a testament to how far he had come since those harrowing days of his youth. But despite the success that surrounded him, Christopher found himself lost in thought, his mind drifting back over the journey that had brought him to this moment.

It had been a long and winding road, one marked by struggle, loss, and a relentless determination to forge a path of his own. From the battlefields of the Civil War, where he had fought not just for the Union, but for the memory of his brother and the hope of a better future, to the corridors of power in New York, Christopher had always believed that his destiny was to serve a greater cause. His rise to the rank of General had been a crowning achievement, a recognition of his leadership and the respect he had earned among his peers. Yet, with that honor came new responsibilities, new battles to fight—battles that were not waged with muskets and bayonets, but with influence, strategy, and a steadfast commitment to justice.

Christopher turned away from the window, his gaze shifting to the map of trade routes that adorned the wall behind his desk. His shipping company had grown rapidly, expanding its reach far beyond the shores of America. He had named the company after his brother

Ryan, a tribute to the sibling he had lost, and the name had become synonymous with integrity and reliability in the world of international trade. The company's success had provided Christopher with the resources he needed to influence the city's political landscape, and he had used that influence to fight for the causes he believed in.

But despite his best efforts, Christopher knew that New York was still a city plagued by corruption and greed. The roots of that corruption ran deep, entwined with the very fabric of the city's political and economic systems. At the heart of it all was William "Boss" Tweed, the notorious leader of Tammany Hall, whose iron grip on the city had allowed him to siphon millions from the coffers of New York's taxpayers. Tweed's power was unmatched, his reach extending into every corner of the city's government, and his influence was bolstered by a network of loyal followers who benefited from his largesse.

Christopher had always been aware of Tweed's activities, but as his own influence grew, so too did his determination to put an end to the corruption that was bleeding the city dry. He had seen firsthand the impact of Tweed's greed—public funds meant for schools, hospitals, and infrastructure projects diverted into the pockets of Tweed and his cronies. The people of New York were suffering, their lives made harder by the theft of resources that should have been used to improve their city. And while many feared Tweed's wrath, Christopher knew that he could not stand idly by while such injustice continued.

The struggle against Tweed and Tammany Hall was not

one that could be won on the battlefield. It required a different kind of warfare—one fought with words, influence, and the careful navigation of the city's complex political landscape. Christopher had learned to wield power in ways that were subtle yet effective, building alliances with reform-minded individuals who shared his vision for a cleaner, more just New York. He had also used his company's success to fund charitable efforts, particularly those aimed at supporting Ireland, his homeland still reeling from the effects of the famine.

Christopher's involvement in the relief effort had garnered him significant support among New York's Irish community, many of whom had lost family members to the famine or had been forced to flee their homeland in search of a better life.

But the fight against Tweed was not an easy one. The man was a master of manipulation, skilled at using his wealth and influence to bend others to his will. He had surrounded himself with loyalists who were willing to do whatever it took to maintain his power, and Christopher knew that taking him down would require not only careful planning but also the courage to stand against a force that had cowed so many before him.

One evening, as Christopher sat in his office reviewing the latest reports on his company's operations, he received a visit from an old friend, John Muldoon. Muldoon had been with Christopher from the early days, helping him build R. P. O'Donaghue & Company into the thriving enterprise it had become. He was a shrewd businessman, but more than that, he was someone Christopher trusted implicitly—one of the few people who knew the full extent of Christopher's ambitions, both in business and in the political arena.

"Christopher," Muldoon said as he entered the office, a grim expression on his face. "We've got a problem."

Christopher looked up from his papers, sensing the seriousness in Muldoon's tone. "What is it, John?"

"Tweed," Muldoon replied, his voice low. "The man's getting desperate. Word on the street is that he's aware of your efforts to rally support against him, and he's not happy about it. I've heard rumors that he's planning to make a move against you—maybe even something drastic."

Christopher leaned back in his chair, his mind racing as he considered the implications of Muldoon's words. He had known that his actions would eventually draw Tweed's ire, but he had hoped to avoid a direct confrontation until he was better prepared. Now, it seemed, time was running out.

"What kind of move are we talking about?" Christopher asked, his voice calm but laced with concern.

Muldoon shook his head. "It's hard to say. Tweed has a lot of people in his pocket—judges, police, even some members of the press. If he decides to go after you, he'll have plenty of ways to do it. I'm just not sure what his plan is."

Christopher nodded, his expression thoughtful. He had faced danger before, both on the battlefield and in the cutthroat world of business, but this was different. Tweed was a man who wielded power like a weapon, and he had no qualms about using it to crush those who opposed him.

"We need to be ready," Christopher said after a moment. "Whatever Tweed's planning, we can't let him catch us off guard. I want you to reach out to our allies—let them know what's going on and see if we can gather any more information about Tweed's plans. In the meantime, I'll make sure our own operations are secure. If Tweed wants a fight, he'll get one—but it'll be on our terms."

Muldoon nodded, already moving towards the door. "I'll get right on it, Christopher. And don't worry—we'll get through this. We've faced worse before."

Christopher watched as Muldoon left the office, his mind already working through the steps he needed to take. The stakes had never been higher, but he was determined to see this fight through to the end. He owed it to the people of New York, to the memory of his brother, and to the values he had spent his entire life fighting for.

In the days that followed, Christopher threw himself into his work, both in his company and in the political arena. He met with reform-minded politicians, business leaders, and community organizers, rallying support for his campaign to clean up the city's government and put an end to Tweed's reign of corruption. He also took steps to secure his company's operations, ensuring that his shipping routes were protected and that his employees were loyal and well-informed.

The tension in the city was palpabl. Christopher's campaign had gained significant momentum, with more and more people rallying to his cause each day. But he knew that Tweed would not go down without a fight, and he was prepared for the possibility that the man might try something desperate to maintain his grip on power.

One evening, as Christopher was returning to his office after a long day of campaigning, he was approached by a man he did not recognize. The man was well-dressed, with a slick demeanor that immediately put Christopher on edge.

"General O'Donaghue," the man said, tipping his hat in a mock show of respect. "A pleasure to finally meet you in person."

Christopher studied the man carefully, noting the smug look in his eyes. "Who are you?"

"The name's O'Leary," the man replied smoothly. "I'm here on behalf of a mutual acquaintance—Mr. Tweed."

Christopher's jaw tightened at the mention of Tweed's name. "And what does Mr. Tweed want?"

O'Leary smiled, a hint of malice in his expression. "Mr. Tweed simply wants to remind you that there are certain... consequences for opposing him. He's willing to be generous, of course—if you're willing to play ball. All you have to do is back off, let things return to the way they were, and everyone walks away happy. No harm done."

Christopher felt a surge of anger rise within him, but he kept his composure. He had expected something like this—a veiled threat disguised as an offer of peace. But he was not about to be intimidated by Tweed or any of his lackeys.

"Tell Mr. Tweed that I'm not interested in his 'generosity,'" Christopher said, his voice firm. "I've made it clear where I stand, and I'm not backing down. If he wants a fight, he'll get one."

O'Leary's smile faded, replaced by a cold, calculating look. "Suit yourself, General. But just remember—when you play with fire, you're bound to get burned."

With that, O'Leary turned on his heel and disappeared into the crowd, leaving Christopher standing alone on the street. Christopher watched him go, his mind racing with the implications of the encounter. Tweed was clearly feeling the pressure, and if he was resorting to threats, it meant that Christopher's campaign was having an impact. But it also meant that the stakes had just been raised, and Christopher would need to be more vigilant than ever.

The year was 1877, and the winds of change were sweeping through New York City. General Christopher O'Donaghue, now firmly established as a key figure in the city's political landscape, was at the heart of the most significant challenge he had ever faced —the downfall of William "Boss" Tweed, the man whose name had become synonymous with corruption. Tweed, once the undisputed master of Tammany Hall and the most powerful man in New York, was finally being brought to justice, and Christopher was determined to see it through to the end.

The journey to this point had been long and arduous. Christopher had spent years building his influence, not just through his shipping empire but also by cultivating relationships with reformers and political figures who shared his vision of a cleaner, more just New York. He had seen firsthand the damage that Tweed's corruption had wrought—the millions stolen from the city's coffers, the public services neglected, and the people who had suffered as a result. For Christopher, this wasn't just a political battle; it was a moral one.

As the investigation into Tweed's activities gained momentum, Christopher found himself at the center of a web of intrigue and scandal. The evidence against Tweed was overwhelming, with documents, witnesses, and financial records all pointing to the vast network of graft that Tweed had orchestrated. Christopher worked closely with Samuel Tilden, the reform-minded governor of New York, and other key figures who were determined to bring Tweed to justice. Together, they built a case that would shake the foundations of Tammany Hall and expose the full extent of Tweed's crimes.

The trial was a spectacle, with the public following every twist and turn of the proceedings. Newspapers printed daily updates, and the courtroom was packed with spectators eager to witness the downfall of the man who had held the city in his grip for so long. Christopher attended the trial regularly, his presence a symbol of the reform movement's resolve. He watched as the prosecution laid out its case, piece by piece, until there was no doubt left in anyone's mind—Tweed was guilty.

But Tweed was not a man who would go down without a fight. He used every tool at his disposal to delay the proceedings, to sow doubt and confusion, and to paint himself as the victim of a political witch hunt. He called in favors, tried to bribe officials, and attempted to leverage his remaining influence to escape the inevitable. But Christopher and his allies were relentless. They countered Tweed's maneuvers at every turn, ensuring that the trial stayed on course.

As the trial reached its climax, the tension in the city was palpable. Everyone knew that this was more than just a trial—it was a battle for the soul of New York. When the jury finally delivered its verdict, finding Tweed guilty on multiple counts of fraud, embezzlement, and corruption, there was a collective sigh of relief. Justice had been served, and Tweed was sentenced to twelve years in prison, a sentence that many felt was too lenient given the magnitude of his crimes.

Christopher was among those who felt that justice had only been partially served. While Tweed was behind bars, the system that had allowed his corruption to flourish was still in place. Christopher knew that the fight was far from over. He continued to work with reformers to push for deeper changes in the city's government, ensuring that the lessons of Tweed's downfall would not be forgotten.

But just as the city was beginning to recover from the shock of Tweed's conviction, news broke that would throw everything into turmoil once again—Tweed had escaped from jail. It was an audacious move, one that stunned the city and reignited the anger of those who had fought so hard to bring him to justice. For Christopher, it was a personal affront. He had put his reputation on the line to see Tweed convicted, and now the man had slipped through their fingers.

The details of Tweed's escape were as audacious as the man himself. He had bribed his guards, used his considerable influence to arrange for a change of scenery under the guise of needing medical treatment, and then simply walked out of the facility. From there, he had fled the country, making his way to Spain in a desperate bid to evade capture.

Christopher was furious. He knew that allowing Tweed to escape would undermine everything they had worked for. The people of New York needed to see that justice could be served, that the powerful were not above the law. Christopher immediately began coordinating with international authorities, using his network of contacts to track Tweed's movements and gather intelligence on his whereabouts.

The hunt for Tweed was a tense and arduous affair. Christopher traveled to Washington, D.C., to meet with officials from the State Department, pushing them to take swift action to secure Tweed's extradition. He also worked with detectives and private investigators, many of whom had been instrumental in building the case against Tweed, to ensure that no stone was left unturned in the search for the fugitive.

As the weeks passed, there were rumors and sightings reported from various parts of Europe, but it wasn't until months later that they received confirmation— Tweed had been apprehended by Spanish authorities. He had been living under an assumed name, but his distinctive appearance had given him away. The Spanish government, eager to maintain good relations with the United States, quickly agreed to extradite Tweed back to New York.

Christopher was relieved but also resolute. The capture of Tweed was a victory, but it was also a reminder of the lengths to which the corrupt would go to protect themselves. When Tweed was finally returned to New York, Christopher was there to oversee his return to custody. The public reaction was a mix of outrage and satisfaction—outrage that Tweed had managed to escape in the first place, but satisfaction that he had been brought back to face the consequences of his actions.

Tweed's recapture was a significant moment in Christopher's career, but it was also a turning point for the city. The incident galvanized the reform movement, leading to a renewed push for changes that would prevent such corruption from taking root again. Christopher continued to work tirelessly, both in his role as a politician and through his influence in the business community, to support these efforts.

As Christopher returned to his work in New York, he was more determined than ever to continue the fight against corruption and injustice. Tweed's downfall had been a significant victory, but Christopher knew that the battle was far from over. There were still those who sought to exploit the system for their own gain, and Christopher was committed to ensuring that they would not succeed.

The city was changing, slowly but surely, and Christopher could see the impact of his efforts everywhere he looked. The streets were safer, the government was more transparent, and the people were more hopeful about the future. But there was still much work to be done, and Christopher knew that he could not rest on his laurels.

As he sat in his office one evening, reviewing the latest

reports on the city's progress, Christopher thought about the legacy he wanted to leave behind. He had come a long way from the streets of Cork, from the boy who had dreamed of a better life in America. He had fought in wars, built a successful business, and risen to the highest levels of political power in the greatest city in the world. But through it all, he had never forgotten where he came from or the values that had guided him on his journey.

Christopher knew that the road ahead would not be easy, but he was ready for whatever challenges lay in his path. He had faced down powerful enemies, overcome impossible odds, and proven that justice could prevail, even in the face of overwhelming corruption. And as long as he had the strength to continue the fight, he would do everything in his power to build a better future for the people of New York and for the generations to come.

The story of Christopher O'Donaghue, the General, the businessman, the reformer, and the humanitarian, was far from over. There were still battles to be fought, victories to be won, and lives to be changed. And as Christopher looked out over the city he had come to love, he knew that he was exactly where he was meant to be—at the forefront of the fight for justice, leading the charge into a brighter, more just future.

The momentum of Christopher's campaign continued to build as Election Day approached. The streets of New York were filled with posters bearing his name, and his supporters rallied with a sense of urgency and hope. The city was at a tipping point, and Christopher was determined to be the catalyst for change.

On Election Day, the city was abuzz with activity. Voters lined up outside polling stations, eager to cast their ballots in what had become one of the most closely watched races in New York's history. Christopher arrived at City Hall, greeted by cheers and applause from supporters gathered outside. He shook hands, exchanging words of encouragement with those who had come out to support him. The excitement was palpable as Christopher prepared to cast his own vote.

As Christopher entered the polling station, he felt a sense of solemnity and resolve. He knew that this was not just a battle for political office; it was a battle for the future of New York City. He cast his ballot with a steady hand, knowing that the outcome of this election would shape the city for years to come.

The hours ticked by slowly as the votes were counted. Christopher and his team gathered in their modest campaign headquarters, the atmosphere filled with anxious energy. They listened to the results being announced over the telegraph, each number bringing them closer to the final outcome.

Finally, the moment arrived. The final results were announced, and the room fell silent as they absorbed the news: Christopher O'Donaghue had been elected the first Irish American Catholic mayor of New York City.

The room erupted in cheers, the tension breaking into joyous celebration. Christopher was congratulated by his team, but his expression remained one of deep reflection. He knew that the real work was just beginning. The people had placed their trust in him, and he would not let them down.

The following day, Christopher stood on the steps of City Hall, addressing a massive crowd of supporters who had gathered to celebrate his victory. The energy in the air was electric, filled with the promise of change and the excitement of a new era.

"Today, we stand at the dawn of a new era for New York City," Christopher said passionately. "Together, we have shown that justice, integrity, and the will of the people can overcome even the most entrenched corruption. This city belongs to all of us, and as your mayor, I pledge to serve you with honor and dedication."

The crowd roared with approval, their faith in Christopher evident in their enthusiastic cheers. Christopher paused, looking out over the sea of faces, each one filled with hope for the future.

"We will fight to end the corruption that has plagued our city for too long," Christopher continued. "We will bring accountability to those who have abused their power. And we will build a New York where every citizen has a voice and a stake in our shared prosperity."

As Christopher spoke, he could see the impact of his words reflected in the faces of the people before him. The city was ready for change, and together, they would make it happen.

Over the coming months, Christopher wasted no time in implementing his reform agenda. He tackled police corruption head-on, dismissing corrupt officers and appointing honest, dedicated individuals to key positions. He demanded accountability and transparency from the NYPD, ensuring that the rule of law was upheld.

Christopher also took on the issue of patronage, ending the practice of awarding government jobs based on political loyalty rather than merit. His administration enacted policies that promoted fairness and equality in hiring, breaking the stranglehold that Tammany Hall had on the city's workforce.

But Christopher didn't stop there. He took on organized vice, cracking down on illegal gambling, prostitution, and other forms of criminal activity that had flourished under Tammany's protection. He worked closely with law enforcement to dismantle these networks, bringing criminals to justice and restoring order to the streets.

Christopher's administration also focused on fiscal responsibility, reducing the tax rate by cutting wasteful spending and redirecting funds to essential services such as public safety, education, and infrastructure. His fiscal policies made New York City a more livable and prosperous place for all its residents.

One of Christopher's most significant achievements was breaking up the Louisiana Lottery, a corrupt enterprise that had been draining money from the city and lining the pockets of criminals. Christopher led a successful campaign to outlaw the lottery, striking a major blow against organized crime and restoring public confidence in the city's governance.

As Christopher worked tirelessly to reform the city, he also returned to his shipping company, where his business continued to thrive under his leadership. The company had expanded its operations, establishing trade routes around the world, and its success was a source of pride for Christopher.

One day, as Christopher walked through the busy offices of R. P. O'Donaghue & Company, John Muldoon approached him with a letter bearing an Irish seal. John's expression was one of excitement and urgency.

"Christopher, you'll want to see this," John said, handing the letter to Christopher. "It's from the Irish Relief Fund. They're asking for our help in sending aid to Ireland. The famine has returned, and they need supplies desperately."

Christopher took the letter, his expression turning serious as he read the plea for help. The memories of his family's struggle during the Great Famine came rushing back, and he knew he must act.

"We'll do more than just help, John," Christopher said firmly. "We're going to lead the relief effort. I want the Constellation ready to sail within the week, loaded with as much food and supplies as we can gather. And make sure the Irish community here knows—they'll want to contribute."

John nodded, understanding the importance of the mission. "Of course, Christopher. I'll see to it personally."

Christopher looked out the window, his gaze distant as he thought of the homeland he left behind but never forgot. The famine had shaped him, had driven him to succeed, and now it was his turn to give back.

The day the Constellation set sail from New York Harbor was one of great significance. The steamship, adorned with the flags of both the United States and Ireland, carried more than just food and supplies—it carried hope, unity, and the love of a people who had never forgotten their roots.

Christopher stood on the dock, addressing the large crowd that had gathered to see the ship off. His voice was filled with emotion as he spoke of the importance of the mission.

"Today, we send more than just supplies—we send hope to our brothers and sisters in Ireland," Christopher said gratefully. "We stand with them in their time of need, just as we have stood together in the face of adversity here in New York. This ship carries not only food and medicine but the love and support of every one of us who calls this city home."

The crowd cheered, their support for the mission evident in their enthusiasm. As the Constellation prepared to set sail, Christopher watched from the dock, his heart filled with pride and resolve.

As the ship slowly pulled away from the harbor, its steam whistle blowing a farewell, Christopher knew that this was just the beginning of a new chapter in his life. He had risen from the streets of New York to the heights of political power, driven by a desire to bring justice, integrity, and prosperity to the city. But his journey was never just about power—it was about honoring his roots, giving back to those in need, and building a legacy that would endure.

Christopher walked through the streets of New York, now a city transformed by his leadership. The buildings were cleaner, the streets safer, and the people more hopeful. He smiled as he saw families enjoying the sunny day in the park, knowing that this was what he had fought for—a better future for the next generation.

As Christopher continued his walk, he reflected on the journey that had brought him to this moment. He had faced countless challenges, had fought battles both on and off the battlefield, but through it all, he had remained true to his principles. He had never forgotten where he came from, and he had never stopped fighting for what was right.

As Christopher walked through the vibrant city, the legacy of his work evident in every corner of New York, he knew that his story was far from over. There were still battles to be fought, still challenges to overcome, but he was ready for whatever the future held. With the people of New York behind him and the memory of those he loved guiding him, Christopher O'Donaghue would continue to rise against the machine, determined to make the city he called home a place of justice, integrity, and hope.

CHAPTER 9: THE REBEL'S RETURN

The cold, mist-laden shores of Ireland stretched around Seamus O'Donaghue like a ghostly veil, the pale moonlight casting an eerie glow over the relentless waves. They crashed against the jagged rocks in rhythmic defiance, as if the land itself resisted the dominion of its oppressors. This night, however, was unlike the countless others spent in the oppressive quiet of British rule. Tonight, the sea carried a cargo that had long been anticipated by some and deeply feared by others. A small, weathered ship emerged from the shadows, its hull darkened by the wear of countless voyages, the timber creaking as it cut cautiously through the treacherous waters. Its destination, hidden from the prying eyes of the British, was known only to a select few.

Seamus stood on the shore, his posture rigid against the biting wind, his eyes fixed on the distant shadow of his income cargo. His once-youthful features were now hard, chiseled by years of conflict, the boy who had left these shores long gone. In his place stood a man shaped by the fires of the American Civil War, a man who had wielded both rifle and dynamite with equal precision. His hands, once calloused by the fields of Ireland, were now rough from years of warfare and survival. His eyes, once wide with the naive hope of youth, now bore the unyielding resolve of a man who had seen too much and endured even more. He hadn't just returned home as a son of Ireland. He had returned as a soldier, a strategist, and, most of all, a rebel with a mission that could no longer be delayed.

The ship's hull was laden with crates, each one carefully hidden beneath tarps, their contents worth more than gold to the men who awaited Seamus's return. These were not simple goods or provisions but instruments of war: rifles, pistols, and, most notably, dynamite.

This cache of explosives had been secured through Seamus's connections during the war, smuggled across the Atlantic with the kind of precision and secrecy that spoke to his meticulous planning

"They've made it," O'Malley said, relief in his voice as he straightened up.

"Aye," Seamus replied. "Let's get to work."

The vessel docked quietly, its arrival shrouded in the thick fog that clung to the coast like a shroud. No sooner had the ship's bow kissed the shore than a group of shadowy figures emerged from the darkness, their faces obscured by the hoods of their cloaks. These were Seamus's comrades, members of the Irish Republican Brotherhood (IRB), men who had sworn their lives to the cause of Irish independence. Without a word, they set to work, unloading the crates with a practiced efficiency that spoke of many such clandestine operations before this one. The only sounds were the faint rustling of the tarps and the distant roar of the sea.

Seamus supervised the operation with the calm demeanor of a man who had been born for such work. He had long ago shed any illusions about the nature of the struggle they were engaged in; this was a fight that would be won with blood, sweat, and steel, not words or pleas for mercy. The weapons they now transported were not just tools of war—they were symbols of resistance, of a determination that had refused to be extinguished despite centuries of oppression.

As the last crate was secured and the group began to disperse into the night, Seamus lingered for a moment on the beach, his gaze sweeping across the dark horizon. He inhaled deeply, the salt air filling his lungs, grounding him in the reality of the task ahead. Ireland was his homeland, but it was not the Ireland he had left behind. It was an Ireland still shackled by the chains of British rule, its people still bowed under the weight of poverty and subjugation. But Seamus had returned to change that, and he was prepared to give everything— even his life—to see it through.

The next day, as the sun's first light filtered through the fog, Seamus found himself in the heart of Dublin, a city that hummed with a nervous energy. It was in a small, inconspicuous building, hidden in plain sight among the bustling streets, that he met with the leaders of the IRB, Thomas Clarke Luby, John O'Leary and Charles J. Kickham. The room was dimly lit, the air thick with the scent of pipe smoke and the unspoken tension of men preparing for war. The table before them was cluttered with maps, documents, and a variety of weapons, each item a testament to the scale of the operations they were about to undertake.

The older leader, Luby, a man in his 40s with a face hardened by years of struggle, addressed the group with the quiet gravitas of someone who knew the stakes of their cause. His voice was steady, his words measured, as he laid out the plan for the coming campaign. "These arms," he began, gesturing to the array of weapons, "will give us the strength to strike at the British like never before. With the dynamite Seamus has brought back, we can cripple their infrastructure, hit them where it hurts."

Seamus listened intently, his focus unwavering as the

leader spoke. When his turn came to address the group, he did so with a voice that carried both the weight of experience and the fervor of conviction. "We're not just fighting for ourselves," he said, his gaze sweeping across the room, meeting the eyes of each man present. "We're fighting for every Irishman and woman who has suffered under British rule. The time for words has passed; now we speak with action."

The room was silent for a moment, the gravity of Seamus's words sinking in. These were men who had long dreamed of this moment, men who had endured persecution, imprisonment, and the constant threat of death for the cause they believed in. Now, with the means to strike back in their hands, there was no turning back.

Seamus continued, outlining the targets they would focus on in the coming months: railways, government buildings, and other symbols of British power that had long been untouchable. The goal was not just to inflict damage but to send a clear message that Ireland would no longer be a colony to be exploited and oppressed. The British had underestimated the resolve of the Irish people, and now they would pay the price.

The men around the table nodded in agreement, their resolve firm. They knew the risks—they had known them since the day they first swore allegiance to the IRB—but the desire for freedom outweighed the fear of death. As the meeting drew to a close, Seamus felt a surge of determination. This was what he had returned for, what he had been preparing for during all those years in America. The road ahead would be perilous, but it was a path he would walk without hesitation.

As the days turned into weeks, Seamus immersed himself in the preparations for the coming rebellion. Dublin, with its narrow streets and ancient buildings, became both a battleground and a refuge. It was here, in the heart of the city, that Seamus took on a new role—one that would prove as vital to the cause as the weapons he had brought back. He became the editor-in-chief of "The Irish People," a newspaper that served as the voice of the nationalist movement, a beacon of resistance against British rule.

The printing press where the paper was produced was hidden deep within the city, a bustling underground operation that worked tirelessly to disseminate the message of Irish independence. The presses churned out copies day and night, each edition filled with articles that challenged British authority, exposed the injustices suffered by the Irish people, and called for an end to the tyranny that had plagued the island for centuries.

Seamus threw himself into his work with the same intensity he had shown on the battlefield. He spent long hours at the press, overseeing every aspect of the paper's production, from the selection of articles to the final proofreading. His desk was always cluttered with papers, ink stains often marking his hands as he pored over the latest edition, making corrections and adding notes. The work was grueling, but it was a labor of love, a way for Seamus to continue the fight even as he planned for more direct action.

"The Irish People" quickly became a thorn in the side of the British authorities. Its circulation grew rapidly, reaching every corner of Ireland, from the bustling streets of Dublin to the remote villages in the countryside. The paper's influence was undeniable; it gave a voice to the voiceless, rallying the Irish people to the cause of independence. It was a call to arms, not just in the literal sense, but in the sense of awakening a nation that had long been lulled into submission.

One evening, as Seamus was reviewing the latest edition, a young reporter approached him, a fresh copy of the paper in his hands. The reporter, barely in his 20s, was one of the many young men inspired by the movement, eager to contribute in any way he could. His face was flushed with excitement as he handed Seamus the paper.

"They're reading, Seamus," the young man said, his voice filled with enthusiasm. "The people are listening. Your words... they're making a difference."

Seamus took the paper, skimming the headlines with a critical eye. The articles were bold, unapologetic in their denunciation of British rule and their call for rebellion. He looked up at the young reporter, a small smile playing at the corners of his mouth.

"This is only the beginning," Seamus replied, his voice resolute. "The British fear the truth as much as they fear our weapons. We'll keep the pressure on, and we won't stop until Ireland is free."

The young reporter nodded, his admiration for Seamus evident in his eyes. He had heard the stories of Seamus's exploits in America, of the battles he had fought and the sacrifices he had made. Now, seeing him in action, he understood why so many looked to Seamus as a leader, as a symbol of the indomitable Irish spirit.

But Seamus knew that the work they were doing was not without its dangers. The British authorities were not blind to the growing influence of "The Irish People," nor were they oblivious to the fact that Seamus was at the center of it all. As the weeks passed, the tension in Dublin began to rise. British soldiers patrolled the streets with increasing frequency, their presence a constant reminder of the oppressive regime that sought to quash any hint of rebellion.

One afternoon, as Seamus made his way through the crowded streets of Dublin, he couldn't help but notice the unease in the air. People moved quickly, heads down, as if trying to avoid the gaze of the soldiers who loomed on every corner. The city, once vibrant and full of life, now felt like a powder keg waiting for a spark.

Seamus pulled his coat tighter around him, the collar turned up to shield his face from both the chill in the air and the watchful eyes of the British. He moved with purpose, his destination a safe house where he was scheduled to meet with senior IRB members. But he could feel it—he was being watched. Every instinct honed during years of war and rebellion screamed at him to stay alert, to be ready for anything.

When he finally reached the safe house, tucked away in one of Dublin's many narrow alleys, he was greeted by the familiar faces of his comrades. The room was as he remembered it—small, dimly lit, the walls lined with maps of Ireland and the table in the center covered with plans and documents. But there was a tension in the air that hadn't been there before, a sense of impending danger that weighed heavily on the men gathered there.

The meeting was brief but intense. The British were tightening their grip on the city, making it increasingly difficult to operate. Two of their printing presses had already been shut down, and more and more of their men were being arrested. The situation was dire, but Seamus refused to let it shake his resolve.

"They may slow us down," Seamus said, his voice firm as he leaned over the table, studying the maps before him, "but they won't stop us. We'll keep the paper running, keep the bombs going off. Every act of defiance brings us closer to our goal."

The men nodded, but Seamus could see the concern in their eyes. These were seasoned rebels, men who had been in the fight for years, but even they could sense that the noose was tightening around them. One of the older members of the group, a man who had been with the IRB since its inception, looked at Seamus with a mix of respect and worry.

"Seamus," the older man said gravely, his voice low, "you're the heart of this movement. If they catch you…"

Seamus cut him off with a wave of his hand, his expression resolute. "Then they'll have to catch me first," he replied, a hint of a smile on his lips. "We knew the risks when we started this fight. I'm not backing down now."

The older man nodded, though the worry in his eyes didn't fade. He had seen too many good men fall, too many dreams crushed under the weight of British tyranny. But he also knew that men like Seamus were rare—men who could inspire others to keep fighting, even when the odds were stacked against them.

As the meeting came to a close, the men dispersed, each heading to their next task with the knowledge that their time might be running out. Seamus lingered for a moment, his mind racing with thoughts of the days ahead. He knew the risks, knew that every step he took could be his last. But he also knew that he couldn't stop, not now, not when they were so close.

The end came swiftly, and without warning.

It was a cold, moonless night when the British finally made their move. Seamus had just completed another successful bombing campaign, targeting a key British installation in Dublin. The explosion had rocked the city, a loud, defiant statement that the Irish resistance was still alive and kicking. But Seamus knew better than to linger. As he moved through the darkened streets, he kept his senses sharp, aware that the British would be out in force, hunting for those responsible.

He had just turned a corner, his heart pounding with the adrenaline of the chase, when he saw them—British soldiers, their weapons drawn, blocking his path. There was no escape. He was surrounded.

Seamus raised his hands, a bitter smile tugging at the corners of his mouth. He had known this day would come, had prepared for it ever since he returned to Ireland. But even now, facing down the barrels of British rifles, he felt no fear. His capture was inevitable, but it was not the end. As long as there were men and women willing to fight, the cause would live on.

The soldiers moved in quickly, their expressions grim as they secured Seamus's hands in iron shackles. As they led him away, Seamus cast one last look at the city he had fought so hard to free. Dublin, with its narrow streets and ancient buildings, was more than just a city to him—it was a symbol of the struggle, a reminder of why he had chosen this path. And though he was being taken away in chains, his spirit remained unbroken, his resolve as strong as ever.

This was not the end.

Seamus's trial was a farce, a predetermined spectacle designed to break the spirit of the Irish resistance. He was brought before a British judge in a dimly lit courtroom, his clothes dirty from the rough treatment he had received, his hands still shackled. The judge, an imposing figure with a face etched in contempt, looked down at Seamus as if he were little more than a troublesome insect to be crushed.

"Seamus O'Donaghue," the judge began, his voice cold and devoid of any emotion, "you stand accused of treason against the Crown. The evidence against you is overwhelming—acts of violence, sedition, and the dissemination of dangerous propaganda. Do you have anything to say in your defense?"

Seamus met the judge's gaze with an unflinching resolve, his voice steady and clear as he responded. "I fight for the freedom of Ireland. I've no defense to make against that. Do your worst."

The courtroom fell silent, the tension palpable as the judge stared at Seamus, his face twisted with anger. This was not the response he had expected, but it was the response he should have anticipated from a man like Seamus O'Donaghue.

"Very well," the judge spat, his voice laced with venom. "You are hereby sentenced to life in penal servitude. You will be taken from this place and imprisoned, never to see the light of day again."

Seamus remained stoic as the sentence was passed, his eyes never leaving the judge's. The chains on his wrists and ankles felt heavy, but they did not weigh down his spirit. He had known this was a possibility from the moment he chose to take up arms against the British, and he had accepted it. The fight for Irish independence was bigger than him, and if his imprisonment could inspire others to continue the struggle, then it was a price he was willing to pay.

As the guards led him away, the camera lingered on Seamus's face, capturing the defiance and determination that still burned within him. He may have been bound in chains, but he was far from defeated.

The cell was dark and damp, the air thick with the smell of mold and decay. Seamus was thrown inside, the door slamming shut behind him with a deafening clang that echoed through the narrow corridors of the prison. For a moment, he stood still, his breath steady as he took in his surroundings. The walls were cold, the floor rough beneath his feet, but it was the silence that struck him the most. After the chaos and noise of the past few months, the quiet was almost suffocating.

Though caged, Seamus O'Donaghue's spirit remained unbroken. His fight was far from over, and even in the darkest of places, he planned his next move.

Seamus took a deep breath, his thoughts racing. He

knew that his imprisonment was just another phase in the struggle, another challenge to overcome. He had always known that the path he walked was fraught with danger, but he had never expected it to be easy. Now, more than ever, he was determined to find a way to continue the fight.

The prison was not the end for Seamus O'Donaghue, though for a time, it felt like it. His days were spent in the darkness of a cell that seemed designed to break men, to crush their spirits under the weight of isolation and despair. But Seamus was not easily broken. Even in the suffocating silence, he refused to surrender his will. His mind was constantly at work, planning, calculating, and waiting for the right moment to act.

Months passed with the slow, agonizing crawl of time that only prisoners know. Seamus became intimately familiar with the walls of his cell, the cracks in the stone, the sounds of the prison—each a reminder of the cage that held him. Yet, he also learned the rhythms of the prison, the movements of the guards, the shifts in routine that could provide an opportunity for escape. Seamus was not alone in his determination; within the prison walls were others like him, men who had fought for Ireland and now found themselves caged like animals. Among them were members of the Irish Republican Brotherhood, men Seamus had known and trusted for years. Together, they formed a bond that transcended the physical confines of the prison, a silent pact to never give up, never give in.

It was during these months that Seamus learned of the plan. Whispers in the dark, passed from cell to cell, spoke of a daring escape. The plan was bold, almost reckless, but it was the only chance they had. Seamus, with his experience and leadership, was at the heart of it. The British had unknowingly placed several key IRB members in the same prison, and these men were determined to use their proximity to stage a breakout that would not only free them but send a powerful message to the British authorities.

The plan hinged on a transfer, one that Seamus and his comrades had anticipated for weeks. The British, wary of keeping so many dangerous men in one place, decided to transfer Seamus and several others to a more secure facility overseas—a move that would take them far from Ireland, perhaps forever. But the IRB had other plans. They had managed to infiltrate the crew of the ship tasked with transporting the prisoners, and with the help of these inside men, Seamus and his comrades would make their escape on the high seas.

The night of the transfer was tense, the air thick with anticipation. Seamus and four other prisoners, known as "The Cuba Five," were marched out of their cells in shackles, their faces drawn but their eyes burning with determination. The guards, hardened men who had seen their share of attempted escapes, were on high alert. They knew these men were dangerous, that they were capable of anything. But they had no idea just how prepared the prisoners were.

As Seamus and his comrades were led onto the British ship, they exchanged glances, subtle nods that confirmed their resolve. The ship, a sturdy vessel with reinforced holds for the prisoners, was heavily guarded.

British soldiers patrolled the deck, their rifles at the ready, while the crew moved about with an air of quiet efficiency. The ship set sail under the cover of darkness, its destination a prison far from the shores of Ireland.

But Seamus and his men had no intention of reaching that destination.

As the ship sailed into the open sea, the plan was set into motion. The IRB members who had infiltrated the crew began their work, moving through the ship with purpose. They sabotaged key systems, cut communication lines, and quietly eliminated the guards who posed the greatest threat. The tension on board was palpable, the air thick with the anticipation of what was to come.

When the moment arrived, it was with a suddenness that took even the most prepared by surprise. The prisoners, their shackles loosened by their inside allies, sprang into action. Seamus led the charge, his body moving with the fluid grace of a man who had spent years honing his skills in combat. The fight was brutal, the confined spaces of the ship amplifying every sound —the clash of weapons, the shouts of men, the thud of bodies hitting the deck.

Seamus fought with a ferocity born of desperation and determination. He knew this was their only chance, that if they failed, they would be doomed to a life of imprisonment far from the country they loved. The ship's deck became a battlefield, the night air filled with the sounds of struggle and the smell of gunpowder.

Despite the odds, Seamus and his men managed to overpower the guards, securing the ship for themselves.

It was a victory that came at a cost—several of the men were injured, and the ship itself was badly damaged. But they had done it. They had taken control of the vessel, and with it, their destiny.

The escape was a triumph, but it was only the beginning of a new chapter. Seamus and his comrades had taken control of the ship, but the waters of the Atlantic still stretched far and wide between them and the safety of a distant shore. Returning to Ireland was not an option— the British would have prepared for them. Instead, they set their sights on America, the land where Seamus had once honed his skills and found his purpose.

Days turned into weeks as they sailed through the perilous Atlantic, battling fierce storms, navigating dwindling supplies, and ever mindful of the threat of British ships that could capture them at any moment. The tension was thick, but Seamus's leadership never faltered. He was a beacon of hope, the fire in his heart fueling the men around him. They were no longer prisoners of the British, but their fight for freedom had only just begun.

Finally, the shores of America came into view, and with them, a sight none of them had expected. As the ship approached New York Harbor, the distant hum of a vast crowd began to fill the air. The harbor itself, usually bustling with the sounds of commerce, now buzzed with a different kind of energy. Thousands of Irish Americans had gathered to greet them—word had spread of their daring escape, and New York had turned out in force to welcome them home.

As the ship drew closer, the docks and streets were lined

with people as far as the eye could see, their green flags waving high in the air. Seamus could hardly believe it—their arrival had become a momentous event, a symbol of Irish defiance. Crowds swelled along the waterfront, packed tightly together, their voices raised in a rapturous cheer. The clamor of excitement was overwhelming, a sea of Irish pride and solidarity.

The moment the ship docked, a roar erupted from the crowd, louder than any battle Seamus had fought in. Men and women surged forward, their hands outstretched, eager to greet the Cuba Five as heroes. Banners bearing the names of Ireland's counties fluttered in the wind, and green ribbons adorned the hats and coats of the cheering crowd. The streets were alive with the music of bagpipes and drums, a cacophony of pride that rang out over the city.

As Seamus and his comrades stepped onto American soil, they were met with thunderous applause. Irish and American flags waved side by side, their union a testament to the shared struggles of the two peoples. Seamus could feel the electric energy in the air—this was more than just a welcome. This was a declaration, a promise from the Irish-American community that their fight was far from forgotten.

"Welcome home!" voices shouted from the crowd, faces beaming with admiration. Seamus and his fellow escapees had become instant legends, their bravery sparking hope in the hearts of Irishmen and women who had endured decades of oppression under British rule.

Flanked by the cheers of thousands, Seamus found himself at the heart of a movement larger than anything he had imagined. New York had turned out to greet them not just as refugees, but as symbols of resistance, as men who had defied the empire and lived to tell the tale. Their arrival had inspired an entire city, and the Irish community, many of whom had fled the famine and persecution back in Ireland, looked upon Seamus and his comrades with pride.

The march through the streets was like a victory parade. As they passed through the crowded avenues, Irish Americans threw flowers at their feet, and children ran beside them, their small hands clutching makeshift Irish flags. The sight of it all—the sea of green, the sound of their voices lifted in song and cheer —was almost overwhelming.

This wasn't just a welcome; it was a statement of unity, a promise that the fight for Ireland's freedom would continue, no matter how far from home they had traveled. Seamus had escaped the British, but now, standing amidst the throngs of his people in New York, he knew that the real battle lay ahead. With new allies, new weapons, and the unyielding support of Irish America, his fight was only just beginning.

In New York, Seamus wasted no time in re-establishing himself. His reputation had preceded him—stories of his exploits in Ireland had made their way across the ocean, and many in the Irish community looked to him as a leader, a man who could continue the fight for Irish independence from American soil. It wasn't long before Seamus found himself at the helm of a new venture: a newspaper dedicated to the Irish cause and the rights of Irish immigrants in America.

The newspaper, which Seamus named "The Irish Voice," quickly became a powerful tool in the fight for Irish independence. It was more than just a paper—it was a rallying cry, a way to unite the scattered Irish community and keep the spirit of rebellion alive. Seamus threw himself into the work with the same intensity he had shown in Dublin. The office was a hive of activity, with reporters, printers, and volunteers working tirelessly to get the paper out to the masses.

Seamus's role as editor-in-chief was demanding, but it was a role he relished. He was in his element, his mind sharp as he crafted editorials, reviewed articles, and coordinated with his staff. The paper's message was clear: Ireland would be free, and the Irish in America would support that fight in every way they could. The paper also became a voice for the Irish immigrant community, advocating for their rights and challenging the discrimination they faced in their new homeland.

But with power came danger. Seamus knew that his influence made him a target, not just for the British, who were still hunting him, but also for those in America who opposed his views. He was treading a fine line, balancing the need to push the cause forward with the need to protect himself and those around him.

It wasn't long before Seamus's activities caught the attention of some of the most powerful—and dangerous—men in New York. Tammany Hall, the infamous political machine that controlled much of the city's politics, saw in Seamus both a threat and an opportunity. Tammany was notorious for its corruption, its leaders more interested in maintaining power than in any moral or ethical considerations. But they were also pragmatic, and they recognized the influence Seamus wielded among the Irish community.

It was in the dimly lit back rooms of Tammany Hall's headquarters that Seamus found himself face-to-face with the city's political elite. Liam O'Sullivan, a man who had once held sway over Seamus's brother Christopher, was among them. Liam was a man of many faces—a charmer when he needed to be, a brute when charm wasn't enough. He was the kind of man who thrived in the murky waters of New York politics, and he had taken a keen interest in Seamus.

"You've done well for yourself, Seamus," Liam said, his voice smooth and laced with a hint of menace. "The paper, the influence… you've got the city in your hands. But remember, power in this town comes with a price."

Seamus met Liam's gaze with an expression that was all sharp angles and unyielding resolve. He knew what Liam was, knew the kind of games he played. But Seamus was no stranger to the darker side of power, and he wasn't about to be intimidated.

"I know the cost, Liam," Seamus replied calmly. "I've paid it before, and I'll pay it again if it means advancing the cause."

Liam's smile widened, a predator sensing the challenge. "I knew there was fire in you, just like your brother. But don't let your ambition blind you to the realities of this city. We look after our own, but we expect loyalty in return."

Seamus nodded, his expression giving nothing away. He understood the game, understood that in a city like

New York, alliances were as dangerous as they were necessary. But he also knew that his loyalty would always be to Ireland first, no matter the cost.

The meeting ended with a handshake, but there was no warmth in it. Seamus left Tammany Hall with a sense of unease, a gnawing awareness that he was stepping into a world where the rules were different, where the stakes were higher, and where the cost of failure could be devastating.

As Seamus walked through the streets of New York that night, the city seemed to press in on him. The lights of Broadway cast long shadows, and the hum of the city's energy buzzed in his ears. He knew he was treading dangerous ground, that every decision he made could have far-reaching consequences. But he also knew that he couldn't stop. The fight for Ireland had brought him here, and it would be that fight that guided his every move.

Yet, despite his determination, there was a weight on Seamus's shoulders that he couldn't shake. He knew his brother, Christopher, was out there, watching, worrying. They had taken different paths, but their bond remained strong, even if it was strained by the choices they had made. Seamus could sense that a confrontation was coming, one that would force them to face the widening gulf between them.

The meeting between the brothers took place in the shadowed streets of New York, beneath the dim glow of a solitary streetlamp. Christopher stood waiting, his silhouette tall and imposing against the backdrop of the city. Seamus approached slowly, his posture defensive but his gaze steady as it met his brother's.

"Seamus... we need to talk," Christopher began, his voice tinged with a mix of concern and frustration.

Seamus stopped a few feet away, his expression guarded. "What's there to talk about, Christopher? You've made your choices, and I've made mine."

Christopher sighed, running a hand through his hair as he stepped closer. "You're getting in too deep, Seamus. Tammany... they're not just a political machine. They're dangerous, corrupt. I know, because I was part of it. I don't want to see you destroyed by the same forces I barely escaped."

Seamus's face hardened, his voice filled with the simmering resentment that had been building for years. "You think I don't know that? I've made sacrifices for our cause, Christopher. You've been out there playing politics while I've been fighting for something real. I'm doing what needs to be done."

Christopher's expression softened, his voice pleading. "I'm not your enemy, Seamus. We're brothers. We've been through too much to let this tear us apart. Please... step back before it's too late."

For a moment, Seamus's resolve wavered, the weight of his brother's words pressing against his own convictions. But the fire of rebellion burned too fiercely within him, and he couldn't turn away from the path he had chosen.

"It's already too late, Christopher," Seamus said, his voice distant, almost resigned. "I'm in this until the end, whatever that may be."

Christopher watched as Seamus turned and walked away, the distance between them growing with each step. The rift that had formed was now a chasm, and Christopher knew that whatever happened next, their lives would never be the same.

As Seamus moved deeper into the corridors of New York's Irish community, his influence expanded rapidly. What had begun as whispers in backroom taverns had evolved into something far more potent—an unstoppable force within the Irish-American diaspora. Tammany Hall had once looked upon Seamus as a potential ally to manipulate, but it was clear now that he had become something more dangerous. He was no mere politician. Under his leadership, the *Clan na Gael* had emerged as the most powerful Irish republican organization in America, and Seamus was pulling strings that even Tammany's elites could only envy.

By the mid-1870s, Seamus was no longer content with the whispers of rebellion. He had grander plans. The escape of the six Fenians from Fremantle Prison in Western Australia had been a significant victory, an audacious rescue that reverberated across the Irish world. Seamus, alongside his comrade John Boyle O'Reilly, had orchestrated the escape aboard the *Catalpa*, ensuring that the men who had fought for Ireland would not rot in British prisons. The operation cemented his position as a leader who could achieve the impossible, a man capable of rallying the Irish cause on both sides of the Atlantic.

But Seamus was not simply an organizer of daring rescues. He was a strategist, a man who understood that the fight for Irish freedom would require both diplomacy and violence. While men like Charles Stewart Parnell sought to bring Home Rule to the forefront of political discourse, Seamus harbored no illusions about the British government's willingness to simply cede control. He believed in a dual approach— one that combined the growing political movement in Ireland with a shadow campaign of violence that would keep the British nervous and off-balance.

It was in this spirit that Seamus initiated the *Skirmishing Fund* in 1877. Ostensibly a means to fund political activism, the fund had a more sinister undercurrent. Seamus funneled resources not only to the Irish Republican Brotherhood (IRB) back home but also to those who were prepared to take more direct action. The Fenians were no longer content to wait for freedom to be handed to them. Under Seamus's guidance, they were planning something much larger— the *Fenian Dynamite Campaign*.

New York had become a center of operations for this global insurgency, and Seamus wielded his influence with precision. He gathered support from wealthy Irish-American businessmen, laborers, and ex-soldiers alike, all of whom saw in him a leader who would stop at nothing to achieve their shared goal. But Seamus was a master of balance. He walked a fine line between the legitimate political efforts of Parnell and the more radical elements that demanded immediate and bloody results.

By 1879, Seamus returned briefly to Ireland, meeting with key leaders in the Fenian movement, including Charles Kickham, John O'Leary, and Michael Davitt. The meeting in Paris was a turning point. Seamus, ever the diplomat when necessary, convinced Davitt and Parnell to work together in what would become known as the *New Departure*, aligning the political aspirations of the Land League with the revolutionary fervor of the IRB. But while he was forging political alliances, Seamus remained steadfast in his belief that no real independence could be won without an armed struggle.

"Irish blood must still be spilled," Seamus had told Kickham after their meeting. "The British will not listen to ballots alone. We must coerce them, make them fear us—not just in Ireland, but wherever their empire reaches."

The words hung in the air, a chilling reminder of Seamus's unrelenting resolve. Even as he helped drive the political momentum of the Home Rule movement, he was already planning for the day when political means would no longer suffice. For Seamus, the *Skirmishing Fund* was merely the first step. The dynamite campaign that followed would make headlines across the world, striking fear into the heart of the British establishment.

But as Seamus's power grew, so did the risks. The British government was well aware of his activities, and his network of contacts—spies, rebels, and politicians alike—was constantly under threat. Even his brother Christopher, now mayor of New York City, had grown increasingly concerned. Christopher had watched from afar as Seamus's influence expanded, worried that his brother's ambitions would lead him down a dangerous path, one that could destroy them both.

Seamus's campaign in Great Britain was a testament to his relentless drive and his unwavering commitment to the cause of Irish independence. He returned to Ireland briefly, gathering his comrades and the resources they needed, before launching a series of bombings in major British cities. London, Glasgow, Manchester— their streets were rocked by explosions that targeted the symbols of British power.

The Fenian Dynamite campaign, as it came to be known, was both audacious and terrifying. Seamus's expertise in explosives, honed during the American Civil War, made him a formidable adversary. The British authorities were thrown into a frenzy, their efforts to capture Seamus and his comrades growing more desperate with each passing day. But Seamus was always one step ahead, using his knowledge and cunning to outmaneuver his pursuers.

Back in New York, Christopher found himself under increasing pressure from the British government. They demanded Seamus's extradition, insisting that he be brought back to stand trial for his crimes. Christopher, now firmly established as Mayor of New York City, was caught in an impossible situation. His duty as a public servant clashed violently with his loyalty to his brother.

Christopher spent long nights in his office, staring at the letters from the British government, the weight of his decision pressing down on him like a physical burden. He knew that whatever choice he made, the consequences would be far-reaching and devastating.

Finally, with a heavy heart, Christopher made his decision. He could not, would not, betray his brother. He picked up a pen and wrote a letter, officially denying the extradition request. As he signed his name, he knew that this decision would seal not only Seamus's fate but his own as well.

But fate is a cruel and unpredictable force.

One night, as Seamus walked the bustling streets of Broadway, lost in thought, he was unaware that his every move was being watched. The city's lights flickered around him, a chaotic symphony of life and energy. But as he crossed a darkened side street, a figure emerged from the shadows, a pistol glinting in the dim light.

Before Seamus could react, a single gunshot rang out, shattering the night's calm. The bullet tore through him, and for a moment, the world seemed to slow, the sounds around him fading into nothingness.

Seamus stumbled, clutching his chest as blood seeped through his fingers. Pain radiated through his body, but it was the shock that gripped him the most—the sudden, cold realization that he had been betrayed.

The crowd around him scattered, their screams echoing in the distance as Seamus collapsed to the ground. The lights of Broadway flickered above him, a cruel reminder of the life that was slipping away.

As the darkness closed in, Seamus's thoughts drifted to Ireland, to the fight he had dedicated his life to, and to the brother he had left behind.

But for Seamus O'Donaghue, this was not the end. The world would think him dead, but in the shadows, the rebellion would continue, fueled by the memory of a man who refused to give up.

CHAPTER 10:
THE FALL OF
AN EMPIRE

The night air in Paris was thick with a certain kind of magic, the kind that lingered in the corners of the city's narrow streets and grand boulevards alike. It was the magic of dreams taking flight, of passions igniting into something more. Tonight, as Rebecca entered the lavish private room within the Moulin Rouge, she could feel that magic thrumming in her veins, heightening every sensation. The room was opulent, its walls adorned with rich tapestries and gilded mirrors reflecting the soft glow of the candelabras. But it was the figure standing by the window that commanded all of Rebecca's attention—Napoleon III, the man who had not only reshaped Paris but had also irrevocably changed her life.

Dressed in his elegant military attire, Napoleon cut an imposing yet strangely approachable figure. The weight of his empire was heavy on his shoulders, but in this moment, as their eyes met, there was a lightness in him that few ever witnessed. Rebecca felt her heart pound with a mixture of excitement and nerves. Though she had performed before countless crowds, it was in these private moments with Napoleon that she felt the most vulnerable—and the most alive.

"Ah, Mademoiselle O'Donaghue," Napoleon greeted her with a warm smile, his voice tinged with affection. "Paris is truly fortunate to have you."

Rebecca curtsied, though there was a twinkle of defiance in her eyes. "The honor is mine, Your Majesty. Though I must admit, I never expected an emperor to enjoy such a lively spectacle."

Napoleon's laughter echoed through the room, rich and unguarded. "Even emperors need an escape from the burdens of state. And where better than in the company of a woman who can make the entire city stop and listen?"

Rebecca's smile softened at his words, a warmth spreading through her chest. This was a man who saw beyond her performances, who understood the fire that drove her. For all his power, Napoleon seemed drawn to her in a way that transcended politics and title.

They spoke of many things that night—the vibrancy of Paris, the changing tides of art and culture, and the dreams they each harbored for the future. Napoleon found himself enchanted by Rebecca's perspective, the way she spoke of the city's artists and poets as if they held the keys to its soul.

"You have a vision for this city, Napoleon, but the people who truly shape it are those who live and breathe its streets every day," Rebecca said, her voice carrying a passionate undertone. "The poets, the painters, even the singers like me. We see a Paris that isn't bound by tradition, one that's alive with possibility."

Napoleon nodded, his expression thoughtful. "You speak as if you know the city better than I do."

Rebecca leaned closer, a mischievous smile playing on her lips. "Perhaps I do, Your Majesty. After all, you're the one locked up in the palace while I'm out there in the heart of it."

Their laughter mingled with the soft strains of music drifting in from the Moulin Rouge below. In that moment, Rebecca felt a connection that was deeper than attraction—it was the beginning of an understanding, a shared vision that drew them both in.

As the evening drew to a close, Napoleon reached out to take her hand, his touch lingering. "There is something about you, Rebecca. You see the world not as it is, but as it could be. I find myself drawn to that vision. And to you."

Rebecca's breath caught in her chest, but she met his gaze with unflinching boldness. "Then perhaps, Your Majesty, we can show each other new ways of seeing."

Paris glittered beneath the night sky, its lights casting long reflections over the Seine. Rebecca O'Donaghue leaned against the balcony railing of her apartment, looking out over the city that had embraced her, elevated her, and transformed her from an Irish singer into a Parisian sensation. But tonight, even the allure of the city couldn't match the anticipation thrumming through her veins. Tonight, she wasn't just Rebecca of the Moulin Rouge—she was meeting Napoleon III.

Rebecca's thoughts drifted to their first encounter, the way his laughter had cut through the murmur of the crowd and the magnetism in his gaze that had drawn her in. She had expected the emperor to be aloof, distant, but he had surprised her with his warmth, his interest in her world. He had seen something in her that no one else had—a spark, a potential for more than just performance.

Now, as a sleek carriage drew up outside her building, Rebecca smoothed her gown and gathered her courage. The emperor's invitation had been direct and tantalizing: "Join me at the Tuileries. There's much to discuss." She could still feel the weight of those words, the promise of something more than just admiration.

Tonight could change everything.

The ride through the streets was brief, but it felt like a lifetime. Rebecca rehearsed her words, unsure of what to expect. When the carriage halted in front of the Tuileries Palace, she took a deep breath, steeling herself as she stepped out. The palace loomed before her, its grand façade aglow with candlelight, and she was struck by the enormity of the world she was stepping into.

A liveried servant guided her through the gilded halls, where every surface seemed to glimmer with opulence. The air was rich with the scent of polished wood and the faint notes of a distant piano, playing a melody that spoke of Parisian elegance. Rebecca tried to calm her racing heart as she followed the servant to a small, private study, where Napoleon waited by the fire, his back to her.

"Your Majesty," she greeted, her voice steady despite the fluttering in her chest.

Napoleon turned, a warm smile spreading across his face as he took her in. "Rebecca, I'm glad you accepted my invitation. Please, sit. I've been looking forward to our conversation."

Rebecca stepped further into the study, her footsteps muffled by the plush carpets underfoot. She took in the room's richness—the heavy drapes, the gleaming oak shelves lined with books, and the soft crackle of the fireplace that filled the space with warmth. It felt both intimate and grand, much like the man who stood before her. She chose a seat opposite Napoleon, who remained standing, gazing into the fire for a moment before turning to face her again, his expression contemplative.

"You know," Napoleon began, his voice tinged with something wistful, "I've always envied artists. Their ability to capture the essence of a moment, to make it last. It's a gift I never had."

Rebecca tilted her head, curiosity dancing in her eyes. "And yet, Your Majesty, you've captured the spirit of an entire city. Paris is your canvas, is it not?"

Napoleon's lips curved into a half-smile. "It's not quite the same, is it? A city, an empire—these things are shaped by power, by compromise. But art... art is honest."

Rebecca leaned forward, her voice dropping to a more intimate tone. "Art and power are not so different, Napoleon. Both have the potential to change the world. The difference lies in how they're wielded."

Napoleon considered her words, a thoughtful look crossing his features. "And you, Rebecca? How do you wield your art? Your voice has stirred the hearts of Parisians, made them dream, made them hope. What do you seek to change?"

She met his gaze directly, unflinching. "I seek to remind people that they are more than the roles they are given. That they can dream beyond the confines of their lives. That's what I want Paris to be—a place where anyone can become anything."

Napoleon studied her for a moment, the firelight casting shadows across his face. "You speak like a revolutionary, Rebecca. And yet, you dance in the halls of the empire."

Rebecca allowed a small smile, her eyes glinting with defiance. "Perhaps the best way to change the world is from within its walls. After all, it's not so different from the stage. You must know your audience before you can move them."

Napoleon let out a soft laugh, his admiration for her growing with every word. "You have a way of seeing things that's... refreshing, unexpected. You challenge me, Rebecca. And I appreciate that more than you know."

Rebecca's heart skipped a beat at the warmth in his tone, the sincerity that cut through the usual formalities. For a moment, the weight of their respective roles seemed to lift, leaving just a man and a woman caught up in a shared understanding.

"I challenge you because you're worth challenging, Napoleon," she replied softly. "You see the potential for greatness in this city, but there's more than one way to achieve it. Paris isn't just a place—it's a dream, a promise. And that promise is carried in the hearts of its people."

Napoleon moved closer, his expression softening as he reached out to gently take her hand. "You make me believe in those dreams, Rebecca. You make me want to be more than just an emperor."

Rebecca's breath hitched at his touch, at the vulnerability in his words. It was a side of him that few, if any, had ever seen. She squeezed his hand lightly, her voice barely above a whisper. "Then let's build something together, something that goes beyond crowns and titles. A city that's not just remembered for its power, but for its soul."

Napoleon's grip on her hand tightened slightly, as if he were holding onto a lifeline. "You speak as though you'll be by my side for years to come, as though you see a future for us beyond these secret moments."

Rebecca met his gaze, a rare softness in her eyes. "I see a future, Napoleon. But only if you're willing to let me be more than a muse."

The silence stretched between them, filled with unspoken possibilities. Napoleon reached up to brush a stray curl from her face, his touch lingering. "You already are, Rebecca. You're more than you know."

Rebecca's heart swelled with a mix of hope and caution. The world outside these walls was full of challenges, of forces that would see them both undone. But in this moment, she allowed herself to believe that perhaps they could defy those odds, that perhaps they could be more than their circumstances.

"Then let's see where this future takes us," she whispered, the firelight reflecting in her eyes. "Let's show Paris what we can create, together."

Napoleon's answering smile was like the first warmth of dawn breaking over a cold winter's night. He pressed a kiss to her hand, a gesture both tender and charged with promise. "Together, Rebecca. We will create a Paris that history will never forget."

Rebecca could still feel the warmth of Napoleon's hand long after he had let go, his words lingering like the last notes of a symphony. The intimacy of their conversation remained with her, a quiet assurance that she was no longer just an entertainer but a woman who could shape the future of Paris itself. And yet, beneath the glow of this new connection, she sensed the delicate balance they walked—a balance between power and desire, between ambition and the secrets they kept from the world.

The days that followed brought more meetings, each one deepening their bond. Napoleon would invite Rebecca to the Tuileries, where they would stroll through the private gardens, speaking of art, philosophy, and the possibilities that lay ahead for France. It was in these stolen moments that they shared their most candid thoughts, the emperor dropping his facade and Rebecca revealing a mind as sharp as it was passionate.

One afternoon, as they walked beneath the blooming chestnut trees, Napoleon paused, glancing over his shoulder as if wary of unseen listeners. "There's talk of trouble brewing beyond our borders, a restlessness in Prussia that concerns me," he admitted, his voice edged with the weight of his responsibilities. "The political landscape is changing faster than even I can keep up with."

Rebecca tilted her head, sensing an opportunity to steer their conversation towards deeper matters. "You've reshaped Paris, Napoleon, turned it into a city that rivals the greatest in the world. But sometimes, greatness attracts envy. What is it that you fear most?"

Napoleon's brow furrowed as he considered her words, his gaze distant. "I fear losing control, Rebecca. Control over the empire, over Paris... even over myself. There are forces at play that I can't always predict. But when I look at you, I see a different kind of power—a strength that lies not in armies or politics but in the heart of the people. You have a way of seeing the city that I've never understood."

Rebecca smiled softly, her fingers brushing the petals of a nearby flower. "Paris is more than politics and monuments, Your Majesty. It's the artists in their studios, the children playing by the river, the lovers who steal kisses in the shadows. You've built the framework, but it's the people who give it life. They're the ones who will remember you—not just as an emperor, but as the man who gave them a city to dream in."

Napoleon turned to her, his expression both earnest and vulnerable. "And how do I reach those people, Rebecca? How do I ensure that they see me as more than just a ruler?"

She met his gaze, her eyes alight with conviction. "Let them see your heart, Napoleon. Show them that you care about their stories, their struggles. Support the artists, the writers—those who give Paris its voice. Let them know that their emperor is listening."

He studied her for a long moment, as if seeing her in a new light. Then he nodded, a slow smile spreading across his face. "You make it sound so simple."

Rebecca's smile widened, a playful glint in her eyes. "It is simple, in a way. You just need the courage to be vulnerable. To trust that the people will see beyond the crown and into the man."

Napoleon reached out, tracing the line of her jaw with a gentle touch. "You have a way of making me believe that such a future is possible. That I can be more than just the symbol I've become."

Rebecca's breath caught, the intimacy of the moment wrapping around them like the warm afternoon sun. "Perhaps that's because I see you for who you are, not just for what you represent. And I believe Paris will, too."

With Rebecca's encouragement, Napoleon began to take small steps toward engaging with the cultural heart of Paris. He attended exhibitions and salons where avant-garde artists displayed their work, often inviting Rebecca to accompany him. Her presence by his side stirred whispers, but it also brought a sense of authenticity to his new interest in the city's vibrant cultural scene.

At one such gathering, held in a gallery near Montmartre, Napoleon and Rebecca mingled with painters, writers, and thinkers who represented the future of Parisian art. The room buzzed with excitement, voices overlapping as people debated the merits of the latest works. Rebecca, dressed in a gown that shimmered like liquid gold, moved through the crowd with ease, introducing Napoleon to the artists she knew and respected.

One young painter, his hands stained with the colors of his latest masterpiece, bowed deeply when Rebecca introduced him to the emperor. "Your Majesty, it is an honor to meet you. We never thought you'd show such interest in our work."

Napoleon's smile was warm but measured. "Paris is a city of innovation, of progress. I want to understand what moves its people, what inspires them. Art is a reflection of the times, is it not?"

Rebecca watched the exchange with pride, knowing that her influence had helped bring Napoleon to this moment. She caught his eye across the room, offering him a small, encouraging nod. And in that glance, they shared a silent promise—a commitment to the vision they were building together.

The next evening, as they dined in a secluded room overlooking the Seine, Napoleon spoke of his dreams for the future. "I want to leave a legacy, Rebecca. One that will endure long after I am gone. But it's not just about power—it's about creating a Paris that will be remembered for its beauty, its culture. And I want you to be a part of that."

Rebecca's heart swelled at his words, but she knew that such dreams came with a cost. She leaned closer, her voice dropping to a whisper. "What about the shadows that loom over us, Napoleon? The whispers of war, the tensions that grow with each passing day?"

Napoleon's expression darkened, the weight of his responsibilities pressing down on him once more. "I am aware of them, Rebecca. The Prussians grow bolder, their ambitions clearer. I fear that conflict is inevitable. But I will not let that diminish what we have built here."

Rebecca reached out, taking his hand in hers, grounding him in the present moment. "Then let's make the most of the time we have. Let's create something that will outlast the darkness, something that Paris can hold onto even if war comes."

Napoleon's gaze softened, and he squeezed her hand

gently. "You speak as if you know the future, as if you see a path I cannot."

She smiled, her voice filled with quiet certainty. "I see a city that will remember us, Napoleon. Not just for the battles fought, but for the art, the music, the dreams that flourished even in uncertain times."

Rebecca awoke the next morning with a sense of purpose that she hadn't felt in years. The words she and Napoleon had exchanged the previous night still echoed in her mind—a promise of a future, of creating something lasting and meaningful together. As she walked through the morning light that bathed Paris in a golden glow, she found herself drawn to the city's hidden corners, the places where life moved outside the grand façades and stately avenues.

It was in one such quiet moment that she discovered her new passion. Passing by a small shop tucked away near the Place des Vosges, Rebecca noticed a display of intricately crafted cameras, their brass fittings glinting in the sunlight. The shopkeeper, an elderly man with a friendly smile, beckoned her inside, eager to share the wonders of his wares.

Rebecca hesitated for a moment but then stepped through the door, her curiosity piqued. As the shopkeeper explained the intricacies of photography— how light and shadow could be captured on glass plates, preserving a moment for eternity—Rebecca felt a spark ignite within her.

"These cameras, they can do more than take portraits, can't they?" she asked, her fingers brushing over the cool metal of a camera's body. "They can tell stories, capture the soul of a place."

The shopkeeper nodded with a knowing smile. "Indeed, mademoiselle. A photograph is more than an image—it's a way of seeing the world, of showing others what you see."

Rebecca left the shop that day with a camera of her own, her mind racing with the possibilities. Over the following weeks, she began to explore Paris through her new lens. She captured the delicate curve of the Seine as it wound through the city, the shadows of children playing in the Jardin des Tuileries, the intricate dance of light and shadow over the façade of the Notre-Dame. But she also sought out the quieter, grittier corners of Paris—the narrow alleys where washerwomen sang as they worked, the markets bustling with vendors and the chatter of countless languages.

One evening, she brought a small stack of photographs to the Tuileries Palace, eager to show them to Napoleon. He greeted her with his usual warmth, but when he saw the camera slung over her shoulder and the carefully wrapped images in her hands, his curiosity was piqued.

"What have you brought me this time, Rebecca?" he asked, gesturing for her to join him by the window where the evening light cast a warm glow over the room.

Rebecca carefully unwrapped the photographs, her fingers trembling with a mix of excitement and nerves. "I've been experimenting with something new," she confessed. "I wanted to show you a different side of Paris—one that doesn't always make it into the halls of the palace."

She handed him a photograph of a narrow alley in Montmartre, where a painter sat hunched over his easel, his face furrowed in concentration. The image captured the man's dedication, the way his brush moved with precision over the canvas, despite the world bustling on around him. Napoleon studied the photograph, his expression shifting from curiosity to genuine admiration.

"You've managed to capture a moment, a feeling," he said softly, his fingers tracing the edges of the photograph. "This... this is Paris in its purest form, isn't it? The passion, the struggle, the artistry."

Rebecca's smile was radiant as she saw the impact her work had on him. "I've always believed that Paris is more than its grand boulevards and monuments. It's the people, the hidden stories. I wanted you to see it through my eyes."

Napoleon set the photograph aside and took her hands, his gaze steady and intense. "You have a gift, Rebecca. You see beyond the surface, beyond the appearances. This is what makes you extraordinary—not just your voice, but your ability to capture the heart of things."

Rebecca felt a surge of emotion at his words. It wasn't often that she felt truly seen, truly understood. And in that moment, she realized that her photography was more than just a hobby—it was a way to express the depth of what she felt for this city, and perhaps for the man who now held her hands in his.

"Will you let me use them?" Napoleon asked, a new light in his eyes. "These images—they show a side of Paris that most people never see. I want to share them, to show the world what you've captured."

Rebecca hesitated, her mind racing. She had taken the photographs for herself, as a way to connect with the city in a new way. But the thought of her work being seen, being used to tell the story of Paris in a way that could reach so many—there was a power in that she couldn't ignore.

"If it can help show people what Paris truly is, then yes," she agreed, her voice filled with quiet determination. "Let's use them, Napoleon. Let's show the world what this city means to us."

Napoleon's smile was like the breaking of dawn, filled with a rare, unguarded joy. He pulled her into a gentle embrace, his voice a low murmur in her ear. "You have no idea what this means to me, Rebecca. Together, we'll create something beautiful."

Rebecca rested her head against his shoulder, her heart swelling with a mixture of hope and resolve. In this moment, she felt as though they were truly partners— not just in their private moments, but in the vision they shared for Paris.

And so, her photographs became more than just images; they became a symbol of their shared vision. Napoleon used them in pamphlets and publications, presenting a Paris that was both modern and timeless, a city that held the promise of art and possibility even amidst its struggles. Rebecca's images of hidden alleyways, bustling markets, and serene riverbanks were distributed far and wide, captivating the hearts of those who saw them.

The city itself began to change in subtle ways,

influenced by the new appreciation for its less polished corners. Artists and poets who had once been relegated to the shadows found their work celebrated in salons and galleries, and the cultural pulse of Paris beat stronger than ever.

But as their vision for Paris began to take shape, so too did the tensions of the world beyond their intimate moments. News of political unrest reached their ears —rumblings from Prussia, whispers of a looming war. The carefree nights they had spent discussing art and philosophy grew shorter, replaced by long hours where Napoleon met with advisors behind closed doors.

Rebecca felt the shift keenly, but she refused to let the fear take hold. Instead, she poured her energy into her photography, capturing the resilience of Paris even as the storm clouds gathered. And through it all, Napoleon continued to find solace in her images, in the hope they represented.

One afternoon, as they walked through the gardens of the Tuileries, Rebecca sensed the weight of his worries pressing down on him like never before. She slipped her hand into his, offering a small, reassuring squeeze.

"Tell me what troubles you, Napoleon," she urged gently. "You don't have to carry this burden alone."

Napoleon paused, glancing at her with a mixture of gratitude and sorrow. "The war is coming, Rebecca. It's no longer a matter of if, but when. And I fear that everything we've built, everything we've dreamed of... it could all be undone."

Rebecca's heart clenched at the vulnerability in his voice. She turned to face him fully, her expression fierce with determination. "We've built something real, something that can't be erased by war or politics. No matter what happens, Paris will remember us, remember what we've tried to achieve."

Napoleon's gaze softened, and for a moment, the shadows lifted from his face. "You have a way of making me believe that, Rebecca. Of making me think that there's a future beyond all this."

"There is a future, Napoleon," she said, her voice filled with conviction. "And we'll find it together."

As the sun dipped low over Paris, casting the city in hues of gold and crimson, Rebecca held on to the hope that their vision for the city could withstand whatever challenges lay ahead. But even she could not have predicted how quickly that vision would be tested, nor how far she would have to go to protect the city she had come to love, and the man who had given her a place in it.

The mood in Paris had grown tense, the city's vibrancy now tinged with a sense of unease. The sounds of lively conversations in cafés and the laughter of crowds on the boulevards had given way to whispered fears about the looming conflict with Prussia. Rebecca sensed the shift with each passing day, feeling the weight of uncertainty settling like a shadow over the city she had come to love.

In the Tuileries, the change was even more palpable. The once lively gatherings and discussions with Napoleon had become rarer, replaced by hurried meetings with military advisors and the constant presence of diplomats. Napoleon's face, usually so open and warm when they were alone, had grown more lined, his expression often distant as he wrestled with decisions that could alter the fate of France.

Rebecca watched him now from the corner of the room as he stood by the window, staring out over the palace gardens with an uncharacteristic stillness. She could see the tension in the set of his shoulders, the exhaustion in the way he leaned against the window frame. She crossed the room quietly, her footsteps soft on the ornate rug, and placed a gentle hand on his arm.

"You look like you're carrying the weight of the world, Napoleon," she said softly, her voice laced with concern.

He turned to her, his features softening at the sight of her, but the worry in his eyes did not fade. "In many ways, I am, Rebecca," he admitted, his voice tinged with a weariness she hadn't heard before. "The tensions with Prussia are rising, and the ministers believe war is inevitable. They say it's a matter of honor, of showing Europe that France is still a power to be reckoned with."

Rebecca's brows furrowed as she studied his face, searching for the man she had come to know behind the mask of the emperor. "And what do you believe, Napoleon? Do you think this war is truly necessary?"

Napoleon hesitated, the question striking a chord within him. He looked out the window again, as if seeking answers in the sprawling cityscape beyond. "I believe that wars have a way of spiraling beyond anyone's control," he said quietly. "I fear what this could mean for France, for Paris. I fear what it could mean for us."

Rebecca's hand tightened on his arm, her heart aching

at the vulnerability in his voice. "Then don't let them push you into it," she urged, her voice gaining strength. "You have the power to make different choices, to steer this country away from the brink. Paris is your city—our city. Think of what we've been building together."

He turned to face her fully, reaching up to cup her cheek with a tenderness that made her breath catch. "You see a future beyond this conflict, Rebecca. You see hope where my ministers see only threats. It's a vision I want to believe in, but there are times when the weight of history feels too great to bear."

Rebecca leaned into his touch, her eyes searching his with an intensity that matched his own. "We cannot control the future, but we can shape it. I believe in you, Napoleon. I believe in what we could create here, even in the face of uncertainty. But you must trust yourself as much as you trust me."

For a moment, Napoleon allowed himself to imagine a world where they could remain untouched by the tides of war, where Paris could continue to flourish under their shared vision. But reality crept back in, the knowledge that the fate of empires often hinged on decisions made in rooms like this one. He let out a slow breath, his hand dropping from her cheek to grasp her hands instead.

"I will try, Rebecca," he promised, though a shadow of doubt lingered in his eyes. "But this war... it feels like a storm that cannot be avoided. I don't know if I can protect everything we've built."

Rebecca held his gaze, her expression resolute even as a chill settled in her bones. She knew he was right—the storm was coming, and there was little they could do to stop it. But she refused to let fear consume her. Instead, she squeezed his hands and offered him the only thing she could in that moment: hope.

"Whatever happens, we will face it together," she said firmly. "And if the storm comes, then we will endure it. Paris is stronger than war, and so are we."

Napoleon pulled her into an embrace, holding her close as if drawing strength from her words. Rebecca closed her eyes, allowing herself a brief moment of peace in his arms, even as the sounds of distant military drills echoed from the courtyard below, a reminder that their time of tranquility was slipping away.

In the days that followed, Rebecca witnessed the gradual transformation of the Tuileries from a place of artistic vision into a hub of military strategy. Maps of Europe sprawled across tables that had once held sketches of Parisian gardens. Uniformed men filled the halls, their hushed discussions carrying the tension of pending battles.

Yet, in the quiet hours of the night, Napoleon would still find his way to her side, seeking solace in her presence when the weight of his decisions became too much to bear. They spoke less of the future they had imagined together, and more of the challenges at hand—of the Prussian forces that seemed to loom ever closer, of the allies that France might need to secure, and of the shifting currents of European politics that threatened to drown them both.

One evening, as they sat together in the dim light of the study, Rebecca ventured a thought that had been lingering in her mind. "Napoleon, you've always seen Paris as a beacon, a symbol of what France could be. But what if... what if we used that light in a different way?"

Napoleon looked at her, curiosity sparking in his weary eyes. "What do you mean?"

Rebecca leaned forward, her voice gaining a fervent edge. "You've seen my photographs, the way they capture the spirit of Paris. What if we used those images, not just to show the beauty of the city, but to remind the world of what's at stake here? To show them what we're fighting for—beyond politics, beyond borders. To make them see Paris as more than just a battleground."

Napoleon's expression shifted as he considered her words, the beginnings of a smile tugging at the corners of his lips. "You believe that photographs could sway the hearts of diplomats and soldiers alike?"

"I believe that images can show what words cannot," Rebecca replied, her passion burning bright. "Let me do this, Napoleon. Let me show the world why this city matters. If I can make them see what I see, then maybe, just maybe, it will make a difference."

He reached out, taking her hand and pressing it gently. "You have a way of making the impossible sound within reach, Rebecca. If anyone can capture the heart of Paris, it's you."

Rebecca's heart swelled with gratitude, with the sense that even in the darkest moments, there was still a chance for them to shape their own destiny. As she gazed into Napoleon's eyes, she saw a glimmer of the man she had fallen in love with—hopeful, determined, ready to defy the odds.

But outside the walls of the Tuileries, the drums of war continued to beat, growing louder with each passing day. And as the specter of conflict drew nearer, Rebecca knew that their time of whispered dreams and quiet nights was running out.

Rebecca threw herself into her new mission, her camera becoming a constant companion as she roamed the streets of Paris, capturing scenes of a city on the brink. She photographed the faces of children playing by the Seine, the worried expressions of shopkeepers closing their shutters as news of the conflict spread, the artists who still sketched by the river's edge as if to hold on to a sense of normalcy. Through her lens, she sought to immortalize the spirit of Paris—a city that refused to bow even as the shadow of war loomed over it.

Each evening, she would bring her photographs back to the Tuileries, where she and Napoleon would sift through them together. It became a new form of dialogue between them, a way to hold on to their vision even as reality pressed in from all sides.

"This one," Napoleon murmured one night, holding up a photograph of a street performer playing a violin beneath the arches of a bridge. "It's... haunting. There's a melancholy to it, but also a kind of defiance."

Rebecca nodded, a bittersweet smile curving her lips. "It's the spirit of Paris, isn't it? To find beauty in even the hardest moments. To keep playing, no matter how dark the days become."

Napoleon's gaze lingered on the image, a heaviness

settling in his chest. "It's a spirit worth fighting for. Worth saving."

Rebecca reached out, brushing her fingers against his. "And that's what you're doing, Napoleon. No matter what happens, remember that."

But even as she spoke the words, a chill ran through her. For the first time, she wondered if their belief in a shared vision would be enough to withstand the storm that was now upon them. And whether the images she captured could truly change the course of a world hurtling toward war.

Rebecca's fingers trembled slightly as she adjusted the focus on her camera, her mind drifting between the present and the unknown future. Her latest photograph captured the silhouette of the Eiffel Tower, framed against a sky bruised by the colors of dusk. It was a scene of fragile beauty, a moment that seemed to hold its breath before night fully descended. But tonight, it wasn't just the tension of Paris that weighed on her—it was the secret she carried, one that had begun to shape every thought and decision.

She slipped the camera back into its case, pressing a hand to her stomach as she did. The realization had struck her just weeks ago, when she'd found herself lingering in front of a shop window, feeling an inexplicable exhaustion and a queasiness that was not typical of her. A visit to the discreet doctor she trusted had confirmed it: she was pregnant, carrying a child that would link her to Napoleon forever.

In the days since, Rebecca had wrestled with the implications of this new reality. She had not yet told

Napoleon, unsure of how to broach the subject when he was already burdened by the looming war. But she could not ignore the growing life within her, nor the way it filled her with a strange, fierce determination. It was as though the child had given her a new lens through which to see the world—a perspective that made her both hopeful and terrified.

That evening, as she entered the study where Napoleon waited, the weight of her secret felt heavier than ever. He was seated by the fire, poring over reports and maps with a furrowed brow, but his expression softened when he saw her.

"Rebecca," he said, setting the papers aside and standing to greet her. "You always bring light into this room, even on the darkest days."

She smiled at his words, but her heart ached with the knowledge of what she had yet to share. "I brought something for you," she said, handing him a new photograph—this one of a mother and child sitting by the Seine, their faces illuminated by the soft glow of a lantern. "I thought you might appreciate the reminder of what we're fighting for."

Napoleon took the photograph, studying it in silence. His expression grew wistful, the tension in his shoulders easing slightly as he traced the outlines of the figures. "It's beautiful," he murmured. "You have a way of capturing... what truly matters."

Rebecca watched him closely, gathering her courage. "There's something else I need to tell you, Napoleon," she said softly, her voice barely above a whisper. "Something I've been carrying with me for a while now."

He looked up, sensing the gravity in her tone, and his hand reached out to clasp hers. "What is it, Rebecca? You know you can tell me anything."

She took a deep breath, steadying herself before she spoke. "I'm pregnant," she confessed, her voice trembling with the weight of the words. "We're going to have a child."

For a moment, time seemed to hang suspended between them. Napoleon's expression shifted from shock to something deeper—an emotion she couldn't quite place. He released a breath as if he had been holding it in for far too long, his grip on her hand tightening.

"A child…" he echoed, his voice rough with emotion. He reached out, gently placing his other hand over hers, just above where their child grew. "Rebecca, I… I don't know what to say."

She searched his face, her own emotions raw and unguarded. "I didn't plan for this, Napoleon. And I know it couldn't come at a worse time. But this child… it's a part of us. A part of the future we've dreamed of."

Napoleon's eyes glistened in the firelight, his voice thick with unspoken fears. "I have dreamed of a future with you, Rebecca, but I never imagined…" He paused, swallowing hard as he tried to find the words. "A child changes everything. It means hope, but also risk— especially now, when everything feels so uncertain."

Rebecca felt tears prick at the corners of her eyes, but she held them back, her gaze steady on his. "I know. But maybe… maybe this is the hope we need. A reason to fight for a future that's more than just survival. A reason to believe that there's something waiting for us on the other side of this war."

Napoleon cupped her face, his thumb brushing away a tear that had escaped despite her resolve. "You have always given me reasons to hope, Rebecca. And now you've given me the greatest one of all." His voice broke slightly as he continued, "I will protect you both, with everything I have. I swear it."

Rebecca leaned into his touch, allowing herself to believe, if only for a moment, that they could be safe, that they could be more than the shadows closing in around them. She wrapped her arms around him, drawing strength from his embrace, and whispered against his shoulder, "We'll find a way, Napoleon. Together."

For a while, they simply held each other, the room filled with the quiet crackle of the fire and the unspoken promise between them. But as they pulled apart, a shared determination glinted in their eyes—a resolve to face whatever came next, for themselves and for the child that now bound them together.

Rebecca awoke one morning to the sound of distant cannon fire, a low rumble that reverberated through the stone walls of the Tuileries. She sat up, her hand instinctively going to her stomach, where the faint flutter of life provided a small, grounding comfort. The sense of foreboding that had lingered for weeks now settled deep in her bones. The war that had once felt like a distant threat was now at their doorstep.

When she joined Napoleon later that day, she found

him surrounded by his military advisors, their voices low and urgent as they discussed the latest reports from the front. Maps covered the walls, marked with red lines that seemed to creep closer to the heart of Paris with each passing day. Napoleon's face, usually so controlled, was drawn with fatigue, his eyes shadowed from too many sleepless nights.

As soon as he saw her, he dismissed his advisors with a curt nod, stepping away from the table strewn with documents. He reached out to take her hand, pulling her into a quiet alcove by the window, away from the prying ears of his officers. His grip was firm, almost desperate, and when he spoke, his voice was barely above a whisper.

"They're closing in on us, Rebecca," he confessed, his eyes searching hers as if seeking a reprieve from the harsh reality that surrounded them. "The Prussians have breached the eastern borders, and the ministers... they want to prepare for a siege."

Rebecca's heart sank at his words, her mind racing through the implications. A siege meant isolation, starvation, a city turned into a battlefield. It meant that the world they had built within the Tuileries would be shattered, replaced by fear and desperation. She squeezed his hand, drawing him closer, as if she could shield him from the shadows gathering outside their walls.

"Napoleon, we can't let them reduce Paris to rubble. Not after everything we've tried to build," she urged, her voice trembling with urgency. "There must be another way—diplomacy, negotiation—anything that could avoid turning this city into a battleground."

Napoleon's expression tightened, and he looked away, his jaw clenched with a mixture of frustration and helplessness. "I have tried, Rebecca. I have sent envoys, made appeals to the other powers. But Bismarck... he wants this war. He wants to see France brought low, to see Paris humiliated. And I fear that he will not rest until he has achieved it."

Rebecca felt a shiver run down her spine at the cold certainty in his words. She had heard of the Prussian chancellor's ruthless reputation, but to hear it confirmed by the man she loved brought the danger into sharp, terrifying focus. She reached up to cup Napoleon's face, forcing him to meet her gaze.

"Then we must show them that Paris is not just a prize to be conquered," she said fiercely. "We must remind them that this city is more than walls and streets—it's a symbol of hope, of culture, of everything that is worth fighting for. And you are the one who can do that, Napoleon. You are the one who can stand between this city and its destruction."

He closed his eyes for a moment, leaning into her touch as if drawing strength from her conviction. "You believe in me so fiercely, Rebecca. Even when I struggle to believe in myself."

"Because I know the man you are," she replied, her voice softening as she pressed her forehead against his. "And I know that no matter what happens, you will fight to protect what we've built together."

But even as she spoke the words, she could feel the fragility of their position—how quickly the tide could turn, how easily the forces of war could sweep away the dreams they had nurtured. She felt the baby shift inside her, a gentle reminder of the future they still hoped to create, and she clung to that hope like a lifeline.

In the days that followed, Paris braced itself for the inevitable clash. The streets that Rebecca had once roamed freely with her camera now echoed with the sound of marching boots and the clatter of artillery being positioned along the city's defenses. The cafés and salons that had once buzzed with talk of art and philosophy were now filled with hushed conversations about rations and evacuations.

Within the Tuileries, the atmosphere grew more strained with each passing hour. Napoleon, torn between his duties as an emperor and his desire to protect the woman he loved, became increasingly withdrawn, his moments of tenderness growing fewer and farther between. And Rebecca, sensing the weight of his burdens, did her best to remain strong, even as the uncertainty gnawed at her.

One evening, after a particularly tense meeting with his generals, Napoleon found her sitting by the window of their private room, staring out over the darkened city. He joined her silently, slipping an arm around her shoulders as he followed her gaze.

"They're building barricades in the streets," she murmured, her voice barely audible over the distant sounds of preparation. "They're preparing for a fight that none of us ever wanted."

Napoleon rested his head against hers, the lines of exhaustion etched deep into his features. "And yet, here we are. A city on the edge of ruin, and I, its emperor, powerless to stop it."

Rebecca turned to him, cupping his face with both hands as she searched his eyes. "You are not powerless, Napoleon. You are a symbol, just as Paris is. If you show strength, the people will follow. If you show compassion, they will believe that there is still hope."

His expression softened, and he reached up to cover her hands with his. "You see so much more than I do, Rebecca. You've always seen a future beyond war, beyond politics. And now, with a child on the way... I wish I could promise you a better world, a safer world."

She smiled through the tears that threatened to spill over, brushing her thumb against his cheek. "All I need is for you to promise me that we will face whatever comes together. That no matter how dark the days become, we will hold on to what we have, to the life we're creating."

Napoleon pressed a kiss to her forehead, his lips lingering against her skin. "I promise you that, my love. I will fight for us, for our child, for the dream of a Paris that can survive even this."

But as they held each other in the dim light of the room, the sounds of distant cannon fire rumbled through the night, a grim reminder that their time was running out. And though they clung to their promises, the specter of war loomed ever closer, casting a shadow that neither of them could ignore.

As the siege of Paris began, the Tuileries transformed into a fortress, its halls filled with the urgent movement of soldiers and advisors. Rebecca watched as Napoleon's focus shifted more and more to the defense of the city, the strain of leadership carving new lines into his face. Yet amidst the chaos, he never failed to find moments to sit with her, to hold her hand and share a quiet word or a tender touch.

One evening, as the cold of autumn settled over the city, Napoleon found her sitting in their private study, her hands resting on the gentle curve of her belly. He knelt beside her, his expression softening as he placed a hand over hers, feeling the faint flutter of life beneath his palm.

"Have you thought of a name yet?" he asked quietly, a small smile tugging at the corners of his lips.

Rebecca tilted her head, considering the question with a wistful look. "I've thought of many, but I can't seem to settle on just one. It feels too much like choosing a future I'm afraid to hope for."

Napoleon's smile faltered, and he leaned in to press a kiss to her temple. "I understand that fear, more than you know. But perhaps... perhaps if we name this child, it will remind us that there is still something to hope for. That no matter what happens, we have something worth fighting for."

Rebecca nodded slowly, her eyes glistening with unshed tears as she met his gaze. "Callan," she whispered, the name slipping from her lips like a prayer. "It means 'little warrior.'"

Napoleon's smile returned, and he pressed another kiss to her temple, a newfound determination shining in his eyes. "Then Callan it is. Our little warrior, born into a world that we will make better—together."

Rebecca rested her head against his shoulder, holding on to the promise of that future even as the sounds of conflict echoed beyond the palace walls. And as the days of siege dragged on, she clung to the hope that they could survive the darkness and emerge into the light— no matter how long the night might last.

The air in the Tuileries Palace felt heavier than ever, as if the very walls were straining under the weight of what was to come. Rebecca watched from the shadows of a side room, her heart clenched with a tension that had become all too familiar in the past weeks. Outside, the sound of marching boots and muffled cries from the city streets echoed through the palace, a reminder that Paris was no longer the city of lights and dreams they had once known.

In the grand study, Napoleon sat at his desk, flanked by his most trusted advisors. A document lay before him— its ink still drying, the words spelling out a fate he had once thought impossible. Rebecca could see the strain etched into his features, the lines that had deepened with each passing day of conflict. He glanced toward her, a silent communication passing between them, one that spoke of shared memories, unfulfilled promises, and the understanding that their time was running out.

"Your Majesty," one of the advisors began, his tone formal and tinged with urgency. "The situation is untenable. The Prussians are advancing, and our forces are in disarray. If you do not abdicate, they will march through Paris unopposed. The people... they need a resolution."

Napoleon's jaw clenched, his gaze flickering back to the

document. "A resolution," he echoed bitterly, his voice barely more than a whisper. "And what resolution will this bring? The end of an era, the dismantling of everything we've built."

Rebecca stepped forward, unable to remain silent any longer. "Napoleon, they may take the crown, but they cannot take what you've given to Paris. What we've created together—no war can erase that."

He looked up at her, his expression softening in the face of her unwavering conviction. For a moment, the burden on his shoulders seemed to lift, and he reached out a hand, beckoning her closer. She took it without hesitation, standing by his side as he faced the assembled ministers.

"Very well," he said at last, his voice rough with a mixture of resignation and defiance. "I will sign the abdication, not for the Prussians, nor for the ministers who stand here today. But for Paris—for the city I love, and for the hope that one day, it may rise again."

He picked up the pen, his hand trembling ever so slightly as he signed his name. Each stroke of the quill seemed to sap a piece of his strength, and Rebecca felt the weight of history pressing down on both of them. When he finally set the pen aside, the silence in the room was deafening.

"It is done," he said quietly, a strange emptiness in his voice. He turned to Rebecca, searching her face for reassurance, for some sign that there was still hope amidst the ruins of his dreams.

Rebecca squeezed his hand, her voice breaking as she whispered, "You are more than an emperor, Napoleon.

You are a man who dared to dream. And that will never be forgotten."

The advisors bowed their heads respectfully, and one by one, they left the room, leaving Napoleon and Rebecca alone in the fading light of the day. The sounds of Paris —both the clamor of the city and the distant thunder of approaching troops—felt like a heartbeat, steady and inevitable.

Napoleon's shoulders sagged as the last of the ministers departed, and he leaned heavily on the edge of the desk, as if the strength had left his legs. Rebecca wrapped her arms around him, holding him close, her tears mingling with his as they shared the weight of his decision. They stood like that for a long time, wrapped in the silence of their shattered dreams, before Napoleon finally pulled back, a shadow of a smile on his lips.

"Come with me, Rebecca," he said, his voice barely more than a breath. "Let's leave this place behind. Let's find somewhere... where we can forget, even if only for a little while."

Rebecca nodded, her heart aching with the knowledge that the man she loved was no longer the ruler of France but a man adrift, seeking refuge from the tides that had swept him away. Together, they gathered the few belongings they would take with them, leaving behind the grandeur of the Tuileries for the uncertain quiet of a life beyond the palace walls.

The air in the villa outside Paris was quiet, a stark contrast to the city they had left behind. It was a small estate nestled among rolling hills, far from the echoes of war and the clamor of politics. For Rebecca, the stillness was both a relief and a torment, offering a chance to gather her thoughts but also forcing her to confront the reality of their situation.

Napoleon had grown quieter since their arrival, the vibrant energy that once defined him now replaced by a lingering weariness. He spent his days in the sun-dappled gardens, walking slowly among the trees or sitting on the veranda, gazing out at the distant fields with a look that seemed to stretch beyond the horizon. Rebecca watched him from a distance, feeling a tightening in her chest each time she saw the slump of his shoulders, the way his hand would drift unconsciously to his chest as if to steady his own heartbeat.

As autumn gave way to winter, the chill seeped into the villa, forcing them to huddle closer to the hearth each evening. Rebecca wrapped herself in shawls, her growing belly a constant reminder of the life they had created even as another life seemed to ebb away. She found herself speaking to Callan in quiet whispers, sharing her hopes for a future that felt increasingly uncertain.

"Your father is a great man," she murmured one evening as she sat by the fire, her hands resting protectively over her stomach. "He has built so much, dreamed so much. I wish you could have seen him when he was full of life, when Paris was ours to shape."

Napoleon, sitting in his armchair nearby, overheard her words and smiled faintly, though the effort seemed to cost him. "You speak as if I am already gone, Rebecca," he chided gently, his voice hoarse from disuse. "But I'm still here, even if I am no longer the man I once was."

Rebecca looked up, startled by the rawness in his tone. She crossed the room to kneel beside his chair, taking his hand in hers. "You are still the man I fell in love with, Napoleon. Even now, I see that same fire in your eyes, the same hope for something better."

Napoleon shook his head, a bitter chuckle escaping his lips. "Hope... it feels like such a fragile thing now. I spent so many years believing that I could reshape the world, that I could bend history to my will. But here I am, hiding in a villa while Paris burns."

Rebecca's grip on his hand tightened, her voice firm. "You are not hiding. You are fighting—fighting for a life that is worth living, for a future that doesn't end in ruin. Callan needs you, I need you."

Napoleon turned to look at her, his eyes glistening with unshed tears. "I fear I have given all I have to give, Rebecca. My body... it grows weaker with each day. The weight of my failures presses down on me, and I find it harder and harder to breathe beneath it."

Rebecca pressed her forehead against his hand, her tears soaking into his skin. "Then let me carry some of that weight, Napoleon. Let me bear it with you."

They remained like that for a long moment, wrapped in the silence of the villa, the fire crackling softly beside them. And in that silence, Rebecca realized just how much she feared losing him—not just as the man she had come to love, but as the partner in the dream they had built together.

The weeks that followed were a blur of quiet desperation. Napoleon's health continued to decline, his once-commanding presence now reduced to a frail shadow. Rebecca cared for him tirelessly, preparing simple meals, bringing him warm blankets, and reading to him from his favorite books. At night, she would sit by his bedside, watching over him as he drifted in and out of fitful sleep, her own exhaustion a distant ache that she ignored in favor of being close to him.

One particularly cold evening, as the wind howled outside the villa's walls, Napoleon reached out for her in the dark, his hand finding hers. His grip was weak, his breathing labored, and Rebecca's heart clenched at the sight of him so vulnerable.

"Rebecca," he rasped, his voice barely audible over the sound of the wind. "Do you remember the first time we met? At the Moulin Rouge?"

She leaned closer, brushing a lock of hair from his forehead. "I remember it like it was yesterday. You were the most powerful man in the room, but you looked at me like I was the only thing that mattered."

Napoleon's lips curled into a faint smile, his eyes closing as he clung to the memory. "I never imagined... that a singer could change my life so completely. You made me believe in dreams again, in a future that was worth fighting for."

Rebecca felt her throat tighten, her tears spilling over as she stroked his cheek. "And you gave me a place in this world, Napoleon. You made me believe that I could be more than just a voice on a stage. You made me believe in us."

His eyes fluttered open, meeting hers with a clarity that took her breath away. "Promise me... promise me you'll keep dreaming, Rebecca. Even after I'm gone. Promise me you'll raise Callan to know that his father... that we tried to make this world a better place."

Rebecca choked back a sob, pressing her lips to his hand. "I promise, Napoleon. I promise with everything that I am."

Napoleon's breath hitched, a shudder running through his frail body. He reached up with trembling fingers to cup her face, his touch as gentle as a falling leaf. "You have been my light in the darkness, Rebecca. You... and Callan. I only wish... I could have given you more time."

Rebecca pressed her cheek into his palm, her tears wetting his skin as she clung to the fading warmth of his touch. "You gave me everything, Napoleon. You gave me a life I never thought I'd have. And I will carry that with me... always."

Napoleon's lips parted, as if he wished to say more, but the strength left him, and his hand fell back to the bed. Rebecca's heart clenched in her chest as she watched the last breath leave his body, a sigh that seemed to carry with it all the dreams they had shared.

For a moment, the world seemed to stop, the air in the room thick with the weight of finality. Rebecca pressed her hand to her mouth, a broken sob escaping her as she clutched his lifeless form to her chest, her grief pouring out in waves.

In the days that followed, the villa became a place of ghosts. Rebecca moved through its halls in a daze, her mind struggling to accept that the man who had once held her so fiercely was now gone. She found herself returning to the garden where Napoleon had often sat, imagining his voice in the rustling leaves, his presence in the shadows that stretched across the ground.

But as the snow began to fall, covering the villa's grounds in a blanket of white, Rebecca knew that she could not remain there forever. There was a child to be born, a promise to keep. She gathered the remnants of their life together—the letters they had exchanged, the photographs she had taken, the sketches he had made of their plans for Paris—and packed them away with care.

Rebecca stood before the windows of the villa, looking out over the snow-covered fields that stretched beyond the horizon. The chill of winter seeped through the glass, mirroring the cold ache that had settled in her chest since Napoleon's death. Yet, amidst the grief, a determination simmered—a refusal to let the man she had loved so fiercely be remembered only for his defeat.

And then, with one last look at the villa where they had shared their final days, she turned her back on the past and began the long journey back to Paris.

She had left the quiet refuge of the villa with a heavy heart, her few belongings packed away, and Callan growing stronger inside her with each passing day. Her journey back to Paris had been one of reflection, of confronting the ghosts of the life she and Napoleon had built together. But now, as she stood in the shadow of the city's crumbling defenses, she knew that her purpose had shifted.

Paris was on the brink of occupation. The Prussian forces, led by the indomitable Otto von Bismarck, were tightening their grip on the city, poised to seize control at any moment. The ministers and generals who remained were desperate, their strategies fraying under the weight of imminent defeat. The city that had once been the heart of Europe now faced a future of humiliation and loss.

Rebecca could not—would not—let that happen.

She leveraged every connection she had forged during her time with Napoleon, calling on those who still respected her influence. It was through these efforts that she secured an audience with Bismarck himself, a meeting that no one believed possible. But Rebecca had always thrived where others faltered, and she knew that this was her chance—perhaps her only chance—to shape the future of Paris.

The meeting was arranged in a nondescript building on the outskirts of the city, far from the prying eyes of soldiers and spies. Rebecca arrived cloaked in a simple black dress, her expression set with a steely resolve. She stepped into the room where Bismarck awaited her, the Iron Chancellor's presence as formidable as the storm clouds gathering over Europe.

He stood by a map spread across a wooden table, his tall frame casting a shadow over the room. When he turned to face her, his eyes held a mixture of curiosity and challenge, as if he were sizing up an unexpected opponent. Rebecca met his gaze unflinchingly, refusing to be intimidated.

"Monsieur Bismarck," she began, her voice steady and measured. "I appreciate your willingness to meet with me. I come to you not as a grieving widow, but as someone who cares deeply for the fate of Paris—and for

Europe."

Bismarck raised an eyebrow, his lips curling into a faint, sardonic smile. "And what does the widow of a fallen emperor hope to accomplish with this conversation, mademoiselle? Paris is on the verge of surrender. What can you offer that might change its fate?"

Rebecca took a breath, steadying her racing heart. This was a man known for his strategic brilliance, for his ruthlessness in pursuit of his goals. But she knew that beneath that exterior lay a pragmatist—someone who could be persuaded by the right argument, by the right vision.

"Paris is more than just a city, Monsieur Bismarck," she said, her voice gaining strength as she spoke. "It is the heart of Europe, the center of art, culture, and intellectual life. To occupy it would be to destroy not just a capital, but a symbol—one that resonates far beyond the borders of France."

Bismarck's expression remained inscrutable, but he gestured for her to continue, intrigued despite himself.

Rebecca pressed on, her words flowing with the passion that had driven her throughout her life. "You have seen the spirit of the French people. They will never accept their capital under foreign rule. If you occupy Paris, you will face not just armies, but the resistance of a united populace. Every street, every building, will become a battleground. And even if you succeed, what will you have gained? A city in ruins? A legacy of resentment that will haunt Germany for generations?"

Bismarck folded his arms, regarding her with a skeptical glint in his eye. "You speak as if you know the will of the French people better than their own leaders. But war is a matter of strategy, not sentiment. Why should I risk losing the advantage we have gained?"

Rebecca leaned closer, her voice lowering as she brought a new angle to her plea. "Because there is another path. A path where you do not become the villain in the story of Europe. If you show restraint, if you allow Paris to retain its dignity, you will position Germany not as a conqueror, but as a stabilizing force in the new order. You could shape the future of Europe—not by destruction, but by diplomacy."

She saw a flicker of interest in his eyes, the hint of a calculation beginning to unfold. This was the opening she needed, and she pressed on, weaving a vision of a different Europe—one where Germany and France could stand as pillars of stability, rather than as eternal enemies.

"Imagine the legacy you could leave behind, Monsieur Bismarck. A Europe that remembers you not just for the wars you waged, but for the peace you forged. Think of the allies you could gain by showing mercy now, of the stability that could follow if you let Paris remain untouched."

For a long moment, silence filled the room, the air thick with tension. Rebecca held her breath, watching as Bismarck weighed her words, his gaze distant as he considered the implications. She knew that she was asking him to see beyond the immediate spoils of war, to imagine a future that required vision rather than brute force.

Finally, Bismarck spoke, his voice softer than she had

expected. "You are a remarkable woman, mademoiselle. Few would have the courage to speak to me as you have today. Fewer still could make me consider an alternative to victory." He paused, his gaze sharpening as he met her eyes. "But words alone cannot change the course of history. There must be assurances—guarantees that this gesture will not be seen as weakness."

Rebecca nodded, understanding the delicate balance he sought. "There are still those in Paris who respect your strength, who would see a peaceful resolution as a sign of wisdom rather than submission. Give me the chance to reach them, to secure their agreement to terms that preserve both the dignity of France and the interests of Germany."

Bismarck studied her for another long moment, then gave a slow, measured nod. "Very well, mademoiselle. You have your chance. But know this—if Paris defies me, if your promises cannot be kept, I will not hesitate to return with force."

Rebecca inclined her head, accepting the challenge. "Understood, Monsieur Bismarck. And I promise you, I will not let Paris—or you—regret this decision."

With that, the meeting came to an end, leaving Rebecca with a monumental task before her. As she left the room, the weight of her responsibility settled heavily on her shoulders. She had bought Paris a chance—one that rested not on armies, but on the strength of her words and the hope that diplomacy could still prevail.

Rebecca returned to Paris with a heavy heart and a sense of quiet pride. The city she had fought so fiercely to protect still stood—its lights flickering like stars against the encroaching darkness of the war. Yet, Paris was changed. The scars of conflict etched themselves into the very walls, and the people moved with a tension that had not existed before. The salons, once alive with the laughter of artists and philosophers, now bore the weight of whispered fears and uncertain futures.

She walked through the familiar streets, clutching a small bundle of Napoleon's letters and sketches close to her chest—remnants of a dream that had burned brightly but too briefly. The cold wind bit at her cheeks, but she kept her head held high, her thoughts lingering on the promise she had made to Napoleon as he lay dying: to keep dreaming, to raise their son in a world that would remember them both for what they had tried to build.

Rebecca's return to the social circles of Paris was met with a mix of curiosity and sympathy. Many still saw her as the tragic figure—the singer who had captured the heart of an emperor, only to lose him in the end. But there was a new strength in her that few understood, a resolve born from the knowledge that she had altered the course of history, even if the world would never fully acknowledge her role.

She threw herself into her work, using her influence to promote the arts and to support those who had been displaced by the war. Her salon became a gathering place once more, but now it was a space where the conversations were laced with a sense of urgency—talk of rebuilding, of preserving the soul of Paris amidst the changes that swept through its streets.

Yet, even amidst her efforts to rebuild, Rebecca felt

a growing sense of isolation. The life she had shared with Napoleon now felt like a distant dream, and the presence of Callan, her son, was both a comfort and a reminder of the complexities she faced. Callan was a boy with his father's eyes, but he was growing up in a world that did not know the man Napoleon had been to her—a world that would judge him for the shadows cast by his legacy.

One evening, as Rebecca stood on the balcony of her modest apartment overlooking the city, she allowed herself a moment of vulnerability. She clutched a photograph she had taken of Paris, one of her last works before the war's end—a scene of the Seine reflecting the twilight sky, the Eiffel Tower standing resilient against the horizon. It was a Paris that had survived, but at a cost that weighed heavily on her heart.

"I've done all I could, Napoleon," she whispered into the night, the cold air carrying her words into the darkness. "But I'm not sure I know what to do next. How do I build a life for our son when I barely know how to live without you?"

She received no answer, only the distant hum of the city and the rustle of wind through the bare branches of the trees. But as she turned back to the warmth of her apartment, she resolved to keep moving forward—for herself, for Callan, and for the memory of the man she had loved.

CHAPTER 11: THE COUNTESS AND THE STATUE

Paris was alive with the sounds of the night, the soft glow of gas lamps casting long shadows over cobblestone streets. The city had transformed since Rebecca first arrived all those years ago, and now, she found herself navigating a world that was both familiar and strange. The salons, once filled with laughter and light, were now tinged with a sense of uncertainty as the echoes of political unrest rippled through the city. Yet, amid this, Rebecca remained a figure of grace and beauty, her presence commanding the attention of everyone in the room.

She moved through the crowd at a grand salon, her smile warm, but her thoughts elsewhere. Since Napoleon's death, Rebecca had been trying to find her place in a city that had once revered her. Callan was never far from her mind, the young boy who was growing up in a world filled with both privilege and the shadow of his father's complex legacy. As she listened to the idle chatter around her, she couldn't help but feel a growing sense of isolation, as though the world she had known was slowly slipping away.

Her thoughts were interrupted when her eyes met those of a man across the room. He stood out among the Parisian elite, his sharp features and noble bearing marking him as someone of significance. This was Count Casimir Markievicz, a Prussian of noble Polish heritage, who had recently arrived in Paris. The intensity of his gaze held her for a moment longer than was polite, and Rebecca felt a flutter of something she hadn't experienced in a long time—curiosity.

Later that evening, as the salon began to wind down, Rebecca found herself seated beside Casimir in a quieter corner of the room. The sounds of the party faded into the background as they engaged in conversation. Casimir was charming, his words laced with a subtle yet undeniable passion that drew her in. He spoke of the beauty of Paris, but more so, he spoke of a life beyond its borders.

"Paris is a city of wonders, Rebecca," he said, his voice low and compelling, "but it is nothing compared to the life I could offer you in Poland. A life of comfort, of security, and most importantly, of love."

Rebecca listened, her heart pounding. The scandals surrounding her relationship with Napoleon III and the birth of Callan had left her isolated, vulnerable. The prospect of a new life was deeply appealing, yet the pain of past betrayals made her cautious.

"You speak of love so easily, Casimir," she replied, her tone guarded. "But love has not always been kind to me. I have a son to think of... his future is everything to me."

Casimir leaned closer, his voice soft but persuasive. "I would treat Callan as my own. You would both have a place of honor in my home, in my life. All I ask is that you give me a chance to prove my love to you."

Rebecca's eyes searched his, looking for any hint of deception, but all she saw was sincerity. The weight of her loneliness and the desire to protect her son pressed down on her, and she found herself nodding slowly. "Then show me, Casimir. Show me what life could be like with you."

Casimir smiled, taking her hand in his. His touch was warm, his grip firm yet gentle. As they sat there, a bond was being forged—one that promised a new beginning, a chance to escape the shadows of the past.

But Rebecca was not alone in Paris. There was another woman who had become a close confidante in recent years, someone who understood the complexities of living in a world where power and influence could be as dangerous as they were alluring. Madame Alana Gonne (Irish: A leanbh Nic Ghoinn), an Irish revolutionary and actress, was much younger than Rebecca, but their friendship had blossomed quickly. Alana, with her fierce intelligence and passion for justice, had won Rebecca's admiration from the moment they met.

Alana had come to Paris in pursuit of a career on the stage, but she quickly found herself drawn into the city's political undercurrents. It was through her relationship with Lucien Millevoye, a married journalist with fervid right-wing politics, that Alana had gained access to information that others could only dream of. It was she who had first warned Rebecca about Casimir, having discovered through her connections that his background was not as it seemed.

"Be careful with him, Rebecca," Alana had said one evening as they walked along the Seine. "I've heard things—rumors from sources I trust. The Russian secret police have their eyes on him, and not for reasons you would like."

Rebecca had dismissed the concerns at first, caught up in the whirlwind of romance that Casimir had swept her into. But as time passed, small inconsistencies in his stories began to gnaw at her. Alana's warnings echoed in her mind, planting seeds of doubt that she could not ignore.

When Casimir invited her to his estate in Poland, Rebecca hesitated. She spoke to Alana about it, seeking her friend's counsel.

"You must go," Alana urged. "See for yourself what his life is truly like. But keep your wits about you, Rebecca. I don't trust him, and neither should you. Promise me you'll be careful."

Rebecca had promised, and with a mix of excitement and trepidation, she and Callan embarked on the journey to Poland. The estate that awaited them was grand, but there was an air of neglect, as if the property had seen better days. Casimir was at her side, his arm around her waist as he guided her into the manor, proudly declaring it to be her new home.

"Welcome to your new home, Rebecca," he said, his voice filled with pride. "This estate has been in my family for generations, and now it is yours as well."

Rebecca smiled, but there was a hint of unease in her eyes as she took in the faded grandeur of the estate. The servants bustled about, preparing the place for its new mistress, but there was a chill in the air that she couldn't shake.

That night, as they dined in the grand dining room, Casimir watched her with a look of intense admiration. "You are the most beautiful woman I have ever known, Rebecca. And now, as my wife, you will be the envy of all Europe."

Rebecca smiled at his words, but the unease from earlier lingered. She had begun to notice inconsistencies in Casimir's stories, small details that didn't quite add up. Still, she pushed her doubts aside, focusing on the promise of a new life for herself and Callan.

"And when will we have that grand wedding you promised me, Count Markievicz?" she teased, trying to lighten the mood, although secretly disappointed with the private reception they had weeks prior to make their nuptials official.

Casimir's smile faltered for a moment, but he quickly recovered. "Soon, my love. There are just a few matters of business I must attend to first. But rest assured, it will be a wedding fit for a queen."

Rebecca nodded, but the camera would have lingered on her expression if this were a film, hinting at the growing doubt within her. She knew something wasn't right, but she couldn't yet bring herself to confront it.

Days turned into weeks, and Rebecca found herself adjusting to life in the manor. She organized the household, made improvements to the estate, and hosted gatherings for the local nobility. Her charm and beauty quickly won them over, but beneath the surface, she remained troubled. Casimir continued to shower her with gifts and promises, but there was an increasing distance between them. He frequently left for "business trips," and when he returned, he was often distracted and evasive.

It was during one of these absences that Rebecca received a letter from Alana. The letter was filled with concern, expressing worry over rumors that had reached Paris about Casimir's true identity. Alana had been digging deeper, using her connections in the Russian secret police, and what she had discovered was damning.

Rebecca's hands trembled as she read Alana's words. Casimir was not who he claimed to be. The title of Count had been taken without right, and there had never been a "Count Markievicz" in Poland. The man she had trusted, the man she had allowed into her life and the life of her son, was a fraud.

The sound of footsteps approaching pulled Rebecca from her thoughts. Casimir entered the room, his expression calm and confident—completely unaware that his secret had been uncovered.

"There you are, my love," he said, smiling. "I've just returned from Warsaw, and I have wonderful news. We'll be hosting a grand ball next month to celebrate our union."

Rebecca stood, her eyes blazing with anger. "There will be no ball, Casimir. I know who you really are."

Casimir froze, the smile fading from his face as he realized what had happened. "Rebecca, listen to me. Whatever you've heard, it's not true. I love you—I've always loved you."

But Rebecca's resolve was unwavering. "You've done nothing but lie to me, Casimir. You took advantage of my trust, and I won't let you continue to deceive me or my son. We're leaving, and you'll never see us again."

Casimir's face hardened, and for a moment, there was a flash of something darker, more menacing in his eyes. "You think you can just walk away? You're my wife, Rebecca. You belong to me."

Rebecca stepped forward, her voice steady and defiant. "I belong to no one. Not you, not anyone. Now, get out of my way."

The tension in the room was palpable, but Casimir eventually relented, stepping aside. Rebecca brushed past him, her expression set in determination as she headed to Callan's room to pack their things.

It was in the early hours of the morning when Rebecca and Callan left the manor. They traveled quickly and quietly, taking only what they could carry. When they finally arrived back in Paris, Rebecca was exhausted but relieved. The city was as vibrant as ever, but she felt like a stranger in a place that had once been her sanctuary.

Madame Alana Gonne was there to greet her, her expression filled with concern and relief. "I'm so glad you're safe, Rebecca. I was worried."

Rebecca embraced her friend, the weight of the past months finally beginning to lift. "Thank you, Alana. I don't know what I would have done without you."

"You don't have to worry about him anymore," Alana said, her tone reassuring. "The Russian secret police are keeping an eye on him. He won't be able to deceive anyone else."

Rebecca nodded, grateful for Alana's support. "I just want to move on, to find a new purpose."

"You will," Alana said confidently. "And you won't have to do it alone."

Rebecca smiled, the first genuine smile she had felt in what seemed like an eternity. She knew she was not alone—she had Callan, she had Alana, and she had the strength to rebuild her life.

One evening, as Rebecca sat in her modest apartment, a letter caught her eye. It was from an old friend, Édouard de Laboulaye, a French political thinker and abolitionist she had met years ago at a gathering with Napoleon. The letter spoke of a grand project he was working on— one that could unite the French and American people in a celebration of liberty.

As she read the words "Statue of Liberty," a spark of interest ignited within her. This project could be her salvation, her way of finding new meaning in her life. She shared the letter with Alana, who immediately saw the potential in it.

"This is it, Rebecca," Alana said, her eyes shining with excitement. "This could be exactly what you need. A chance to start over, to create something lasting."

Rebecca nodded, the spark within her growing. "You're right. This could be my way of honoring the ideals Napoleon and I shared, and of finding new meaning in my life."

"And I'll be with you every step of the way," Alana added. "We'll do this together."

The decision was made, and Rebecca threw herself into the project with renewed vigor. She met with Édouard de Laboulaye, who explained his vision for the Statue of Liberty—a gift from the French people to the United States. Rebecca was captivated by the idea and immediately offered her help, determined to make the project a success.

She used her connections in Paris to organize fundraising events, hosting elegant soirées where she passionately spoke about the importance of the statue and its symbolism for both nations. Alana was by her side at every event, using her charm and wit to rally support for the cause.

Rebecca worked closely with sculptor Frédéric Auguste Bartholdi and engineer Gustave Eiffel, contributing her own ideas to the design and construction of the statue. She spent countless hours in meetings, sketching out ideas, and inspecting the progress of the work. The project became more than just a task—it became her mission, her way of honoring the ideals she and Napoleon had shared.

As the statue began to take shape, Rebecca's involvement grew. She became the project's de facto manager, coordinating the efforts of everyone involved and ensuring that the statue would be ready on time. Her determination and passion inspired those around her, and the project moved forward with renewed energy.

But even as Rebecca dedicated herself to the Statue of Liberty, she knew that the time had come for a new chapter in her life. The project would soon be completed, and she would need to find a new home, a new purpose.

It was Alana who suggested that they take the statue to America themselves. "Why not?" she said with a grin. "It's the perfect opportunity to start fresh, to see the New World. And I've always wanted to visit New York."

Rebecca considered the idea, and the more she thought about it, the more it appealed to her. America represented hope, opportunity, and a chance to leave behind the pain of the past.

The decision was made, and Rebecca and Alana began to prepare for the journey. They knew it would not be easy, but they were ready for the challenge. They would take the Statue of Liberty to America, and in doing so, they would begin a new chapter in their lives.

As the day of their departure approached, Rebecca stood on the balcony of her apartment, looking out over the city that had been her home for so many years. She felt a sense of peace, knowing that she had done everything she could to honor Napoleon's memory and to build a life for herself and Callan.

But now it was time to move on, to embrace the future and all the possibilities it held. She turned to Alana, who stood beside her, and smiled.

"Are you ready for this?" she asked, her voice filled with determination.

Alana grinned, her eyes sparkling with excitement. "More than ready. Let's go make history, Rebecca."

With that, they turned and walked back inside, ready to face whatever the future held. They had a mission to complete, a statue to deliver, and a new world to explore.

Rebecca and Alana stood at the prow of the ship as it approached the bustling harbor of New York City. The early morning light bathed the skyline in a warm, golden hue, and the towering buildings seemed to welcome them to a land of endless possibilities. Beside Rebecca, Callan's eyes were wide with wonder, taking in the sights of this new world with the innocent curiosity of a child. Alana, ever the adventurer, was practically buzzing with excitement, her enthusiasm infectious.

"This is it," Alana said, her voice tinged with awe. "The

land where dreams come true."

Rebecca smiled, her heart swelling with a mix of emotions—relief, hope, and a touch of apprehension. She had left so much behind in Paris, but she knew that this new chapter was full of promise. They had brought the pieces of the Statue of Liberty across the Atlantic, a symbol of the very ideals that had driven Rebecca all her life—freedom, resilience, and the pursuit of a better future.

As the ship docked, the harbor was alive with activity. Workers and officials bustled about, eager to catch a glimpse of the statue that would soon stand as a beacon of liberty to all who arrived on these shores. Rebecca's heart skipped a beat as she stepped off the ship, her feet touching American soil for the first time.

Waiting on the dock was a group of officials, led by none other than the then-Mayor of New York City, Christopher O'Donaghue. He had aged since the last time Rebecca had seen him, more than a decade prior whilst touring America; his once-youthful face now marked with lines of responsibility and the weight of leadership. But his eyes still held the same warmth, the same spark that had defined him all those years ago.

Rebecca's breath caught in her throat as their eyes met. For a moment, time seemed to stand still. Christopher's expression shifted from one of formal greeting to one of stunned recognition.

"Rebecca?" he said, his voice barely above a whisper.

Rebecca stepped forward, her heart pounding. "Christopher... is it really you?"

They stood there, a few feet apart, both overwhelmed

by the realization that after all these years, they were finally reunited. Tears welled up in Rebecca's eyes, and she saw the same emotion mirrored in her brother's gaze.

Christopher closed the distance between them in a few strides, and before she knew it, Rebecca was enveloped in his arms. The years of separation, the pain of loss, and the uncertainty of their fates melted away as they embraced, holding onto each other as if afraid to let go.

"I wasn't sure if I would ever see you again," Rebecca whispered, her voice choked with emotion. "I never imagined... oh, how I've missed you."

Christopher pulled back slightly, his hands resting on her shoulders as he looked at her with a mixture of pride and amazement. "And look at you, Rebecca. The Countess of Paris, bringing the Statue of Liberty to America. You've done so much... I can hardly believe it."

Rebecca smiled through her tears, her heart filled with a sense of completeness she hadn't felt in years. "I did it for all of us, Christopher. For the family we lost... and for the future we still have. This is our new beginning."

Christopher nodded, his eyes glistening with tears he was too proud to shed. "We've both come so far... and there's so much more to do."

As they stood there, reunited after so many years apart, the towering figure of the Statue of Liberty loomed in the background, a symbol of hope and resilience. It was more than just a monument—it was a testament to the strength of the human spirit, the enduring bond of family, and the belief that no matter how dark the past, the future always holds the promise of light.

The next few days were a whirlwind of activity as the pieces of the statue were unloaded and transported to their final destination. Rebecca, Christopher, and Alana worked tirelessly, coordinating with the officials, ensuring that every detail was perfect. The project that had consumed so much of Rebecca's life was finally coming to fruition, and she was determined to see it through to the end.

On the day of the statue's unveiling, a massive crowd gathered at the harbor, eager to witness the historic moment. Rebecca stood beside Christopher and Alana, her heart swelling with pride as the final piece of the statue was put into place. The crowd erupted into cheers as the veil was lifted, revealing the Statue of Liberty in all its glory, her torch held high, a beacon of freedom and hope for all who saw her.

As the cheers echoed across the harbor, Rebecca felt a deep sense of fulfillment. She had come to America seeking a new beginning, and now, standing beside her brother and her closest friend, she knew that she had found it. The Statue of Liberty was more than just a monument—it was a symbol of everything she had fought for, everything she had lost, and everything she had gained.

Later that evening, as the sun set over the city, Rebecca stood on the balcony of her new apartment, looking out over the harbor where the statue now stood. The lights of New York City twinkled in the distance, and for the first time in a long while, Rebecca felt a sense of peace.

Alana joined her on the balcony, a glass of wine in hand. "To new beginnings," she said, raising her glass.

Rebecca smiled, clinking her glass against Alana's. "To new beginnings," she echoed, her voice filled with hope.

As they stood there, gazing out at the city that would be their new home, Rebecca knew that the future was bright. She had faced love, loss, and betrayal, but through it all, she had emerged stronger, more determined than ever to build a life of purpose and meaning.

And with the Statue of Liberty standing tall in the harbor, a symbol of the ideals she held dear, Rebecca knew that she had finally found her place in the world.

The journey had been long and difficult, but as the stars began to twinkle in the night sky, Rebecca felt a deep sense of satisfaction. She had done it—she had honored Napoleon's memory, built a life for herself and Callan, and forged a future that was filled with promise.

As she turned to walk back inside, Alana at her side, Rebecca knew that whatever challenges lay ahead, she was ready to face them. She had come this far, and there was no turning back now. The future was hers for the taking, and she was ready to embrace it with open arms.

The chapter of her life in Paris was over, but the story of her life in America was just beginning. And with Christopher, Alana, and Callan by her side, Rebecca knew that there was nothing she couldn't achieve. The world was full of possibilities, and she was ready to seize them all.

CHAPTER 12: O'DONAGHUE REUNION

Seamus O'Donaghue stepped off the ship and into the bustling chaos of New York Harbor, his boots landing heavily on the wooden dock. The salty air of the Atlantic clung to his clothes, a mix of brine and sweat that he barely noticed after years of travel and struggle. His face, worn by the years, carried the marks of battles fought far from the land he once called home. America had changed him, hardened him, but beneath the grizzled exterior was still the heart of an Irishman—stubborn, fierce, and unyielding.

The harbor buzzed with activity. Immigrants disembarked from ships, their faces filled with hope or trepidation, while dockworkers moved crates and barrels with the efficiency of men who had long forgotten the meaning of a slow day. The Statue of Liberty stood partially assembled on Bedloe's Island, her torch raised defiantly against the sky, as if offering a silent promise to those who arrived on these shores.

Seamus looked up at the towering skyline of New York City, the buildings piercing the sky like the ambitions of the men who had built them. He was no stranger to ambition. His entire life had been driven by it—the ambition to free his homeland, the ambition to survive, the ambition to carve out a place for himself in a world that seemed determined to crush him.

His thoughts were interrupted by the sound of a familiar voice, high-pitched with excitement, cutting through the din of the harbor.

"Uncle Seamus! Uncle Seamus!"

Seamus turned just in time to see Callan Markievicz, his now 14-year-old nephew, barreling toward him with the reckless abandon of youth. A rare smile softened Seamus's stern features as he knelt down, bracing himself for the impact. Callan launched himself into Seamus's arms, and Seamus caught him, pulling the boy into a tight embrace.

"Look at you, Callan!" Seamus said, ruffling the boy's tousled dark hair. "You've shot up like a beanstalk since I last saw you."

Callan grinned, his eyes shining with admiration as he looked up at his uncle. The boy's energy was infectious, a bright contrast to the weariness Seamus carried. As they pulled apart, Seamus's gaze shifted, and he saw them—his brother Christopher and his sister Rebecca, walking toward him through the crowd.

Christopher O'Donaghue, tall and imposing in his tailored suit, moved with the confidence of a man who had risen far beyond his humble beginnings. The years had added a few lines to his face, but they had also brought him power, the kind of power that commanded respect in a city like New York. Rebecca walked beside him, elegant and poised as ever, her eyes sparkling with the same excitement that had lit up Callan's face. Despite everything, she had not lost that light within her, the one that made her the center of any room she entered.

Christopher reached Seamus first, extending a hand. For a moment, the two brothers simply looked at each other, their expressions unreadable. Then Seamus took Christopher's hand, and they shook, the gesture firm but tinged with the tension of years spent apart.

"Christopher," Seamus said, his voice steady.

"Seamus," Christopher replied with a nod, his tone equally measured.

Rebecca stepped forward, breaking the tension with a warm embrace. She wrapped her arms around Seamus, and he returned the gesture, though the movement caused him to wince, a sharp pain shooting through his side. Rebecca noticed immediately, pulling back with concern etched across her face.

"Seamus, are you hurt? What's wrong?" she asked, her voice laced with worry.

Seamus started to brush off her concern, but Christopher interjected before he could speak, his voice calm but carrying an edge of urgency.

"There's a lot we need to catch up on," Christopher said. "But first, let's get you back to my place on Fifth Avenue. You need to rest before dinner. We'll have some good old Irish stew and a few pots of Guinness—just like old times."

Seamus nodded, still wincing slightly as he picked up his bag. But before they could move on, a figure emerged from the crowd—a young woman, strikingly beautiful, with dark hair cascading over her shoulders and a determined look in her eyes. She moved with a grace that caught everyone's attention, and as she approached, Seamus's expression softened further.

"Rebecca, Christopher," Seamus said, turning toward the woman. "This is Marissa Collins."

Rebecca's eyes widened in surprise, and then a delighted smile spread across her face as she stepped forward to greet Marissa, who was visibly pregnant.

"Marissa, it's so wonderful to meet you!" Rebecca exclaimed, taking Marissa's hands in hers. "And… you're expecting? Seamus, you've been keeping secrets!"

Marissa smiled, a little shy but clearly happy to be welcomed into the family. Rebecca's joy was infectious, and she held Marissa's hands warmly.

"Well, you two best hurry up and get married before the baby arrives," Rebecca teased. "Can't have the little one born out of wedlock!"

Seamus chuckled, feeling a bit sheepish, but there was a glint of pride in his eyes as he looked at Marissa. "We've been talking about it. If it's a boy, we're thinking of naming him Michael—after our uncle. And if it's a girl… Ailish, after Marissa's mother."

Rebecca's eyes misted with emotion at the mention of their beloved uncle Michael, who had been a guiding light in their lives until his untimely death. She squeezed Seamus's hand, her voice softening with affection. "They're beautiful names, Seamus. Uncle Michael would be so proud."

Christopher stepped forward, his voice taking on a more serious tone as he greeted Marissa. "Marissa, it's a pleasure. Seamus, why don't you let Marissa head home and get some rest? We'll catch up over dinner."

Seamus hesitated for a moment, glancing at Marissa with a look of concern, but she smiled reassuringly. "I'll be fine, Seamus. Go spend time with your family. I'll see you tonight."

Seamus gave her a gentle kiss on the cheek, his voice tender. "Take care of yourself and the little one."

Marissa nodded, smiling warmly at Seamus before she turned and headed back toward the city.

The three O'Donaghues made their way to the waiting carriage, the tension between the brothers still lingering, but softened by Rebecca's presence and the excitement of their reunion. Seamus couldn't help but notice the grandeur of the carriage, the polished wood and fine upholstery—a far cry from the rough transport he had become accustomed to. It was another sign of how far Christopher had come since their days in Ireland.

As they traveled through the bustling streets of New York City, Seamus took in the sights and sounds with a sense of awe. The city was alive with energy, a place where anything seemed possible. But beneath that awe was a deep-seated wariness—Seamus had learned the hard way that nothing was ever as it seemed, and the streets of New York, like those of any city, could turn on you in an instant.

When they arrived at Christopher's mansion on Fifth Avenue, Seamus was struck by the sheer opulence of the place. The towering brownstone was covered in ivy, its stately presence a testament to the wealth and power Christopher had amassed in this new world. The carriage pulled up to the front entrance, and Christopher was the first to step out, his posture rigid with authority.

He helped Rebecca down, followed by Seamus, who took a moment to absorb the grandeur of his brother's home. The mansion's facade was impressive, but it was the interior that truly took Seamus's breath away. As they entered the grand foyer, the rich tapestries, gleaming chandeliers, and ornate furnishings created an atmosphere of luxury that was almost overwhelming. It was hard to reconcile this lavish setting with the memories Seamus carried of their humble beginnings in Ireland.

But as Christopher led them through the mansion, Seamus couldn't shake the feeling that there was something more to all of this—something that went beyond wealth and power. There was an undercurrent of purpose beneath the opulence, a sense that Christopher had built this life not just for himself, but for a greater cause.

The dining room where they finally gathered was an inviting blend of elegance and comfort, with a large table set for an intimate family dinner. The centerpiece was a pot of Irish stew, its rich aroma filling the room and evoking memories of simpler times. Freshly baked bread and butter were laid out beside the stew, and the fire crackled warmly in the hearth, adding to the cozy atmosphere.

As they sat around the table, the conversation flowed easily, filled with laughter and memories. They spoke of their childhood, the struggles they had faced, and the bonds that had held them together despite the years and the miles that had separated them. Seamus found himself relaxing in the warmth of their company, the tension that had gripped him since his arrival slowly easing.

But even as they reminisced, Seamus couldn't ignore the sense of something looming on the horizon, something that had yet to be revealed. He caught Christopher's eye several times during the meal, noting the thoughtful, almost guarded expression on his brother's face. Whatever Christopher had planned, Seamus knew it was more than just a family reunion.

As they finished their meal, the mood grew more somber, the conversation shifting from lighthearted memories to more serious reflections on their past struggles and losses. It was Rebecca who finally broke the silence, her voice filled with emotion as she reached out to place a hand on each of her brothers' arms.

"We've lost so much," she said softly, her eyes brimming with tears. "But we've found each other again. That's something to be grateful for."

Christopher nodded, but the weight of his thoughts was evident in his posture. He took a deep breath, as if steeling himself for what he was about to say.

"There's something I need to tell you both," Christopher began, his voice steady but tinged with a gravity that made Seamus and Rebecca exchange glances. "Everything I've done here, all the wealth I've accumulated, the connections I've made—it's all been for one purpose. To take back what was stolen from us. To free Ireland."

Seamus's eyes narrowed slightly as he processed his brother's words. "You've been planning this all along?" he asked, his voice cautious. "Building an empire here in America to strike back at the British?"

Christopher met his gaze with unwavering resolve. "Yes," he replied firmly. "I never forgot what they did to us, what they did to our people. But I knew I couldn't fight them with just anger and bitterness. I needed power, influence. And now, I have both."

Rebecca's expression shifted from shock to admiration, her voice trembling with the realization of what Christopher had sacrificed. "Christopher... you've been protecting us, all this time?"

Christopher nodded, his expression softening as he looked at his sister. "I've used my position to shield you, Seamus. The British have been after you for years, and I've kept them at bay. I've waited for the right moment, and now, with all of us together, we can make a real difference."

Seamus leaned forward, the tension in his shoulders easing as he realized the truth. "I thought you'd turned your back on us. On Ireland. But you were just biding your time, weren't you?"

Christopher stepped closer, placing a hand on Seamus's shoulder, his voice filled with conviction. "We've all been fighting our own battles, but now it's time to fight together. With Rebecca's influence in politics, your leadership of the Clan na Gael, and the resources I've amassed, we can bring Ireland to freedom."

Rebecca looked between her brothers, her heart swelling with pride and determination. She knew the path ahead would be dangerous, but she was ready to stand by her brothers, to fight for the future they all deserved. "We'll do it together," she said passionately. "The O'Donaghues will be the force that brings down British tyranny."

The siblings sat in silence for a moment, their resolve solidifying in the flickering firelight. It was a moment of unity, a moment where the weight of their shared history was acknowledged, and the path forward was made clear.

Just as they were about to continue discussing their plans, the door to the dining room creaked open, and they all turned to see Jenny, Christopher's wife, standing in the doorway, her face pale and her expression troubled.

"Christopher," she said softly, holding out a sealed envelope. "This just arrived... it's from Australia."

Christopher frowned as he took the envelope from her, his eyes narrowing in concern. The atmosphere in the room shifted immediately, the sense of anticipation thickening as Christopher broke the seal and unfolded the telegram. His eyes scanned the page quickly, his expression shifting from confusion to shock as he absorbed the message.

"What is it?" Rebecca asked, her voice tense with worry.

Christopher didn't answer immediately, his mind racing as he tried to process the implications of the telegram. Finally, he looked up, his face a mask of grim determination.

"We need to talk," he said, his voice low and urgent. "But not here. Let's go to my study."

Seamus and Rebecca exchanged puzzled glances, but they knew better than to question Christopher's judgment. The three of them rose from the table and followed Christopher out of the dining room, Jenny watching them go with a look of concern. The dinner that had started with warmth and nostalgia was now tinged with a sense of foreboding, as if the telegram had brought with it the promise of new challenges, new dangers.

As they made their way to Christopher's private study, Seamus couldn't shake the feeling that whatever was in that telegram was about to change everything. The future they had just begun to plan for—the future of Ireland, their family's legacy—now seemed more uncertain than ever. But Seamus knew one thing for sure: whatever came next, they would face it together, as a family.

And with that resolve, they entered the study, ready to confront the next chapter in their lives.

FINAL CHAPTER: THE IRON ROAD

The Australian outback stretched endlessly into the night, a vast, unforgiving landscape that held secrets as old as the earth itself. The sky above was a deep, starless black, the only sound the eerie wail of the wind as it whipped across the barren land. The ground was hard, cracked by the relentless sun that had baked it for centuries, but now cooled by the night air, it seemed almost to breathe in the silence.

For several long moments, there was nothing but darkness. The wind's mournful howl grew louder, carrying with it the weight of the desolate wilderness, a land where survival was a daily battle and mercy was as rare as rain.

Then, gradually, the darkness began to lift, and the faint outlines of a figure emerged. Ned Kelly, his eyes hidden behind the narrow slits of his iron helmet. His breath was slow and steady, his mind sharp and alert despite the late hour. The cold metal of the helmet pressed against his skin, a constant reminder of the battles he had fought and the ones still to come.

The moonlight caught the edge of the iron, casting a harsh, silvery gleam that cut through the darkness like a blade. Kelly's eyes remained closed, as if he were lost in thought, or perhaps preparing himself for what lay ahead. The helmet was his armor, his identity, and his symbol of defiance against a world that had shown him no kindness.

Suddenly, his eyes snapped open, fierce and filled with a burning resolve. There was no hesitation, no fear—only the unyielding determination of a man who had nothing left to lose. The outback was his battlefield, the place where his fate would be decided, and he was ready for whatever came next.

To be continued....

If you enjoyed The Famine, please consider leaving a review—your feedback helps keep the story alive and reach more readers. To stay updated on the next books in The Irish Series, exclusive content, and behind-the-scenes insights, visit www.bookstale.com and join the journey!

HISTORICAL CHARACTERS:

1. **James Rowan O'Beirne (1839–1917)** was an Irish-American soldier, lawyer, and journalist, known for his involvement in the American Civil War and his connection to the Irish nationalist cause. Born in County Kerry, Ireland, O'Beirne immigrated to the United States with his family at a young age. He grew up in New York and eventually became a prominent figure in both the legal profession and the Irish-American community. In *"The Famine,"* Christopher O'Donaghue's character is inspired by O'Beirne's heorics in the Battle of Fair Oaks, being shot in the lunch and being awarded the Medal of Honour, and his later role in the manhunt for John Wilkes Booth.

2. **W.R. Grace (William Russell Grace, 1832– 1904)** was an Irish-American businessman and first Catholic mayor of New York City. In the novel, he represents the Irish immigrant success story in America, influencing Christopher O'Donaghue's endeavors. His legacy in the book ties into the themes of perseverance, ambition, and the pursuit of

power in a foreign land.

3. **Catherine Hayes (1818–1861)** was a celebrated Irish soprano, known as "the Swan of Erin." In *"The Famine,"* Rebecca O'Donaghue's character is heavily inspired by Hayes, mirroring her rise to fame as a soprano in Europe. Rebecca's musical career, filled with both success and heartbreak, reflects Hayes's journey, intertwining with the novel's broader themes of cultural and national identity.

4. **Jeremiah O'Donovan Rossa (1831–1915)** was a prominent Irish nationalist and Fenian leader. Seamus O'Donaghue's character in *"The Famine"* is partly modeled after Rossa, particularly in his radical activities and involvement in the Fenian Dynamite Campaign. Seamus's story highlights the extremities of the fight for Irish independence, showcasing the lengths to which individuals would go to liberate their homeland.

5. **John Devoy (1842–1928)** was an Irish nationalist leader and journalist who played a significant role in the Irish independence movement, and another character Seamus' character is inspired by. As a member of the Irish Republican Brotherhood, he was arrested for treason and exiled to the United States, where he became a prominent figure in the Fenian Brotherhood and Clan na Gael. Devoy was instrumental in organizing Irish-American support for Irish nationalism, including funding revolutionary activities and

influencing political discourse.

6. **Maud Gonne (1866–1953)** was an Irish revolutionary, suffragette, and actress, renowned for her passionate support of Irish nationalism. In the novel, Madame Alana Gonne is inspired by Maud Gonne, embodying her spirit of rebellion and her close relationship with Rebecca O'Donaghue. This character's narrative involves political intrigue, personal sacrifice, and a deep commitment to the Irish cause.

7. **Virginia Oldoini, Countess of Castiglione (1837–1899),** was a famous Italian aristocrat and mistress to Napoleon III. In *"The Famine,"* she serves as inspiration for Rebecca's character, particularly in her role as a political influencer and confidante to Napoleon III. Rebecca's relationship with Napoleon mirrors the Countess's influence on the Emperor, blending personal and political ambitions.

8. **Ned Kelly (1854–1880)** was an Australian outlaw and folk hero, known for his defiance against British colonial rule. In *The Famine*, Ryan O'Donaghue adopts the name "Ned Kelly" after escaping from his Australian prison camp, taking on the identity of a dying Irish prisoner during the harrowing voyage to Australia. Though historically, the real Ned Kelly was born in Australia, *The Famine* reimagines the name as a mantle of Irish resistance, carried by Ryan as he fights his way back to freedom. This reinvention of

Kelly's identity serves as a powerful symbol of rebellion, survival, and the Irish spirit of defiance against oppression.

9. **Major Denis Mahon (1787-1847)** was the Irish landlord of Strokestown in County Roscommon who was shot and killed during the Great Famine of Ireland. His death is considered the first murder of a landlord during the Great Famine and to this day there is debate over the real reason for his murder and the identity of those responsible. In *"The Famine,"* his character is seen driving the O'Donaghue's out of their home, but being killed as result by their mother.

10. **General Winfield Scott Hancock (1824–1886)** was a senior Union commander known for his leadership at Gettysburg. In *The Famine*, Hancock mentors Christopher O'Donaghue, recognizing his leadership potential and offering him a path to higher command. Hancock's role in post-war Reconstruction mirrors Christopher's own struggles with military and political power.

11. **Napoleon III (1808–1873),** the Emperor of the French, ruled from 1852 until his defeat in the Franco-Prussian War in 1870. In *"The Famine,"* he is central to the narrative, depicted in a fictional relationship with Rebecca O'Donaghue. This relationship explores his political and personal struggles, particularly through the lens of Rebecca's influence on his policies and his eventual downfall.

12. **William M. Tweed (Boss Tweed) (1823–1878)**, known as "Boss Tweed," was an American politician and head of Tammany Hall, New York's Democratic political machine. In *"The Famine,"* Tweed represents the corruption and political power struggles within New York, linked to Christopher O'Donaghue's rise to influence. His presence in the novel underscores the moral complexities of political ambition.

13. **John Wilkes Booth (1838–1865)** was the assassin of President Abraham Lincoln. Although not a central figure in the novel, Booth's actions and the era he represents are alluded to, connecting the turbulent period of the American Civil War with the O'Donaghue family's narrative. His legacy serves as a backdrop to the broader themes of violence and political extremism.

14. **Sergeant Boston Corbett (1832–1894)** was the soldier who shot John Wilkes Booth. In *The Famine*, Christopher questions the suspicious circumstances of Booth's death, reflecting real-life controversies over whether Booth was silenced by higher powers.

15. **William R. Grace (1832–1904)** was the first Roman Catholic mayor of New York City and founder of W.R. Grace and Company. In the novel, Grace is mentioned in connection with Christopher O'Donaghue's life in New York, representing the Irish-American influence on

the city's political landscape. His character symbolizes the success and challenges faced by Irish immigrants in America.

16. **Countess Constance Markievicz (1868–1927)** was an Irish politician, revolutionary, and the first woman elected to the British Parliament. In *"The Famine,"* aspects of Rebecca O'Donaghue's character are inspired by Markievicz, particularly her involvement in Irish nationalism and her leadership qualities. The novel reflects Markievicz's pioneering role in women's participation in politics.

17. **Lucien Millevoye (1850–1918)** was a French journalist and politician. In the novel, Millevoye's relationship with Madame Alana Gonne provides the necessary intrigue and political connections to uncover Casimir's false background. His character adds depth to the narrative's exploration of political manipulation and espionage in 19th-century Europe.

18. **Joseph Oller (1839–1922)** was a Spanish-French entrepreneur and co-founder of the Moulin Rouge. In *"The Famine,"* Oller's role is adapted to be closely tied to Rebecca's rise to fame in Paris. His character helps create the vibrant backdrop of the Moulin Rouge, where Rebecca's talents as a performer are showcased, reflecting the artistic and cultural revolution of the time.

19. **Charles Zidler (1831–1897)** was a French

entreprefeur and co-founder of the Moulin Rouge. Alongside Joseph Oller, Zidler's character in the novel plays a crucial role in Rebecca O'Donaghue's career. Their partnership in founding the Moulin Rouge creates a historical setting that highlights the blend of entertainment, politics, and societal change in late 19th-century Paris.

20. **Frédéric Auguste Bartholdi (1834–1904)** was the French sculptor best known for designing the Statue of Liberty. In *"The Famine,"* Bartholdi's role is significant as Rebecca becomes involved in the statue's creation. The novel integrates Bartholdi's work into the narrative, symbolizing the transatlantic ties of freedom and the importance of public art in shaping national identity.

21. **Gustave Eiffel (1832–1923)** was a French civil engineer, known for designing the Eiffel Tower and the internal structure of the Statue of Liberty. In the novel, Eiffel's collaboration with Bartholdi and Rebecca highlights the intersection of engineering and artistry. His presence in the narrative underscores the era's spirit of innovation and the monumental achievements of the time.

22. **Édouard de Laboulaye (1811–1883)** was a French political thinker and key figure in the conception of the Statue of Liberty. In *"The Famine,"* Laboulaye's character serves as a link between Rebecca's ambitions and the

grand project of the statue. His inclusion in the story emphasizes the ideological connections between France and the United States during the 19th century.

23. **John Francis O'Mahony (1816–1877)** was a founder of the Fenian Brotherhood, an Irish revolutionary organization. In *"The Famine,"* his ideas and leadership inspire Seamus O'Donaghue's revolutionary activities. O'Mahony's presence in the novel reinforces the theme of Irish nationalism and the global fight for independence.

24. **Tammany Hall Leaders:** Tammany Hall was a political machine that dominated New York City politics in the 19th century, led by various figures like Boss Tweed. In the novel, these leaders are referenced in relation to Christopher O'Donaghue's rise in New York. Their inclusion highlights the complex interplay between power, corruption, and immigrant influence in American politics.

25. **La Goulue (Louise Weber)(1866–1929)** was a famous French can-can dancer and a star at the Moulin Rouge. In *"The Famine,"* her persona is integrated into Rebecca's stage career, where Rebecca adopts the nickname La Goulue. This blending of characters reflects the novel's exploration of fame, identity, and the cultural vibrancy of Paris during the Belle Époque.

26. **Thomas Francis Meagher (1823–1867)** was an Irish nationalist, soldier, and politician.

Known for his fiery oratory and leadership during the Young Ireland movement, Meagher was sentenced to exile in Tasmania after the failed Rebellion of 1848. Later, he escaped to the United States, where he became a Union general during the American Civil War and eventually served as Acting Governor of Montana.

27. **Thomas Francis Meagher (1823–1867)** was an Irish nationalist, orator, and Union General in the American Civil War. In *The Famine*, he plays a crucial role as Ryan O'Donaghue's (alias "Ned Kelly") right-hand man in the Australian outback, where the two men form a deep bond during their time in the penal colonies. Meagher, exiled to Australia for his involvement in the 1848 Young Ireland Rebellion, is depicted as a mentor and strategist, helping Ryan navigate the brutal conditions of British imprisonment before ultimately planning his escape.

Meagher's journey later mirrors Ryan's own as he escapes Australia and rises to prominence in the United States, becoming a key figure and founder of the Irish Brigade during the Civil War, and helping Christopher and Seamus. An essential historical detail not included in *The Famine* is that Meagher was the first to receive the Irish tricolor flag on March 7, 1848, in Paris, France. He was given the flag by French revolutionaries as a symbol of solidarity between Ireland's struggle for independence and the revolutionary movements in France. This symbol of Irish unity—green for Catholics, orange for Protestants, and white for peace—becomes a central motif in our country's fight for a united Ireland.

28. **The Cuba Five** refers to five Irish Fenian prisoners captured by British authorities while attempting to escape from Ireland in 1866. The five men were John Devoy, Jeremiah O'Donovan Rossa, Charles Underwood O'Connell, Henry Mullady and John McClure. Unlike the Fremantle escapees, these men were key figures in Irish-American Fenian networks and their capture symbolized British oppression of the nationalist movement. In *The Famine*, their plight is used to galvanize Seamus O'Donaghue, and his parallel depictions of Rossa and Devoy, and the Irish-American community, reinforcing the transatlantic struggle for Irish independence.

29. **Count Casimir Markievicz (1874–1932)** was a Polish nobleman, artist, and the husband of Constance Markievicz, the Irish revolutionary and suffragette. Though less politically active than his wife, Casimir was a talented painter and playwright, known for his Bohemian lifestyle and his contributions to the arts in Europe. His marriage to Constance introduced him to the world of Irish nationalism, but the couple eventually separated as Constance became more deeply involved in politics and rebellion.

30. **Manuel García (1805–1906)** was a Spanish-born opera singer, vocal coach, and composer, widely regarded as one of the most influential figures in the development of vocal technique. He was also the father of the famous soprano Adelina Patti. In "The Famine," Garcia's character serves as a model for Rebecca O'Donaghue's musical career. His expertise in vocal pedagogy and his status as a renowned performer in Europe inform Rebecca's rise to prominence. Garcia's contributions to vocal technique and his establishment of the Garcia School of Singing are reflected in Rebecca's own training and musical success.

31. **Captain Edward Doherty** (1831–1897) was an Irish-born officer in the Union Army during the American Civil War. He is most famous for his role in the capture of John Wilkes Booth, the assassin of President Abraham Lincoln. Doherty was born in County Wexford, Ireland, and immigrated to the United States in his youth. Before the war, he worked as a schoolteacher and a policeman in New York City.

HISTORICAL EVENTS:

1. **The Great Irish Famine (1845–1852)**: As the central backdrop of the novel, the Irish Famine is depicted in devastating detail, showing how British policies exacerbated the suffering of the Irish people. The novel explores the forced **evictions, mass starvation, and emigration** that shaped the O'Donaghue family's fate.The brutal landlordism, the destruction of Irish tenant farming, and the failure of British relief efforts are key themes that drive the novel's narrative.

2. **The Young Irelander Rebellion (1848)**: The Young Ireland movement, led by figures like Thomas Francis Meagher, sought to overthrow British rule. The rebellion's failure led to the arrest and exile of many revolutionaries, including Meagher, who was transported to Australia—where his path intersects with Ryan O'Donaghue in the novel. This uprising serves as a **precursor to later Irish revolutionary movements**, influencing Seamus O'Donaghue's militant ideology.

3. **The Transatlantic Migration Boom (1840s– 1890s)**: The novel explores the mass

emigration of Irish refugees to America and Australia, depicting the horrors of coffin ships, forced labor, and the struggle to survive in foreign lands. This serves as the foundation for the O'Donaghue family's global journey.

4. **Franco-Prussian War (1870-1871):** The Franco-Prussian War was a conflict between the French Empire and the Kingdom of Prussia, leading to the fall of Napoleon III and the establishment of the German Empire. In *"The Famine,"* this war serves as a backdrop to the unraveling of Rebecca and Napoleon III's relationship. The war's impact on Paris and the fall of the empire are crucial turning points in the narrative.

5. **Battle of Fair Oaks (1862):** The Battle of Fair Oaks was a crucial conflict during the American Civil War, fought between the Union and Confederate forces in Virginia. In this battle, James Rowan O'Beirne was shot in the lung but continued to fight with remarkable bravery. For his valor and determination under fire, O'Beirne was awarded the **Medal of Honor**, a testament to his extraordinary courage and commitment to the Union cause.

6. **The Lincoln Assassination (1865) & Aftermath:** The assassination of President Abraham Lincoln by John Wilkes Booth is a key turning point in the novel. Christopher O'Donaghue is drawn into the manhunt for Booth and his conspirators, which ties the novel's themes of political violence and

conspiracy to American history.

7. **The Irish Republican Brotherhood's (IRB) Growth in America (1860s–1880s)**: The novel highlights the rise of the IRB in exile, especially in New York, where Seamus O'Donaghue aligns himself with radical Irish revolutionaries. Irish-American fundraising, arms smuggling, and political lobbying are depicted as critical to keeping the nationalist movement alive.

8. **The Rise of Tammany Hall (Mid-Late 19th Century)**: The political dominance of **Tammany Hall in** New York is a major subplot in the novel, with Christopher O'Donaghue becoming entangled in its corrupt machinery. The struggle between Irish immigrants seeking power and the institutionalized corruption they encounter is a central theme.

9. **The Fenian Raids on Canada (1866–1871)**: The Fenian Brotherhood, made up of Irish-American veterans of the Civil War, launched a series of armed incursions into British Canada between 1866 and 1871. Their goal was to seize Canadian territory, hold it hostage, and use it to bargain for Irish independence from Britain. In *The Famine*, Seamus O'Donaghue is actively involved in these raids, using his connections in New York and among Irish-American war veterans to support the effort. The raids ultimately fail, but their inclusion in the novel reinforces the willingness of Irish exiles to continue their war against Britain

from across the Atlantic.

10. **The Fenian Rising in Ireland (1867)**: Taking place around the same time as the Fenian Raids in Canada, the 1867 Fenian Rising was an armed rebellion in Dublin, Cork, and other parts of Ireland, organized by the Irish Republican Brotherhood (IRB). It was poorly coordinated and ultimately crushed by the British, with many leaders executed or transported to penal colonies like Australia. In *The Famine*, Seamus O'Donaghue supports the rising from afar, working through underground networks to fund and arm the rebels. The failure of the rebellion deepens his disillusionment with Irish uprisings, reinforcing his decision to take the fight beyond Ireland through other means.

11. **Reconstruction of Paris (1853-1870)**: The reconstruction of Paris under Baron Haussmann involved the modernization of the city's infrastructure, creating the wide boulevards and iconic architecture seen today. In *"The Famine,"* this transformation of Paris is closely tied to Rebecca's story, as she photographs the city's new landmarks and uses these images to support Napoleon III's reign. The reconstruction symbolizes both progress and the loss of the old Paris.

12. **Statue of Liberty Construction (1875-1886)**: The construction of the Statue of Liberty, a gift from France to the United States, symbolizes freedom and democracy. In the novel, Rebecca

O'Donaghue becomes deeply involved in the project, using her influence to ensure its completion. The statue's construction serves as a metaphor for the transatlantic ideals of liberty and the enduring connection between France and the United States.

13. **Ned Kelly's Final Stand (1880)** Ned Kelly, the infamous Australian outlaw and folk hero, faced his legendary final stand on June 28, 1880, at the Glenrowan Inn in Victoria, Australia. Trapped by the police, Kelly and his gang donned homemade suits of bulletproof armor fashioned from ploughshares, creating an iconic image of rebellion. The police surrounded the inn, leading to a fierce gunfight that lasted through the night. Kelly, the last man standing, emerged from the smoke at dawn, armed and clad in his iron armor. Though he withstood a hail of bullets to his torso, arms, and legs, he was ultimately captured after being shot in the legs and brought to the ground.

14. **The Fremantle Fenian Prisoner Escape (1876)** The Fremantle Fenian Prisoner Escape, also known as the "Catalpa Rescue," was a dramatic event in the history of Irish nationalist movements. In 1876, six Irish political prisoners—members of the Fenian Brotherhood—managed to escape from the infamous Fremantle Prison in Western Australia, where they had been held since their conviction for their role in the Irish

nationalist movement. These prisoners had been sent to Australia as part of the British government's policy of transporting Irish rebels to penal colonies after their capture.

15. **The Paris Commune (1871)**: Following the Franco-Prussian War, the Paris Commune was a radical socialist uprising that briefly took control of Paris. In *The Famine*, Rebecca O'Donaghue finds herself entangled in this revolutionary chaos, navigating the shifting political landscape while trying to survive in a city under siege. The fall of the Commune and the brutal suppression of its supporters by government forces mirror other failed revolutionary efforts depicted in the book.

16. **Fenian Dynamite Campaign (1881-1885)**: The Fenian Dynamite Campaign was a series of bombing attacks carried out by Irish nationalists in England. In *"The Famine,"* Seamus O'Donaghue's activities are modeled after this campaign, illustrating the lengths to which Irish revolutionaries would go to fight British rule. The campaign's inclusion underscores the novel's themes of resistance and the fight for independence.

17. **Moulin Rouge Opening (1889):** The Moulin Rouge, a famous cabaret in Paris, opened in 1889 and became a symbol of the city's nightlife and cultural revolution. In the novel, the Moulin Rouge is where Rebecca O'Donaghue's talents as a performer are fully realized. The opening of the venue marks a

significant moment in her career and reflects the novel's exploration of art, entertainment, and societal change. Historical dates have been changed to align with the story timeline

HISTORICAL PLACES:

1. **Tuileries Palace (Paris, France)** was the royal residence of the French monarchy before its destruction during the Paris Commune in 1871. In *The Famine*, the palace is a central setting for Rebecca O'Donaghue's relationship with Napoleon III, symbolizing the height of imperial power and decadence. As Napoleon's empire begins to crumble, the fall of the Tuileries mirrors both the personal and political downfall of its rulers, reinforcing themes of impermanence, revolution, and exile.

2. **New York City (USA)** serves as a major backdrop in *The Famine*, particularly in Christopher O'Donaghue's rise through the city's corrupt political machine. The novel captures the contrasts of New York—from the brutal realities of immigrant slums in the Five Points to the wealth and influence of Fifth Avenue's elite. As Christopher navigates the power struggles of Tammany Hall, the city itself reflects the opportunities and obstacles faced by Irish immigrants in the late 19th century.

3. **Parisian Salons (France)** were cultural hubs where intellectuals, artists, and political figures gathered to discuss ideas. In *The Famine*, Rebecca O'Donaghue uses these salons to cement her influence in Parisian high society, forging connections with key figures like Napoleon III, Virginia Oldoini, and radical revolutionaries. These settings symbolize the intersection of art, politics, and seduction, where Rebecca masters the power of persuasion.

4. **Fifth Avenue, New York (USA)** in the 1880s was a symbol of Gilded Age wealth and high society, lined with lavish mansions and exclusive social clubs. In *The Famine*, Christopher O'Donaghue's access to this world signifies his ascendancy in New York's political elite, yet it also highlights the stark contrast between the Irish working class and America's ruling aristocracy.

5. **Manhattan Docks and W.R. Grace's Shipping Headquarters (USA)** played a crucial role in New York's booming maritime trade. In *The Famine*, the docks are depicted as a center of Irish labor and smuggling networks, where Christopher O'Donaghue engages in both legitimate business dealings and underground activities. The influence of William Russell Grace, a major figure in shipping and Irish-American politics, is deeply felt in these waterfront dealings.

6. **The Coffin Ships (1845–1852, Transatlantic)**

were overcrowded, disease-ridden vessels that carried Irish emigrants fleeing the Great Famine to America, Canada, and Australia. In *The Famine*, the horrors of these voyages are vividly depicted through the O'Donaghue family's journey, where passengers suffer from starvation, disease, and the ruthless greed of shipowners. These ships serve as a grim symbol of desperation, survival, and the cost of exile.

7. **Kilmainham Gaol (Dublin, Ireland)** was a notorious British prison used to hold Irish revolutionaries. In *The Famine*, Seamus O'Donaghue is deeply connected to Kilmainham, where fellow rebels are imprisoned, tortured, and executed. The gaol's bleak walls reflect the brutality of British rule and the sacrifices made by Irish nationalists in their fight for freedom.

8. **Clerkenwell Prison (London, England)** became infamous in 1867 when the Fenians attempted to bomb it to rescue their captured comrades. In *The Famine*, Seamus O'Donaghue is involved in the planning of this bold attack, which serves as a testament to the desperation and determination of the Irish resistance movement in exile.

9. **St. Patrick's Cathedral (New York, USA)** was the spiritual and political center of Irish Catholic life in America. In *The Famine*, Christopher O'Donaghue attends a key political gathering at the cathedral,

illustrating the close ties between the Church, Irish immigrants, and the Democratic political machine in 19th-century New York.

10. **Freemasons' Tavern (London, England)** was a hub for radical political groups and secret societies in the 19th century. In *The Famine*, it is a meeting point for Irish revolutionaries, British spies, and European political dissidents, where clandestine deals and betrayals shape the course of the rebellion.

11. **The Bowery (New York, USA)** was a rough, working-class district known for crime, gang activity, and immigrant struggles. In *The Famine*, Seamus O'Donaghue finds allies among the Irish underworld of the Bowery, using it as a base for his revolutionary activities and smuggling operations.

12. **The Brooklyn Bridge (New York, USA)**, completed in 1883, was an engineering marvel that symbolized America's industrial expansion. In *The Famine*, the bridge's construction is witnessed by Christopher O'Donaghue, marking New York's transformation into a modern metropolis. The bridge's rising towers stand in contrast to the struggles of the city's Irish immigrants.

13. **Strokestown Park (County Roscommon, Ireland)** was the estate of Major Denis Mahon, a landlord infamous for his brutal evictions during the Great Famine. In *The Famine*, the O'Donaghue family is forced from their home as part of Mahon's land clearances, a tragic

moment that encapsulates the cruelty of British rule and the forced displacement of the Irish people.

14. **Château de Fontainebleau (France)** was a French royal residence where Napoleon III and his court gathered. In *The Famine*, Rebecca O'Donaghue visits the château, experiencing the luxury of the French elite before witnessing the empire's decline. Fontainebleau represents both privilege and the fragility of power.

15. **The Five Points (New York, USA)** was the most notorious slum in 19th-century America, infamous for poverty, crime, and immigrant struggles. In The Famine, Christopher O'Donaghue's early days in New York bring him through the gang-controlled streets of the Five Points, where he sees firsthand the brutal reality of Irish immigrant life.

16. **Port Arthur Penal Colony (Tasmania, Australia)** was a harsh British prison settlement where Irish rebels and political prisoners were sent. In *The Famine*, Ryan O'Donaghue (Ned Kelly) is sentenced to hard labor in an Australian prison camp, reflecting the real-life fate of Thomas Francis Meagher and other Irish exiles. His escape from captivity is a pivotal moment in the novel, symbolizing his rejection of British authority.

HISTORICAL ORGANISATIONS AND MOVEMENTS:

1. **The Fenian Brotherhood (1858–1890s):** A secret Irish revolutionary organization founded in the United States to support the Irish Republican Brotherhood (IRB) in its fight against British rule. In *The Famine*, Seamus O'Donaghue is deeply involved in the Fenian Brotherhood's American operations, helping to raise funds, organize weapons shipments, and plan military actions such as the Fenian Raids on Canada (1866–1871).

2. **Clan na Gael (1867–1900s):** An influential Irish-American nationalist group that succeeded the Fenian Brotherhood and played a major role in supporting Irish revolutionary activities.In *The Famine*, Clan na Gael's secret meetings and financial backing are crucial to Seamus O'Donaghue's efforts to arm the Irish resistance, showing the transatlantic nature of the nationalist struggle.

3. **Tammany Hall (1789–1930s):** The Democratic political machine in New York, notorious for

corruption but also instrumental in helping Irish immigrants gain political power.In *The Famine*, Christopher O'Donaghue is drawn into Tammany Hall's world, using its influence to rise within New York's Irish-American elite while navigating the dangers of its deeply corrupt system.

4. **The Molly Maguires (Mid-19th Century):** A secret society of Irish coal miners in Pennsylvania who violently resisted exploitation by mine owners. In *The Famine*, the Molly Maguires are referenced as part of the broader Irish struggle in America, representing the extreme conditions faced by Irish laborers and the radical means some took to fight back.

5. **The Communards (1871):** The radical faction of French revolutionaries who led the Paris Commune, fighting against both French royalists and Prussian forces. In *The Famine*, Rebecca's time in Paris intersects with members of the Communards, reinforcing her exposure to European revolutionary ideals.

6. **The Ribbonmen (Early-Mid 19th Century):** A secret Irish agrarian society that violently resisted British landlords and evictions. In *The Famine*, the Ribbonmen's tactics of assassinating landlords and burning estates are referenced in relation to Major Denis Mahon's assassination, which mirrors real-life land conflicts in Ireland.

7. **The Bohemian and Avant-Garde Movements (Paris, 19th Century):** A cultural movement

that embraced artistic freedom, political dissent, and radical new ideas. In *The Famine*, Rebecca O'Donaghue becomes part of this world, using her connections in Parisian salons and artistic circles to navigate political intrigue and secure her place in French high society.

8. **The Phoenix National and Literary Society (1856–1859):** A predecessor to the Irish Republican Brotherhood, founded by Jeremisah Rossa to promote nationalist thought and Gaelic revival. In *The Famine*, Seamus O'Donaghue's early radicalization is linked to the Phoenix Society, which provides the ideological foundation for his later involvement with the Fenians and IRB.

9. **The Irish Brigade (Union Army, American Civil War, 1861–1865):** A famed military unit composed mainly of Irish immigrants who fought for the Union. In *The Famine*, Christopher O'Donaghue serves in the Irish Brigade, experiencing the horrors of the American Civil War while forging strong bonds with fellow Irish soldiers, including Thomas Francis Meagher, the brigade's commander.

THE FAMINE NOVEL: COMPREHENSIVE TIMELINE OF EVENTS

1840s:

- **1845**: The Great Famine begins in Ireland, ravaging the causing widespread starvation and disease

- **1847**: After the death of their parents, the young O'Donaghue siblings flee the countryside to the streets of cork. A run in with the law results in the two older brothers having to emigrate. Ryan to Australia and Christopher to America.

- **1848**: Ryan O'Donaghue, following being sent to Australia on the Transport ships, escapes from the penal colony, and begins his life as an outlaw.

- **1849**: Uncle Michael dies when Rebecca is 5 years old. Seamus, her older brother, who is 8 at the time, steps into a more significant role, helping to manage the family's affairs and taking on responsibilities that would shape his future in nationalist activities.

- **Late 1840s**: Christopher O'Donaghue,, begins to establish himself in America, building connections in New York and eventually aligning with political groups, such as Tammany Hall. His ambition grows as he starts to see the potential of power and influence in the New World.

1850s:

- **1855**: Ned Kelly made his last stand with the police in Glenrowan, Australia
- **1856**: Seamus founds the Phoenix Society, which later evolves into a more radical nationalist organization. His increasing involvement in Irish independence efforts sets the stage for his future as a revolutionary leader.
- **1859**: Rebecca, now a young teen, makes her debut at the Dublin Opera House. Her extraordinary talent quickly earns her recognition, and she begins to attract attention from influential figures.

1860s:

- **1861-1865**: The American Civil War rages, and Christopher O'Donaghue, by now an established figure in New York, sees an opportunity to leverage the war to distance himself from unruly forces in NYC.

- **1861**: Rebecca moves to Paris and begins studying under Manuel Garcia, a renowned vocal teacher. Her success in the Parisian opera scene is swift, and she soon becomes a prominent figure, as a global singing star.

- **1862-1865**: Seamus travels to the United States, where he meets with other Irish nationalists and secures weapons and explosives from his connections in the Union Army. He returns to Ireland with these materials, preparing for future uprisings.

- **1865**: Rebecca becomes the star attraction at the Moulin Rouge, adopting the stage name La Goulue. Her performances become legendary, and she helps to popularize the can-can dance, cementing her status as a cultural icon in Paris. She befriends Napoleon III and becomes his mistress.

- **1865**: The assassination of President Abraham Lincoln shakes the United States. Christoper O'Donaghue, the eldest of the O'Donaghue brothers, who had joined the Union Army, is tasked to hunt down his assassin.

- **1869-1870**: The Franco-Prussian War begins, leading to the fall of Napoleon III. Rebecca remains by Napoleon's side as his health deteriorates, and she witnesses the collapse of the empire they had hoped to sustain.

1870s:

- **1870**: Napoleon III abdicates after France's defeat in the Franco-Prussian War. He and Rebecca retreat to a private villa, where Napoleon spends his final days. Their son, Callan, is born during this period.

- **1871**: Rebecca convinces Otto von Bismarck "Iron Chancellor" not to occupy Paris with the Prussian army

- **1875**: Rebecca befriends Madame Alana Gonne, a young Irish actress and revolutionary. Alana provides Rebecca with critical information about Count Casimir Markievicz's true identity, exposing his deceit.

- **1875-1876**: Rebecca's (now titled Countess Markievicz) relationship with her new husband Casimir Markievicz, a Polish nobleman, ends after she discovers his fraudulent background. Rebecca returns to Paris, focused on her son and her work in social causes.

- **1875-1876**: Seamus is successful in the planning and execution of the escape of 6 Fenians from Fremantle prison, Australia

- **1878**: Christopher O'Donaghue solidifies his power in New York City, becoming a major political figure and know for fighting the corruption in the Tammany Hall. He uses his influence to protect Seamus from British authorities and to plan for future actions in support of Irish independence.

- **1878**: Rebecca continues her life in Paris, contributing to social reforms and artistic movements, and becomes a prominent figure in Parisian society. She takes charge of the project to deliver the Statue of Liberty to America

- **1878-79**: Christopher O'Donaghue uses the resource from his shipping company R.P. O'Donaghue Shipping to contribute to the Irish famine relief fund one-fourth the cargo of provisions sent in his steamship Constellation

---

1880s:

- **1880:** Christopher O'Donaghue is sworn in as the first Roman Catholic Mayor of New York City

- **1881-1885**: Seamus O'Donaghue leads the Fenian Dynamite Campaign, financed by his skirmishing fund, a series of bombing attacks in Great Britain aimed at weakening British rule and supporting Irish independence.

- **1885**: Rebecca and her son Callan arrive in New York Harbor with the disassembled pieces of the Statue of Liberty. This marks a significant moment of reunion and reflection for the O'Donaghue family as they reconnect with Christopher, who has become a powerful figure in New York, as its first catholic Mayor.

- **August 1885**: Seamus having returned from a recent trip across the Atlantic, meet Christopher and Rebecca at the docks, where he introduces his pregnant partner, Marissa Collins, and discuss their future together and the names of their unborn child—Michael if it's a boy, after Seamus's late uncle, and Ailish if it's a girl, after Marissa's mother.

- **August 1885**: The O'Donaghue siblings—Seamus, Christopher, and Rebecca—reunite in New York. They discuss their past struggles and future plans, especially in relation to Irish independence. During this reunion, Christopher's wife, Jenny, interrupts the meeting to deliver an urgent telegram from Australia, signaling a new chapter in their lives.

Final Scene:

- **1855:** In the Australian Outback, a close-up of Ned Kelly's eyes under his infamous helmet symbolizes the enduring spirit of resistance and the global fight against oppression. Left with a sense of anticipation for what is to come.

SYNOPSIS OF
THE FAMINE

The Famine is an expansive historical novel that spans four decades (1845-1885), following the lives of the O'Donaghue siblings—Rebecca, Seamus, Christopher, and Ryan—as they navigate survival, personal ambitions, and political upheavals across multiple continents. Set against the backdrop of one of the darkest chapters in Irish history, the story begins with the Great Irish Famine and takes readers through the transformations each sibling undergoes as they confront global events such as the Irish fight for independence, the US Civil War, and the political turbulence of 19th-century Europe and Australia.

The novel begins in 1845 with the onset of the Irish Potato Famine, a catastrophic event that devastates the lives of millions. The O'Donaghue family lives in the countryside of Cork, Ireland, struggling to survive as famine spreads across the land. Their parents die early on, leaving the children orphaned and vulnerable. After this, the unwinding tales of the four siblings as they encounter very different paths to one another spanning countries and continents is spellbinding.

The second eldest sibling, Ryan O'Donaghue, represents

a very different path. After leaving Ireland, Ryan ends up in Australia, having been transported as a convict after being caught stealing a loaf of bread. While the authorities initially sought Ryan for a minor crime, they discovered he was also wanted for the murder of Major Denis, a crime committed by his mother, Ann, during an act of defence for the family. Ryan's journey in Australia is one of survival, as he navigates the brutal realities of the penal colony system. While not involved in a rebellion before his transportation, his life in Australia reflects the struggles of the many convicts who were forcibly displaced by the British Empire. In the outback, Ryan becomes a survivor and a symbol of resilience. He adopts the name Ned Kelly, after a fallen companion on the journey over from Ireland, to evade capture by the authorities following escape from the prison, and inspired by the real life events of Ned Kelly, vividly portrays this as the fictionalised alias as the outback's most famed outlaws. His story is filled with hardship and the drive to forge a new life in a harsh new world.

Meanwhile, Christopher O'Donaghue escapes Ireland for America, where he becomes embroiled in the corrupt but powerful Tammany Hall political machine in New York City. In contrast to his siblings' radicalism and idealism, Christopher's journey is one of compromise and survival. He quickly rises to power, adopting the persona of William R. Grace, a fictionalized version inspired by the real-life political and business figure of the same name. Christopher navigates a world of greed, power, and influence, gaining wealth and security for himself in exchange for his moral compromises. His political maneuvering places him in control of significant immigrant communities, and he is portrayed as a man of pragmatism, whose survival instincts trump idealism. But as his influence grows, so does his awareness of the deep divisions between his newfound American identity and the Irish roots that he can never fully shake. Christopher's political career culminates in a delicate balancing act between supporting the Irish cause back home and managing his empire in New York, where maintaining power requires him to make increasingly dangerous alliances.

Seamus O'Donaghue, the youngest brother, responds to the devastation of the famine by throwing himself into revolutionary activism. While Rebecca, his baby sister, seeks personal escape, Seamus seeks collective justice. He becomes deeply involved with the Irish Republican Brotherhood (IRB), an underground movement that aims to overthrow British rule in Ireland. His path is one of violence and defiance, mirroring the real-life Fenian movement that orchestrated a series of bombings across Great Britain. As a revolutionary leader, Seamus grapples with the moral complexity of his actions, as well as the loss and destruction caused by his dedication to the cause. He becomes a fugitive, living in the shadows, and gradually the ideals of revolution harden into obsession. Despite being driven by love for his homeland, Seamus risks losing his humanity to the violence he perpetrates. His inner turmoil is fueled by the constant danger of capture, and by the widening gap between himself and the peaceful reformers of the Irish nationalist movement.

It is Rebecca, the youngest of the siblings, who

immediately becomes the heart of the family. Her striking voice becomes her refuge, a source of joy amidst the suffering. Rebecca's story takes a dramatic turn when Sir Reginald Townsend, an English nobleman, overhears her singing and recognizes her talent. She is offered the chance to leave Ireland and pursue a career as a singer in Europe. Despite the immense emotional toll of leaving her home and her brother Seamus behind, Rebecca accepts, understanding that this may be her only opportunity to escape the life of poverty and starvation. Her decision also reflects the family's growing desperation.

In Paris, Rebecca rises through the opera houses of Europe, her voice captivating audiences. Under the tutelage of the renowned vocal teacher Manuel Garcia, Rebecca becomes a celebrated soprano, performing in prestigious venues and eventually joining the avant-garde circles of Paris. She moves in the highest echelons of society, where she influences the policies of Napoleon III, especially around education reform for women and the working class. However, Rebecca's personal life becomes increasingly complicated as she enters a secretive romantic relationship with the Emperor himself, which ultimately ends in heartbreak and personal scandal. Throughout her journey, Rebecca carries with her the memory of her suffering family back in Ireland, and the loss and pain from the famine shape her character as she struggles with the contradictions of wealth, fame, and personal integrity.

Throughout *The Famine*, real historical events such as the US Civil War, the Fenian bombings, and the Franco-Prussian War act as pivotal turning points for the characters. Christopher's involvement with Tammany Hall is directly influenced by his interactions with real-life figures, while Rebecca's ascent in Paris places her in proximity to power and policy reform during Napoleon III's reign. Ryan's journey reflects the realities of transportation to Australia, and Seamus's actions embody the revolutionary spirit of Irish nationalism, modelled after figures like Jeremiah O'Donovan Rossa and John Devoy.

The novel's central theme revolves around the complex notions of identity, resilience, and survival. Each sibling grapples with what it means to be Irish in a world where their homeland is ravaged by famine and British colonialism. While Rebecca tries to escape her roots by embracing European culture and fame, Seamus fights to preserve Ireland's spirit through rebellion. Christopher reinvents himself in America, blending into the politics of a new world, and Ryan, in Australia, lives a life marked by both exile and resistance.

Their individual arcs converge in the final chapters as the siblings, after years of separation, reunite in New York. The tension between Christopher's newfound wealth and Seamus's radicalism comes to a head, but it is Rebecca's influence that becomes a unifying force. Together, the O'Donaghue siblings must navigate the consequences of their past actions and the choices they've made. The novel closes with a reunion tinged with hope, but also uncertainty, as the characters face the world they have helped shape—each in their own way, through art, revolution, politics, and survival.

In *The Famine*, the personal stories of the O'Donaghue siblings are set against a broad historical canvas, blending fiction with real events to create a rich, immersive narrative that captures the human experience amidst some of the most turbulent events of the 19th century. The novel explores not only the impact of the famine itself but also the long-lasting effects it had on Irish identity and the Irish diaspora. Through the trials and triumphs of Rebecca, Seamus, Christopher, and Ryan, the novel pays tribute to the resilience of the Irish spirit and the enduring legacy of a people who, despite immense suffering, continued to fight for survival, dignity, andfreedom.

ABOUT THE AUTHOR

 Born in Belfast during the Troubles, Ryan Donaghy grew up with a deep awareness of the forces that shape history—both the grand conflicts that divide nations and the personal struggles that define families. At the age of six, he and his family left Northern Ireland to escape persecution, finding refuge in New Zealand before eventually returning home. That early displacement left him with a lifelong curiosity about Ireland's past, its resilience, and the echoes of history that still shape its people today.

Despite his love for history, Ryan took a different path, building a career in finance, marketing, and entrepreneurship that spanned the globe— from Australia to Latin America, from Red Bull's headquarters to launching his own tech startup. But when a surfing accident left him largely immobile, he found himself at an unexpected crossroads. Unable to travel, unable to move with ease, he turned to a lifelong passion he had never fully pursued—storytelling.

What started as a simple script idea for a historical epic evolved into something much greater. The Famine was born not out of a desire to be a novelist, but from a need to tell a story that had never been fully told on a grand scale. Weaving his own family's dynamics into the narrative, Ryan reimagined himself and his siblings as characters in 1845, walking the same path as those who lived through one of Ireland's darkest chapters. His background in history, his love for cultural storytelling, and his admiration for Wilbur Smith's multi-generational sagas all shaped the book's sweeping scope—one that blends fact and fiction, real historical figures with imagined legacies.

Though *The Famine* is his debut novel, it is only the beginning. His planned series will follow the O'Donaghue family across generations and continents, exploring the ripple effects of history through the lives of those who dared to change it.

Now based in Belfast, Northern Ireland, Ryan continues to write, blending adventure, history, and personal experience into stories that transport readers across time and place.

 mybookstale@gmail.com

bookstale_com

bookstale

www.bookstale.com

HOME RULE

"Home Rule: A Nation's Awakening", the second book in the Irish Series written by Ryan Donaghy, is a historical fiction novel set against the backdrop of the Irish Home Rule movement in the late 19th century, weaving together the lives of ordinary individuals caught in extraordinary circumstances. The O'Donaghue family, torn apart by the Great Famine of the 1840s, becomes the central focus as they grapple with the social, economic, and political turmoil of the era, exploring the complexities of British colonialism and the enduring fight for Irish self-governance. The story unfolds across continents, from the rolling countryside of Victoria, Australia, to the bustling streets of London and the vibrant landscapes of South America, connecting diverse perspectives on the Irish struggle.

The novel opens in 1865 Melbourne, Australia, where Ryan O'Donaghue, now known as Ryan Duffy, style after the legacy of Sir Charles Gavan Duffy, lives a life far removed from his origins. Once the notorious Irish outlaw Ned Kelly, Ryan escaped the gallows through the intervention of Judge Redmond Barry and forged a new identity as a respected businessman and politician. He's married to Maeve and has two sons, John and Frank, when Barry convinces him to at least try to leave the past behind. However, Ryan remains haunted by his past and drawn into the clandestine activities of the Ribbonmen, a secret society fighting against British oppression in Australia.

The early chapters explore Ryan's internal conflict and the challenges of balancing his desire for a peaceful life with his ingrained sense of justice and commitment to Irish freedom. He forges an uneasy alliance with the Kulin Aboriginals, recognizing their shared struggle against British colonial rule. This alliance brings both promise and peril, as Ryan navigates the complex dynamics of race, land ownership, and political ambition. The first part culminates in a raid orchestrated by the Ribbonmen to disrupt British supply lines and arm the Aboriginal tribes. The raid is a success, but it comes at a heavy cost, blurring the lines between justified resistance and outright violence. Ryan is further tested when Judge Barry, his mentor and protector, dies, leaving him exposed to new threats. This loss is compounded by the growing recklessness of his friend John Toohey, whose thirst for action threatens to spiral into open warfare with the British. This sets off a chain of events culminating in Toohey's arrest and execution, triggering riots and ultimately leading to the tragic deaths of Maeve and John.

Consumed by grief and guilt, Ryan flees Australia with his surviving son, Frank, seeking solace and a new purpose in the exotic landscapes of South America. They stumble upon the remnants of his broken family when seeing the "R.P. O'Donoghue Shipping," the boat his brother Christopher owned. The scene is set for a possible return to action for the O'Donoghue family.

Meanwhile, across the Atlantic, Christopher

O'Donaghue, who heads up the shipping line, and his sister Rebecca, a celebrated opera singer, and political activist in Europe, find themselves increasingly intertwined with the movement for Irish Home Rule. Rebecca, inspired by the success of women in power and politics, uses her influence and wealth to support the cause, while Seamus, always driven by a restless spirit and unbending resolve, becomes embroiled in a campaign of bombings and sabotage across England. Their actions draw the attention of British intelligence, and a network of spies and informants begins to weave a web of deceit around the O'Donaghue family. The discovery of a treacherous scheme by the British intelligence and the lengths to which they will go to subvert Irish autonomy from English rule becomes the central conflict moving forward.

As the O'Donaghue siblings rise in prominence, they attract both admiration and animosity, their personal lives becoming increasingly intertwined with the political landscape. Rebecca becomes entangled in a passionate and dangerous love affair with Charles Stewart Parnell, the charismatic leader of the Irish Parliamentary Party, threatening to undermine his reputation and the fragile coalition he has built. Their intense relationship is used as leverage to the British against the family.

As the novel progresses, the political climate in Ireland intensifies, leading to both great advancements and great steps back. The Home Rule movement gains momentum, but it is also plagued by internal divisions and external threats. The novel culminates in a series of dramatic events that test the strength of the

O'Donaghue family and force them to confront their deepest loyalties.

What will be discovered on the battlefields of Cuba, as the United States and Spain prepare for War? What price is Parnell willing to pay? How far will Seamus go? What role will Michael, Seamus' son, take on as he gets pulled closer to the cause?

Rebecca, torn between her love for Parnell and her commitment to Irish self-governance, must make impossible choices that could determine the fate of both her family and her country. She finds herself increasingly alienated from the world in which she has built, and it is at the heart of this great political and family storm that the question of whether she will be willing to sacrifice everything for her people looms. Will she return to that familiar setting, with new vigor? Or will it become her prison, a reminder of promises broken and dreams unfulfilled?

What does Christopher do as he sees the plans of the British reach American shores? A shrewd businessman and skilled political tactician, he's never been one to show his hand easily. Christopher has always navigated the treacherous seas of international finance with a calm facade and a keen eye for opportunity.

As it moves towards its climax, "Home Rule" explores the themes of family, love, betrayal, sacrifice, and the enduring power of hope. The novel confronts the complexities of Irish identity, the legacy of colonialism, and the difficult choices individuals must make when caught between personal desires and the demands of a larger cause. What does it mean to be truly free? What is the price of autonomy? And how can a nation heal from centuries of oppression and division?

The O'Donaghue family, forever bound by their shared history and their unwavering commitment to Ireland, stands as a testament to the resilience of the human spirit and the enduring power of family in the face of adversity. The question remains: Can they forge a new future for themselves and for Ireland, or will they be forever haunted by the ghosts of their past? Who will be called to take up arms, and to what cause? To what degree will their commitment to one another hold as they fight against old allies and new foes? Who will survive as this family learns that not all battles are fought on the field.

COMING SOON!

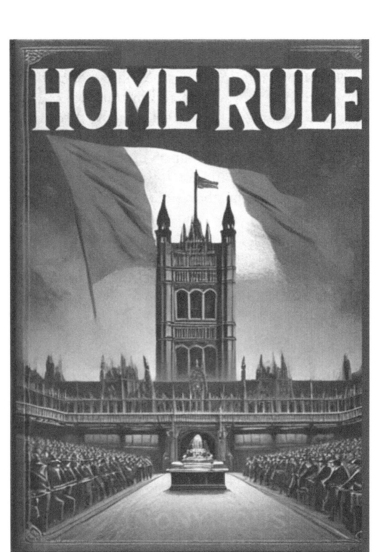

Made in United States
Cleveland, OH
12 June 2025

17692105R00225